"*The Lost Girl of Astor Street* is a delicious read! Stephanie Morrill gives readers a historical mystery full of heart and brimming with the vibrant atmosphere of 1920s Chicago. The moment I finished, I was ready to flip it over and begin again."

—SHANNON DITTEMORE, AUTHOR
OF THE ANGEL EYES TRILOGY

"Morrill delivers a story that has it all—mystery, the mafia, and a heroine you can't help but root for. If *Veronica Mars* met the Roaring Twenties, you'd end up with *The Lost Girl of Astor Street*!"

—ROSEANNA M. WHITE, AUTHOR
OF THE LOST HEIRESS

"Spunky Piper Sail is more interested in investigating her best friend's death than in society's expectations for a young woman in 1924. She's curious, intelligent, and gutsy, and while she's not immune to a handsome man, she's not needy. Reminiscent of Philip Pullman's Sally Lockhart series in all the best ways! I thoroughly enjoyed *The Lost Girl of Astor Street*."

—MAUREEN DOYLE MCQUERRY, AWARD-
WINNING AUTHOR OF THE PECULIARS
AND THE TIME OUT OF TIME DUET: THE
TELLING STONE AND BEYOND THE DOOR

"Witty and compelling, *The Lost Girl of Astor Street* is as thick with romance as it is with evolving mysteries. Piper Sail is a 1920s heroine to root for, and the dashing Mariano Cassano a detective sure to win more hearts than just her own. A truly fresh and engaging story that not only kept me guessing until the very end, but that left me with a satisfied sigh for *more please!*"

—JOANNE BISCHOF, AWARD-WINNING AUTHOR
OF THE LADY AND THE LIONHEART

"Step back to a more glamorous time with the captivating story of Piper Sail, a sassy young woman with a penchant for finding trouble. As a mystery unfolds, you'll be turning the pages and cheering on a heroine you won't forget."

—JENNY B. JONES, AWARD-WINNING
AUTHOR OF *CAN'T LET YOU GO* AND THE
KATIE PARKER PRODUCTION SERIES

"Thoroughly engaging. Fast-paced, filled with vivid details, and featuring a delightful heroine, it was a joy to read. It's a keeper, for sure."

—*NEW YORK TIMES* AND *USA TODAY*
BESTSELLING AUTHOR SHELLEY SHEPARD GRAY

"In *The Lost Girl of Astor Street*, Morrill invites us on a wild ride through teen eyes down the crime-ridden, mob-infested streets of Chicago in the 1920s. Laden with mystery and laced with romance, this intriguing who-done-it read is a testament to friendship, courage, and first love that you won't soon forget!"

—BETSY ST. AMANT, AUTHOR OF
ALL'S FAIR IN LOVE & CUPCAKES
AND *LOVE ARRIVES IN PIECES*

"Stephanie Morrill delivers an engrossing mystery that takes readers into the jazz clubs, illicit speakeasies, and gangster neighborhoods of 1920s Chicago in a search for a missing girl. The intrigue, romance, and glamorous Roaring Twenties setting will draw readers in."

—JILL WILLIAMSON, CHRISTY AWARD–WINNING
AUTHOR OF *BY DARKNESS HID* AND *CAPTIVES*

"Stephanie Morrill paints a vivid picture of 1920s Chicago with strong, relatable characters and their intriguing relationships. You won't be able to stop wondering what will happen next as the clever heroine works to solve the mystery of *The Lost Girl of Astor Street*."

—MELANIE DICKERSON, AUTHOR OF
THE GOLDEN BRAID AND
THE BEAUTIFUL PRETENDER

THE
LOST GIRL
~*~ OF ~*~
ASTOR STREET

STEPHANIE MORRILL

BLINK

BLINK

The Lost Girl of Astor Street
Copyright © 2017 by Stephanie Morrill

This title is also available as a Blink ebook.

Requests for information should be addressed to:
Blink, *3900 Sparks Dr. SE, Grand Rapids, Michigan 49546*

ISBN 978-0-310-75838-9

Cover design: Kirk DouPonce, Dog Eared Design
Interior design: Denise Froehlich

Printed in the United States of America

17 18 19 20 21 22 23 24 25 /LSC/ 18 17 16 15 14 13 12 11 10 9 8 7 6 5 4 3 2 1

"It was hardly *my* seat. Those are public benches. And he only did it to goad you." Her eyes spark with mischief as she grins at me. "Did you and Mr. Crane have an enjoyable conversation?"

"Did you leave me alone with him on purpose?"

Lydia giggles and shrugs. "Maybe."

Heat climbs up my neck and burns my cheeks. Did Jeremiah think I was trying to finagle alone time with him?

Lydia turns a sweet smile on Matthew, who sweeps open the back door for us. "Good afternoon, ladies. Sorry to be late."

"No trouble at all." Lydia slides through to the other side to create room for me.

I refuse to offer such comforts. If he'd been on time, I wouldn't have had to spar with Jeremiah in the first place. I step one foot in the car, then pause. "Do you know if Walter is home yet?"

He tips his flat cap. "I haven't heard, Miss Sail."

Matthew closes the door behind me once my limbs are tucked safely inside. "He had better return today," I say to Lydia. "Home is almost insufferable without him around."

Lydia fusses with a tendril of long, flame-red hair. Her mother, unfortunately, won't hear of her bobbing it. And Lydia won't hear of doing something of which her parents disapprove. "Piper, you really should consider giving up that friendship. You're getting too old to be friends with boys."

"We're not going to have this conversation yet again, are we? I've told you—it's not like that with Walter and me."

"It *hasn't* been, but it'll change if you stay on this course. You don't really want to be a baseball player's wife, do you? Surely even you couldn't be happy in that situation."

I glance up front as Matthew folds his tall frame behind the wheel. I wait until the engine thunders to life before answering.

be seen. And Lydia is still making conversation with Mae, who's hardly preferable to Jeremiah.

The wind again gusts off the lake and threatens to carry away my brimless cloche. I trap it on my head with my hand.

"I see you haven't changed."

Jeremiah's gaze is fastened to the hand I've pressed to my head. The hand that bears this week's punishments from Ms. Underhill. Embarrassment sours my stomach. I don't know his sister well, but my guess is that proper Emma Crane doesn't come home from her day at Presley's with bruised knuckles.

I tuck my hand into my coat pocket. "I trust the newspaper business is as strong as ever."

Jeremiah opens his mouth to respond, and then stops himself.

Lydia has rejoined us. "Pardon my interruption, but Matthew is here."

"Miss LeVine." Jeremiah sweeps his trilby off his head and holds it over his heart. "Please forgive me for taking your seat. Miss Sail objected most vehemently on your behalf."

Lydia beams a smile at him as if he has offered an actual apology instead of one that mocks. "It's forgotten. Have a good day, Mr. Crane."

"Thank you for being so gracious." Jeremiah winks at me as he settles his hat back on his head. "Stay out of trouble, Miss Sail."

Laughter spills from Lydia. "If you knew Piper"—she links her arm through mine, pulling me toward the idling car—"you would know that's quite impossible."

Jeremiah chuckles behind us.

"Excuse me." I keep my voice low and my chin high. "I was trying to stand up for you. He took your seat."

Behind me, Lydia groans.

Jeremiah turns and assumes a face of surprise. "Why, Miss Sail. I had no idea the two of you had intentions on this bench." He makes a show of scooting over. "Plenty of room for both you and Miss LeVine."

Jeremiah's trilby sits askew, and his right eye squints in the mid-afternoon sun. His gaze holds a dare. Other girls at school describe him as "dashing." I daresay Jeremiah believes his own press.

I take the seat, careful to leave space between me and Jeremiah, as well as room for Lydia to sit. But when I glance to my left, I see Lydia has abandoned my cause in favor of social-izing with Mae Husboldt and her insipid friends. Beyond them, the sun glares off Lake Michigan, making my eyes water.

"It seems Miss LeVine's heart was not so set on this bench after all."

I turn and push a smile onto my face. "Do you intend to con-sole yourself with that notion, Mr. Crane?" I arrange the folds of my straight black uniform skirt, shielding my legs from the Chicago wind, chilly even in May. "They must not keep you busy enough at the newspaper if you have time to think up schemes like taking seats from nice girls like Lydia LeVine."

Jeremiah's smile stays steady. "I'm just here for my sister."

At his core, Jeremiah is a newspaper man—imperturbable. I have no problems imagining him digging for interviews and pounding away at his typewriter. Or someday taking over his father's role as owner.

Not that I spend a lot of time thinking about Jeremiah Crane.

"Of course you are." I look with hope to the cluster of Fords and Buicks, but the LeVine family's Duesenberg is nowhere to

CHAPTER ONE

CHICAGO, ILLINOIS

MAY 12, 1924

If he doesn't know it already, Jeremiah Crane is about to learn that I'm not the type of girl to be pushed around. Standing behind him, I watch as he stretches his long arms across the back of the wooden bench, feigning ignorance of my presence. I glare down at the top of Jeremiah's new hat, which he probably bought because it looks just like the trilby Rudolph Valentino wore in last month's issue of *Photoplay*.

Lydia touches my elbow and pitches her voice low. "Don't make trouble with him, Piper. Just let it go."

Probably wise advice. Lydia's most always is.

Our fellow Presley's School for Girls classmates stream around us on the sidewalk, monotonous in black-and-white uniforms as they head to the L station or the automobiles idling in the pickup line.

I turn away from the bench, but the outright rudeness of Jeremiah's action—plopping himself right in the middle when he *knew* Lydia and I were about to sit there—and the possibility that he thinks I'll just lay down and take it makes me pivot around again. This is 1924, after all. A girl has the right to be heard.

I plant my hands on my hips. "Excuse me, Mr. Crane, but my friend and I were about to sit there."

7

"First of all, Walter is like a brother. Secondly, even if he weren't, you of all people, Lydia LeVine, are hardly in a position to lecture me on propriety when—"

Lydia's ice-blue eyes spear me. "Not a word about that." Her gaze skitters to the back of Matthew's head and her cheeks flush red.

I glance at Matthew's profile. I can't exactly fault Lydia's fondness for him. While he doesn't have the rakish, worldly charm of Jeremiah Crane—which I care nothing for, of course—there's a quiet confidence about him that all men would do well to have.

Still. Lydia is a darling of the Astor Street district. Not just wealthy and well-bred, but sweet too. She could have anyone. Why Matthew?

Maybe Mrs. LeVine is right. Maybe I *am* a bad influence on her daughter.

Lydia scratches behind her ear. Then on her arm. "Do I have something on me? I'm so itchy today."

"I don't see anything."

"It's weird to have dry skin this time of year, right?"

My heart seems to pause in my chest. Is this some side effect of her illness?

"And at least he has goals. Dreams." Lydia's voice is so quiet that even I can hardly hear her. She scratches at the nape of her neck again. "Walter's whole life is baseball. What happens if he never becomes a professional? If he gets injured? I'm just looking out for you, Piper. You deserve more than a paycheck-to-paycheck life."

I raise my eyebrows at her. "I'm running out of ways to say this—I have no intentions of marrying Walter. But what kind of life do you think you'd have with—"

She gives me the same harsh look I've seen Mrs. LeVine wear when she wants Lydia's little sisters to shut their mouths.

The car is so loud that there's no way Matthew can hear, but I humor her sensitivities and utilize our code name. "Pickles. What kind of life do you think you'd have with Pickles?"

Lydia giggles, and the flush of embarrassment fades to a becoming shade of pink. She leans forward and taps Matthew's shoulder with a gloved hand. "Matthew? I'll need you to drop me at the Barrows' home today."

My body goes stiff. Is Lydia truly planning to watch Cole today?

Lydia leans back in her seat. Scratches the back of her leg. "This dry weather must be what has me so itchy."

I look out the window, my mind churning as I take in the tall buildings of Lake Shore Drive. Maybe I'm overreacting and Lydia is merely paying a social visit to Mrs. Barrow. "Why are you going to the Barrows'?"

"They still haven't found a new nanny, so I'm watching Cole when I can."

If only I could come right out and tell Lydia *why* she's in no shape to care for a small child. *You can't tell anyone*—Mrs. LeVine's cautionary words ring in my ear—*not even Lydia*.

Still. I have to say *something*. "Do your parents know?"

Lydia's blue eyes widen. "Of course."

"And they don't mind?"

"Why ever would they? Mrs. Barrow is desperate for help. It's horrible, the situation they're in. What sort of person— especially a nanny by trade—leaves a family when the mother is weeks out from the birth of a second child? To go work in some speakeasy, of all places?"

"It *is* horrible. But . . ." I weigh my words before letting them out. "Are you sure you're feeling up to it today?"

Lydia directs her gaze forward. Her jaw clenches and her pert nose is in the air. "Of course."

I open my mouth, but the words I want to say—*you really shouldn't*—stick in my throat. I'm not accustomed to handing out cautionary advice.

"Mrs. Barrow is lucky to have you," I say instead.

"It's no trouble. Cole is such a dear."

My snort of laughter is apparently audible over the roar of the engine. Lydia grins at me. "He is, I swear. You just happen to hate all children."

"Just because I've yet to meet a child I enjoy doesn't mean I hate all children."

"You don't even like your own nephew."

"Who would? Howie cries all the time."

"He's a baby. And he's darling."

"And you're the nicest person in the world."

Lydia shakes her head at me and then gazes out at Lake Michigan, blue-gray and choppy. "I wonder if the water has warmed at all."

"I doubt it."

Previous summers, we spent oodles of time on its shores. Sand gritty between our toes as we ate hot dogs slathered with tangy mustard and spicy onions. Seagulls cawing and boys playing a showy game of ball nearby. Lydia's never put more than her ankles in the lake, I'm sure. And I suppose that's a good thing. Even if her parents haven't banned her from caring for children, they must have banned swimming. Right?

Matthew steers off bustling Lake Shore Drive and onto the

relative quiet of Astor Street. My oldest brother lives in the suburbs now, and when he visits he complains about the noise of our neighborhood, how a man can't even smoke his pipe in the privacy of his yard.

True, our yard is the size of a hatbox and barely has room for the few shrubs within the wrought iron fence. On one side, our stone walls graze the brick home of the Lincoln family, and on the other we have hardly a foot of space between us and the Applegates. No, not much space for a man who wants to smoke his pipe in solitude. But it's where Mother once lived and loved us, and anytime I imagine myself leaving this fall for college, my eyes sting with tears.

"Thank you, Matthew," I say as I push open the door.

"Of course, Miss Sail." After over a year of bringing me home from school, I've finally convinced him to stay seated and let me get my own door. But he always looks rather uncomfortable about it.

"Depending on how long I'm at the Barrows', I might ring you later tonight," Lydia calls out the window. "Mother and Father have tickets to the ballet, so it'll just be me, Hannah, and Sarah."

I wave as I unhook the gate of my front yard. "Talk to you then."

She flutters her fingers in a farewell wave. With her smile and eyes gleaming bright, Lydia looks so healthy. Another image of Lydia flits through my mind—her head angled awkwardly back, her arms stiff against her chest, her breathing strangely erratic.

Matthew chugs away to carry her around the block to the Barrow residence. I press my eyes closed, as if that can shut out the image of the Other Lydia. *She'll be fine*, I tell myself.

The LeVines seem able to convince themselves of this. Why can't I?

The gate clanks shut behind me, and I mount the stone steps to my front door. I draw my house key from my bag, but the doorknob twists in my hand, and I push open the heavy door with my hip. Inside, it's silent. I pull off my saddle shoes and drop them by the base of the stairs.

"Where's Lydia?" My brother Nick's voice startles me from the living room. He's in Father's chair with a notebook open and his mouth drawn in its usual frown.

"I didn't know you'd be here."

"Well, I am." His fingers fidget with a tassel on the arm of the chair. "Did Lydia have somewhere else to be?"

I pull off my cloche and bite my lip so I don't laugh at my besotted brother. We've grown up with the LeVines, but it's as if six months ago he woke up and realized Lydia is a young lady and not just a girl.

"Lydia is showing her charitable side over at the Barrows' house. She's taking care of Cole so Mrs. Barrow can put her feet up, I guess."

"I didn't need to know *where* she was, Piper." Nick's face grows redder with each word he speaks. "It's just that Lydia frequently comes in with you, and the two of you make so much noise that I might have needed to go to the library to study."

"Right. Well, no. Lydia won't be coming over this afternoon."

"Okay, good." Nick makes a show of settling against the back of the armchair. "Then I won't bother with going to the library."

"Is Walter home yet?"

"Try the kitchen."

My feet take off in an unladylike rush. The yeasty scent of

bread dough greets me as I push through the dining room door and into the kitchen. Joyce is scrubbing her hands at the sink and glances over her shoulder at me.

"He was here, Piper, but I sent him to the market to pick up my order." She shuts off the faucet and smiles at me as she dries her hands on her apron. "You'll have to make do with my company for now."

"How did he look? Is he injured again?"

"He looks much better than when he came home earlier in the season. He assures me that other than a bruised shin, he's fine." Joyce drapes a kitchen towel over two rising mounds of dough. "No broken fingers. No black eyes. Hopefully, that means he's learned his lesson about interfering when two other players decide to brawl."

"We can hope so, at least."

With its peeling wallpaper and functional feel, the kitchen isn't the prettiest room in the house, but it's still my favorite. After school, I almost always find our housekeeper, Joyce, in here starting supper. She'll let me sit and talk to her about whatever is on my mind, unlike the men in the house. Joyce even looks a bit like my mother; she's rounder, but has similar almond-colored eyes and sandy hair.

"How was school today?"

I pull open the door of the refrigerator. "It was school."

Joyce sighs. "Never have I seen a girl with a mind as fine as yours dislike school so much. Don't you know how lucky you are, Piper?"

I set my glass and the bottle of milk on the counter. "I don't mean to sound ungrateful." But that's exactly how I sound. Joyce would have loved to send Walter to a nice school, a school like she probably went to before her life took a cruel turn.

16

"Gracious, girl. Again?"

I look up and find Joyce's gaze is on my bruised right hand, the one clutching the milk bottle. I shrug and pay careful attention as I unscrew the cap.

"Ms. Underhill?"

"How'd you guess?" I keep my gaze on the flour-dusted floor. This is always the worst part of Ms. Underhill's discipline—bearing the weight of Joyce's disappointment.

Usually Joyce launches into a lecture about keeping my sassy mouth shut in Home Economics and letting that sweet Miss LeVine teach me a thing or two. Today, she sighs and says, "You should put some ice on it before it swells any worse."

I feel her gaze on me as I select a chunk of ice, wrap it in a knobby dish towel, and press it to my knuckles. "I wasn't mouthing off today, I swear. I missed a step in my pattern, is all."

Joyce's eyebrows arch. "And is there a reason you missed a step? Perhaps you were too busy chatting or passing notes to pay closer attention?"

I bite my lip and look away.

Her "Mm-hmm," has a distinct *That's-what-I-thought* snap to it.

My knuckles are painfully cold, but that's okay. Next they'll be numb. The routine is familiar by now.

"Piper, I know you've been raised in a house of boys. You know things a girl shouldn't know at age eighteen." She stirs the potato soup simmering on the stove and then turns to me. Her eyes are piercing. "But you're a young lady. It would do you well to start acting like one."

The only sound in the kitchen is the whir of the gas stove and the occasional bubble from the pot. Words slide around in my head—*I'm trying my best. Ms. Underhill just doesn't like me.* But Joyce would only say that I did that to myself when I—ahem—borrowed Ms. Underhill's shapeless cardigan last fall and snuck Lydia and me a pastry from the teacher's room. Or when my infamous ride down the stairwell banister resulted in knocking her over. Or when—

Footsteps pound up the back stairs, and then the door shoves open. In swaggers Walter Thatcher, grinning over the box of groceries.

"There's a sight for my homesick eyes—Piper Caroline Sail." He settles the cardboard box on the counter and sweeps off his flat cap.

I find myself hesitating, cataloging the changes in him these last weeks. His already dark skin has grown even darker from California's sunshine, and his black hair is clipped shorter. But his broad smile is the same, and when he opens his arms, I rush to embrace him. The scents of the grocery store—spices and cardboard—cling to his tweed suit. Walter squeezes me against his thick chest before holding me out at a distance.

"With your hair like that, I might not have guessed it was you. I might've thought you were a blonde Clara Bow."

I touch my bobbed hair. "Father was finally convinced."

"Or, rather, Miss Miller talked him into it," Joyce says as she unloads canned goods onto the counter.

I scrunch my nose at the mention of Jane. Joyce's mouth twitches with a smile when she sees. No lecture this time.

But with Walter in the room, even the mention of my father's girlfriend can't spoil my mood. My gaze skims down the length of Walter and up again. "You're quite tan. I think I'd like to spend part of my year living in California as well."

Walter leans against the counter. "Maybe you could stow away in my suitcase when I leave next."

Joyce clears her throat. "The son I raised would never make such a bawdy suggestion."

Walter grins at his mother and pecks a kiss to her cheek. "Don't fret, Mother. Piper knows well that I'm teasing."

"Why don't the two of you go for a walk?" Joyce suggests. "Leave me in peace to do my work."

"Can you believe this, Pippy?" Walter settles his hat back onto his black curls. "Not even home a day and already my mother is shooing me out the door."

Joyce smiles at him and turns back to her soup.

Walter winks at me, and I realize just how lonely it's been since he left in the spring to play minor league ball out west. Initially after Mother died, I was like a pet of sorts to my brothers and Walter. And then as Tim and Nick grew into their adult lives, it became just me and Walter. At eighteen years old, I should be growing into my adult self as well, but behaving like a lady feels like wearing an ill-fitting costume.

Nick is still in Father's chair, hunkered over the notebook. "Where are you two going?"

"For a walk. Wanna come?"

Nick heaves a sigh as he smooths his sheet of paper. "No, you go ahead. I have a test tomorrow."

Apparently, becoming a lawyer takes lots of time and energy, even if your father is already one of the most sought-after defense attorneys in Chicago.

"And be safe!" Nick calls after us.

I glance at Walter and roll my eyes as I pull on my hat. That's become Nick's constant parting advice since he started studying criminal cases. Ignorance is bliss, it seems, because I never give safety a moment's thought when I leave the house. Not in a neighborhood like ours, anyway.

Walter holds the wrought iron gate open for me. "Folks will think I'm high class, strolling with a Presley's girl."

I glance down at my long black skirt, the sweater, and bow. "Blast. I forgot I still had on my uniform."

"You look fine. Though I'm not fond of seeing your knuckles in that shade of gray."

"I bring it upon myself." I clasp my hands behind my back as the wind bites at us. I probably should have grabbed my coat. "Tell me all about how your season is going. No splints or black eyes, I see."

"That's because I'm warming the bench." Walter's words have a bitter edge to them. His jaw is set, and his eyes focus farther down tree-lined Astor Street.

Time to dust off my you-can-do-this speech. "I know that's frustrating, Walter, but you told me yourself that's just part of the game. It'll be your turn soon. I'm sure of it."

Mrs. LeVine is climbing the steps of her front porch, her handbag over her shoulder. She either doesn't see me or pretends not to. Having lived only three houses down from me since I was two years old, she's had a front row seat to all the antics that make me a less-than-ideal friend for her prized daughter. I have no doubt that my tendency to walk alongside a man of Walter's position is on her extensive list of my flaws.

Walter takes a deep breath. "I've actually decided to give up baseball."

My feet stop walking, but Walter presses a hand into the small of my back and urges me onward, around the corner.

"How can you even think that, Walter? Since I met you, being a baseball player is basically all you've talked about."

"I know. But I didn't really know then what it would be like."

"What do you mean? You love it."

"When I get to play, yeah."

It's a good thing Walter's hand is pressing me forward, guiding me around a mother pushing her baby in a pram, because I'm so busy staring at him, trying to decode him, that I might have run into them. I've known Walter since I was thirteen, when my mother fell ill and Joyce took the live-in housekeeping job. But the boy I've known these last five years, so determined to strike out on his own, to provide a living for himself and his mother, is a stranger in this moment.

"Everyone warms the bench sometimes, Walter."

He winces. "Not everyone."

"You're nineteen, and this is your first team. Don't you think it's a bit premature to give up on baseball because you're not a starter yet? Not everyone is Babe Ruth."

Walter looks away, his chin jutting defiantly. "The money isn't good either. And you should see the dives we sleep in when we're on the road."

"But it won't always be like that."

"I don't want to be poor all my life."

"Who does? We're not talking about your whole life. We're talking about now."

"I should learn a trade or something." Walter kicks at a pebble that's dared to wander from a garden and onto the sidewalk. "Build me some kind of dependable future."

"Dependable future?" A laugh bubbles out of me. "I'm sorry, are you really Walter Thatcher? Because I've never heard you use a phrase like that before. I figured you'd only start talking like that when—" My feet stop walking again, and I press my hand over my mouth.

This time Walter doesn't force me onward. He stops and gazes at me.

"That's it, isn't it? You've met someone."

His only response is to stare back.

"I'm right, aren't I?"

He holds my gaze as he takes in a breath. "Yes. There is someone."

"I knew it!" Walter continues walking, and I sashay along-side him, tugging at his hand. "How'd you meet? What's her name? What's she like? Did she come to your games and swoon over you? Or—" I gasp again. "Or does she not like baseball? Is that why I'm hearing all this talk about giving it up?"

Walter smiles, looking more like his normal self. "No, she likes baseball. It's more that . . . Well, she comes from a family with money—"

"Ah, now we're getting somewhere." I link my arm through his as we start up State, the street that runs parallel to mine. "A rich girl."

"You wouldn't know it, though, from talking to her. She's very humble."

I roll my eyes. "You must really be over the moon. People always say that about girls with money, and it's so rarely true. Except for Lydia." Wait a minute. "Is it Lydia? It is, isn't it?"

Walter chuckles. "No, it's not Lydia." He squeezes my arm. "I know she's your best friend, and I don't want to offend, but I wouldn't describe her as a girl who you can't tell comes from money."

"Lydia's so sweet, though. So selfless."

"She is, yes." Walter hesitates. "But in a rich girl kind of way."

"How can you say that? She's up the street this very minute helping out Mrs. Barrow with Cole. If that's not sweet, then I don't know what is."

Walter smiles at me like my oldest brother, Tim, does when he finds me amusing. "I don't want to fight about Lydia."

"Fine." Lydia isn't perfect, of course, but she's always polite to Walter when they happen to be together. Even if she *does* disapprove of us being friends.

Quarrelling isn't how I want to spend our limited time together. I shake away my annoyance. "Well, whoever she is and however much pin money she's accustomed to, I hope she knows how lucky she is to have caught your eye, Walter. But you should know that I will personally flog you if you give up baseball for her. Because unless you're ready to marry her now—" My feet stop moving. "You're not, are you?"

"No. Audrey still has some school to finish. And it's early still. We've only been out a few times."

That's a relief. I've always expected Walter to marry, of course, but knowing I have time to adjust to the idea is nice. "It seems to me, then, that there's still time for you to give baseball a try before you need a 'dependable future,' as you put it."

Walter is quiet for the next block, and I can tell by the way he repeatedly buttons and unbuttons his coat that it's a thoughtful kind of silence. "I suppose I'm just frustrated over how little playing time I've had recently," he finally says. "You're right. I'm still young, and I always expected there to be hard work. It's just harder than I thought it would be, being out there all alone without Mother or you."

"Well, you have Audrey now."

His mouth quirks in a soft smile. "True."

I squeeze his arm. "You're close, I can feel it. I hate to think of you giving up when you've worked so hard. And—"

My gaze catches on something strange ahead on the sidewalk. A crumpled girl with long flames of hair who's wearing a uniform identical to mine.

A scream rips through the bright blue afternoon—my own.

grasp my skirt to provide my knees freedom to run. "Lydia!" I'm yelling even though I know she can't hear, that she's not with us.

With Walter's long legs and athleticism, he beats me to her bent frame. But he just gapes at her, same as I must have during the seizure I witnessed last month. I collapse beside Lydia and call to mind the questions I heard Dr. LeVine asking Mrs. LeVine last time. *How long did it last? What were her arms doing? Her legs? Did she lose control of her faculties?*

Even with my attempt to frame the moment in a list of scientific details, the sight of Lydia seizing has me biting in another scream. Her neck is angled back, and her eyes are rolled up, unseeing. Her throat makes a repetitive clicking noise, like the skipping needle on a record that needs turning over. Her arms are both extended, as if she'd been pushing someone away when the seizure struck, and her knees are tucked up beneath her rumpled, urine-soaked Presley school skirt.

"Oh!" Blood. A stream of crimson leaks onto the concrete. I want to curl into a ball and weep, but instead I lean closer to the sidewalk until I can see the source of the blood. A scrape on her right temple.

"What's happening?" Walter's words are hoarse.

"She's having a seizure." My voice is quiet but steady. "She must have been standing when it happened."

"What do we do? How do we make her stop?" Panic oozes from him.

"We can't." My hands smooth Lydia's hair, her skirt. "She has to come out of it on her own. But we need to get her home."

"I'll run for Matthew."

"No, she'd die if he saw her this way." I glance around to get my bearings. It's a miracle no one has seen yet. "Can you carry her? We can cut between those houses to the alley and then take her through the LeVines' back door. If you can carry her, I'll run ahead to phone for her father."

The repetitive clicking stops and a groan gurgles in Lydia's throat. Her legs stretch indiscriminately, nudging her skirt up and scraping her silk stockings along the concrete.

The fear that had squeezed my heart eases. "She's coming out of it." I lean close to her face. Her eyes are no longer rolled. Now they're milky, unseeing slits. "Lydia? Can you hear me?" The corner of her mouth twitches up, but it seems involuntary.

I stand and brush crumbs of concrete from my hands. "It'll be a while before she's really aware. If it's like last time."

"Should I pick her up?"

"Yes."

Walter presses his flat cap firmer onto his head and crouches beside Lydia. A shudder runs through him, and then he lifts her up into his arms.

I nod to the narrow gap between the houses. "Can you squeeze through there?"

"Just run, Piper. I'll get her there."

"Try not to be seen," I call as I hike my skirts up over my knees and take off. The gap between the houses is so narrow that I can hardly run without one of my elbows brushing against the brick siding. I burst into the alley, look both ways, and run south to the LeVines' home.

Their back door is locked. I pound on the door while keeping my gaze up the alley, waiting for Walter to come through with Lydia.

Tabitha opens the door, a broom in one hand and a scowl on her weathered, brown face. "Miz Sail, what on earth are you—"

"Lydia," I pant out. "Call Dr. LeVine."

The broom clatters to the floor as Tabitha rushes for the telephone.

Footsteps echo in the alley. Walter runs with Lydia clutched to him. The Chicago wind whips her red curls, and also Walter's hat from his head. But he pays no mind, just runs with her, and my heart seems to explode with appreciation for him.

"Missus!" Tabitha calls from deeper in the house. "It's Miz Sail. Somethin's wrong with Miz Lydia!"

I scrape dishes and food to the far end of the kitchen counter, grab a handful of towels to cushion Lydia's head, and then I rush to hold open the door for Walter.

As he eases Lydia through the doorway, Mrs. LeVine storms into the kitchen. "Where was she? What happened?"

"We found her on the sidewalk near the Barrows'. It looks like she was walking home when the seizure hit. She was still seizing when we found her. We saw maybe a minute of it."

Walter settles Lydia onto the counter and backs away as Mrs. LeVine leans over her daughter's motionless body. She presses two fingers to Lydia's wrist, and with her other hand smooths down her skirt. She gasps at the blood-soaked strands of hair.

I can't make my voice go above a whisper. "I think that's where she hit the sidewalk."

Walter clears his throat. "It doesn't look very deep, ma'am. Head wounds just bleed a lot."

He glances at me, and his mouth flickers with a reassuring smile. Walter's shirt is wet with something. Urine, I think. Heat rushes to my cheeks on behalf of my ladylike friend.

Mrs. LeVine keeps her gaze on Lydia's hauntingly still face. "Thank you for carrying her home, Walter." And then, almost to herself, "Why would she have been walking? Where was Matthew?"

"I don't know." Taking a full breath seems impossible. "I know he was taking her to watch Cole, but that's all."

Lydia shifts on the counter, groans. But then becomes still again.

Tabitha bustles into the room. "Dr. LeVine is on his way, Missus." Her gaze falls on Lydia, and her shoulders slump. "Oh, Miz Lydia . . ."

"Tabitha, fetch me a wet rag." The shock seems to have worn off Mrs. LeVine. "And keep the girls out of the kitchen. I don't want them seeing their sister like this."

"Yes, Missus." Tabitha hands her the rag and scurries away to find Hannah and Sarah.

Mrs. LeVine presses the rag to the head wound and turns a severe gaze toward us. "Thank you for delivering her, but I'll ask that you please allow us to handle this matter as a family now."

"Yes, of course." I trail my hand along Lydia's arm. Her normally fair skin is chalk white, but there's comfort in the warmth of it. In the rhythmic rise and fall of her chest.

"Piper, I trust that you will continue to be discreet in the matter of Lydia's health."

"Of course."

Her gaze flicks to Walter and then back at me. "And that you will impart the importance of discretion to Walter as well."

"Yes, ma'am. Neither of us will breathe a word. Might I—" I hesitate a second. "Might I ring later to check on her?"

Mrs. LeVine's mouth purses. "Will that not raise too much attention in your house?"

"No, not at all. I know how to be covert when I use the telephone."

"Yes, of course." Mrs. LeVine's gaze, so like Lydia's and yet so different, flicks up and down me. "I daresay you do."

I flush and take a step backward. "We'll leave you to care for Lydia now."

"Remember, Piper," Mrs. LeVine calls as Walter holds open the back door for me. "Not a word. Not even to Lydia."

"Not a word," I vow.

With a farewell nod of his head, Walter closes the door behind us.

The chill of the wind, which had been an ignorable nuisance before, whips down the alley. My right ankle is sore, and it's no wonder, running at such a pace.

"I don't think I've ever been so scared in all my life," Walter confesses.

My knees tremble, and I lean against him as we walk along the grit of the alley. "I'm so thankful you were with me. I couldn't have carried her."

"How long has this been going on?"

"I learned of it only a month ago. I was at the LeVines'. Lydia and I were making fudge, and we sat a spell to rest while it cooled. And . . ." I swallow as emotion rises high in my throat. "We had been sitting there in the living room, just chatting, when Sarah came twirling through the room. And when I looked back to Lydia, she was . . ."

Her head had been angled back, as though she were trying to see the bit of ceiling just behind her view. Her hands, which had been in her lap, were now pulled against her collarbone, the wrists bent in.

"Lydia?" I had dropped my glass of iced tea, though I wouldn't realize it until later. "Lydia?"

I must have been louder than I thought, because Mrs. LeVine had rushed into the room, Hannah and Sarah close behind her. "Get her on her side!" she ordered, even as she eased Lydia out of the chair and onto the ground. "Girls—leave the room at once."

A scream stuck in my throat at the sight of prim and frilly Lydia biting her tongue as though it was a bit of chewing gum. Her unblinking, rolled eyes seemed inhuman.

Mrs. LeVine had glanced at her wristwatch. "Piper, get the girls out of here, and call Dr. LeVine." But I had been frozen there. She turned, and looked up at me with a glare even more severe than Ms. Underhill's. "Go, Piper. Piper!"

Walter's voice blends with the memory of Mrs. LeVine's. "Piper?"

I shake myself from the LeVines' living room and back into the present. "That seizure lasted eight minutes, I was told. It felt like forever. When her father finally got there, Mrs. LeVine took me aside and made it clear I was to tell absolutely no one about what I had seen. Not my father, not friends at school. She asked that I not even mention it to Lydia."

Walter's forehead scrunches as he frowns at me.

I pitch my voice low. "They're worried about Dr. LeVine's practice. About what would happen if word got out that his daughter has been having unexplained seizures for several months now."

His face doesn't lose the serious countenance. "Can it be cured?"

"Dr. LeVine says it can. That it's a matter of finding the right combination of medicines." I take a deep breath. "He says the seizures don't *hurt* her. That she's sore afterward and often comes to with a headache, but doesn't remember a thing. So I guess even if she does have pain, she doesn't remember feeling it."

"Well. That's a small comfort, I suppose."

I picture Lydia as her beautiful self. Carefully curled red hair, skin aglow, and blue eyes lively. *That* is Lydia. I hold the image in my mind as the Other Lydia—her arms tucked awkwardly and her eyes rolled up—tries to crowd her out.

"This is 1924, for heaven's sake." I infuse my voice with false bravado. "We can make automobiles, telephones, and electricity. So surely this can be solved as well."

Walter smiles down at me. "Yes, you're right. And Dr. LeVine is one of the best in the city. Lydia couldn't be in better hands."

"Right."

We slow to a stop at the back door of our home. He glances down at his shirt, soiled with Lydia's blood and urine.

"You can't put that in the wash, or Joyce will ask about it. I'll have to replace it for you. Your hat too. What are your measurements?"

"Piper, one less shirt is no problem." He threads the buttons of his suit coat through their holes. "I'm going to get cleaned up, and then I'll be back down."

He disappears into the house, and I sink onto the bare wood steps. My ankle feels as though it might be swelling, and my legs quiver beneath my school skirt. I stare at the back of the brick house behind ours as my head swirls to all sorts of dangerous places.

Can I trust Dr. LeVine when he says this is curable? Or is it like when Mother came down with influenza in the summer of '19? When they told me she would be fine. And then she was not.

Lydia held my hand all through Mother's funeral. Didn't offer trite words of comfort, just pressed her palm against mine and stood there with me. How could I survive losing someone else I love? Especially without Lydia to see me through?

I take an angry swipe at the tears that fall. Lydia's *not* dying. Dr. LeVine told me so, and I will choose to trust him.

Only I can't block out the memory of my mother's parting words to me. Of the way she beckoned me close and spoke with labored breaths. "You're a smart girl, Piper. Trust yourself." The last cohesive sentences she chose before slipping into an unsettled sleep from which she never awoke.

The words shiver through me with every breath I take—*trust yourself.* I find I can't ignore that the seizures are happening with more frequency. Nor can I talk myself out of the fear that Dr. LeVine prioritizes secrecy more than Lydia's healing.

"I beg you to reconsider this." Lydia's words are spoken through pinched lips. Her gaze trails after the Hart, Schaffner & Marx employee as he ducks into the back room. "Really, Piper. Buying a shirt for a man is far too bold a gesture. How could Walter *not* read into such a gift?"

"It's my fault his shirt was ruined. I'm trying to be fair, not flirtatious."

Lydia yawns. "And why would you have thrown a mud ball at him in the first place? You're not a child anymore, Piper."

I shrug and feign interest in the display of neckties, running the cool silk between my fingers. The store smells of cedar and mint and is oppressively quiet, like a library. The only other patron at the men's clothing store is also a woman. Her back is to us as she surveys men's suits, but even from here I can tell she's nearly as tall as my brothers and old enough to be in here for a respectable reason—a suit for her husband, most likely. She keeps glancing at us. Probably curious about why two adolescent girls are in a men's clothing store.

I resolve to ignore her silent questions. "Besides, Walter is seeing someone in California. He told me so yesterday. He's quite smitten."

"And how did you feel when he told you that?"

I shrug again. "It's strange to think of him married. He wouldn't come home as much. That makes me sad. But of course, I suppose I'll be moving out before too long."

"But you weren't jealous?"

"No. Same as I wouldn't be if I learned Nick were marrying. I've told you—Walter's like my brother." I smile as she attempts to cover up another yawn. "Am I boring you?"

Her smile has a sleepy tinge to it and her eyelids are heavy. "Not at all. I'm just so tired for some reason today."

Lydia scratches the back of her neck as she stares at a display of cuff links. She looks so healthy, so utterly normal, it's impossible to believe the state I found her in yesterday afternoon. Her mouth turns up in a smile, and her cheeks grow pinker with every passing second.

"Are those cufflinks amusing you, Lydia LeVine?"

Lydia startles and then gives a wistful sigh. "Oh, Piper. How can I lecture you about giving Walter a present when I'm standing here dreaming about giving a gift of my own?"

"What possible purpose does Matthew have for gold cufflinks?"

"Would you keep your voice down?" Lydia glances over her shoulder at the other woman, who looks away. I cannot imagine why we're of such interest to her. "I wish you didn't disapprove so strongly of me and Matthew. It gives me very little hope of Mother and Father giving us their blessing."

I take in my beautiful friend. "You could have anyone, Lydia. Heaven knows you already have beaux lining up—"

Lydia arches doubtful eyebrows. "I don't see Jeremiah Crane hanging around school to talk to *me*."

"He's not there to talk to me either. He's there to pick up Emma."

Lydia shakes her head. "You're normally so intuitive, Piper."

"Just please don't rush this thing with Matthew, okay?"

Lydia's jaw tightens. Even if the sales clerk hadn't picked that moment to return, I don't think she would have given the promise I sought.

The clerk looks down his long nose at us. "Shall I wrap this and the hat in the same box, Miss?"

"Please."

Lydia is quiet while we wait, and I occupy myself with wrapping the tie of my uniform around my finger and then unwrapping it. On the drive here from school, I had used a considerable amount of energy restraining myself from yelling at Matthew for not being with Lydia when she had her seizure.

When I had called the LeVine residence last night, Tabitha

had—in words so hushed I could barely hear them—told me that Matthew had gone to the market to pick up the grocery order, having expected Lydia to remain at the Barrows' residence for at least an hour. Tabitha, perhaps sensing my ire, assured me that he'd been distraught to learn Lydia had not only walked home but had one of her spells and been hurt.

One of her "spells." Ha.

"Is something unsatisfactory, Miss Sail?"

I blink and realize that I just snorted at the package the clerk offered me. "No, nothing at all. Thank you for your assistance."

"Thank you for your business."

As we exit the clothing store, Matthew smiles and sweeps open the back door of the Duesenberg for us. He touches the brim of his flat cap as I pass by him. "It looks as though the stop was a success."

"It was. Thank you." The brusqueness in my voice seems to go unnoticed by him.

It's unfair to be so angry with Matthew when he was only trying to be efficient with his work time, but I can't seem to silence the accusations in my head. That if Matthew had been there, if Lydia hadn't been left alone yesterday afternoon, somehow the seizure never would have happened.

I look back to the door, where Lydia stands beaming up at Matthew. She speaks in too private a voice for me to overhear, but whatever it is, Matthew smiles too. With a pang, I think of Lydia's blush as she gazed at the cufflinks inside the store. Where is my sensible and proper friend?

I dread the moment I become sweet on someone. It seems to turn your brain to mush.

"Oh, Matthew." Lydia's voice is breathy with laughter as she ducks inside the car.

STEPHANIE MORRILL

The door closes behind her, and I tuck my parcel between us. Lydia arranges her red curls over her shoulder as she watches Matthew slide around the front of the car. Under the wide brim of her hat, and with the way she styled her hair today, I can't even see the scrape from yesterday. But something—frustration? Exhaustion? Stupidity?—makes me ask anyway.

"How did you hurt yourself, Lydia?"

Her chuckle holds embarrassment as her fingertips graze her temple. "Oh dear, can you see it? It looks worse than it is, I assure you." She presses her fingers to her mouth to cover a yawn. "Just one of my fainting spells. You're the first to ask about it today. I thought I had concealed it nicely."

I keep my gaze on the straps of my black shoes. They turn to blurs.

Matthew climbs in the car, and Lydia leans forward. "My, that wind today!"

As he pulls out into traffic, she continues to chat with him in the animated, artful way we've learned in etiquette classes.

Watching her flirt somehow makes the truth feel like a smack in the face—Lydia has no idea about the seizures. And neither does Matthew, it seems. If Dr. and Mrs. LeVine can be trusted, it's only me, Walter, and Tabitha who know details. Being the only one in the car who's aware that Lydia could transform at any second, could become that girl I saw on the sidewalk yesterday, leaves me incapable of capturing a full breath. As if the truth is like a hand clasped over my mouth.

Lydia should know. Matthew, who drives Lydia and her sisters so often, should know.

But I made my promise to Mrs. LeVine. While I have no scruples about borrowing Ms. Underhill's cardigan to snatch a pastry, or sliding down the school banister in my swimming costume, breaking a promise is a line I won't cross. What does a girl have, really, if her word cannot be trusted?

As Matthew steers us toward the Astor Street district, and as Lydia persists in drawing conversation out of him, my gaze stays on the choppy gray waters of Lake Michigan. The ache in my knuckles is dull despite the lashes Ms. Underhill inflicted today when my mouth got the best of me.

"What kind of lazy work is this, Miss Sail?" She had held up the mess of green fabric for the class to see. "Is this the bodice of a dress or a bird's nest?"

Only dimwitted Mae Husboldt was rude enough to play along and laugh.

I took a measured breath, determined to behave in a way that would make Joyce proud. That wouldn't make Lydia scold me afterward. "Yes, I believe I've made a mistake or two in my stitches."

"A mistake or two? More like ten." She had allowed a beat of silence in her abuse, as if anticipating Mae's giggles. "Here you've sewn the right side together with the wrong side. You'll have to take it all apart. Start over. There won't be time for you to finish it for the fashion show, I'm afraid."

This earned a reaction from the other girls—an exhale of horror.

She thrust the bodice back to me, and the haughty expression she wore made it seem as though she thought this might be a devastating blow to me. Like all my hopes were pinned on this dress being displayed in the Presley's School for Girls Fashion Show, a long-standing tradition during the week of graduation. "Yes, Ms. Underhill."

My meekness only seemed to spur her. "I wonder about your future, Miss Sail. Such a fine mind in there, and yet, what will become of you?"

"Well." I pulled my seam ripper along the bodice, and the sound of severing threads filled the air. "I doubt I'll be a seamstress."

And it was no surprise to me when she ordered me to stretch my hand out across the table.

Lydia's loud laughter calls me back to the car. Matthew, who's normally so quiet, speaks with enthusiasm about something that requires a faux Irish accent. Not a bad one, either.

Somehow Lydia has managed to draw him out.

It's funny. I've asked myself the same question that Ms. Underhill did today. What will become of a girl like me who lacks patience for sewing, who doesn't understand the art of flirting, and who is more skilled with a right hook than the kind used for crocheting?

I've received my acceptance notices from Vassar, Smith, and Bryn Mawr, but what will the point of it all be? What do I want to *do* with my life? Despite my bobbed hair and beliefs that women should be equal with men, I wouldn't describe myself as a flapper. Nor do I see myself as the happy housewife with a brood of children. These days, is there room for a place in-between?

And yet I've always thought I had Lydia pegged. I assumed she would marry early, to someone with bright prospects who worked in real estate or medicine. They would have babies for whom she'd knit booties and sweaters, but only after she'd held fund-raisers for the less fortunate in Chicago and attended parties with other socialites.

That Lydia LeVine would have a life like her mother's, like

my mother's, has always seemed a given. Only now as I watch her send Matthew encouraging smiles, and as I think about how hurt she seemed at the clothing store when I had spoken against the two of them, the question seems to apply to her as well.

Lydia laughs loud, makes an excuse of brushing a bit of fuzz from Matthew's shoulder.

Oh, Lydia. What will become of you?

Whhat's this for?"

Walter's voice calls me out of the confusingly romantic world of Catherine and Heathcliff. His broad shoulders practically fill the doorway as he holds up the shirt.

"It's for wearing." I turn the page. "They call it a shirt."

"Pippy." But his amusement leaks through his growl. "I told you that you didn't need to replace it."

"And I told you that I was going to." I smile sweetly. "Anything else?"

"You're a very stubborn woman. Are you aware of that?"

Bessie Smith's "Baby, Won't You Please Come Home" crashes to a close, and I stand to flip the record. "I am. Have you tried it on? Does it fit?"

"Like it was tailor made. I don't want to ask how you knew my size."

"Because you don't want to know that I snuck into your room?"

"No. I don't want to know that."

"Then it's good you aren't asking."

"Pippy . . ."

The soulful melodies of Bessie Smith start up again, and I turn my back to the Victrola to smile at my worried friend. "I didn't snoop at all, I promise. I only looked at your shirt to see what size it was, and I didn't even think of hunting for your correspondence with Audrey."

Now Walter smiles. "Well. Thank you. For the shirt and hat. You didn't need to."

I gesture to his attire—knickerbockers and gaiters. "You're playing somewhere?"

Walter nods. "With Jimmy and the fellas. For old time's sake."

"Can I come?"

Walter glances at my pale clothing, hardly ideal for a baseball game. I smooth my cream skirt. "I could change quickly."

Walter opens his mouth, but it's Joyce who speaks as she comes through with a basket of folded laundry. "Your father wants you home for dinner tonight, Piper."

I groan. "Does that mean Jane is eating with us?"

Joyce purses her lips. "He did not mention Miss Miller to me, no. Just you and Nicholas."

"Perhaps they've parted ways."

Joyce only gives me a look.

"Well, enjoy dinner." Walter nods to his mother as he fits his baseball cap on his head. "I'll just grab my bat and glove and be off."

Joyce watches him go, and then affixes the basket to her hip. She gives me an evaluating look. "It would serve you well to get used to the idea of Miss Miller."

I sink back to my seat on the couch. "I'm quite comfortable disliking her, but thank you."

"I imagine the idea of liking her feels like a betrayal to your mother, but you would *honor* her memory by being kind. You would show that Elsie Sail raised a lady."

"My mother died before she could raise a lady." The words cause an ache in my chest.

"Piper." Joyce's voice dips low and warm. "We all have hard

things in this life. But good can come from them, if we choose to see it."

I look at Joyce and note the lines that fan out from her dark eyes. See hair that was once sandy streaked with gray now gray streaked with sandy. Yes, Joyce certainly knows what it's like to be dealt a bad hand. Not that she would ever breathe a word of her history to me, but Walter has.

Joyce was raised in a middle-class family in Peoria, Illinois. She had a steady beau and plans for college when she found herself pregnant. Walter says she never has divulged details about his father—was it the boyfriend? Another man who took advantage? A mistake of passion? Regardless, Joyce's parents sent her to Chicago for an abortion and she never returned home.

Joyce certainly knows a little something about not letting life get you down. But still.

"I won't treat Jane like she's some sort of blessing."

Joyce's mouth flickers in a frown. "Then, Piper, how will she ever become one?"

I lower my gaze to my book and refuse to say any of the caustic words locked behind my lips. Joyce lingers only a moment longer before carrying on her way to the family bedrooms.

A breath I had been holding leaks out. I stare at the words on the page until they blur.

The rap on the front door jolts me from my daze. How long have I just been sitting here? Nick, who's coming down the stairs with a briefcase in hand, opens the door.

Lydia stomps inside. Her blue eyes are ice as she rips her wide-brimmed hat from her head. "I'm furious."

"Yes, I see that." I snap shut my novel. "What's going on?"

"It's my parents. Would you believe—" She catches sight of

Nick in her peripheral vision. "Oh, hello." Her smile is a shade bashful. "How are you this afternoon?"

"I'm doing fine. I would inquire about you, but I think I already know the answer." He winks at her, but Nick's attempts to flirt only embarrass her further.

Lydia laughs lightly and ducks her head.

I give Nick a pointed look, and he clears his throat. "Well, I'm on my way to the library to study with some friends." He holds up his briefcase as if submitting evidence. "I'll see you later."

She murmurs a good-bye and then perches beside me on the couch. Lydia fusses with her beaded handbag until the front door closes behind Nick, and then she giggles. "That was foolish of me. Why didn't I think to greet the person who opened the door before I spoke?"

"Because you're angry. He's sweet on you, you know."

"You think everyone is sweet on me. And anger is no excuse for bad manners." Her face pinches. "But, yes. I'm furious."

"What happened?"

"Mother and Daddy have confined me to the house." Lydia collapses onto the couch, in a startlingly unladylike manner. "They've even pulled me out of school."

"With not even two weeks before graduation? Why would they do that?"

Lydia regards me with a serious gaze. "It's these fainting spells I have. Apparently, they're more of a concern than Mother and Daddy have let on."

Seizures. The correction sits on my tongue, and I bite it back.

Lydia's chin trembles. "They say it's nothing I need to worry about, and then . . ." She takes a deep breath. "Then they go and pull me out of school, and now they're making me . . ."

43

Tears overtake her. Lydia falls against my shoulder and releases a loud sob.

I wrap her in a tight hug. "It'll be okay, Lydia. It will."

Footsteps thunder down the hall and Walter bursts into the living room. "What's wrong? Oh." He takes in the scene of me and Lydia on the couch. "I'm sorry, I heard crying. I'm sorry."

He backs out of the room.

"He's gone," I murmur to Lydia.

"No doubt he thought it was you crying yourself silly in here. Not that you'd ever do such a foolish thing." Lydia fumbles in her bag and retrieves a handkerchief. "But he thought it must be you, and he rushed to help, because that's just how it is for you."

She dabs at her eyes with a damp handkerchief. I pull a fresh one from my cardigan pocket and hand it to her. "There were a lot of false implications in those statements, but you're upset so that's okay."

Lydia clutches the offered hankie but doesn't use it. She looks at me with red-rimmed eyes. "They're sending me to the Mayo Clinic in Minnesota." Her voice is flat, as if she used up all her emotion moments ago. "To some doctor friend of Daddy's who thinks a special diet can help me with my condition."

Always such delicate terms with the LeVines. Lydia's *condition*, Lydia's *episodes*, Lydia's *spells*. But they can frame it however they want if they're being smart enough to get her expert help.

"This is a good thing, Lydia." I'm afraid she can hear the relief in my voice, see it on my face. Can she tell I know more than she does? "You're going to get better."

Lydia's mouth is in a firm line as she looks at me.

"Don't you *want* to get better?"

"Of course I want to get better. But I don't want to be shipped off to Minnesota like this! Not when . . ." She pushes herself off the couch and turns the Victrola bell toward the wall, quieting Bessie Smith. "How can you hear yourself think with that playing so loud?"

"Not when *what*, Lydia?"

She twists the hankie in her hands, and I see my initials—embroidered by Lydia—fold in on themselves. "Not when Matthew is showing signs of having feelings for me."

It's all I can do to keep my eyes from rolling. To not say the exasperated *Oh, Lydia* that's ripe on my tongue. Why do girls allow themselves to be so foolish when it comes to men? Why does being in love seem to fill their heads with nothing but empty space and giggles? Even my practical, duty-driven, even-tempered friend.

As the silence grows, so does the shade of pink of Lydia's cheeks. "Maybe I'm wrong, but I think he does, anyway. This afternoon, when you and I were getting back in the car at the store, he even touched me. Put his hand on my back as I got in the car, just like Daddy does with Mother. Perhaps I'm imagining things . . ."

"Lydia. If Matthew has half a brain, he's in love with you. But that's not going to change just because you spend a few days at a hospital in Minnesota."

"More like a month or two." Lydia perches on the edge of the couch. "Maybe more."

"Fine, a few months then. Perhaps some time and a change of society would even be a good test to know if this is real."

Lydia chews on her lower lip for a moment. "Or maybe I just won't go."

"You can't be serious, Lydia. This . . . condition of yours is no small thing. You have to get help. You can't jeopardize your health just because you fancy yourself in love."

Lydia's blue eyes turn flinty. "I know you're afraid of growing up, but that doesn't mean you get to pin your fears on me, Piper Sail. I *know* I love Matthew. If he asked me to marry him today, I'd have no hesitation saying yes."

"Lydia." The horror I'm feeling—or at least part of it—is surely evident on my face. "It's one thing to carry a torch for your chauffeur, to flirt with him as he's driving you around. It's quite another to be his wife."

She turns away from me, nose in the air. "I didn't know you were capable of such snobbery."

"I don't wish to be a snob, I wish to be practical." My voice rises with each word, and maybe if I'm loud enough, she'll actually listen. "But whether you want to hear it or not, I can't imagine you being content in some low-rent apartment, wearing a homemade dress as you fix beans for the third night in a row."

Lydia shoves my handkerchief into her pocket and wrestles her handbag closed. "Oh, so you think *me* a snob?"

"Not at all. I think you're a girl who's grown up in a fine house. Who doesn't know how to cook or do laundry or go a month without a new bauble." I can't believe the words coming next will be *mine* directed to *Lydia*. "I beg you to be cautious. To think this through."

My friend just looks at me. Doesn't speak, but doesn't stand to leave either.

She scratches behind her knee. "It's the medicine, Daddy said." Her words are quiet and tear-soaked. "The medicine makes me feel like I have bugs crawling on me. It makes me paranoid too. I kept thinking this black car was following me. Or like at the store today. I was convinced that woman was listening to every word we said. Following me." She chuckles humorlessly. "Last night, I fell asleep at the dinner table. Right in the middle of eating my pot roast."

I press my eyes closed, hoping it'll keep tears from spilling. "This is why you need to go to the Mayo Clinic. So we can get you healthy."

"What if I can't get healthy?"

Her words push all the air from my lungs, like when I fell out of a tree as a kid and couldn't seem to take a breath. "Don't say that, Lydia. We're not going to think like that."

She fiddles with the clasp of her bag. "I think we both know these fainting spells of mine aren't merely fainting spells. They're getting closer together. And for all we know—"

I squeeze my eyes tight. *Don't say it. Please.*

"—the next one I have could be my end."

The wailing of Bessie's voice is the only sound of the room. I open my eyes and study Lydia. The matter-of-fact line of her mouth. The blue eyes that hold only reason, not fear. "You're going to get healthy, Lydia. You . . . you just *are.*"

"We can pray to that end, and I certainly do. But death is a part of life. We both know firsthand that, for some, it comes earlier than seems natural." She takes in a deep, resolved breath. "And when I may not have a tomorrow on this earth, it leaves me reluctant to sacrifice the happiness available to me today."

I can only look at her.

Lydia rises from the couch with straight-backed grace that showcases her good breeding. "I need to tell the Barrows I can no longer watch Cole, but I'm going to go home and tell Matthew how I feel." The slight waver in her voice is the only indicator of her nerves. "I'll do it without your support, but having it would mean the world to me."

I'm taller than she, but standing here beside her, it feels as though I'm a child and Lydia is hopping onto the train of womanhood. And what else can a best friend do when a farewell comes but give a hug, promise to write often, and wave good-bye?

"What will you say to him?"

She takes a deep breath. "I don't know. Perhaps I'll see if he's free to go out tonight." Her laugh is high and wheezy. "I have absolutely no idea."

"I'm sure you'll think of something brilliant. And I'm sure you don't need to. He cares about you. It's obvious."

Lydia grins, and for a moment we're both just girls. "You think that about everyone." She squeezes me close. "But thank you."

I hold open the door for her, and my friend who wears adulthood with such ease steps out. She shivers. "I was so furious on my way over, I guess I didn't notice the wind. Doesn't the weather know it's almost summer?"

"Here." I unhook my coat from the rack and hand it to her.

"Thank you." Lydia wraps it tight around her. "Maybe wearing it will help me to be brave like you. I'll bring it back later tonight."

I wave the offer away. "Wear it on your date. But ring me later."

Her smile is nervous, but her eyes bright. "I will."

Watching her walk down the steps, it seems impossible to believe she won't be able to call Matthew her own by the end of the evening. "Want me to walk you home?"

Lydia laughs. "I can manage the three houses, I think. But thank you."

Still, I stand on the front porch and watch until she unlatches her gate. "Farewell, my friend."

Though it would be impossible for her to hear me, Lydia looks up and calls a chipper, "Good-bye!" before giving me one last wave and smile.

"You're very quiet tonight, Piper." Father arches his silver eyebrows at me as he cuts through his steak. "Is something troubling you?"

I shake away thoughts of Lydia and Matthew. Of the silent telephone. "No." I put on a smile for Father and Nick. "Not at all."

"Did school go well today?"

"It did."

Father continues to look at me as he chews. A lawyer trick of his to keep someone talking. I pick up my glass of milk with my left hand and tuck my bruised right hand under my pleated skirt.

"We're studying poetry in English, and I find it rather boring."

Father chuckles. "You get that from me, I'm afraid. Your mother loved it. She used to recite Psalms to me." He pops a bite of steak into his mouth. "From the Bible."

"I'm familiar with Psalms, Father. *I* pay attention on Sunday mornings."

Father winks at me. "Good for you, Piper." He swirls the red wine in his glass and holds it up as if offering me a toast. "Don't tell Reverend on me."

Despite alcohol being illegal, I don't imagine Reverend would be too shocked to learn Father continues to enjoy a nightly glass of wine.

The table falls into silence, with the exception of chewing and Nick's rustling newspaper. Dinners when Mother was still with us were alive with conversation. Mostly between her and Father, but also us kids. She certainly never would have allowed Nick to read the newspaper during marked family time.

Nick turns the page. "Looks like a promising season for the Cubs. Jigger Statz will be back."

"I would have more faith in the organization if they would sign Walter." I stab my boiled carrots. "But I suppose there's always next season."

Father pours himself another glass of red and offers the bottle to my brother. "Nick, you help with the Cassanos' cases. You should enjoy some of the spoils."

As Father and Nick lapse into lawyer speak about the evidence that earned a dismissal of the charges against a client, my thoughts drift to Walter and our conversation yesterday. Would he still want to play for the Cubs now that Audrey is in the picture? It rattles me to think how tempted he is to give up his first love—baseball—because of a few good dates.

Why did both my dear friends have to fall in love at the same time? It leaves me woefully short of sane people with whom I can converse.

"We were lucky to end up with Judge Hill." Nick swirls his wine, imitating Father. "He's smart enough to see which police have been bought by the Finnegans."

Father shakes his head. "The statement from Giovanni's son sealed the deal, I think." He glances at me. Smiles. "But let's not speak of such gruesome matters in front of Piper. Especially not tonight." The way he lays his napkin beside his plate and leans back in his chair calls to mind Joyce saying he'd requested Nick and I be present for dinner. "I have some good news to share with you both."

I brace myself for the blow that I've anticipated these last six months.

"I have asked Jane to marry me, and she has agreed. She wanted to be here when I told you, but I decided it would be best to tell you myself."

Of course she wanted to be here. She wanted to look down her snub nose at me in her moment of victory. Even though I have expected the news, my mouth fills with a bitter taste, and it's not just from the boiled Brussels sprouts.

Father smooths the tablecloth. He's nervous. "I had hoped Tim and Gretchen could join us for dinner as well, but they had other commitments, so I had to tell your brother on the phone this afternoon."

And how did my oldest brother feel when he heard Father is about to marry a woman who's a year younger than himself? Maybe it's different for men. Maybe Tim finds it admirable that Father can win a lady so young.

My stomach clenches like a fist.

Nick puts on the smile he uses when practicing being in a courtroom. "Congratulations, Pop. When's the big day?"

A beat of silence. "June fourteenth."

The words are a knife, and I suck in a breath. "Is that really necessary?"

"I'm sorry, Piper. I know it's hard." Father's gaze holds sympathy, and I wish that meant something to me. "With this short of notice, it was the only available date."

The little girl inside me is stomping her feet, screaming herself hoarse. *How dare you!* she screams. *How dare you get married on Mother's birthday!*

The dining room fills with the screech of my chair pushing back on the wood floor.

"Wait, Piper. I know how it devastated you to lose your mother." Father's voice has an urgency, and I think I'm getting a taste of what juries see when Timothy Sail Senior pleads his client's case. "It destroyed me to lose Elsie. It's why I never pursued remarriage, despite knowing she would have wanted you to grow up with a mother—"

"I *have* a mother."

Father's eyes are tender as he gazes at me. "Of course you do. I should have said 'Mother would have wanted you to have a *female* to talk to.'"

"I have Joyce."

"Who's wonderful, and who has made our loss tolerable these last five years. But Jane is a modern woman of society. There are so many opportunities for young women these days, and she'll be able to guide you through these years as you attend college and look for a husband."

Nick snorts as he pushes his bite of steak through gravy. I'm too emotionally ravaged to spare him a nasty look, but Father sends him one before turning back to me.

"I'm sorry the timing has worked out this way, Piper."

As if this is completely out of his control.

I look away from him, keep my jaw locked. "May I be excused?"

Father hesitates. "Perhaps . . . Perhaps Jane and I could be married later in the summer. But the next available date is August ninth, and I just can't bring myself to do that."

"It doesn't matter." Or rather, the damage has already been done. Just knowing that Father is willing to have the wedding on what would have been Mother's birthday is what hurts.

"What's August ninth?" Nick asks around the food in his mouth.

"The anniversary of Mother's death," I say when Father is silent. I look my father in the eye. "May I be excused?"

He rakes in a breath. "I know my remarrying would've been hard for you regardless. I'm just sorry I've made it harder."

"I have poetry to read."

"Fine. You're excused."

As I turn from the table, Joyce enters the dining room. "Sorry to interrupt, but there's a telephone call for you, Piper."

"You can take it in my office, honey."

If Father expects a thank-you, he doesn't get one. I drag myself to his office. I'm not in the mood to be happy for Lydia, to hear every detail of her conversation with Matthew. I just want to be alone in my room where I can think and cry.

In the graying light of the room, I flop onto Father's office chair and pull the candlestick phone onto my lap. "Hello, Lydia."

There's silence. "Piper"—*not* a female voice—"this is Dr. LeVine. I thought Lydia might be there. Is she not?"

"No, sir. She was here around five o'clock, but she didn't stay long."

"Oh." And then again, but with a different note, "Oh. We thought she would dine with your family."

So she's getting her date, and I don't even get the courtesy of being told that I'm the cover story? That's just ducky. Regular Lydia wouldn't do anything so dishonest, but this new Lydia who fancies herself in love? She's probably dancing the night away at the Green Door Tavern.

"When did she leave?" Dr. LeVine's voice is curt.

"I don't remember. She didn't stay terribly long." I swallow. How can I salvage this? "I believe she was going to stop by the Barrows'. Perhaps she's dining with them?"

Of course they'll just say she isn't, but really, if Lydia wants me to lie for her, she has to clue me in ahead of time.

"If you see her, please tell her we want her at home."

"Sure, Dr. LeVine." But he's hung up.

I sigh and hang the earpiece back on its hook. The one night I need Lydia to be her steadfast, tender-hearted self, she's sneaking around.

"She'll get over it," Nick is saying to Father in the dining room. "You and Jane can't design your whole life around Piper."

My back stiffens. Is it too much to ask for a little sensitivity for Mother's birthday?

Father's voice is too low for me to make out, but I don't care to eavesdrop. My stocking feet whisper against the hardwood floors as I stalk up two flights of stairs to my bedroom. I shut the door behind me with such force, the glass shade on my lamp rattles.

I take in my room—so full of my mother—with dry eyes. The white iron bed and pink bedding that she picked out when I was too young to know I didn't like pink. The desk she surprised me with when I was ten and in love with writing stories. The armoire that was hers . . . until she no longer needed it.

I sit in the rocking chair that she used with all three of us children and wait for the tears to come. I know Father's right, that Mother would have encouraged remarriage. Would have likely told me that she wasn't using her birthday anymore, so Father and Jane might as well have it. My guess is she would have liked Jane and her fussy, girly ways, because Mother liked everyone.

But would she like this girl that I am? Bitterness over losing her has certainly festered in my heart these last five years. And in embracing the resentment, perhaps I've overlooked becoming a lady whom Elsie Sail would have been proud to call her daughter.

"Why, I can't believe my eyes. Is that possibly Miss Sail walking alone?"

I turn and find Jeremiah Crane standing along the walkway of Presley's the next afternoon. His trilby tips at an angle, his mouth is set in a smirk, and his hands are in the pockets of his trousers. The combination of which makes up a rather rakish picture.

I hesitate, and then step out of the flow of girls to join Jeremiah. "And how are you today, Mr. Crane?"

"Very well, thank you." Jeremiah makes a show of glancing about. "Where is your Miss LeVine this afternoon? I hardly recognized you without her."

Of course. Lydia's red hair and lovely face have always attracted male attention. I tip my face up to the warm sunlight in hopes that Jeremiah won't read into any disappointment that might be evident. "At home, I believe."

Probably suffering from punishment so severe, she couldn't have even imagined it.

"Have they come for you, Miss Sail?" Jeremiah asks teasingly.

I look to Jeremiah and find him grinning, his gaze attached to something behind me. But when I try to follow his eye line,

I see nothing but vehicles and parents. My confusion must be clear because Jeremiah nods toward the street. "See those two men who just got out of the touring sedan by the streetlamp?"

"Yes." One looks near Father's age, and is thick, with a belly that implies he doesn't let Prohibition tamper the amount of beer he drinks. The other is trim with olive skin and, from this distance at least, seems quite young. Maybe only three or four years older than me.

"That car they just got out of is a detective bureau vehicle." Jeremiah leans against the railing and crosses his arms over his chest. There's a spark of mischief in his slate-blue eyes. "Have pastries gone missing from the teacher's lounge again, Miss Sail?"

My cheeks heat. "I can neither confirm nor deny that."

Jeremiah releases a loud laugh. "What other response would I expect from a lawyer's daughter?"

"Surely you Cranes have plenty to discuss at the dinner table." I clap a hand to my hat as a gust of wind sweeps across campus. "It seems you wouldn't have to sink to mere secondary school gossip."

"Is it mere gossip that you slid down the stairwell banister in only your bathing costume?"

My face burns even hotter. "That . . . that's being taken out of context."

"Or that you stole a frog from the science teacher's classroom?"

"*Liberated* is the word I would choose, but that's never been proven."

"Or that you have the highest marks in the school?"

Why's he razzing me so hard? It's not like I went out of my way to talk to him. *He* called out to *me*.

"I believe it's time for me to be going, Mr. Crane." I take a step backward. "Good day."

"Wait, Miss Sail. Do you . . ." Jeremiah clutches his hat in his hands, rotating it in an absent manner. "Do you go to the movies often?"

My breath catches in my chest. Is he . . . ?

"Emma and I saw *The Thief of Baghdad* last night." Jeremiah mashes his hat back onto his head. "I thought maybe you might like to see it. That maybe, if you were free this Friday evening, we could go together."

There's no longer mischief lighting Jeremiah's eyes. My brain is incapable of forming an intellectual response. A date? He's asking *me* on a date?

"Excuse me? Are you Miss Piper Sail?"

I turn toward the unfamiliar baritone and find myself face to face with the two detectives Jeremiah pointed out to me minutes ago. "Yes, I am."

The older man is several steps up on the stairway, as if he were leading the way to the school doors. But the younger one stands on the same step as me. Both tip their hats, and the younger one speaks. "I'm Detective Cassano, and this is Detective O'Malley. Could we have a minute of your time to ask a few questions?"

What could they possibly . . . ? "Of course. About what?"

As if their heads are connected, both detectives look to Jeremiah.

"I don't mind if he hears." I straighten my shoulders, remind myself of the truth. "I haven't done anything wrong."

"Of course not, Miss," says Detective Cassano. "We're here in service of the LeVine family."

My surroundings dim with two exceptions—the grave

expression on the detective's face, and the way my heart seems intent to fly right out of my chest. "The LeVine family?"

"Dr. Charles LeVine?"

"Yes, I know. I'm best friends with their daughter."

"That's why we're here. We hoped you could provide insight to her whereabouts."

Oh, Lydia. What have you done?

"H-her whereabouts?" I swallow to steady my voice. "How do you mean?"

My stomach turns to ice as both detectives sweep their hats off their heads.

"I apologize to have to tell you, Miss Sail. We thought you would know by now." Detective Cassano's words are measured, as if being selected carefully. "Lydia LeVine has been reported missing."

58

CHAPTER
FOUR

Jeremiah's hands grasp my shoulders, hold me steady, and that's when I realize I swayed.

"I'm sorry we're the bearers of troubling news, Miss Sail." Detective Cassano glances to his older counterpart before training his eyes back on me. "I'm sure it's alarming to learn about your friend in this manner. We're hoping you can help us locate her."

"Of course." My words are so high and breathy, I barely recognize them as my own. "I'll do whatever I can."

Detective O'Malley fits his homburg back on his round head. "Cassano, I'll head in to have a word with the headmistress." He nods to me. "My apologies, Miss Sail." While his words are brusque, his gaze is sincere.

"Thank you, detective."

They sound like lines from a school play rather than my real life. *Reported missing. Thank you, detective.*

At the most, Lydia was supposed to be going on a date. Just a date.

From his inside pocket, the detective pulls a small notepad and a stub of a pencil. "I know it's hard, Miss Sail, but I need to ask you a few questions about Lydia. When was the last time you saw her?"

Around us, Presley's girls clatter down the stone steps, passing us curious looks as they bend their bobbed heads together and whisper. I almost sway on my feet again, but I stop myself in time.

"Yesterday, around five o'clock. She was only over for about fifteen minutes, and then she left."

"What was Lydia like during that time? Anything unusual about her behavior?"

Everything.

In fact, it was hard to remember anything that *hadn't* been unusual. From Lydia's anger, to her talk about her health, to her determination to finally tell Matthew how she felt. *If he asked me to marry him today, I'd have no hesitation saying yes.* The words reverberate in my ears.

Surely not. Even as brave and reckless as she seemed yesterday afternoon, surely she wouldn't have gone so far as to actually run away with Matthew.

Or would she?

Jeremiah's hand presses into my waist. "Piper, I think you should sit down."

I had swayed again.

"Miss Sail, while I understand you being alarmed over your friend, I assure you that this sort of thing is not unusual." Detective Cassano gazes at me from under the brim of his hat. Despite the firm line of his jaw and his sharp eyes, there's a softness about his manner. "The majority of the time, we find the young lady with a friend or boyfriend. So while we're taking this seriously, of course, you should know that the results usually are not as distressing as they initially seem."

"Thank you, that's comforting." I take a swallow of dry air. "You asked about Lydia's behavior. She came over because she'd been fighting with her parents. When she arrived at my house, she was upset."

"What had they been fighting about?"

"Dr. and Mrs. LeVine wanted Lydia to go to Minnesota for a few months, and she didn't want to go. She . . ." I press my eyes closed, the betrayal bitter on the tip of my tongue. Lydia will understand, right? He's a detective. I can't lie. "She believed herself in love with someone, and she didn't want to be gone so long."

Detective Cassano's eyebrows rise. "Who was it?"

"The family's chauffeur. Matthew. I'm sorry, I don't know his last name."

"What's going on here?" Walter's voice booms into the conversation, and I turn to find him mounting Presley's limestone steps two at a time to reach us. I've never thought of Walter being frightening, but with his broad shoulders and the scowl on his face, I'm not surprised the girls in his path skitter out of the way.

"What are you doing here?"

"Picking you up." Walter's tone says this ought to be obvious to me. He puts a protective arm around me, bumping Jeremiah.

Jeremiah yanks his hand away and nearly knocks into his sister as she joins us.

"This is Detective Cassano," I say to Walter. "Apparently Lydia—"

Walter's hold on me tightens as he turns to the detective. "Is it really necessary to question her?"

Walter knows? But of course; the news is probably all over the neighborhood.

Detective Cassano spares a glance for Walter. "Seeing as

she's Miss LeVine's best friend, I assumed Miss Sail wouldn't mind providing information."

"And you couldn't do it in the privacy of her own home?" Walter's words come through clenched teeth.

Walter is making such a scene that most Presley's girls have given up covertly observing and now openly stare. That stupid Mae Husboldt giggles behind her hand.

I tug at Walter's sleeve. "Calm down. I'm happy to answer his questions."

Detective Cassano angles his body away from Walter. "Miss Sail, back to what you were saying about Matthew. Were the two of them romantically involved?"

I can feel Walter gaping at me. "Not exactly. Lydia liked him, but I think I was the only one who knew. Except last night . . ." My hands tremble, and I clasp them together. "When she left my house, she said she was going to tell Matthew how she felt. I think she was hoping for a date. She said she would call me to tell me how it went, but she never did."

The detective glances at me, his eyes perceptive like a bird of prey, but also somehow compassionate. "Had you noticed, or had she mentioned, anyone suspicious hanging around?"

"No."

"What about strange behavior from people she knew? Her mother? Father? Sisters?"

"No. Everyone had been very normal."

He seems to hesitate a moment. "Even Matthew?"

"Matthew seemed fine. He was quiet, but Matthew is always quiet."

Without looking up from the notes he's taking, he asks, "Even with Lydia?"

I attempt a calming breath, but the air shakes as it comes in and out. "Whenever I was around them, yes."

Detective Cassano holds my gaze as he reaches into his breast pocket. He hands me a thick, cream-colored card. "Here's the number at the station. If you think of anything else we should know, please call and have them put you through to Detective O'Malley or myself."

It isn't until I reach for the card that I realize my hand still trembles. Detective Cassano presses the card into my palm, and then grasps my hand, steadying it. "We're going to do everything we can to get your friend back, Miss Sail. I know it's hard, but try not to worry. We take every case seriously, but as I said, many turn into nothing."

The world around him—my classmates, the flowering trees, the bright blue sky—is framed in black. I remind myself to take a breath. "Thank you, detective."

He tips his hat at me and jogs up the stairs to the front door.

Walter's fingertips press into my shoulders. "C'mon, Piper. Let's get you home."

My brain buzzes with an incoherent mess of thoughts—Lydia's smile as she waved farewell to me yesterday, the dreamy look on her face as she considered purchasing cufflinks for Matthew, the way she asked to have my support.

If he asked me to marry him today, I'd have no hesitation saying yes. Her words keep echoing in my head.

Walter tucks me inside Father's Chrysler. I gaze up the emerald lawn of Presley's, across which Jeremiah guides Emma to his car. He must see me looking, because he offers a small wave. I wave back.

"I hate that I was late." Walter yanks his door closed. "Mrs.

Lincoln caught me as I was walking out to the car, and she wanted to talk all about Lydia. You know how she is." He turns to face me. "How are you? Did that detective scare you?"

I take a deep breath. Detective Cassano's card is still grasped in my hand, and I stare at it. "I'm alarmed, of course. But he can't help that."

"He shouldn't have talked to you at school. He should have waited until you were home."

"I think he just happened to see me there. They were there for the headmistress, not me."

"Still." Walter faces forward and jabs the shifter into gear. "It's inconsiderate."

"Have they spoken to Matthew yet? Is *he* home?"

"I don't know." Walter gives me a sidelong glance as he edges the car into traffic. "So Lydia and Matthew?"

"Kind of. I mean, that's what she wanted, and I never could talk her out of it. She wouldn't listen to me. And now this."

Whatever *this* is.

"Matthew is a good man. He wouldn't have run off with her." Then a moment later, "I don't think so, anyway."

But an even worse thought percolates within me. If she *didn't* run off with Matthew . . . where is she?

I shake the dark thought away. There's no reason to think along those lines. Not yet. "Let's stop at the LeVines'. I want to see how I can help."

I want to look in her armoire and see that clothes are missing. That *Persuasion* is no longer on her bedside table. And I want to see that she's left my coat—which she would never be careless enough to take with her—folded neatly on her bed with a note tucked in the pocket. *Next time I see you, I'll be Matthew's wife!* it might read.

"I don't think that's a good idea, Piper. The police were there a lot of the day, the street has been crawling with reporters, and the LeVines are likely exhausted. Why don't you telephone them instead?"

"I don't want to telephone them." The pitch of my voice climbs higher with each word. "I want to go there and figure out what's going on."

"It will all be okay, Pippy." Walter reaches for my hand and crushes it in his. "It really will."

I avert my gaze out the window, to the high rises of Lake Shore Drive that Matthew drove me by just the day before. I try to believe Walter, but fear clogs my throat. I'm not going to cry. Not when there are dozens of possibilities as to where Lydia could be right now.

I wipe away an insistent tear.

Okay, so I might cry a *little*, but I'm not going to fall apart. I clamp my teeth over my trembling lower lip. *It's going to be okay.* That's what Walter said, anyway.

But I find I can't even allow myself to trust Walter.

***

Joyce opens the front door as I dash up the patio steps. She folds her arms around me, and I stand stiff in her embrace, unable to lean in. The rough fabric of her work dress rubs against my cheek, and I soak in the lavender and lye scents that cling to her.

"I know, honey," she says in my ear.

Father, Jane, and Nick sit in the living room wearing somber faces. Nick's eyes are red and puffy.

"Oh, Piper, you poor darling." Jane rushes to me, arms

outstretched. The scalloped tiers of her velvet afternoon dress sway, and her floral scent clouds my head as she cups my face in her hands. "How are you, dear?"

Her hazel eyes stare into mine with a pity that pokes to life a fire in my belly.

"I'm fine." The words are louder, sharper than I anticipate. "We don't know anything yet, so there's no reason to not be fine."

Jane's fingers stiffen against my skin, but if she's hurt, she covers it with a smile. "Yes, that's right. It's frightening, of course, but it's premature to be *too* alarmed."

Father fits his arm around my shoulders, causing Jane's hands to fall away. Her fussy scent is replaced by that of pipe smoke. "The police will want to talk to you, dear—"

"They already have." Walter's gruff voice breaks into the conversation. "I got there late, and one of the detectives was grilling her."

"He was only asking questions." I look up to Father. "Have you spoken to the LeVines?"

He nods. "I left a message with their housekeeper, conveying our sympathies and our willingness to help however we can."

"I'd like to go over there—"

"Absolutely not, Piper. We're not going to intrude on them during this difficult time."

"Your father is right." Jane loops her bejeweled arm through Father's. "We want you right here, where we can be sure you're safe."

"I'll bring Walter with me. It's three houses away."

"It doesn't even take that much sometimes." Nick's raw voice enters the conversation. "I read this case in class last week where—"

"Son." Father shakes his head. "Not now."

Nick paces to the couch and perches on the edge. Then he stands, mutters something that involves the word "smoke," and heads out back.

Father squeezes my shoulders. "Your heart is in the right place, Piper, and there'll be a time to pay a visit. I just don't think it's today."

"Excuse me." Joyce's low voice cuts into the conversation. "But the LeVines telephoned earlier, asking that Piper please come over when she returned from school."

I feel everyone's gaze on me as I look up at Father. He works his lower lip back and forth and his blue eyes are unfocused, two clear signs that he's thinking this over. His mind is so creative in its logic, that even now when I have a clear request from the LeVines, I find myself bracing for Father to come at this from an angle I can't anticipate, to still find a way to keep me home.

But all he says is, "Take Walter with you."

With its limestone bricks, tall bay windows, and the fleurs-de-lis carved in the arch over the door, the LeVines' house creates a grander impression than ours. It's the type of place where even the details are maintained—bushes pruned into shape, toys tucked away, books dusted and spines aligned on shelves.

Tabitha answers my knock with downcast eyes and no smile.

"I'll wait out here for you," Walter says, and I don't bother to argue.

Tabitha takes my hat and handbag. "They're in the living room."

The air is too warm and absent of the lemony, clean smell I associate with the LeVines. I never knew that fear had a feel, but I know now that Tabitha has closed the door. Fear is sticky. Suffocating.

Dr. and Mrs. LeVine are in their respective chairs, though they've been dragged from the front window to the phone table, which sits between them. Dr. LeVine has a collection of papers in his lap, and Mrs. LeVine clutches a hankie, which she twists this way and that. It's the closest I've ever seen her come to sitting idle.

When Mrs. LeVine sees me, she rises to her feet, wraps her arms around me in a tight hug, and weeps. Mrs. LeVine, who rarely shows emotion during Lydia's seizures. Who thinks I'm a bad influence on her daughters. Who sometimes winces—albeit discreetly—when she comes home and finds I'm at the house.

I pat her back with several stiff flicks of my wrist. "I came as soon as I could. Thank you for phoning."

"We're so glad to see you, Piper." Dr. LeVine's voice is weary.

Mrs. LeVine releases me and presses her handkerchief to her eyes. "I'm sorry, dear. I've soaked your shoulder."

Dear. "There's no reason to apologize. It's just a uniform."

"I couldn't help thinking that at this time of day, Lydia would be coming home in *her* Presley's uniform . . ." Her chin trembles as her sentence fades away.

Blast my insensitivity. Why didn't I think to change before rushing over here? Lydia certainly would have, had things been reversed.

Tears prick my eyes. "I'm so sorry. I wasn't thinking—"

"Have the police spoken to you yet?" Dr. LeVine's words are brusque as he reaches for his pipe.

"Yes." I settle onto the edge of the couch and fold my hands in my lap. "Two detectives were at school to speak with Headmistress Robinson. One of them recognized me somehow. I don't think I was very much help."

Mrs. LeVine dabs at her eyes as she takes her seat again. "So Lydia hadn't spoken to you about leaving?"

"No, ma'am. Well, except for Minnesota."

"But she didn't say she wanted to run away or anything?"

Saying she would accept a marriage proposal isn't the same thing, right?

I shake my head.

Dr. LeVine packs tobacco into his pipe. "It's not like our Lydia to do something rash like run away, all because Edna and I made a decision she didn't like. But I find myself hoping all the same. The alternatives . . ."

A sob bursts from Mrs. LeVine. "I'll go ask Tabitha to put on some coffee." She bustles from the room with the handkerchief pressed to her mouth, muffling the noise.

When I catch Dr. LeVine subtly wiping away a tear, my own eyes pool.

He leans to hand me a fresh handkerchief from his pocket and then settles into his wingback chair to smoke. "We were confining her to the house until our appointment at the Mayo Clinic." His voice is graveled. "She was angry, as I'm sure you already know, Piper. She wanted to tell you and to let the Barrow family know she could no longer watch Cole for them. Considering what she's gone through these last six months, it seemed only fair. And so harmless . . ."

I've wadded my uniform skirt into my fists. I release it. Smooth it. "You can't blame yourself, Dr. LeVine."

"When we spoke to the Barrows, they said Lydia never arrived." Emotion catches in Dr. LeVine's voice. He covers his mouth with one of his large, life-saving hands. "I can't bear to think she might have been taken." The vulnerability of him, of the stoic doctor who served in the Great War, takes away my breath. "But I also can't think of why my Lydia might trick us."

"Her room has been searched, I assume? Which clothes are missing? Did she leave a letter?"

When Dr. LeVine shakes his head, it feels as if another brick crumbles from my certainty that this is nothing to panic about. "Everything is exactly in its place."

"And . . . and no one else is missing?" There's a wobble in my voice.

Dr. LeVine's gaze sharpens to a point. "Who else would you expect to be missing?"

I swallow hard. "I only wondered if she went with a friend. If one of the other ladies of Lydia's acquaintance is gone too."

"No. You . . ." He hesitates. "You're Lydia's closest friend. We can't imagine her running off with anyone else."

"Had the staff observed anything different about Lydia?" My heart beats so loud in my chest, I wonder if Dr. LeVine can hear. "I assume you've talked to Matthew, asked if he overheard any-thing she might have said in the car?"

"We did. Matthew said there was no indication that she was planning to run away."

I can't seem to take a deep breath. Lydia is gone. But Matthew is not.

"Matthew is taking this very hard, actually. He feels responsible, like he should have driven her around the block. And while, of course, I wish we *had* asked Matthew to drive her . . ." Dr. LeVine's eyes go misty again. He straightens and taps the ash from his pipe.

"There has to be someone who saw her." The words seem to tumble out of me. "Have we walked the neighborhood? Interviewed neighbors to see who saw what? I could talk to—"

"Piper." Dr. LeVine's stern tone matches his gaze. "The police are handling this."

"I'm sure they are. But I know Lydia and the police don't, so I might see things that they wouldn't—"

"No. It's a bad idea for you to get yourself tangled up in this. Especially when we don't know . . ." His voice breaks. "When we don't know what happened to her."

Tears clog my throat. I swallow them and do my best to keep my voice level. "I understand your concern, Dr. LeVine, and I appreciate it. But time is critical, and don't you think we need everyone possible looking for her—"

"I don't think little girls need to be out there poking around, no. I know you've been raised in a different kind of family, Piper, but this is a job for men. You would only get in the way. We don't need detectives out there looking for *you* as well." He stands. "If you'll excuse us, we have matters to attend to."

My knees tremble as I stand. "Please tell Mrs. LeVine I said farewell."

His nod is curt. I collect my belongings in the entryway and walk out the front door into the peony-scented afternoon. Only then, when I can breathe easier, do I realize how life-sucking the fear within their home had been.

"I'm walking around back to have a word with Matthew. You don't have to come."

Walter glowers beneath the brim of his flat cap. "You really think I'm going to let you go anywhere alone?"

I study Walter. He's already puffed himself up to his full height and breadth. He morphs into big brother mode faster than the two who are my brothers by blood. "But I don't know how keen he'll be on talking if you're with me."

Walter crosses his arms over his chest. "You'll have to find out, because I'm not letting you out of my sight."

"Fine." I thunder down the stairs. The LeVines' house is too close to the neighbors' to get to the alley—we'll have to go around the corner.

"Look, Piper." Walter takes hold of my arm as we walk. "I'll take you to see Matthew, but after this, you need to just stay out of the way and let the detectives handle things."

My jaw tightens.

"Piper." Walter's tone is somber. "I want to know you're safe."

"And I want to know Lydia is safe."

Matthew is where I hoped we'd find him, in the company of only the Deusenberg and a bucket of soapy water. He pauses his work as we approach, but he doesn't look wary or embarrassed or anything useful. He looks like stoic Matthew. The sleeves of his shirt are rolled up on his tanned forearms, and he squints in the afternoon sunlight.

"What can I do for you, Miss Sail?"

The questions that have spun in my mind since Detective Cassano told me Lydia had been reported missing—is she with Matthew? Did she run off with him?—tangle in my mouth. As I look at him, his round face, his even gaze, the slight creases fanning from the corners of his eyes, new questions form. How old is Matthew? And where is he from? Besides being quiet and polite, what do we really know about him?

"You've come to ask me about Miss LeVine." His words are matter-of-fact.

"Yes." I force myself to say it louder. "Yes."

Matthew's nostrils flare with his exhale, and he swipes his sudsy rag across the top of the car. "If only she'd asked me to drive her. I'd have driven her six inches if it meant she was with someone. A girl in Lydia's condition shouldn't be left alone."

My stomach pitches, and I brace myself against the hot car. "Matthew, do you mean . . ." Tears swell inside me. "Does that mean . . . ?"

Matthew pauses. Waits.

"Do you not know where she is?" Emotion pulses with every syllable.

"'Course I don't, Miss Sail." It's the first time I've ever heard Matthew sound offended. "You can't honestly think I'd have anything to do with this."

"I thought . . . I mean, Lydia told me that . . ." My inhales and exhales are involuntary bursts, as if I ran to the LeVines' house. "I had hoped that maybe you and Lydia had . . ."

His expression is like a giant question mark.

"Run off together."

"Miss Sail . . ." Red splotches bloom on Matthew's cheeks. "I'm . . . I'm flattered, I suppose. But you can't possibly think your Miss LeVine would have any interest in a fella like me."

"But she told me she was going to tell you." My words are coming out high and gaspy again.

Matthew's eyes are trained on the hood of the car. "Tell me what?"

"That she loves you."

A muscle in his jaw ticks. "No disrespect intended, Miss, but I think you must be all balled up."

"I'm *not*. Lydia loves you. When she left my house yesterday, she said she was coming home to tell you. I watched her walk through the gate."

Matthew looks at me, mouth downturned and eyes brimming. He looks as though he pities me. "She must have been teasing you."

"Lydia doesn't believe in teasing."

"Then it must've been a misunderstanding."

"It wasn't a misunderstanding." I stomp my foot. "If she's not with you, Matthew, then where is she? Where is she?"

Walter is here, his thick arms around me, holding me back. "It's okay, Pippy."

"She didn't tell him." My words are a blubbery mess against the shirt I bought only yesterday. "She never told him. They're not together, she's just . . . gone."

My mind plays out ugly scenarios—Lydia snatched from the street. Lydia crying for help, calling for me, but I'm oblivious inside my house. Lydia terrified and unable to fight off her captors.

"I'm sorry I made things worse." Matthew's words are hoarse.

Walter's arms gather me against him and squeeze. "Piper was holding on to hope."

"We're all trying to. I'm sorry, Miss Sail." Through my blurred eyes, I find Matthew regarding me with more emotion than I thought him capable. "I'm sorry I didn't keep her safe."

At that, his chin trembles, and he busies himself with the bucket of suds.

"Let's get you home," Walter murmurs as he guides me up the alley.

"She's out there, Walter. We have to find her."

"Lots of people are looking." Walter's words are low and soothing. "They're doing their best."

But what if their best isn't enough?

P iper?" Joyce stands in the doorway of the living room. Her pale blue work dress has damp patches from washing dinner dishes and she holds a rag in her hand. "Jeremiah Crane is on the phone for you."

Walter stops digging through the box of screws and Nick's heel stops tapping against the floor.

"Can you tell him I'm not available to speak right now? That I'll ring him tomorrow?"

"Of course." Joyce's footsteps whisper down the hall, back to Father's office.

"What's he calling for?"

I open my mouth to answer Walter.

"He's keen on her." Nick taps his pipe against the desk. "He called earlier too."

I almost say he's *not* keen on me, but then I recall this afternoon's invitation to the movies. The memory is foggy, as if perhaps it was only a dream.

I press my fountain pen to the page of my notebook. *Lydia watched Cole for the Barrow family during the last month because their nanny left to work at John Barleycorn. She once told me that she didn't like being there if it was just Mr. Barrow, because—*

"How can you study at a time like this?" Nick's voice is filled with disgust as he folds shut the newspaper. "I haven't been able to get a blasted thing done all afternoon, I'm so worried."

"I'm not studying. And sitting there, smoking your pipe, and staring at the paper won't bring Lydia home."

I tap my pen a few times. What were Lydia's exact words about Mr. Barrow?

She was "unsettled in his presence," she once said to me, and she mused that maybe that was why their nanny had quit. That it was better to be a waitress at a speakeasy, where being flirted with is a known part of the job.

"Piper, what are you working on?" Walter's voice sounds nervous, as if he already knows the answer to his question.

"One second." I finish my thought about possible motives for Mr. Barrow—could Lydia have learned something about him that he didn't like?—and then look up. "I'm writing down anything about Lydia that seems like it could be important. Things Lydia said or reasons others might have had a grudge against her or the family. That sort of thing."

This is met with silence. Nick's mouth hangs open slightly and Walter seems to have forgotten he was in the middle of finding a screw to repair the leg of the end table.

"When I'm done, I'll give it to the detectives, and hopefully it'll help them." I poise my pen above the page and consider the next name.

"Piper . . ." Walter sets down the box of screws. "I know it's hard to wait, but I think you should just let the detectives do their work."

"I'm letting them do their work." My pen flows in smooth letters across the line, emitting the comforting smell of ink. "They felt it necessary to question me, and Detective Cassano gave me their card. I'm just answering his questions more thoroughly."

Matthew has been the LeVine family's chauffeur for over a year—

"Where do you think she is?" Nick's voice is a notch above a whisper.

I look at my brother, his blond hair tousled from his hat. Behind his spectacles, his eyes, blue like Father's, spark with fear. I think of the way he had been looking at Lydia these last few months. It had been similar to how Lydia had looked at Matthew.

"I don't know," I say.

What if Nick had discovered how Lydia felt about Matthew? What if yesterday, instead of heading to school like he said, he had lingered outside and listened to our conversation? And what if he had decided to wait around the corner for Lydia to try and talk to her? Only it didn't go well, and his hurt and jealousy made him—

No. This is my brother. He cares about Lydia. Yes, he's temperamental and big-headed, but violent? No way.

"Where are you going?" Walter asks as I stand. The screw he'd been holding clatters back into the box.

"I'm going to use the telephone in Father's office. I'll be right back."

Father used to spend most evenings at his desk, reviewing cases as he enjoyed a glass of scotch. But nine months ago, when he met the new-to-town court reporter, Jane Miller, all that changed. Now the cherry wood desk is frequently empty at night, and the framed portrait of Mother sits in the dark unless Joyce comes in to answer the telephone.

I close Father's office door with a click. The room smells of tobacco and neglect, and the only sound in the office is the clock, ticking away seconds with frightening speed. Lydia's absence has done peculiar things to my perception of time. In my heart, she's been missing for an eternity, and minutes are being siphoned away far too rapidly.

I pull Detective Cassano's card from the pocket of my skirt. I hold the earpiece in my left hand and move a trembling finger to dial the first number. There's no need to be nervous. I'll just be leaving a message asking him to please telephone me tomorrow.

"Detective division." The female voice is abrupt and nasally.

"Hi. I'd like to leave a message for either Detective Cassano or O'Malley, please."

"One moment."

In the silence, I stare at my page, at the black dot where I started to write my brother's name. It looks like an ordinary blot of ink, but I know better. How could I ever write my own brother's name in here? What if he saw?

"Cassano."

I blink at the notebook, at the blot of ink. He's still at work?

"Hello?"

"Yes, hi, detective. This is Piper Sail. We spoke earlier at Presley's about my friend Lydia LeVine, who—"

"I know who you are, Miss Sail."

"Oh, okay." I look at my notebook, at the list of people and their stories. A list of people whom Lydia loves.

"Is there something you need, Miss Sail?"

"Yes, actually. When we spoke at the school earlier, I wasn't much help. It was the shock of the news, I suppose."

"That's very common." Detective Cassano's voice has a gentle quality to it, and it calls to mind the way he held my hand steady at school. "It's why I carry cards with me, because it's hard to think logically in the face of news like that."

I glance at my notes again. Do any of the stories even make sense? Do any of them matter?

"I wondered if you or Detective O'Malley had any time tomorrow to meet me. I spent some time thinking through everyone Lydia interacts with, and I made some notes that may be helpful. I could come to the station if that's more convenient."

"That won't be necessary. We're meeting with Dr. and Mrs. LeVine tomorrow afternoon, and it would be easy to stop by your place as well. Say around three o'clock? Or will you still be at school?"

My eyes slide shut. That's so far from now. "Three o' clock is fine. Thank you."

"I hear hesitancy in your voice, Miss Sail. Has something important come up?"

"No, I just . . . I hate waiting." Tears reduce my voice to a scratchy whisper. "I'm so afraid for her. She would never take off on her own like this."

"We're going to do everything we can to get Miss LeVine back home with you and her family."

"Detective Cassano . . ." I trace the blotter on Father's desk. "Please be honest with me. You said these situations are frequently nothing. How often is that true?"

His silence pushes my tears over the rims of my eyes.

"You seem to be a very intelligent young woman, Miss Sail." His words are husky and low. "And with your father's profession, I'm sure you're not ignorant of the crimes that occur in our city."

He knows what my father does? I bite down on my lip in an effort to stop my chin from trembling.

"But missing girls frequently have just run off with a beau or for effect, so—"

"But Matthew is here, and Lydia never would have run away on her own. She just *wouldn't*."

"Even so, it's still possible she's alive and well."

"If Lydia were able to, she would call. She would know we were worried about her."

Detective Cassano seems to hesitate. "By 'alive and well,' I don't necessarily mean that she would be free to call home. She could still have been taken and just not be able to call."

"Oh. If a girl is taken, where are you most likely to find her?"

My question is met with silence. "I'll be blunt, Miss Sail. I'm uncomfortable talking about this with a young lady."

I huff out an impatient breath. "You'll have to get over that, detective, because I care much more about finding my friend than I do your comfort."

"If I thought there was a benefit to telling you"—there seems to be a smile in his words—"then I would. But you knowing the possibilities of where Lydia might be won't help get her home. Just know that we're checking everywhere we can think of."

Despite how Detective Cassano seems amused by me, I don't think I'll be able to convince him these are details I should be privy to. But there are other questions he might answer. "Have you talked to our neighbors? Did anyone see her?"

"We've talked to most."

"Did anyone see her?"

He hesitates. "Miss Sail . . ."

"Why don't you call me Piper?" I poise my pen above my notepad. "Who have you not talked to? In the morning, I could talk to them, and then when we meet tomorrow afternoon, I could tell you if I've learned anything."

"Miss Sail—"

"Piper."

Another hesitation. "Piper, I admire your tenacity. And Miss LeVine is a lucky girl to have a friend like you. We don't know exactly what happened to her, but . . . the evidence suggests she didn't simply run away from home—"

"Of course not. I told you, Lydia would never do that."

"Right. So, with that in mind, can you see why I might not want to send you knocking on doors?"

"I can help." I want my voice to sound strong, but my words bleed with desperation. "I really can. Lydia's been my best friend since we were toddlers. I know how she thinks and I know who she knows. I can be helpful."

Detective Cassano exhales long and slow. "I get how hard it is to sit and wait. And, after talking to your headmistress today, I have no doubt that you would knock on doors or even take the L to the shadiest neighborhoods to look for her there. So while I really appreciate your spirit, and while I look forward to meeting with you tomorrow and going over your notes, it doesn't seem very safe to have you do anything more."

I feel myself flushing. What all did Headmistress Robinson tell them about me? "I'm many things, Detective Cassano. But safe isn't one of them."

There seems to be a tinge of amusement in his voice when he says, "I'll see you tomorrow at three, Miss Sail."

I awake the next morning to bright sunshine streaming into my room. My eyes are raw and crusted, and my lips chapped after a night of weeping.

At two this morning, I had dragged myself down to the kitchen for a glass of water. The memory of what I'd seen when I went downstairs makes me shudder even now. Father had been asleep in his armchair, an empty tumbler in his lap and a shotgun propped beside him. The gun froze me on the bottom stair, made my blood roar through my veins. Guns have always unnerved me. ("Good," my father once said when I told him this. "Then stay away from them.")

I couldn't take my eyes off the firearm. Why was it out? Why was his chair angled toward the front door?

I crept to his chair, careful to avoid the side with the gun, and removed the tumbler from his limp hand. I draped an afghan over him and carried his empty glass to the kitchen. Just the smell of the strong liquor burned my throat.

As I rinsed it, my mind wouldn't let go of the gun. Lydia being gone had us all on edge. Is that what this was?

"What are you doing up?"

Walter's voice drew a yelp out of me. He filled the doorway of the kitchen staircase, the one that led to Joyce's living quarters. He wore striped pajamas, and his curls were rumpled, but he seemed too alert to have been awakened by me.

"You scared me."

"Sorry." He studied my face a moment. "You look like you haven't slept at all."

I combed my fingers through my hair. "Probably because I haven't."

"Want to get some air?"

"Sure."

Walter pulled a flannel blanket from the linen closet and draped it around my shoulders once we'd settled onto the back stoop. We sat in silence for a while, the rhythm of breathing and the comfort of being with a friend lulling me like a bedtime song.

I yawned. "I could sleep, I think, but somehow it feels wrong. Like I have no right to be comfortable in my bed when Lydia isn't in hers."

"Doesn't help her any for you to lose sleep."

"I know it's senseless. But I'm a girl."

"You're not the senseless type, though. And don't change that."

We fell silent again, and my mind drifted to the notebook sitting up on my desk, the one I intended to give to Detective Cassano. In the last hour, my writings had started to sound like those of a lunatic. I had gone so far as to brainstorm reasons why my future stepmother or Ms. Underhill might have taken Lydia.

"Oh, Walter, where is she?" Tears brewed from exhaustion and anxiety dripped from my eyes. "The detective said it looks like she didn't just run away, but who would have taken her?"

He coaxed me against his shoulder. "I don't know. But it makes me never want to let you or Mother out of my sight again."

The scenario that had plagued my thoughts all night long finally emerged. "What if someone *did* take her and she has a seizure?"

Walter's breath caught, and I knew he too was thinking of the Other Lydia. Lydia with the rolled-back eyes, absent mind, and soiled skirts. "I don't know."

"Father's asleep in the front room. He . . . he has his gun out."

"He's just nervous, is all. Eighteen-year-old girl goes missing from the neighborhood. Not only does he have an eighteen-year-old girl, but also a long list of criminal-types who he's angered over the years." Walter squeezed my shoulder. "Nothing for you to be worried about, though."

Now as I stretch awake in the late-morning sun, last night's conversation seems far away. Outside, birds hum merry songs and the lemon-yellow light declares that this is a beautiful late-spring morning. I should have been at school hours ago. Right now, I would be sitting in Ms. Underhill's stupid class, making a dress that will never fit me right and suffering her distaste for me.

What I wouldn't give to be living that day instead of this one.

My stomach groans with hunger. No surprise considering it's after eleven, and I only picked at my supper last night. But instead of finding breakfast, I cross the room to my desk. The notebook sits where I left it before venturing downstairs. I rip out the last page, full of incoherent rambling, and review my other notes. A list of neighbors and their relationships with the LeVine family. A list of all the household staff I could remember, and who had been fired when and for what reason. A list of any members of the community whom Dr. and Mrs. LeVine didn't seem to get along with (that list was the shortest by far), and another list of everything I could remember talking about recently with Lydia.

I think of the gun lying against Father's chair and poise my pen above the notebook. But what about that could possibly be helpful to the detectives? Walter was probably right; my best friend went missing from three houses down, and it naturally made my father paranoid. That's all it was.

I close my eyes and pray—something I've done more in the last day than in the last five years combined—that even a single item I've written down might be useful to bringing Lydia home.

85

Detective Cassano opens the gate at 2:57. He smiles and tips his homburg when he sees me sitting on the front steps. "Good afternoon, Miss Sail."

"It's Piper, please." My hands are clammy against the notebook I clutch. "And good afternoon, detective."

He stops at the bottom of the stairs and rests his elbow against the rail. I can just make out the lump of his holstered gun. "If you insist on me calling you Piper, then it seems you should call me Mariano."

Mariano Cassano. It has a musical quality to it, like a familiar but forgotten tune. "I've never known a Mariano before."

His lips curl into a slight smile. "Family name."

"Mine too. It was my mother's maiden name. Father wanted to call me Caroline, after his mother, but mine insisted on Piper. So I'm Piper Caroline."

Detective Cassano's—Mariano's—dark gaze stays steady on me as I share more about my name than he likely cares to hear. Is he as young as he looks? He's handsome, with his olive skin and strong jaw. He might even be strikingly handsome, were I of the mindset to be struck.

"Are you able to take a walk around the block with me, Piper? I thought you could help familiarize me with the neighbors."

My heart leaps—that sounds like I might actually be useful. "Of course. Just let me tell my family."

I pull open the door, dash down the hallway toward the kitchen, and practically run into Walter. "Oh, hi. I'm taking a walk with Detective Cassano. I'll be back in a bit."

His face folds into a deep frown. "I'll come with you."

"You don't need to."

"I don't think your father would like the idea of you walking around the neighborhood alone."

"I'll be with the police, I'm fine." Walter hesitates, and I put my hands on my hips. "I'm not asking permission, you know. This is just a courtesy so that you know where I am."

"Fine," Walter says as I retreat. "See you later."

I rush outside without bothering to grab a hat.

Mariano has his back to the door when I come out, and he turns to smile at me. "This is good of you, Piper. Neighborhoods can be impossible to understand without an insider's perspective."

"I'm just happy to feel useful. To be able to do something other than sit by the phone and wait." I charge through the gate that he holds open for me. "Did you see Dr. and Mrs. LeVine?"

He nods.

"And?"

Mariano glances at me, his brown eyes searching. "They were how you'd expect. Tired. Scared."

"I was there yesterday after school, and I don't think Mrs. LeVine ever stopped crying."

"They said you had come by. I got the impression you were a great comfort to them."

"I hope so." Because that's not the impression I left with. I hug my notebook to my chest. "They've never particularly cared for me."

Mariano's face creases with his frown. "Why do you say that?"

"Because they don't." My laugh holds no humor. "Lydia . . . Well, she's as close to perfect as they come. Sweet and kind-hearted and well-mannered. We were a strange match, and her parents wouldn't have minded Lydia spending time with other friends."

"Are you not sweet, kind-hearted, and well-mannered, Piper?"

"No. I'm not."

He chuckles at this, though amusing him wasn't my intention. "And how long have you lived here?"

"As long as I can remember. I was two when we moved in."

"So you know all the neighbors, then?"

I nod and, feeling bashful, hand him the notebook. "I made this. Just in case . . . You know. In case something happened to her." I tuck my hair behind my ears and swallow a gulp of air. "I don't know how helpful this will be, but I tried to think of everyone I could who might have had even a slight grudge against the LeVine family. I listed neighbors in there. With a map."

I feign interest in Mrs. Jensen's peonies as Mariano looks through my notebook. I should brace myself for the likely response—that it'd be better for everyone if I stayed out of this. That the professionals are more than capable of handling Lydia's case. But I can't stop myself from thinking he might appreciate my efforts. Detective Mariano Cassano seems to be the only person who realizes that what I know could matter.

Mariano taps on an open page. "What's this one?"

"Oh." Heat stains my cheeks. "I tried to document every conversation Lydia and I had in the last week. Just in case it was of any importance."

Mariano's footsteps slow. "She hoped to *marry* Matthew?" He looks at me. "Things were that serious?"

"Yes. I mean, no." I shake my head. "I don't know, honestly.

I think she was just feeling theatrical when she said that. But when you first told me she was missing, I wondered if maybe she'd run off with him."

Mariano stops walking, and his thoughts are clearly far away. "I talked to Matthew extensively yesterday and today. He insisted that if Lydia had feelings for him, he was unaware."

I read skepticism in Mariano's expression. "He told me the same. But when Lydia left my house on Tuesday, she said she was going to tell him as soon as she got home." In my memory, I see her waving to me from her gate, beaming. Tears flood my eyes. "I'm so sorry." I reach into the pocket of my gray skirt only to find it empty.

"No apologies necessary." Mariano pulls a handkerchief from the breast pocket of his suit. "If I may say so, Piper, I think you've shown remarkable strength these twenty-four hours."

I attempt to laugh, but it sounds more like a hiccup. "I don't think it's sunk in yet, to be honest."

"That's normal, I promise. In your opinion, how does Matthew feel about Lydia?"

I dab my eyes with Mariano's handkerchief, which has a minty, clean smell. "I don't know for sure."

"I'd like to know your thoughts."

I bite my lower lip as I look up at him. "Matthew has always seemed very closed off to me. My brother Nick was much more obvious. I could tell he fancied her. But Matthew . . ." I sigh. "I don't understand how he *couldn't*, but I also can't point to evidence he did either."

I hold Mariano's handkerchief out to him, but he shakes his head. "Hold on to it for now."

"Thank you." I grasp it between my fingers and find we've

wandered off Astor Street and toward State. All without me mentioning a single neighbor. "I'm sorry, I'm being a terrible tour guide, aren't I?"

Mariano holds up the notebook. "You've more than made up for it, Piper. Thank you for this."

When he tucks it inside his coat, I catch another glimpse of the gun holstered around his waist. Fear skitters up my spine, which is silly. He's a detective. Of course he wears a gun. There's something about Mariano Cassano, though—his age? His face?—that makes me forget this is his job.

With a spark of intimidation, I realize that suggests he's excellent at what he does.

My notebook seems suddenly childish. "I hope it's helpful. I just wanted to feel like I'd done something."

"I know the feeling." He clasps his hands behind his back as we turn onto State Street. "Yesterday, you told me that Lydia was angry about being sent to Minnesota. Was that related to her feelings for Matthew?"

"Yes. She seemed to think it would mess everything up if she had to spend a few months at the hospital there, and I thought it would be a good test of her feelings. But of course I know lots of details about her seizures and she doesn't, so I suppose it's easier for me to prioritize her getting healthy." The tears strangle my final words, and a humorless laugh bubbles out of me as I press Mariano's handkerchief to my eyes. "You were smart to let me hang on to this."

But he's not walking beside me anymore. I turn and find he's stopped on the sidewalk. "What do you mean, she had seizures?"

His question causes an icy blast of disbelief to run through me. "Did they not tell you?" It seems impossible. I knew the

LeVines guarded Lydia's condition carefully, but . . . "Lydia has recurring seizures. A type of epilepsy, I think. Though they would never dare say that word."

I half expect his face to relax, for him to laugh and say, "Oh, right, that. Of course they told me *that*."

But he doesn't. He only stares.

"You hadn't been told."

He shakes his head. "No."

I take a deep breath. "I can't believe they didn't tell you." The words fall out before I can think better of them. "They're very private about it due to Dr. LeVine's profession. Even Lydia didn't know. She thought they were just fainting spells. I only knew because I happened to witness two."

From his pocket, Mariano pulls out my notebook. "Is all that in here? The seizures?"

"Everything is. Everything that seemed as if it might help."

Mariano stares at the notebook a moment and then slides it back in his pocket. When he looks at me, his gaze feels heavy. "Thank you, Piper." He resumes walking, his hands deep in his trouser pockets, his narrow shoulders hunched.

He's quiet. The only sounds are the young green leaves rustling in the afternoon wind and the passing cars. Is the same question—why did the LeVines not tell the detectives about Lydia's seizures?—pulsing in his head like it is mine?

"I assume you know the family who lives in this house."

I glance at the Barrows' tall, narrow brick home. "Yes, of course. The Barrow family lives here. Lydia watches their son sometimes."

"Lydia told you she planned to visit them that evening, correct?"

"Yes."

"Do you know them well?"

I shrug. "Not really."

"Have you ever cared for their son?"

"Children and dogs terrify me. They have both."

"It's a funny thing." Mariano adjusts his tie. "O'Malley and I visited them yesterday and this morning. Lydia never arrived, both Mr. and Mrs. Barrow say. But the young boy has been acting peculiar since that night. Or so I gather from something the mother said. We never actually saw the boy."

Despite the warmth of the afternoon sun, my arms prickle with goose bumps. "Peculiar how?"

"This morning, his mother said he's been sullen. They didn't want him knowing that Lydia was missing, didn't want to frighten him. But she made a comment this morning that he must sense something has happened, because she hasn't been able to get him to speak a word."

Mariano turns to me, and his eyes seem assessing. Seem to ask, *can I trust you?* "Perhaps it's nothing. Perhaps my suspicion is only because of something that happened in my family when my mother died."

My heart squeezes. *I've been there*, my soul wants to say to his. *I know the pain.*

"She died in labor with my youngest brother. My second-youngest brother, Alessandro, was five at the time, same as the Barrows' son. And after Mama's funeral, we could barely get him to speak. Mostly, he just clung to my sister. He screamed in his sleep sometimes, but it was months before he would really talk. The doctor had seen it before, with children who witnessed something traumatic. It didn't make sense to us at first, because we didn't think Alessandro had seen anything."

Mariano's Adam's apple bobs as he casts his gaze on a passing car. "But we found out later that Alessandro had snuck into the room during all the commotion. That he had been in there for the screaming, and then . . . then for the silence."

When Mariano turns to me, his eyes are dry but his face makes my heart ache. "Perhaps it's a coincidence, Cole Barrow's silence. But it bothers me. And his parents won't let us near him. Would you mind, Piper? I've no business asking it of you, but seeing as you know Cole, if you happened to be around him in the next day or two, I would like to know your opinion of his behavior."

"Yes." The word emerges breathless. I'm being asked to help! "Of course."

"Though, if you pay a visit, I would suggest you do it at a time when it's only Mrs. Barrow and her son. And I would bring someone with you. Your brother, perhaps."

"I will." As Mariano and I walk past where Walter and I found Lydia seizing, I clutch the handkerchief tighter and seek to distract myself from the memory. "I'm sorry to hear about your mother. How old were you when she died?"

"Seven."

I wince. "Are you able to remember her very well?"

His look is questioning.

"My mother died when I was thirteen, and I don't remember as clearly as I wish. Seven would be much worse."

"Losing a good mother is never well-timed." Mariano's smile is wry. "I try to feel grateful that I had seven years. My brothers had far less."

"How many brothers and sisters do you have?"

Mariano's gaze hangs on me for a moment. He opens his mouth. Shuts it. Opens it again. "I'm sorry, I'm just surprised. I can't recall anyone I've investigated asking *me* questions."

My stomach flips at the term. "Am I being investigated?"

"Oh, not like that. You're part of the investigation, I mean. And usually no one is too interested in my childhood." Mariano tweaks his tie. "I'm the second oldest. My sister is twenty-three, and my brothers are nineteen and fourteen."

Emma Crane is seated on her front porch, perusing the newspaper and drinking a glass of milk. She gives me a slight smile and wave but doesn't call out.

"Were you all born in the states?"

"Yes, though Gianna, just barely. My parents had only been in Chicago a few weeks when she was born. She arrived a month earlier than anticipated."

I shudder involuntarily. "How terrifying for them. Your mother must have been very brave."

He doesn't say anything, but the warm look he gives makes me feel as though I've done something special.

"Thank you for the walk, Piper," Mariano says several minutes later as he holds open the gate to my yard. "You were very helpful."

"Good."

He walks alongside me to the front door. "And if you do happen to speak to Cole, please telephone me to let me know what you think."

"I will." I bite back the urge to thank him for giving me a task.

Mariano tips his hat. "Good afternoon, Piper."

"Good-bye."

But before he reaches the bottom step, he pivots and climbs the stone steps once more. Mariano stops on the stair below mine, making us the same height. "I'm probably just being overly cautious, but I would recommend you not visit the LeVine house by yourself."

The words wrap around my heart with icy fingers.

"I'm sure it's just paranoia getting the best of me." There's warmth on my arm, and I glance down to find Mariano's hand resting on the crook of my elbow. "But I think it'd be best—safest—if you stay away from there for now."

I nod because I can't seem to speak. With a farewell squeeze of my arm, he strides purposefully through the gate.

Walter's rag pauses midwipe of the glass. "I cannot believe he's asked this of you." He turns away from the windowpane to look at me. "Is he the police, or are you?"

"But the Barrows won't let the police talk to Cole." I fuss with the pearl necklace Father gave me on my eighteenth birthday. "It's something I can do to be helpful."

In the reflection of the window, I catch Walter scowling as he returns to cleaning. "Haven't you been plenty helpful already? I mean, how long was that walk yesterday? An hour?"

The air is heavy with the threat of rain, and his words make me want to start my own storm right here on the front porch. Plenty helpful? What does that even mean? But I know from experience that digging in my heels only makes Walter dig his in deeper, and I need him.

"Ignoring your gross exaggeration, what better use of my time could there possibly be but to provide information that might help us recover Lydia safely?"

Walter methodically wipes the window dry. He hangs the towel over the edge of the bucket of vinegar water, and then comes to stand near me, where the front porch meets the walkway. His knickers are grubby from a morning of working in the yard and his cheeks are smudged with dirt. But he doesn't talk, just looks at me.

"Please come with me. Nick is at the library, and I don't want to go alone."

Walter rests against the porch rail. "It scares me, you poking around in this business with Lydia."

"Mariano wouldn't have asked me to do it if he thought it was dangerous."

"Mariano?"

"Detective Cassano."

Walter huffs an exhale. "You and the detective are on a first-name basis?"

Embarrassment flares within me. "I'm just trying to do what I can to get Lydia home, and it's not going to hurt things to be friendly with one of the detectives working on her case. That's all this is."

"I still don't like the idea of him sending you on errands," Walter mutters as he kicks at the ground with the toe of his work boot. "You can save your eyelash batting for the detective, though. Give me a few minutes to get cleaned up, and I'll walk you over there."

I bite my lip but can't hold in my annoyance. "I didn't bat my eyelashes."

Walter's mouth flickers with a smile as he slips past me.

"I didn't!" I call after him.

Oh well. He can think whatever he wants so long as he accompanies me to the Barrows' house. Perhaps he would even venture over to the LeVines' with me . . . I've had a terrible kicked-in-the-gut feeling since yesterday, when Mariano cautioned me against going over there. Is it because they hid Lydia's seizures? Is that some sort of sign of bigger secrets?

I think of how Dr. LeVine behaved after the first seizure

of Lydia's that I witnessed, his deep frown as he studied her. He had asked Mrs. LeVine scads of questions and jotted her answers in a slender black notebook. He was a loving, concerned father.

Wasn't he?

"I cannot stress to you enough how important it is that you keep this secret." Mrs. LeVine's eyes had been sharp, probing. "Dr. LeVine's livelihood depends upon it."

And how far would he go to protect his livelihood? Far enough to shield the illness from his own daughter. Far enough to pull her out of school just shy of graduation and secret her away to the Mayo Clinic. But far enough to cover up something more sinister?

And where, exactly, might he keep that notebook?

Father's gleaming Chrysler coupe pulls up to our house, and out spills Jane, laughing as if she hasn't a care in the world. Her raven bob shines in the midmorning sun beneath a close-fitting cloche hat. Her tennis whites infuriate me. Perhaps it's unfair to feel lives should go on hold because Lydia is missing, but it seems outright selfish that they should go play a game of tennis at the club at a time like this.

"Hello."

My ice-cold greeting causes Jane's laugh to die in the air. "Oh, hello, dear."

"Piper." Father frowns as he comes around the car. "What are you doing out here by yourself?"

"Waiting for Walter."

"I would prefer you wait inside." Father gestures to the door, and I obey. Maybe that will keep him from asking too many questions about where Walter and I plan to go.

Jane's eyes hold sympathy as she walks beside me up the stairs. "How are you doing, Piper? You must be terrified."

I force my chin high. "I'm choosing to hope."

As we walk through the door my father opens for us, Jane rests her hand on my arm. The cluster of diamonds on her left ring finger wink in the afternoon sunlight. I'm actually disappointed by how swell her engagement ring is. I would prefer something ostentatious that I could make fun of. "I'm just sure someone knows something, especially in this neighborhood, where everyone watches out for each other."

"Well, if that's true, they're keeping quiet."

Jane hangs her handbag on the rack. "The LeVines should offer money for information, in my opinion. The right amount of money can get anyone to talk."

Of course that's what Jane would think, because that's the type of person *she* is. Here it's not even lunchtime, and she's bejeweled and made up as if heading to a nightclub.

"It's also a great motivator for people to lie." Father leafs through the mail on the entry table.

"Well, at least the police seem to be doing a thorough investigation. That's what Lydia's mother told me when I called on her. One never knows these days, with everything the police have on their laps." Jane notes something displeasing on her thumbnail. She frowns and scrubs at it. "Though Edna says one of the detectives is extremely young."

I catch sight of Walter in the hallway in clean trousers and a freshly scrubbed face. "Yes, Detective Cassano is young, but he seems very sharp."

Jane's carefully penciled eyebrows raise, and she smirks at my father. "They allow Cassanos on the police force?"

Father shrugs. "My understanding is he's a good sort. Have a nice time, kids."

My teeth grind together as I push the front door open. A good sort? What does that mean? Mariano has no more choice about being born to an Italian family than I did to third-generation Americans. Why should they not allow him to serve our city?

"Can you believe her?" I huff to Walter as I stomp down the front steps. "She's so fake and judgmental. What does my father see in her?"

"Piper . . ." Walter speaks my name as an admonishment.

"Is it the pretty packaging? Because all that stuff comes with a price tag, you know. That kind of upkeep costs money."

Walter holds open the gate for me. "And why am I getting lectured?"

"Because you're a man, and you're here."

I clamp my teeth over my lower lip, working hard to keep it all inside—the screaming, the tears, the angry words. Not until we've rounded the corner of Astor Street do I feel I can finally speak without exploding.

"I know it isn't fair to ask my father to be a bachelor forever, but that's really what I wanted. I wanted him to keep missing my mother and keep pouring himself into his work. And with Jane, it feels—" I have to bite my trembling lower lip until the threat of tears has passed. Walter's gaze is on me, I can feel it, but he remains quiet. "Jane makes me feel like I've lost Mother all over again. Even though I know she would have encouraged Father to remarry."

"Maybe now isn't the best time to visit the Barrows." Walter's voice is gentle. "Maybe instead we should see a movie. Get your mind off things."

Get my mind off things? "That's what you do when you did poorly on a test or a friend won't talk to you. I'm not going to go see a movie when Lydia needs me."

"You seeing a movie isn't going to change the situation with Lydia." His hand cups around my arm. "I know you feel guilty that you were the last to see her, but you don't have to solve this."

I yank my arm away from him and glare. "So if it was me, you would be content to just lounge around the house? Go to the cinema? Play ball with Jimmy and them? Because if it were you, I sure wouldn't. I would be knocking on every door, Walter Thatcher, until the detectives knocked on *my* door and said you wouldn't be coming home."

What if that happens?

What if Lydia isn't coming home?

It's impossible to take a breath despite how I gasp for it, and the world tilts beneath me.

"Pippy, it's going to be okay." Walter crushes me against him. His heart pounds beneath my ear as I struggle for breath. "It's going to be okay."

But my brain won't stop thundering, *what if it isn't?*

Mrs. Barrow's hand runs over her impossibly pregnant stomach in an absent way. "I can't tell you how shocked I was when the police knocked on our door. Dr. LeVine had called the night before, of course, to ask after Lydia. But when I hung up with him, I had assumed it was all some sort of miscommunication."

"I did too." My words come out quiet even though I don't intend for them to.

Mrs. Barrow dabs at her eyes with a hanky, and I'm endeared by how red and puffy they are. "Such a sweet girl. She was so wonderful to help me out when our nanny up and quit for that waitressing job. Our new nanny started this week, but Lydia and Cole had a special connection." She lowers her volume. "We haven't told him yet about what's happened. He's been in the strangest mood this week, and I don't want to upset him further. He must sense it's almost time for the baby to be born. They say children can tell these things."

Walter shifts beside me, but if Mrs. Barrow senses his embarrassment, she doesn't show it. Mrs. Barrow doesn't look much older than me, which is a bit unnerving. Her high cheekbones and catlike eyes make me think of women I see in advertisements, and even with her round stomach, she's somehow elegant.

"Lydia always speaks so warmly of Cole." The dog—a yippy rat of a thing with sharp teeth—scratches at the door where he's been shut away, and I raise my volume to drown it out. "I know she'll be delighted to see him again. Where is he?"

When Mrs. Barrow regards me, her face is full of sympathy. "Oh, Miss Sail. I admire your hope. And perhaps I'll borrow some of it, because I fear—" She cuts off her words with a bright smile directed beyond me. "Hello, Cole. Where's Dottie?"

Cole stands in the doorway, a sullen expression on his face, and a toy car clutched in one hand. "Kitchen." His gaze shifts to me. "You're Lydia's friend."

He speaks in that little-kid way. Dottie is in the "titchen" and I'm Lydia's "fwiend."

"Hi, Cole. Yes, I am." He keeps looking at me in that soul-seeing way children have about them. I try not to squirm. "How are you?"

He looks down at his sailor shirt and flicks at a button.

"Darling, don't be rude. Miss Sail asked how you are."

Cole keeps flicking. His blond curls are orderly, not at all like every other time I've seen him, where they're windblown and streaked with dirt.

Mrs. Barrow sighs. "This is what I'm talking about." Her voice has a confiding quality to it, despite Cole standing right there. "Ordinarily, he would talk your ear off. He just isn't himself these days." She turns her furrowed brow back to Cole. "Are you feeling all right, sweetie?"

He doesn't answer her, but instead looks at me. "Is Lydia coming over?"

All I can do is stare back. Tears fill my eyes. "I . . ."

"Remember, dear? Lydia is busy with big-kid school. That's why she hasn't been over recently."

Cole looks at me, as if waiting for me to confirm or deny this story. I can't seem to make words come out of my mouth.

"Cole, honey, I think I hear Papa outside. Would you run and check for Mama?"

My sharp inhale draws Walter's gaze. I push a smile onto my face. Walter is here, and I'm in the presence of David Barrow's wife, son, and unborn child. Surely I'm safe.

Cole doesn't run. He ambles to the window. And in my head, I recall Lydia's breezy voice one day in the car. *I'm exhausted. I swear Cole doesn't walk anywhere. He's always running.*

"Well, Cole. Is he here?" Mrs. Barrow asks.

The door opens and in strides Mr. Barrow, looking very Big City Businessman in his three-piece suit and fedora. He drops his hat on Cole's head. "Hello, Mr. Barrow." His voice is deep and jovial. "Is the Missus around?"

Cole only stands there. He doesn't even look up at his father.

And again, I hear Lydia. *I always feel unsettled around Mr. Barrow, but he must be a good father, because Cole runs and jumps on him whenever he comes home.*

Mrs. Barrow laughs with too much gusto. "Hello, dear. You remember Miss Piper Sail? And this is her friend, Walter."

Mr. Barrow's gaze swings to us on the couch. He's not a particularly handsome man, but he dresses and carries himself in a commanding way. "Of course. You're lovelier every time I see you, it seems."

"We were just leaving."

"They had come by to say hello. We were discussing the . . . the current news in the neighborhood."

Mr. Barrow's face flickers with understanding. "Yes, well, I'm glad to see you're not out walking alone, Miss Sail. I'll show you to the door."

This seems rather absurd considering I can see the door from here, and unease tingles in my chest.

"Thank you for calling," Mrs. Barrow says.

"It was our pleasure. Thank you for putting your dog away."

"Of course. If you're not used to them, they can be quite a lot to deal with. Good-bye, now."

"Good-bye."

Mr. Barrow follows us outside. The door clicks closed behind him. "I don't want you coming around and upsetting Mrs. Barrow with your talk of Lydia." His voice is quiet but also, somehow, threatening. "The pregnancy has been hard enough on her, and she doesn't need the stress of thinking about some girl who got herself taken."

My hands curl into fists. "Some girl who got herself taken?"

Mr. Barrow smiles in a thin-lipped way. "I trust this is the last time we'll have to have this conversation."

He turns on his heel and shuts the door, leaving me with the flavor of unspoken, venomous words on my tongue.

Walter tugs at my arm. "Let's go, Piper. He's not worth the energy."

But I disagree. I think looking into Mr. David Barrow and where he was Tuesday around 5:20 might be worth a *lot* of my energy.

First, however, I intend to track down Dr. LeVine's notebook.

When Mariano told me he didn't think I should go to the LeVines' anymore, he probably just meant when the family is there. Right?

That's what I'm banking on, anyway, as I watch Tabitha leave the house, her shopping sack on her shoulder as she sets out to do her normal Saturday errands. Matthew drove Dr. and Mrs. LeVine to an appointment of some kind with Mariano and Detective O'Malley, and Hannah and Sarah have been shipped away to relatives in the suburbs so they won't be underfoot.

I pull the LeVines' house key from its hiding spot, slink around to the back door, and let myself in. My heart feels ready to catapult right out of my chest, and "What ifs?" circle my thoughts like birds of prey. But I have to ignore them. Getting my hands on that notebook, learning if there's anything else Dr. LeVine hid about Lydia, must take priority over my fears.

Bread dough rises on the kitchen counter. My mind's eye sees the scene from the last time I stood in this kitchen—Lydia unconscious and bleeding from her fall. Her soiled Presley's uniform. Everything had seemed so bad that afternoon, and now . . .

I must focus. I brush tears from my eyes and make my way to Lydia's father's dark office.

The room is soaked in prestige. A bookshelf takes up the back wall, crammed with medical texts. Framed artwork of battle scenes and certificates of Dr. LeVine's awards and degrees take up the rest of the wall space. A rolltop desk sits atop a blue-and-red rug, which seems just feminine enough for Mrs. LeVine to have done the choosing.

What am I looking for, exactly? The notebook of course, but something else too. Something that might prove Dr. LeVine cares more about his daughter than he does his reputation.

Whatever clues I'm looking for, I'm not going to find them standing in the doorway, am I? I take a deep breath and step into the office.

A knock sounds on the front door. I slam my hands over my mouth to squelch my scream.

I take a deep breath. My heart drums so loudly, it's hard to think. No one from the family would knock, right? I'll very quietly go to the front door and see who it is.

I peek out the parlor window and sigh with relief. Only the gardener. He whistles something jaunty as he starts trimming the shrubs.

Not a threat. But, still, I shouldn't dally about.

Dr. LeVine keeps his desk very neat. I carefully leaf through a small stack of folders and papers—a medical magazine, several files for patients I don't recognize. Nothing that seems significant. But, of course, I don't know exactly what I'm looking for.

I pull open the top drawer. Pens and pads of paper. The second drawer is full of used medical instruments—vials missing stoppers, stethoscopes without various parts. Nothing of interest. I tug at the third drawer, but it doesn't budge.

Because it's locked. Hmm.

Where would I keep a key to a locked desk drawer? With sinking disappointment, I realize that I would keep it on my person, along with my house and automobile keys.

But I also might hide a spare in my office. Just in case.

Where, though? I pick up the framed photographs on his desk, flip them around. Nothing. Of course, putting it with something that Tabitha would routinely pick up and dust wouldn't be a good choice. I turn in a full circle. The bookshelf alone creates hundreds of hiding places.

I heave a sigh and pull out volume after volume of medical textbook. Nothing.

I stick a hair pin into the lock and jimmy it around, like they do in movies. Nothing.

I feel around under the desk for anything that might be taped there. Nothing.

I look on the backs of his framed art. Nothing.

I pull up the rug under Dr. LeVine's desk. Noth—

Something.

My fingertips brush against cool metal, and I peel the rug back farther. The key is brass and shaped differently than keys to doors or cars. Indeed, it makes a beautiful clicking sound when I stick it inside the desk lock and turn.

The drawer slides open.

Mariano looks up from my hastily scribbled notes. "I would ask how you came by this information, but I'm not sure I want to know."

The spark in his eyes, however, tells a different story.

I lean back in the chair that sits by Mariano's desk and cross my ankles. "I happened to find myself in the right place at the right time, is all."

"How interesting." His voice is flat, his expression unreadable. He rests his elbows on his desk. "I was pretty sure I had voiced some concerns about you visiting with the family."

"Well, I didn't visit them in the traditional sense of the word."

Mariano continues to look at me. His mouth is a line and his gaze sharp. Even though heat creeps up my neck and face, likely staining my cheeks red, I refuse to look away.

The detective department is a blur of life around us. Cigarette smoke casts a haze over the room of ringing telephones and scraping chairs. The air tastes of burned coffee and pencil shavings. I don't know how Mariano manages to think in an office that feels like a train station.

Mariano looks away first, down at the notepad on which I'd spent as much time as I dared writing notes. "So, tell me what I'm looking at."

I scoot up against the desk, where I can see my scribbling. "There was a bundle of correspondence with a doctor friend at the Mayo Clinic, the one he planned to take Lydia to. I documented anything that seemed important in those letters on the next page. There was also the diary of Lydia's episodes. That's what I went in there for."

I swallow back the emotion that clogs my throat. "You can read the list for yourself, but he talks about all the different doses of medication he tried and how she reacted." I run my finger down the list. "Feeling like she had bugs all over her, hearing sounds nobody else did, paranoia about being followed or people talking about her, excessive sleepiness. I witnessed a lot of that.

"But the most interesting thing, I think"—I flip away the diary of Lydia's reactions for another page—"was a patient file on Margaret Finnegan."

Mariano's dark eyebrows arch.

I nod. "When I realized that she was one of *the* Finnegans— you know, like the Irish gang family—I thought it was worth paying attention to. The notes are all there, but the gist is that six months ago, Margaret was treated by Dr. LeVine for an infected gall bladder. Directly after, she came down with a different infection and died. Her brothers pressed charges, but there wasn't enough evidence to convict Dr. LeVine of malpractice. And the Finnegans were . . . well, I copied down some of the correspondence. They were upset."

Mariano scans the notes. "Were there any outright threats?"

"They didn't threaten, no. But they were certainly not pleased."

"Maybe that's why Dr. LeVine chose not to mention the Finnegans when we asked about anyone who might have bad feelings toward his family . . . ?"

When Mariano looks at me, I can read the same question on his face that's occupied my mind all afternoon. Is Lydia's disappearance about payback?

The thought makes my breathing come in shallow bursts instead of long, even strokes. Father is careful to censor what he says around me about work, but Nick isn't, and he has a slew of names for the Irish gang that controls the North Side—charmless thugs, brainless brutes, dumb paddies.

"Could I get you some coffee, Piper?" Mariano's low words are like a life preserver in my sea of fears, calling me back.

"No, thank you." Something drips onto my wrist. "Oh, blast, I'm crying."

"You're allowed to cry, Piper."

I unfasten my handbag and pull out the handkerchief Mariano had loaned me just a few days before. "I brought this to return. I'm afraid I'm going to need to use it, though."

Mariano leans back in his chair, his hands laced together behind his head. "Well, that solves the mystery of why you carry such a large handbag." His lips curl in a smile. "Stolen handkerchiefs, of course."

When he smiles, lines form on his cheeks. Not like dimples, exactly. More like parentheses, framing in his smile. The effect is charming; I don't even feel bothered that it's at my expense.

Mariano brings all four legs of his chair back to the ground. "As a lawyer's daughter, I'm sure you know that none of this would be admissible in court, since there was no search warrant. Just"—Mariano gestures to the notes I gave him—"creative fact finding. But it does motivate me to stop in on the Finnegans and see what they might know about your Lydia."

"Is that safe?" My mind holds images of crime scene photographs, men splayed in odd angles.

He grimaces. "As you might guess, my relationship with the Finnegan family isn't exactly warm and fuzzy."

"I'm sure they don't like detectives."

"Oh, they like some." His smile is wry. "Not me, though. Not with who my family is in the business." Mariano shrugs away the implied story, as if he thinks he might be telling me something I already know. Are other men in his family detectives? "But I'll be fine. O'Malley will be with me, of course."

The squeeze in my chest eases knowing he won't be alone. "Okay, good. You can keep those notes, if you'd like. And I did pay a visit to the Barrows yesterday. I'm wondering, did Mr. Barrow tell you where he was at the time Lydia was taken?"

"You're not asking me to share details of an investigation, are you?"

I make a show of fluttering my eyes several times. "Of course I am."

Now he smiles. "Why do you ask?"

But his smile fades as I recount for him what happened when Walter and I went over there yesterday. I detail how different Cole was from the boy Lydia had always described, and how Mr. Barrow surprised us by coming home early. And that he made it clear that another visit would be unwelcome.

I hook my thumb around my necklace and trace the length of the strand of pearls. "So, I'm thinking about brushing up on my childcare skills."

Mariano's eyes narrow. "Childcare skills."

"Yes. I'm terrible with kids. Just ask my sister-in-law. And since I'm getting older, and I'm, well, female and all, I think it's time that I learn how to care for a child."

I can't read his expression. He doesn't seem pleased or angry or fearful or . . . anything, really. He's just looking at me with those intense eyes of his.

A shadow falls over Mariano's desk as Detective O'Malley joins us. He tips his hat to me. "Miss Sail, pardon the interruption. Cassano, could I speak with you for a minute?"

"Of course. Excuse me, Piper."

The two men step away, and I push the damp handkerchief deeper into my bag. My gaze catches on this morning's issue of *The Daily Chicagoan* perched precariously on the edge of Mariano's messy desk. *Wealthy Detroit girl found alive in the underbelly of Chicago* reads a headline near the bottom of the page. My heart hiccups at the byline—Jeremiah Crane.

Nineteen-year-old Willa Mae Hermann of the Detroit Hermanns went missing last month while on her way to Milwaukee to visit her aunt. Her father, mother, and four younger siblings had given her up for dead when they received a phone call from Willa Mae herself. Willa Mae made the phone call from Johnny's Lunchroom on Clark Street in Chicago's North Side—

"Piper, I'm sorry"—Mariano yanks his suit jacket from the back of his chair—"but I've got to go. I'll ring you later. Hey, Jones!"

An officer several desks away looks up.

"Could you escort her out?" Mariano calls over his shoulder.

There isn't even time to say good-bye before he and Detective O'Malley forge their way through the office.

Jones heaves a gusty sigh as he scoots back from his desk. I skim the article about how Willa Mae escaped the brothel she had been sold to—shudder—and her claims of being beaten and locked in a closet when she refused to comply with her captors.

I hope Mariano isn't the only one who rings me tonight. Hopefully Jeremiah's patience hasn't been exhausted, and he intends to call me yet again this evening.

Tonight, I believe, I will feel up to a conversation.

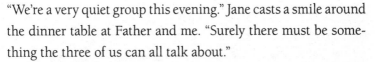

"We're a very quiet group this evening." Jane casts a smile around the dinner table at Father and me. "Surely there must be something the three of us can all talk about."

Father smiles thinly at her. "Sorry, dear. I'm afraid my mind is on a case, and Piper isn't much for chit-chat these days."

I spear a wedge of boiled potato. "Having a missing best friend will do that to a girl."

"There's no need to be snide." Father pats my hand. "We understand this is a difficult time for you."

Jane slices elegant bites of her pork chop. "Perhaps it would cheer you to know that I went with that peach color you liked so well for the bridesmaids' dresses."

I don't recall the peach color or liking it so well. The little girl in me wants to tell Jane this, but a voice that sounds like Lydia's curbs my instincts. *Piper, it won't hurt you to smile and say, "How nice."*

"How nice." My teeth are gritted, and perhaps Father notices, because he jumps in with a question for Jane about the reception hall. While they chat, I mentally slip away to thoughts about

Lydia, the Finnegan gang, and a war-hero doctor who's brilliant enough to save lives on the front lines, but doesn't seem to understand how to help detectives find his daughter.

After dinner, as I carry plates to the kitchen for Joyce, there's a knock on the front door.

"I'll get it," I tell her as she turns off the faucet.

"You sure?"

"It's no problem." As I rush from the kitchen, my hopes soar that it might be Mariano. That whatever he and Detective O'Malley hurried off to this afternoon was related to Lydia. And now perhaps he's come to tell me in person that she's been returned home safely . . .

But I open the door to the grave faces of Jeremiah and Emma Crane. Jeremiah sweeps his hat off his head and clutches it in front of him. "We would have telephoned first, but our line was occupied. May we come in?"

"Of course." I hold the door open wider. "May I take your hats?"

I hang his trilby and her brimmed cloche on the coatrack, and then lead them into the living room. Father and Jane are still in the dining room, discussing the wedding guest list over cups of coffee. "Have a seat."

Jeremiah and Emma settle onto the couch beside each other. While they share a family resemblance, with the sandy hair and blue eyes, Jeremiah has a certain sheen to him that makes Emma appear washed-out. Like when Joyce takes the slipcovers off the arms of the couch, the rest of the fabric then looks faded.

Emma folds her hands primly on her lap. "We wanted to see how you're holding up."

The way they smile at me, heads tilted and no teeth showing, takes me back to how people smiled at Mother's funeral.

"I don't know, honestly." I perch on an armchair and smooth my skirt over my bare knees. My silk stockings snagged on my way home from Mariano's office and now are buried somewhere in my bag with his handkerchief. With Jeremiah and Emma looking so proper, I wish I had bothered to put on a fresh pair when I came home.

"I can't even imagine, Miss Sail." Jeremiah's voice holds more sympathy than I would expect, but I suppose empathy is a smart skill for a man who's destined to take over one of the biggest daily newspapers in Chicago.

"I was actually planning to ring you tonight." Surprise registers on both their faces, but I press on as if I didn't notice. "I saw your article about Willa Mae Hermann of Detroit. And I wondered . . . I wondered how you came to know of her."

Emma's cheeks pinken, but Jeremiah's gaze is unflinching. "She called us. That's almost always how it works for cases like this. We get a call."

"Were you the one who spoke to her?"

"I took a train to Detroit to interview her."

"And you think her story is true?"

"I wouldn't have reported it if I thought otherwise. There's no reason for a girl to make up a story like that."

Emma's voice—sweet and almost musical—breaks into the conversation. "I feel she's bold for coming forward. Many girls in Willa Mae's situation might have kept quiet for the embarrassment of it all."

Including Lydia, should this turn out to be her situation. I can almost hear her saying she just wants to put the whole thing behind her, that she doesn't want Matthew to find out. "I agree, Emma. She's very brave. And I was glad to see it reported."

"You're worried Lydia might be in the same situation, aren't you?" Her words are direct, but her tone soft.

"I am. I know they say white slavery is more buzz than sting . . ."

Jeremiah snorts. "The reason the politicians say that, Miss Sail, is because they don't want to have to be responsible for it. But I'll tell you the truth—for every Willa Mae Hermann who escapes, there's dozens of girls who don't."

Emma flashes me a sympathetic glance before looking to her brother. "That's not very uplifting, Jeremiah."

He nods to me. "My apologies, Miss Sail."

"Considering the frankness of this conversation, I think you had better call me Piper."

Jeremiah's mouth curls into a smile. A real smile, not his rakish grin or the closed-mouth pitying one from when he arrived. "Piper."

I try to smile back at him, but I'm not sure I succeed. This should have been an exciting moment, having Jeremiah Crane drop by. We would have talked over superficial things, perhaps. The baseball season and Bessie Smith and Agatha Christie's latest novel. I would have called Lydia and giggled with her. She would have preached to me out of our etiquette textbook on what to say and how to smile.

But instead, his first visit is somber and dark.

"Have the police any leads?" Emma's voice breaks into my mental wanderings. Was I just sitting here staring off? "We had detectives come to our house, the same ones who were at school that day. But they weren't sharing details, of course."

"They've talked to all the neighbors in hope that someone saw something. But so far, no one did."

"In a neighborhood like ours, doesn't it seem unlikely?" There's a suspicious tinge in Emma's voice.

I think I like her.

"I agree." Jeremiah settles against the back of the couch, looking so relaxed, I half expect him to loosen his tie. "If nothing else, you'd think Mrs. Applegate would have seen something. When I was a kid, Mama always said she never had to worry, because Mrs. Applegate had an eye on me at all times."

"That's because you're trouble from the tips of your hair to the toes on your feet, brother dear."

Jeremiah winks at me. "Everybody seems like trouble when compared to you, sweet Emma."

I feel like I should jest back, but the part of me that knows how to be witty and flirtatious has been crowded out by emotions like dread and anxiety. "Jeremiah, did you take many notes during your conversation with Willa Mae? I would be interested in seeing them."

The smiles on their faces fade.

"Yes, I took lots of notes." His words are careful. "But I don't know how helpful they would be if your hope is to find Lydia."

"I just thought there might be something in there. Does she know who kidnapped her? What happened after that? Did she ever see any of the other girls, or was she isolated?"

Jeremiah's gaze is steady on me. He opens his mouth. Closes it. Looks to Emma and then back at me. "The details that I didn't put in the article . . . they're so ill-suited for the public. I wouldn't want to put you in the troubling position of reading them, Piper."

"You're not putting me in it. I'm asking it of you."

"But you don't know what's in there. I do. And I don't think it's a good idea."

Silence descends on the room. I hold Jeremiah's gaze until he looks away.

Emma stands. "We should be going. I'm sure you don't feel like entertaining. We just wanted you to know we're thinking about you."

Jeremiah stands as well.

"Thank you." My words are stiff, despite my sincerity. "Hopefully, next time we get together, we'll be celebrating her return."

Kindness shines in Emma's eyes. "I pray diligently for Lydia to be returned home safely."

Tears—which seem so much closer to the surface than ever before—spring in my eyes. "Thank you, Emma. I've started to feel as though I'm the only one who still thinks she'll be found . . ." The tightness in my chest won't let me squeeze out the word *alive*. It's a wonderful word that I should be able to shout—alive!—but it's lodged in my lungs.

When Jeremiah's fingertips graze the underside of my elbow, I know I faded out on them again. "Telephone if you need anything. Anything at all."

I look at him, the fellow who's antagonized me on a regular basis for the last year, yet now extends comfort in some of the darkest days I've ever known. "I need Lydia."

The words are raw, and if I had more sense of myself, I would probably want to snatch them back and shove them away. But I don't care that Jeremiah looks at me with pity or that Emma's eyes shine with tears. My sense of pride is so far gone that I don't even care that they might still be able to hear me when I close the front door behind them, slide to the floor, and sob.

L ots of Presley's girls take the L."

But Father only repeats, "Walter will drive you," and underlines a sentence on the document he's reading.

"But—"

Father sits up straight in his desk chair and gives me a stern look. "I know you're practically a grown woman, and that before too many more months you'll be away at college, but for now, I need to know you're being watched over at all times. Can you understand that?"

His face may be stern, but his eyes are full of fear.

"Yes, Father," I murmur.

"Thank you." He reaches for his cup of black coffee. "Is there anything else?"

I think of him slack-jawed with sleep, a gun at his side, and his chair swiveled expectantly toward the front door. If I don't ask him, the questions will keep pestering me.

"The first night we knew about Lydia, I came downstairs in the middle of the night." I glance at him. He's watching me, mouth pressed in a line. "You were asleep in your chair. You had your gun with you."

He takes a long drink of his coffee. The steam curls into the air between us. "And that scared you, didn't it?"

"Yes, sir."

Father sighs and rests his cup on his desk. "I'm sorry to

have scared you, Piper. But *I* was scared. I'm a single father, with a daughter whose best friend has vanished from the neighborhood. I guess it made me feel better to have the gun with me. I was overreacting, of course." He reaches across his desk for my hand. "As a lawyer, I sometimes make men angry. Very nasty men. And my imagination ran wild."

"What were you imagining?" I can't seem to make my words louder than a whisper.

He regards me a moment. "Nothing that I could substantiate with evidence. It was just farfetched worrying, okay?"

"Okay, Daddy." I haven't called him that in years, but with my tiny hand pressed inside his large one, the term seems to fit the moment.

He squeezes my fingers before releasing me. "I hope your school day goes well. I know it'll be a hard one for you."

It will. But not for the reason he thinks.

He glances at the leather shopping bag on my shoulder, and I suck in a breath as I anticipate him asking about it. But I leave without any questions. Perhaps he thinks carrying a shopping bag instead of a handbag is some new rage among the secondary-school crowd.

Walter is quiet on the drive until he pulls alongside the front sidewalk of Presley's. He puts on the brake and watches the crowd of girls heading up to the doors. "I wish I could go in there with you. I hate that you have to do this alone."

It's not hard to fake the wobble in my voice. "I can handle it."

If I tell Walter what I have planned for today, he won't let me out of his sight, and this is something I need to do.

I slide out of the car, my shopping bag thumping against my

calf in a way that seems incriminating. But Walter only says, "See you at three" as I shut the door.

I wave good-bye and start up the sidewalk.

I dawdle my way to the front doors, keeping an eye on the Ford as Walter inches through Presley's traffic. The girls stream around me, walking in content pairs or groups. They beat their gums about parties and summer plans, but their chatter fades to a whisper when they brush past me.

No one says a word to me. I wouldn't have expected this to hurt so deeply.

I had hoped I could slink away once Walter was out of sight, but there are far too many eyes trained on me for that. I'll have to go inside and try to use a telephone in there.

I stroll through the doors, becoming one of the many girls in saddle shoes and an ankle-length black skirt. Several glance at the shopping bag hanging off my shoulder—*they* know it's out of place—but still no one breathes a word to me. And as the time draws near for class to begin, when I know Headmistress Robinson is in the chapel for morning prayers, I slip into her office.

The room hasn't changed since the last time I was in here, "borrowing" several sheets of her personalized stationery. The same photographs are gathered on the edge of the desk, the same cup of sharpened pencils, and the same candlestick telephone.

I pull out the card and dial the number.

"Detective Cassano." His words have a gruff, almost sleepy sound.

"Hi, it's Piper."

There's a pause. "Are you not at school today?"

"I am, actually, but I needed to let you know something.

Before I tell you this"—I suck in a swift, fortifying breath—"I want to make it clear that I'm not calling to ask permission."

"I'm already nervous."

Footsteps echo in the hallway and my heart rate doubles. I'm in here because . . . ? I left a book at home? I'm feeling sick? I'm emotionally traumatized?

The footsteps travel farther down the hall, and breath whooshes from my lungs.

"Piper, are you still there?"

I drop my voice low. "Yes, sorry. I thought someone was about to come in here."

"Where exactly are you?"

"The headmistress's office. Look, I'm going up to Clark Street today, to that lunchroom where Willa Mae made her phone call. I want to ask around about Lydia. I'm only telling you because I want someone to know. Just . . . in case."

"And you're picking me." His statement is slow, measured.

"You're the one person I know who won't try to stop me."

"Don't be so sure of that, Piper. A girl like you . . ." Mariano's voice drops to a hush as well. "Look, it's not a good idea for you, of all people, to go walking around by yourself in a part of town that's controlled by the North Side Gang. Let's not tempt fate."

"I told you, I'm not calling to ask your permission. I'm calling so someone knows where I am."

"We've gone to every vice district there is with a photograph of Lydia, including the North Side. This isn't something you need to concern yourself with."

"Detective Cassano, I think you're smart enough to know that in a situation like this, a girl like me might be able to get answers when a uniformed officer can't."

"I thought we'd dispensed with the formalities."

"Well, you're not acting like Mariano right now. You're acting like Detective Cassano." I glance at the clock. Morning prayers will be over soon. "Now, I'll be getting on the L at Schiller, and I intend to get off at—"

"Piper, stop."

"I want *somebody* to have this information." I clutch close the paper on which I scribbled my plan this morning. "If you don't want it, then I'll leave it taped under the headmistress's desk, and if something goes awry—"

"I'm coming with you."

I'm glad Mariano isn't here to see the surprise on my face. "That's not necessary, Mariano. I don't expect you to drop what you had planned to—"

"My job right now is to recover Lydia LeVine. I would rather not lose you in the process."

The thought of Mariano coming with me, of not having to venture into Johnny's Lunchroom alone, makes relief slide through my veins. Yet my words still come out razor-sharp. "You won't show up looking like a cop, will you? Because I don't see that helping me any."

"If you promise you'll wait at school for me, I promise I won't blow your cover, Detective Sail."

I glance at the clock. It's definitely time to get out of here. "There's a bench at the corner of Irving and Lake Shore. I'll meet you there." Footsteps echo in the hall again. "And if by chance I'm not there, come into the school and tell them I'm needed for something."

I hang up before he responds.

And just a second before the headmistress opens the door to her office.

The surprise on her face is quickly replaced with fury, and a deep crease forms between her silver eyebrows as she scowls at me. "Miss Sail—"

My response is a reflex. I cover my face with my hands and burst into loud, fake tears.

"I know I shouldn't be in here, but it's just so awful, ma'am. I can't stand it, I can't." I don't let myself peek. I don't want her seeing that my cheeks are dry. "It feels so terrible to be at Presley's without Lydia. She loves it here so much. She views you as a role model." Was that too much? Too late now . . . "And I just feel closer to her when I'm in your office."

Behind my hands, I squeeze my eyes tight, pushing out a dribble of tears before I risk uncovering my face.

Headmistress Robinson's expression has softened. It's still not soft by any stretch, but the crease between her brows is gone.

"I know you and Miss LeVine are very close." She glances at the two wooden chairs in her office, the ones for students, but remains standing. "Her disappearance is a shock to us all. If you feel you are unfit for school, Miss Sail, I suggest you go home. If, however, you decide that crying and feeling sorry for yourself will not do anybody any good, you may head to your first class."

This woman is a stone.

Or aware that I'm faking.

Here she is, practically gift wrapping a reason for me to walk out the school doors, but my pride buckles with the implication of weakness. "I'll go to my class, thank you." I rise, back straight and chin jutted.

I skirt around her at the door, inhaling the smell of

peppermint candy, which she uses to cover up her cigarette habit. I feel her cold, suspecting gaze follow me down the hallway.

The most discreet exit is in the back, by the lunchroom, which is empty. I help myself to two chicken sandwiches in the ice box and tuck them into my sack. I duck into the pantry and wriggle out of my uniform, which I wore over a pale blue day dress that matches the color of Lydia's eyes. I had originally dressed in a dull gray, hoping to ward off unwanted male attention, and then realized if I intended to flirt answers out of anyone, I would need to look at least somewhat fetching.

I jam my discarded Presley's uniform into the bag, along with the sandwiches, a notebook, Lydia's senior portrait, and several other items that seemed like they might be helpful—a length of rope, a roll of tape, and Nick's pocket knife, which I hope he has no occasion to miss today. I hesitate a second before pulling it from the bag and tucking it into my pocket. The thought of using it sends a shiver through me . . . but so does the thought of being caught unprepared.

With the shopping bag secured over my shoulder, I slip out the back door and into the crisp morning air.

The bench is unoccupied, and I take a seat. I lost track of time while putting on my show for Ms. Robinson. Will Mariano drive or take the train? He better not show up here in the touring sedan that Jeremiah so easily identified as being a detective's vehicle . . .

My thoughts roam the afternoon ahead. Walking to the train station with Mariano, finding Johnny's Lunchroom. This makes my stomach twist with a different brand of anxiety than I felt when I imagined doing this alone. Aside from my brothers and Walter, I've never spent extended time alone in a man's company.

Not that this is a date in even the loosest interpretation of the word, but that doesn't keep my stomach from feeling like a rag that someone has grabbed either end of and twisted tight.

Ten minutes pass before I catch sight of Mariano. I never noticed how distinct his gait is—he has a sort of swagger to him, arms loose at his side, shoulders squared. I sling the shopping bag over my shoulder and rush down the sidewalk.

But when I reach him, I'm unable to speak. I want to tell him *thank you for coming, thank you for letting me interrupt your day,* but the words catch in my throat.

He sticks his hands in his trouser pockets and rocks back on his heels. "Am I holding up under scrutiny, Detective? I did my best to not look like a cop, but I'm afraid there's only so much a man can do to disguise his true identity."

"You look good." Heat races up the back of my neck. "I mean, you don't look like a detective."

He touches his flat cap. "I changed my hat."

"I see that."

Mariano smiles. Had we met under more normal circumstances, a party or a school function, I would have hoped he'd come ask me to dance.

But we didn't meet under normal circumstances. I shift my bag higher on my shoulder and step into the crosswalk. "If I'd been thinking clearly when we spoke on the telephone, I would have suggested meeting you at the station. That would have saved you time and energy."

"But then I would have had to tell you no, and that would have taken time and energy as well."

I glance at him. "I suppose you're aware that you're very stubborn."

"*I'm* stubborn?" Mariano's laugh rumbles. "*You're* the one who phoned me to say she was venturing into known gang territory wearing a very pretty dress."

My heart hitches in my chest. "It's the daytime. I can't imagine it's so dangerous in the daytime."

That's what I had told myself all day yesterday during church and a slow Sunday afternoon, but Mariano snorts in reply.

The train station is alive with Chicagoans bustling about the city, their coats left unbuttoned, packages and briefcases dangling from arms. The air has the smell of a workday—a mix of coffee beans, newsprint, and shoe polish.

Mariano hands over the coins for our fare.

"I dragged you all the way out here, though," I protest as we're waved into the station. "I'm positive this wasn't on your list of things to do today."

"Oh, you're positive, are you?" Mariano turns to me with arched eyebrows. "When you were at my desk Saturday, were you peeking at my calendar, Piper?"

I roll my eyes. "Of course not. I'm taking an educated guess."

Mariano's hand is light against my back as he guides me through the fray of people toward the platform. "I'm glad you called me. I wouldn't want to find out you did this alone."

I tense, despite my mad urge to lean against him, to let his weight support mine and slow the fissures of fear that weaken me at the core. But I don't think a needy female would impress Mariano Cassano. Nor do I want him suspecting that I manipulated him out here with an ulterior motive.

"Well, I have lunch covered, anyway." I pat my bag. "I swiped sandwiches from the school cafeteria."

"Ah, good." Mariano's hands are in his pockets again, giving him a boyish look. "Because I don't know where we would find lunch during our investigation of Johnny's *Lunchroom*."

I turn away, my nose in the air, and try to bite back my smile. Mariano laughs loud enough that I can hear it above the squeal of the approaching train. "I'm only teasing you, Piper. My stomach thanks you for thinking of it."

After we've waited for passengers to exit, Mariano holds out a hand to help me across the threshold. The train is stuffy, and I pick a window seat underneath a fan. Mariano settles beside me in the green plush seat, his knee bumping mine.

As the train lurches onward down the tracks, I cross my arms around my bag, securing it against my chest. "I've never done anything like this. Do we need some kind of a cover story?"

Mariano's mouth pooches as he considers my question. "This is one of those times when the truth will serve us just fine. My guess is that anyone we talk to will have seen the news about Lydia in the paper. You tell them you saw Willa Mae's story, and you felt hopeful. Simple as that."

"And what about you?" The train curves and we bend with it. "Who do we say you are?"

"When people ask you about Walter, what do you say?"

"Walter?" It's strange, the twist of guilt in my gut. Should I have told Walter what I was doing? Should I have given him a chance to come with me, to help? I turn my gaze out the window. "He and I haven't done many undercover investigations together, so I've never had to answer for him."

"But surely you have to explain him to others sometimes."

Do I? "In the neighborhood, people know he works for my family. I suppose they feel that's a sufficient reason for seeing us out together."

"What about outside of the neighborhood?" Mariano hooks his ankle over the opposite leg. "When the two of you are out, what do most think?"

"How should I know what they think? Maybe they think he's my brother or my bodyguard. I don't know. Times are changing. Even if people knew that Walter worked for my family, I doubt they would give it any thought."

"Don't make the mistake of assuming that just because you don't think on it, no one else does." Mariano shifts in his seat, and again his knee bumps mine. This time it settles there. "I suppose I'm too narrow to make for a convincing bodyguard, so we had better go with the brother angle."

"But we look nothing alike." A man on the other end of the aisle appears to be angling for a better view of my legs, and I rearrange my skirt to cover my knees. "And I disagree about the bodyguard thing. While you aren't big like Walter, you have an air about you that suggests you aren't a man to be messed with."

Mariano doesn't answer. When I glance at him, I find his gaze full of questions. Does he think I'm flirting with him?

Am I?

I look away. "I think I should do the talking." My voice seems terse to my ears. "It'll be less threatening to talk to some secondary-school girl like me. Any advice for how to get information out of people?"

"I think I should be asking you. You seem to know what you're doing."

I shake my head. "I'm just winging it."

"You've got good instincts." His gaze is on me again, but I keep my face turned toward the window. "Most young society ladies in your situation would have fallen apart. But you're too strong for that."

"Your praise is too lofty, Mariano. I don't intend to waste time falling apart when we don't know if anything has happened to Lydia. If that reality changes"—there's a tremor in my voice that hopefully the train covers—"you will not think me strong at all."

"Grief is not weakness." Mariano's words soothe the rattle of fear in my heart. "And I would never accuse you of it, Piper."

I don't mean to look at him, but I can't seem to not. Mariano's face is a man's, no doubt, but there's a boyish softness to him when he regards me that makes my heart quicken. "Thank you."

The bodyguard idea was a smart choice. I don't imagine that anyone who sees us here, staring at each other, would buy that we're brother and sister.

"Closed," I groan. "Why didn't I think of that? I assumed all places like this were open for breakfast too."

Mariano glances at his wristwatch. "But it opens in thirty minutes. That's not so bad."

"We can't just *stand* out here."

"No. We'll walk around. Experience Clark Street in its Monday midmorning glory."

Impatience bites at me as I drag myself away from the eatery. I had expected this neighborhood would look tired after a weekend full of debauchery. That men would be passed out on the streets and trash would sour the alleys. But instead, the street is quiet and reasonably clean. A bit more broken glass in the gutters and not the same manicured feel as Astor Street, but it seems . . . fine.

"I'm just wasting your time, Mariano," I say on a sigh. "I didn't think to check what time Johnny's opened, and this neighborhood seems perfectly safe—"

"Don't let its quiet appearance deceive you." Mariano's voice is low. "This place is . . . It would not be good for you to be found alone here, Piper. And I don't care about Johnny's being closed. In my line of work, you learn to be patient. Let's find someone else we can talk to while we wait."

"Okay. I had thought after Johnny's, I would talk to the police. The station is just—"

Mariano snorts. "Let's not waste our time. They've all been bought."

"What do you mean?"

Mariano gives me a skeptical look. "Given who your father is, I assumed you would know. This part of town is mostly controlled by the Finnegan brothers."

"Father doesn't really talk to me about his work. My brothers know all about it, of course, but he's careful about what he says to me. Some of his clients are even mobsters, I think."

Mariano opens his mouth . . . closes it.

Did I say something I shouldn't have? Maybe that's not even true. "I don't know for sure. I could be wrong."

"No, I . . . I think you're right." Mariano's discomfort with the topic is evident in the way he tweaks his tie back and forth.

"They have as much of a right to legal representation as anyone else, my father says." I shouldn't have added that last part. Makes me sound like a little girl who can't think for herself.

Mariano pulls off his flat cap. Puts it back on. "But your father doesn't talk to you at all about his clients, then?"

"Not really."

I wish I hadn't said anything. If Mariano grew up in a family of police detectives, maybe he doesn't like defense attorneys? I had never considered the politics that might exist between them. We need a subject change.

"So, if it's not a good idea to talk to the police around here, where do we start?"

Mariano doesn't seem to mind the shift in conversation. "Let's head this way for a couple blocks. We'll be right by a . . . Well, a place that's known for . . ." He clears his throat. "The local businessmen might have seen Lydia, if she's around here."

It's charming, his embarrassment. "I promise I won't be too scandalized if you speak the word *bordello* to me, Detective."

He rakes in a breath, a mix of amusement and caution in his eyes. "I know you're no wilting violet, Piper, but I've seen far too much of places like that. It's hard for me to speak casually about them."

I turn those words over in my head as we continue up Clark. Mariano isn't touching me, but he's walking much closer than he did when we roamed Astor Street. And not like he's trying to cozy up to me, but like he's protecting me. Somehow, he manages to strike the perfect balance of shielding me without crossing the line into sheltering.

Mariano gestures to a storefront—O'Connor's Laundry. "Let's try here."

The air inside is hot, damp, and pungent with lye. The whir of machines and the slosh of water make me doubt anyone but Mariano hears the "Hello?" I call out.

But a few seconds later, a ginger-haired woman ambles out to the counter. Her eyes shift from me to Mariano and back to me. "Here to pick up?" Her accent is thickly Irish.

"Hi!" I put on a bright smile before remembering this isn't like selling raffle tickets for the school carnival. "No, actually. We're looking for someone."

The woman rolls her eyes. *Rolls her eyes.* "Of course y'are. Ever since tat Detroit lass turned up on Clark Street, everyone's come pokin' around, looking for someone."

"Yes, well." I pull Lydia's school picture from my bag. "All the same, my best friend was taken from our neighborhood, and I just wondered if you'd seen—"

"How daft are ya?" She doesn't so much as glance at Lydia's photograph. "You tink dey let dem girls walk around for us all to see?"

"There's no need for name calling, ma'am." Mariano's words are clipped.

"If you could just look at her." I move the picture into her line of vision. This woman can call me whatever she likes so long as she looks at the picture. "She's really sick. It's important that we find her."

With a huff, the woman makes a show of looking at Lydia's photograph. "Like I told ya—no. I ain't never seen de girl. Only people who does see de girls is de ones who hires tem."

Why didn't I think of that? "Of course! Are there men here that I can ask?"

Her eyes become slits. "You want me to go get my God-fearing husband so you can ask him if he's seen your friend?"

Embarrassment streaks up my neck and blooms on my

cheeks. "I'm sorry, I didn't mean to imply . . . I'm just very worried about my friend."

"She ain't here, and I got tings to do with my time." The woman turns and waddles away, igniting my fury.

"Thanks so much for your concern!" I call after her, my voice lit with sarcasm. "Your effort really means a lot!"

But she pays no mind to me. "Is this really how people feel about someone who goes missing?" I jab open the door and march through. "That it isn't their problem?"

"I know how personal this is to you, Piper." Mariano's voice is low and soothing in my ear. "But you have to stay clearheaded at a time like this, okay? If you stop thinking clearly, you start making mistakes."

"What if it were them? Or their child?" My breath rattles in and out of me. Lydia's photograph vibrates in my clutched fingers. "Will they all be like this? So callous to Lydia's situation?" My voice morphs to some mocking tone that I don't even recognize. "Well, it's not my problem she got herself taken. It's not my problem she has seizures."

"Hey." Mariano stands in front of me and snaps his fingers in front of my eyes. "Breathe, Piper."

I tell myself to take deep breaths, but the air barely scrapes my windpipe before my body expels it, and I'm growing dizzier with each passing moment.

"Take a deep breath with me, okay?" Mariano fills my vision as he sucks in a deep inhale and then exhales out his mouth.

After several tries, I'm able to mirror his actions. The anger boiling in my chest fades to a simmer, and I realize my head is so still because Mariano's hands have anchored it. His thumbs press into my cheekbones.

The pressure of his hold softens as my breathing regulates. "Better?"

I nod, and he releases me. My cheeks must be like neon lights. He won't think me so strong now, will he?

I take one more deep breath before trusting myself to speak. "How long until the lunchroom opens?"

Mariano looks at me for a long moment, and I fear he's about to ask if I'm really strong enough to go in there. But he glances at his watch. "About fifteen minutes. Let's see what else is open up here and then head back."

The butcher doesn't recognize Lydia, but he's kind about it. As is the tailor we speak to.

"You know who would be good to talk to?" The tailor rolls the end of the measuring tape around his finger. "The man who owns the lunchroom a few blocks down—Johnny Walker."

"Why's that?" Mariano asks before I can share that we were already on our way to see him.

"Well." The tailor's gaze skitters to me and then away. "It's not really fittin' for a lady's ears."

"I'm fine—"

Mariano flicks me a *just go along with it* kind of glance. "I'll be right out, Piper."

My chin juts, but I turn on my heel and stalk out the door without further protest. It won't do Lydia any good for me to pout.

Outside, I lean against the brick building and let my gaze wander the rows of businesses. Where was Willa Mae? Behind one of those ordinary-looking windows? Is that where we'll find Lydia too?

Mariano emerges a minute later, calling, "Thank you, Mr. Gorecki!" over his shoulder.

"So? What is it?" I trot alongside Mariano, who's nudging me toward the lunchroom. "What'd he say?"

"You already know the stuff about Willa Mae. And apparently Mr. Walker has a bit of a reputation for, well, spending time with ladies who . . . Well, with women of a certain . . . I mean—"

"Prostitutes."

Mariano rubs his chin. "Yeah. Mr. Gorecki also thinks he might be involved in gambling or laundering in some way. That perhaps the money funnels through the lunchroom on its way to the Finnegans."

My heart quickens at the thought that we might be just a few breaths away from Lydia. That this Johnny Walker, however vile his personal choices might be, could be what saves her. "Mariano"—my words are breathy from our pace—"I think it'd be best for me to go into the lunchroom alone."

Mariano snorts a laugh. "Think again, Piper Sail."

"I'm serious. I have a better chance of getting him to talk if I'm in there by myself."

Mariano stops walking and gives me an incredulous look. "Did you not hear what I just said?" He ticks it off on his fingers. "Prostitution. Gambling. Money laundering. Finnegan. So, no, you're not going in there by yourself."

I cross my arms over my chest. "Just because a man partakes in a number of vices doesn't mean it's unsafe for me to order a cup of coffee in his restaurant."

"No, Piper."

"How about you give me five minutes in there? You wait right outside, where you can hear me if I scream, and then you can come in if you'd like. But don't act like you're with me if I'm making progress."

"We're not doing any undercover operations that involve me needing to be close enough for rescue in case you need to scream. I'm coming in with you, and that's that."

Beyond Mariano, up the sidewalk, is a dog. He's skinny but tall, and he's trotting toward us. I tug at Mariano's coat. "Let's keep moving. Let's cross the street."

Mariano glances over his shoulder, and then turns back to me with a wry smile. "Well, look at that. You *are* afraid of something."

"I've never claimed otherwise." I tug at his elbow. "Let's get going."

"Going to the heart of gang territory by yourself? Not scary. Being alone with a man who I've just told you has a bad reputation? Not scary. But a stray dog you're three times the size of? Terrifying, apparently."

"Dogs don't like me, okay? They never have." The dog is now galloping toward us, his long tongue flopping out of his mouth. "My archenemies in this world are children, dogs, and my Home Economics teacher, so if we could *please* move faster . . ."

As the dog closes in, my body reacts without my permission—I screech and take off running.

"Piper, don't!" Mariano calls. "That'll make him chase you. Just stand still."

The dog barks. He's closer than I imagined, and another scream bubbles out of my throat. I cower against the cool brick of a building and brace for the impact. For the feel of teeth breaking through skin. "Mariano! Help!"

The dog's wet nose touches my leg, and his paw presses against my thigh.

"Your bag, Piper." Mariano's words are laced with laughter.

I crack open an eye. Mariano stands on the sidewalk, hands on his narrow hips, smirking. The dog has braced himself against me with one paw. He's a skinny thing, with dirt-brown fur matted against his body. His nose is buried in my shopping bag. The bag that holds two chicken sandwiches.

With a trembling hand, I reach past the dog's muzzle and into the bag to retrieve the packed lunch. I chuck the sandwiches as far as I can. The dog barks gleefully and sprints after them.

An exhale shudders out of me. "That was terrifying."

"I know. I was terrified that you'd run back to the train station without me."

I brush dirt from my dress. "I don't like dogs."

"I noticed."

I eye the mutt, whose mangy tail wags as he feasts. "Let's get away from here."

Mariano offers me his arm, and my knees are so weak that I don't even mind leaning on him as we walk to the lunchroom.

It isn't until we're inside and seated at the counter that I realize my master plan to flirt the details out of the proprietor has been foiled.

Stupid dog.

CHAPTER
NINE

Y ou're Johnny Walker?"

The man's straight teeth gleam white, and he winks a dark eye. "Unless you want me to go by a different name, little lady."

"I just thought . . ." I start the sentence before I realize there's no good way to finish. *I just thought you'd look more like a man who couldn't get a date unless he paid them.* "I didn't expect you to be Italian." I try fluttering my eyelashes like I've seen Mae do with Jeremiah. "Why, you look like you could be Valentino's brother."

I swallow. It's not that much of a stretch. Johnny Walker certainly has a face worthy of the silver screen, and he can't be much older than early thirties. Still, it's an uncomfortably forward thing to say to a man. Especially an older man.

But Johnny only smooths his narrow mustache and winks at me again. "Always fancied myself more like Douglas Fairbanks, but you ladies go crazy for Valentino."

"Oh, Fairbanks was dashing as Robin Hood, but there's just something about Italian men." I punctuate this with what I hope sounds like a shy, girlish giggle. I don't let myself look at Mariano, who sits stiffly on the stool beside me.

As ridiculous as Mariano must find my flirting, Johnny leans against the counter. His smile is wolfish, and the weight of Nick's pocket knife is suddenly comforting.

"He's a busy man, Piper." Mariano's brusque words break into the silence. "Ask him what we came for."

Johnny glances at Mariano for the first time, and anxiety squeezes my lungs. Will he recognize him? How often is Mariano around here? I *knew* it'd be better for me to come in alone.

"This is my bodyguard." The words spill out. "My daddy is very protective."

Johnny turns back to me. "A beautiful girl like you? That's smart. Now, how can I help?"

"I'm looking for someone."

"Ah." Johnny's word seems to say, *of course you are.*

"I'm sure you've had tons of people in here since that article came out about the girl from Detroit using your telephone."

"It's just the strangest thing." Johnny straightens. "This neighborhood is tight-knit. We live here, work here, and play here. Why, all my girls live within a block of this place." He makes a sweeping motion to indicate the waitresses. "Ally over there lives just upstairs, even. It's nutty to think something like what happened to the Detroit girl was going on in our backyard, because it's just not like that here."

I dig in my bag for Lydia's photograph. "And I'm sorry to have to take up your time with one more—"

"I don't mind, Miss." He takes the picture from my hand with an indulgent smile, and I feel my own waver. Feel my eyes turn watery.

"Forgive me." I fumble for my handkerchief. "Lydia went missing last week, and I just can't seem to stop crying."

The sound of shattering dishes fills the room, and I jump.

Several tables away, one of the waitresses crouches on the ground beside a shattered coffee mug. She keeps her back to us—to her boss—but her shoulders are hunched in embarrassment.

"Happens to everyone, doll face." Johnny turns back to me and lowers his voice. "Tall dames make for the clumsiest waitresses."

I smile because he expects me to. As he holds my gaze, seeming to have forgotten the photograph he's clutching, I make a show of dabbing my eyes. "I know it's a long shot, Mr. Walker, but do you recognize her? She has red hair and blue eyes."

My breathing hitches as he studies the picture.

"Seen this girl in the papers, but nowhere around here." His voice holds apology.

The hope within me crumbles, and tears spill over.

"Sorry, doll. Wish I could help." He rests Lydia's photograph on the gleaming lunch counter. "She's a pretty young thing."

"And sweet too." My hanky is smudged gray from eye kohl. "Not at all like me."

Johnny's hand is heavy and unwelcome on my shoulder. "Leave your telephone number with the waitress, honey, and I'll call if I see her. We could even hang up a notice in the front window, if you'd like. Lots of people come through my doors, after all."

I sniffle and smile up at him, despite wanting to yank away from the weight of his hand. "Thank you, Mr. Walker."

He gives me a squeeze and steps back as the waitress, who must have made quick work cleaning up the broken ceramic, delivers our lunch. "Thanks, doll. And when this young lady finishes her lunch, you bring her whatever dessert she fancies. On the house."

Johnny takes a step away but pauses at Mariano. He studies

him a moment, and then winks. "One for her guard too. You've got a hard job, son."

Mariano grunts, never breaking character, but embarrassment flames my cheeks.

"Sorry about your friend." The soft words come from the waitress, who's staring at Lydia's picture, still face-up on the edge of the counter. The waitress is, indeed, unusually tall. "She sounded like a lovely girl."

After the way the laundress reacted to Lydia, the compassion of a stranger overwhelms me, and I can't even manage a thank you before she walks away, her auburn bob swishing.

"Well, that was quite a show you put on." Mariano says, his voice low despite no one being around. "When I investigate someone, the best offer I get is for a knuckle duster. You, on the other hand, get free dessert."

"For my bodyguard too." I reach for my fizzing Coca-Cola. "Flirting is miserable work. How do girls do it all the time?"

"You seemed to know what you were doing."

I snort.

"I mean it." Mariano glances around, but the closest people to us are the old men drinking coffee at the opposite end of the counter. "He was so charmed, he didn't know what to do with himself."

I want to throw one of my french fries at him, but that seems too childish. Even for me. "You're trying to flatter me so I don't feel so mortified by what I just did, but it won't work."

"Piper." The warmth he infuses in my name draws my gaze. "You're doing everything you can to get your friend back. That's admirable." Beneath the counter, Mariano's foot bumps against mine. "And it's not true, you know. I've yet to have the honor of meeting Lydia, who I'm sure is very sweet. But you are too."

Those blasted tears burn my eyes again. I can't remember a single person referring to me as sweet. Ever. "I'm really not."

"You're a force, for sure. A hurricane, really. But there's a part of you that's surprisingly tender." He winks. "Mushy, even."

My stomach folds in on itself in a pleasant, unfamiliar way as I turn my attention back to my lunch. What does it mean that Mariano sees something inside me that no one else—not even me—ever has?

The dog sits outside the lunchroom door, and my fingers sink into Mariano's arms when he trots near.

"Shoo." I make a waving motion. "Shoo, dog. I don't have more food."

The dog's head cocks to the right, and his tail flaps back and forth.

Mariano laughs. "Piper, I think you've got a fan."

"I don't want a fan. I don't like dogs." I tuck myself behind Mariano as the dog sniffs me. "Especially big dogs."

"Well, this one sure likes you." Mariano holds out his hand, but the dog flinches away, drawing his tail up between his legs as he cowers. "He's harmless, poor thing."

Mariano crouches, leaving me exposed, and holds out his hand. The dog sniffs it and whimpers. "My mother had a cocker spaniel." He's looking at the dog, but speaking to me. "And after she died, the dog was never quite the same. She took to sleeping in the closet, on Mama's house slippers. Piper, just hold your hand out. He won't hurt you."

"No, thanks. He attacked me no more than an hour ago."

I feel Mariano's chuckle through his suit coat. "He hardly attacked you. He's hungry." Mariano takes my hand in his and tugs me down beside him.

He's holding my hand. Detective Mariano Cassano—handsome and under the impression that I'm mushy inside—is holding my hand.

"He's a good one, Piper. He must have belonged to someone not too long ago. He still has a collar on. No tags, though."

The collar is loose around his scruffy fur. Our attention has set him trembling, and he stares up at us with woeful brown eyes.

"What happened to your mother's dog? Do you still have her?"

"She died a few years ago." Mariano's voice droops under the weight of sadness. "Father cried. Which he hadn't done since she passed. But it was like losing another piece of her, you know?"

"It's funny how it can hit you like that, missing someone all over again. Even years later." I stand, knees popping. "About a year ago, I was over at the LeVines'. Sarah, one of Lydia's little sisters, broke a lamp when she was playing. Mrs. LeVine was so furious, going on and on about how much it cost." Tears clog my throat. "My mother never cared a whit about anything like that. It's my father who loves the grandeur. The right address, the right furniture, the right parties."

Mariano stands too. "I imagine you're a lot like your mother."

"I hope so."

He's still holding my hand. "We should get you back to school."

I like him. Not because of his handsome face, but his heart.

The kind way he's looking at me now. His soft Italian accent when he says *mama*. His concern over Lydia. The freedom I feel around him to be myself.

Something wet grazes my knee, and I jump away when I see it's the dog, sniffing me.

Mariano laughs. He holds out his hand once more to the dog, but it flinches away. "I don't know which of you is more nervous."

For the first time, I look at a dog and feel something besides nerves flare to life within me. He seems to desperately want our attention, and yet is too fearful to accept any affection. "Poor boy. Someone must have been cruel to him." I chew on my lower lip. "We can't just leave him . . . can we?"

Mariano shrugs. "I can't have a dog in my apartment. Nor will he let us touch him."

"True." I offer my trembling hand, but Mariano's right that I don't need to be nervous. The dog only sniffs it before ducking his head. "I guess we'll have to leave him."

Mariano presses his hand against my back and urges me down the sidewalk. "C'mon. Let's get you back to school. I need to call into the office, but I think there's a public telephone by the train station."

As we put space between us and Johnny's Lunchroom, my heart sags. "I really thought we might find her."

Mariano sighs. "I know you did. And maybe we got closer than we realize today. Sometimes little things that seem inconsequential add up." His voice darkens as he adds, "I can't believe you actually left your phone number for that despicable Johnny Walker."

I shiver as I think of how Johnny winked at me when

I scribbled my telephone number on the back of my receipt. "What else should I have done? He may have some shady deals going, but if he can help get Lydia back, it's worth it."

"Somehow, I don't think that's how he viewed it. I think he sees it as an excuse to call up a pretty girl."

My cheeks flush at the compliment, regardless of the gruff manner with which it was delivered. Nails click along the sidewalk behind us. I glance over my shoulder and find the dog trotting several feet back. "We have a shadow."

Mariano glances over his shoulder. "Well, how about that."

When we stop walking, the dog stops too. His long tail makes a tentative brushing sound against the sidewalk. *Shh, shh, shh.*

"Would they let him on the train, do you think?"

"Sure. If we had a length of rope or something to—" He watches as I dig in my bag. "Don't tell me."

The dog's tail wags faster when he sees me reaching into the sack.

I pull the rope out triumphantly. "You ask, and I deliver."

"Do I even want to know why you thought you might need that?"

"Probably not."

I crouch on the ground, and the dog sniffs at the rope and gives it a lick. "Does it taste like a chicken sandwich?" My fingers tremble as I slip the rope through the dog's collar and tie a quick knot. With the way he cowers, it's easy to not be debilitated by nerves.

"If Johnny Walker calls, tell me you won't go meet him without me. Promise me that."

I squint up at Mariano, who's silhouetted by the midday sun. "I'm not stupid, Mariano."

"No, you're not. Not at all. But you *are* desperate. I don't care what he says on the phone when he calls, wait for me before you go anywhere with him. Okay?"

"I won't go anywhere without my bodyguard." The teasing tone in my voice draws a smile—albeit a brief one—out of Mariano.

I expect the dog to resist the rope, but instead he trots several feet away from us as we continue along the sidewalk.

Pedestrians thicken as we draw closer to the train station, and the dog must decide I'm the lesser of two evils—in the end, he trots close enough that he actually brushes my leg. I try not to cringe away from him.

Once we arrive, Mariano gestures to the office. "I'm going to borrow their phone. Can you and your furry sidekick wait out here for me?"

Sidekick. Not a bad name for a dog. I point to the women's restroom. "I'll get changed and meet you here."

As I change back into my Presley's skirt and blouse, I mull over how to explain my new "sidekick" to my family. Perhaps, because the weather was mild today, I ate my lunch outside and the dog found me?

And how exactly am I going to conceal this guy at school? There will still be several hours left before dismissal. Perhaps I could stow him in the groundskeeper's gardening shed? Lawrence has always been kind to me. In exchange for keeping quiet, I could promise him a bottle of Father's good stuff—a swell upgrade from the bathtub gin Lawrence normally drinks.

I finish changing before Mariano finishes his phone call, and I stand in the busy station with the dog. He's so riddled with anxiety, he huddles against me. I should pat his head or something, but I can't talk myself into it.

Could I tell Walter the truth about today? It's not like I ventured up here alone, so he can't get too mad, right? Though he might be hurt that I didn't tell him my plan this morning when he brought me to school . . .

"What sounds better," I ask Mariano when he emerges from the office. "That I ate lunch outside and found the dog there, or that—" Mariano's gaze is serious, his mouth downturned. "What's wrong? Was there bad news?"

Is it Lydia? The question forms in my throat, but I can't force it out.

Mariano doesn't even dig up a smile for me. "In my line of work, there's always bad news."

He looks so defeated, I can't seem to help myself. I put a hand on his arm. "I'm sorry."

Mariano covers my hand with his own. Squeezes. "Let's get you home, Piper."

And other than a few polite niceties, those are the last words he says before delivering me back to school.

Sidekick's tail thumps on the grass when he sees me approaching.

"Real gem of a dog ya got here," Lawrence drawls in his Texas accent. "Needs a good cleanin', though. And a good meal."

"Thanks for hiding him for me, Lawrence." Sidekick flinches away from my hand, but he must catch a whiff of the roll I snitched from the school cafeteria for him, because he pushes his nose against my coat pocket. I tear off a bite and place it on my palm for him to lick off. "Good boy, Sidekick."

"It's my weddin' anniversary next week, and my wife'll sure appreciate that bottle of wine." Lawrence gestures toward the west side of campus. "Headmistress usually comes out this here door, so I'd suggest you take him over to the east and wait for your ride there."

"Thanks, Lawrence. I'll deliver your payment tomorrow."

He tips his hat and smiles his gap-toothed grin. "Have a good evenin', Miz Sail."

Sidekick and I sneak to the corner of Lake Shore and Irving, where Walter will make his turn toward Presley's. We've only been waiting about a minute when Walter pulls up along the curb.

I open the back door for Sidekick, who isn't convinced that he should enter until I toss in a chunk of bread.

I grin at Walter. "I'm bringing home a friend."

"Life is never dull with you. I thought you hated dogs."

"This one is kind of growing on me." I slide into the passenger seat as Sidekick sets about pacing the backseat. "Will Joyce be mad?"

Walter shrugs. "Dunno." He grins when Sidekick's head appears between us, his long, pink tongue hanging out one side of his mouth. "So was it give-away-stray-dogs day at Presley's?"

The story that I spent all afternoon cooking up sits heavy on my tongue. The lie would ruin everything between us, wouldn't it?

Walter's smile flickers. "Your silence is scaring me."

I try to arrange my features in a reassuring, confident kind of way. "Do you remember the article I showed you? The one with the girl from Detroit who escaped from a brothel?"

A slow blink. "Yes."

"Well, the newspaper said she made her phone call from this place called Johnny's Lunchroom up on Clark Street—"

Walter's eyes slide closed. "Piper, you didn't."

I take a deep breath. "I looked at a map and saw it wasn't so far from school. So after you dropped me off this morning, I—"

His eyes snap open. "How could you do that, Piper? How could you take a risk like that? If Lydia got taken on Astor Street, can't you see how much more dangerous it is for you to be alone in a neighborhood where—"

"But I didn't go by myself. Mariano came with me."

"Mariano." Walter repeats the name in a flat way.

"I called him this morning just so someone would know where I was, and then he said—"

Walter's mouth twists into a snarl. "It was probably his idea, wasn't it? That you should come with him. As if he's *so* concerned about Lydia."

"He is concerned about Lydia! It's his job, Walter."

"And flirting with you? Is that part of his job too? Is that how he finds missing girls?"

Sidekick whimpers and cowers farther behind my seat. "You're scaring Sidekick."

Walter's mouth sets in a firm line. "I wish I were scaring *you*. You can't take risks like that, Piper. You just . . . can't."

"That's why I didn't tell you this morning. I knew you'd tell me no. I knew you'd stop me."

"Because it's dangerous! Because I don't want you ending up like Lydia. Why does that make me the bad guy?"

I inhale slowly through my nose, trying to calm myself before words come out that I'll regret. I reach to the backseat and pat Sidekick's head stiffly. "It's okay. You're safe."

"I want to keep *you* safe." Walter's words are quiet.

"I know you do. But I can't sit around being sad and scared. Not when it feels like there's a ticking clock. If she has another seizure . . ." Tears threaten to overtake my words, and I clamp down on my bottom lip.

We sit there for a bit, the muffled sounds of traffic and pedestrians around us. Finally, Walter rakes in a breath and turns the ignition. "Let's go home."

Walter is silent as I feed Joyce my story about eating lunch outside and Sidekick finding me. I spend my afternoon bathing and brushing and cutting out mats from his fur. It's easier to touch him like this, when it's about accomplishing a task rather than offering affection. Sidekick makes no protest, just leans on me occasionally. When Joyce—who'd been reluctant to the idea of a big, possibly flea-ridden dog entering her clean house—sees him again, she warms to the idea of a pet. His fur isn't brown, but rather the color of fresh cream, and there isn't a flea in sight.

Joyce shelves the cans of dog food that Walter and I bought at the store on our way home. "Once these patches grow back in, you'll be a real beauty."

Sidekick only cowers at the praise.

When I leave the kitchen, he slinks alongside me, gaze darting about as if danger might be anywhere. "Settle in, Sidekick. It's your new home."

But in my room, he only stands in the corner and watches as I unload my shopping bag. I put my dress in the laundry hamper and then stare at the photograph of Lydia. The demure smile, the curled hair. All so very Lydia.

"I'm trying to bring you home," I whisper.

I sink onto my bed. Something beneath me crinkles.

I stand and find a long white envelope with my name scratched on in painstaking capital letters. No stamp or address. Clearly, it didn't come by post. Fear prickles up the back of my neck as my gaze slides to my third-story window.

Closed, but not locked.

I rip it open and flip over the pages to find the signature.

Matthew.

My breath whooshes out of my lungs, and I sink to my bed to devour his words.

Miss Sail,

You should know straight away that I lied to you that day in the alley, when you asked me about Lydia, if I knew how she felt about me. Yes, I knew. And I want you to know before I tell you any of this that I loved her too. As much as a man like me is capable of loving, anyway.

I lied because I was sure that if the police knew my past, they'd have me in a cell in no time, and I wanted to be here when we got Lydia back. I don't have much hope of that anymore.

Before coming to Chicago, I lived in Kansas City, where I worked for a man named Jim Burk. He was a small-time criminal who imagined himself more important than he was. His cousins are Patrick and Colin Finnegan, and I think Jim thought of himself as a branch of their operation. Anyway, I didn't much care how Jim painted himself. All I cared about was that I made good money, which I did.

If I wasn't working, I was out in the town having a good time. (My mama raised me not to talk to ladies about this sort of thing, and I'm sorry to do so, but I want you to know the whole truth.) I usually went out with a buddy named Tommy. Tommy lived next door to me and seemed like a good guy. What I didn't know—and how could I have, considering he drank more than me?—was that he was a Prohibition agent. And he was using me to trap Jim Burk.

Well, I was dumb enough to fall for it. And one night, when we were picking up a delivery at the river, Tommy was there with a team. The Burks aren't the type to go quietly, and I was one of the few left when the shooting was done.

But I was as good as dead, because one of the men killed was Alan, Jim's oldest son. Alan was a good guy too. Drank too much, maybe, but laughed a lot. He was married, had a kid on the way. Jim had a temper on him, and I knew that if I didn't get out of town, I'd be six feet under.

So that's what I did. Blew out of town. Changed my name and everything.

Anyway. Lydia and me. I've always liked women, but there was something special about her. She wasn't just another pretty, rich girl. I know you know what I mean. The day she went missing,

Lydia had come out to the garage and told me she was going to Minnesota for a while to see a doctor. She was all nervous, and I couldn't figure out why until she said she loved me.

We talked for a while, maybe twenty minutes or so. She wanted to sneak out that night. Go somewhere, just the two of us, before she had to leave for Minnesota. But she had to go see the Barrows, she said. Had to tell them she couldn't watch their kid any longer. You know Lydia. Couldn't help but be responsible. Except for when it came to me, I suppose.

The thing is, Miss Sail, I felt like we were being watched while we talked. At the time, I told myself I was just nervous about getting caught. But now I wonder if we were actually being watched. I can't shake the feeling that Lydia getting taken was somehow my fault. And that was even before yesterday.

I was running errands for the family, and I think I saw Maeve, Alan's widow. She was talking to a man I recognized from the papers as one of the Finnegan brothers, Jim Burk's cousin. I knew then that I had to get away from here before they came after me, and I hadn't even been home yet. At home, I found my cat dead. I'll spare you the details, but he looked like he'd been dragged through hell. My neighbor said he'd once had a dog look like that after it died, and they'd found later that it had inhaled poison from a fumigation.

When I was packing up to get out of town, I found my cat had dragged a tuna sandwich out of my coat pocket. Tabitha had left it out for me the day before, but I don't like tuna, so I'd just taken it and planned to throw it out later. I don't have any proof it was Maeve and the Burk family, of course, but I've never been one to believe in coincidences.

When things settle down, I'll call you. I only wish I'd left before they got to Lydia. I'm sorry, Miss Sail. She deserved better. She deserved everything.

Matthew

As the sun sinks in the sky and casts beams of golden light in my bedroom, I alternate between seething—how can he leave? How can he stand to tuck tail and run?—and despairing. Sidekick watches me pace my room, watches me do the only thing a person *can* do at a time like this. Cry out to God.

If, indeed, you can muster the belief that he's there in a time like this.

"Want to get some fresh air?"

I look up from my book and find Nick standing in the doorway of the living room, hands in his trouser pockets, eyes red. "No, thank you. I'm busy."

"Waiting for the phone to ring doesn't make you busy."

Heat blossoms on the back of my neck. "I'm reading."

"And when was the last time you turned the page?" Nick doesn't wait for an answer, which is good, because I don't have much of one to give him. "Don't you think that new mutt of yours could use some exercise? Just a quick walk around the block."

I glance at Sidekick, who has wedged himself between my feet. "Fine." I snap shut my book. "A quick walk."

It could be good for me to get away from the telephone. I've called Mariano twice now to tell him about the letter from Matthew and heard nothing back. Is it his day off? Is he busy with another case? Or is it that I've simply misunderstood the dynamic between us? Perhaps I think of Lydia's case as being more important to Mariano than it actually is. After all, I have one person I'm looking for, and heaven only knows how many cases Mariano has piled on his desk.

I pull on my coat from last season, ignoring the new fur-trimmed one Father and Jane bought to replace the one I loaned to Lydia. The department store tags still hang from the unwanted garment.

Sidekick seems more content on the leash than he does in the house, and he trots alongside me as we exit.

"Thank you for coming with me." Nick's voice has a rattle to it as he jogs down the front steps. "I couldn't take being in the house any longer. All this waiting . . . I feel like I might go mad." When he looks at me, with circles under his red eyes, I wonder if I look as dreadful as he. "I know you know how I feel about Lydia."

"I do."

His larynx bobs. "Does *she* know?"

"I don't think so."

He exhales slowly. "It seems unreal. Like a nightmare." He turns up the collar of his coat against the nip of the breeze. "What's going on down there?"

Three houses down, at the LeVines' fancy stone residence, men in bowler hats and long coats loiter on the sidewalk.

"I bet it's reporters." Nick adjusts his wire-rimmed glasses. "I've seen some out here before. Never like *this* though."

My stomach lurches. Why would there be a group of reporters outside, unless—

The same fear thumping in my heart seems to streak across Nick's face, and despite the skirts of my dress, I match my strides to his as we hurry along the sidewalk. Sidekick trots along, tongue hanging out, clearly enjoying the accelerated pace.

I scan the faces for clues of how grave the newsbreak is, but no one seems particularly grim. If Lydia were found dead, however, *would* the reporters be grim? Or would they—

Nick clasps a hand on the arm of a reporter scribbling on a notepad. "Hey, old boy. What's all the fuss about around here?"

Nick's voice is so chummy, I think he must know the man, but the reporter only gives him a cursory glance. "I don't know who you work for, sport, but I don't hand out scoops to the competition."

A man nearby snorts, "Scoop? Larry, every paper in town is here."

I finally find my voice, loud and laced with desperation. "Is it Lydia? Is she . . . ?"

Silence ripples through the crowd of men.

Larry shakes his head, his gaze going soft. "No, miss. Nothing like that. It's the family's chauffeur. Up and left."

The relief is dizzying. "Thank God."

"You a friend of the family, miss?"

"Lydia's my best friend." The words earn me an elbow in my ribs from Nick. He appears to be trying to send me some kind of message through eye contact, but—

"Why do you think the chauffeur would have left? Did he and Lydia have some kind of relationship?" Larry has a fresh page open, and holds his pencil poised to document my words.

"I . . ."

"She's not interested in being interviewed, thank you." Nick's hand grasps my arm, pulling me through the crowd of men. Sidekick seems intent on wedging himself between my legs, and Nick's hand on my arm is the only thing that keeps me from falling when I stumble over him.

The reporters call out questions to me—Any theories on why the chauffeur left? Was Lydia unhappy? Did the chauffeur have a special interest in Lydia?—but Nick tucks me under his arm and pulls me through the crowd. Folded against him, the cigarette smell of his coat is cloying, but I don't move away.

For a moment, I fear they'll follow, but the reporters seem more interested in staying close to the LeVines' house. When I glance over my shoulder, I see why—the distinctive touring sedan is parked outside the LeVines' house. Mariano and O'Malley must be there to talk about Matthew.

Once we've turned the corner, Nick releases me. "You okay?"

I nod.

"You sure?"

I take in a wobbling breath. "For a moment, I was sure they were going to tell us that Lydia was dead. So, yes, I'm fine."

Nick's fingers tremble as they reach inside his breast pocket and retrieve his pack of cigarettes. "They're like leeches."

I take another deep breath. "It's just their job."

Nick lights his cigarette and inhales deeply. "What do you think about Matthew? Was he already planning to leave? Are they trumping up a bunch of nothing? Or . . . ?"

I glance at my brother. "Matthew wouldn't have hurt Lydia. He . . . he cares about her."

Nick's expression is guarded as we turn down State Street. "Cares about her? Because she was his employer's daughter, or . . . ?"

This is going to be splashed all over the papers anyway, right? Better that he hear it from me. "Cares about her as in the way you care about Lydia."

Nick winces. "I suppose I can't blame him for that." He takes another long drag of his cigarette. "And what does she think of him?"

I swallow. "You're asking me to betray my best friend's confidence, Nick."

He barks out a humorless laugh. "That's answer enough right there."

What can I say to that? Sidekick tugs toward a bush in the Barrows' front yard, sniffs, and lifts his leg.

Nick drops his cigarette butt and steps on it with the toe of his loafer. "Why did Matthew leave, then?"

"It's . . ." My mind whirls with the details of the letter that I've already read dozens of times since yesterday afternoon. "It's complicated."

"Well, I'm not some prodigy like Tim, but I imagine I can handle a few details about the private life of a *servant*." Nick's voice has a dangerous bite to it, one I haven't heard for a very long time. Not since Mother died and we learned Nick dealt with grief by getting mean.

"Matthew left me a letter." I try to summarize Matthew's history in as few words as possible, but even then we've turned back onto Astor Street by the time I'm done.

"Have you told the police about this?"

"That's why I've been sitting by the telephone. I left several messages for Mariano, but he hasn't called me back."

"Probably because you've pestered him to death."

The comment cuts. Is it true? Did yesterday's excursion in the North push Mariano over the edge? He was awfully quiet during the train ride back to school . . .

"You girls never seem to know how to fall for the *right* guy." Nick jingles the loose change in his pocket. "What a mess."

As our house comes into view, I spot a tall, feminine figure waiting by our front gate. "Who's that?"

"Beats me." Nick squints. "Friend of Jane's?"

"Loitering outside our house?"

Nick shrugs.

As we draw closer, it's clear that whoever she is, she's waiting for us. She stands nearly as tall as my brothers, a brimmed cloche pulled low over her bobbed hair, and her coat collar turned up.

"Good day, miss." Nick's voice is jovial, a jarring juxtaposition to the sour mood he's been in with me.

"Good day." The woman's words are soft and pleasant. "Sorry to intrude upon you like this."

"No trouble at all. What can we do for you?"

She takes in a breath and seems to hesitate. Her gaze moves to me. "You're Piper Sail, aren't you?"

I tighten my grip on Sidekick's leash, despite how he cowers at my feet. "I am."

Her smile is tinged with sympathy, and she seems familiar somehow. "I wanted to apologize for my colleagues scaring you off earlier. I can imagine this week has been hard enough for you, with your best friend missing, and then to not even be able to take a walk in your own neighborhood . . ." She shakes her head. "Almost makes me ashamed to be a journalist."

So that's where I recognize her from. "You're a journalist?"

She nods and sticks out a hand. "Alana Kirkwood. *Kansas City Star*. Nice to meet you."

Sidekick's leash is wrapped around my right hand, and I unwind it to shake her hand. "Nice to meet you too."

Nick leans against the wrought iron fence. "Kansas City sent a reporter up to cover Lydia?"

Alana turns her large eyes toward him. She's very striking.

Probably serves her well in a profession dominated by men. "To cover Jacob Dunn, actually. Or Matthew, as you probably knew him. The chauffeur. He left behind some very angry, very powerful people in Kansas City, so it's a public interest story for our readership."

"You sure made it up here fast."

Alana shrugs. "I'll take any excuse I can to come to Chicago." She gives Nick a slow wink that has me fighting off an eye roll, and then turns her smile to me. "Miss Sail, I want to tell *your* story, the way *you* want it told. I'll even give you full access to the article before it's published so you can be sure I got every detail right. We can start anywhere you like. Maybe with Jacob and where you think he might have gone—"

I hold up my hand. "I thought you came to apologize for your colleagues. Now *you're* soliciting an interview?"

"I just thought—"

"I'm not interested in speaking to the press. Good day, Miss Kirkwood."

"But it'll help Lydia," Alana calls after me. "Information you have could help me get to Jacob."

That's too irritating a comment to leave alone. "Helping *you* look good by getting Jacob is of no interest to me. Nor will it help Lydia, because I know he didn't have anything to do with her disappearance. Put *that* in your article, Miss Kirkwood."

I want to bang the gate door shut, but I can't with Nick trailing after me. He calls a "Sorry" that Alana Kirkwood doesn't at all deserve.

"Don't ask me to go on any more walks," I snap at my brother once the front door is closed behind him.

Nick only glares at me, as if I've somehow done something

wrong. "I'm so surprised you've never been asked on a date, Piper. You're such a *pleasure* to be around."

I throw my shoe at his retreating figure, clocking him in the back of the head.

"Ow!" Nick whirls around, his eyes blazing. "Get control of yourself, Piper."

As he stalks up the stairs, I lean against the wall. My breath comes in rapid gasps, and my eyes are unfocused. Nick's parting words thump in my brain, and I try to talk my lungs into holding on to a breath of air instead of immediately casting it out.

I need to calm down. Lydia is still out there. She needs me to think clearly. She needs me to find her. I think of Mariano on Clark Street yesterday, taking deep breaths and encouraging me to do the same.

Slowly, my breathing eases to a normal pace.

I'm going to call and leave Mariano another message. And I'll leave him another one tonight, if I have to. I don't care if he *does* find me annoying. Lydia is worth far more than what other people think of me.

Walter clears his throat and shifts his hands on the steering wheel. "So. How was school?"

I look at him. Does he really think I'm in the mood to beat my gums about my school day?

Walter sighs as he veers onto Astor Street. "I only have a few days left in town. I just thought it would be nice to not spend the entire drive home in silence. Pardon me."

"I haven't been silent the *entire* drive."

"True. You did speak to me long enough to find out if anyone called for you. That's not exactly the type of . . ."

Walter's words fade away when I see it—the touring sedan parked outside my gate.

Mariano is seated on the top step, and my heart seems to climb up into my throat. It's the way he's sitting—elbows on his knees, head drooped—that makes me shove open the door before Walter has come to a complete stop. That makes me ignore Walter's hollering about being patient, letting him park the car.

"What is it?" I fumble with the gate latch and fling it open. Mariano stands, and I see his face is creased with fatigue and heartache. "Is there . . ." My vision has already blurred. "Is there news?"

"I'm so sorry, Piper." His voice is graveled. Regretful.

Mariano swallows hard before saying the words I've dreaded since the moment we met. "We found her body."

Dead.

She's dead.

She's dead, and I can't seem to cry.

I know Mariano is telling the truth. I know the truth is devastatingly unchangeable. But those facts just flutter around my head without landing on my heart.

I sink to the steps. "Where was she found?" My voice has a cold, unrecognizable quality to it.

"The river."

I shiver as his words conjure images of Lydia's pale-skinned body floating lifelessly in the murky water. "Here?"

Walter has joined us. "Let's not do this now, Piper."

At another time I would have snarled at him to not boss me around, but a numbness has spread throughout me. "When *should* we do it?" Walter doesn't reply, and I look back to Mariano, waiting.

"They found her on Monday in the Lower West Side."

Monday. He and I were pointlessly sniffing around the North on Clark Street. I think of his downcast expression when he rejoined me at the train station, after he'd called into the office. It matches the one he wears now. "That was the bad news, wasn't it? When you called into work?"

Mariano nods.

"Do we know who did it?"

"Not yet."

My nostrils flare with my exhale. Whoever did this is still walking around. The thought makes my nails dig into my palms. "What happened to her? Can they tell?"

He shifts his attention to Walter before looking back to me. "Maybe you should absorb the shock first, Piper."

"He's right." Walter looks down the street, eyeing the mob of reporters outside the LeVines' gate. "Let's get you inside."

"No, I want to know. I want to get it done with."

Mariano's gaze holds mine. "Are you sure?"

I'm not. I won't be able to unhear those details. Won't be able to unsee them play out in my imagination. But I also can't find who did this—can't bring him to justice—if I bury my head. "Yes."

Mariano reaches inside his jacket pocket and withdraws a trifolded sheet of white paper.

"What's that?" Walter asks.

But Mariano looks at me when he answers. "The coroner's report."

"You can't let her see that!" Walter's voice rises high with indignation. "Those aren't details she needs."

"Maybe they're details she wants," Mariano says in that quiet but authoritative way of his. He holds out the piece of paper. "I removed the photographs."

Walter paces several steps away, then several steps back, and then away again. His frustration is palpable.

I don't open it, though. Just hold the paper between my thumb and forefinger. "I called you. A lot."

"I wanted to call back. I was afraid I would say too much, and we didn't know for sure yet."

I run my fingers down the crease of the coroner's report. "I had information."

Walter stops pacing and stares at me.

Mariano frowns. "You didn't say so in your message."

"I didn't know I had to bribe you to call me." Anger bubbles in my stomach, but the words are still coming out calm and cold. "Matthew left me a letter before he blew out of town."

Mariano whips his notebook from his breast pocket. "What'd it say? Can I see it?" He's morphed from Mariano to Detective Cassano in less than a second.

As I summarize Matthew's parting words, Mariano's pencil scratches continually against his paper. I feel Walter gaping at me, much like Nick did when I told him everything on our walk. My words, and even Mariano and Walter, feel miles away from where my head is.

Lydia is dead. And just like with my mother, I can't *do* anything. It's done, and it's forever.

"But he didn't say where he was going?" Mariano asks.

Apparently, I had stopped talking. "No."

"Any guesses? Anything you can think of from your time with him?"

I shake my head. "He was always very quiet. Very . . . careful."

Mariano absently taps his pencil against the notepad. "Taking this into account . . . Well, Piper. He skipped town the same day we found the body. I'm sure I don't need to explain to you how this looks. He was the closest thing we had to a suspect even before an organized crime connection." Mariano's gaze goes unfocused as he stares off at nothing in particular. "Finnegans. Yet again."

"But why would he give me that letter if he did it? Why would he have stuck around for so long after she went missing?"

Went missing. The vagueness of those words has infuriated me this last week, and now I wish I could cling to them a bit longer. When she was only missing, there was still a chance of finding her alive. My head throbs with the pain of unshed tears.

"If he had nothing to hide, why leave at all? He had given us an alibi—albeit one that we couldn't completely nail down. Why not stick around?"

"Fear for his life. Doubt of a fair trial. This is Chicago, after all."

"That's a harsh statement from a lawyer's daughter."

I hold up the still-folded coroner's report. "The world is harsh."

Mariano's gaze softens as he regards me. "I won't argue that point with you, Piper."

Walter sits beside me and rests a large hand on my shoulder. "What happens now, detective?"

"We'll keep trying to find Matthew. I'd like to get that letter from you, Piper. Doesn't need to be right now, though." Mariano folds his notebook shut and tucks it back into his pocket. "We'll continue to make it clear that we only want him for questioning, but the press will continue to skewer him. After a few weeks of fruitless searching, the case will probably go cold. The LeVines might hire private detectives, but we won't be able to do anything else."

Walter exhales long and slow. "You don't seem to believe in sugarcoating."

"That's out of respect for my audience." Mariano nods at

me. "Walter, if you wouldn't mind giving me and Miss Sail a moment, I have some questions I'd like to ask her in private."

Walter's jaw clenches. "Is now really the best time?"

Mariano regards him for a moment. "Yes."

Walter, who I've seen make countless diving catches and hustle doubles, now seems physically taxed by the act of standing. Moments later, the front door clicks shut.

I expect Mariano to sit, but he remains standing and crosses his arms over his chest. Though not broad, there's certainly something intimidating about him. Even in a moment like this, when I know he's on my side. "Can you think of any reason why someone might have confused you and Lydia?"

At a different time, I would have laughed. "No. We look nothing alike. Why?"

His gaze is evaluating.

"What is it, Mariano?"

"The Finnegans. It seems to keep coming back to them. I just . . ." Mariano tugs his tie loose. "What do you know about them?"

"Not much. I think I already told you that my father has had a case or two that involved them. But like I said, he doesn't talk to me about his work."

"The Finnegans are up-and-comers in town. Brothers. They want to be the next Torrio and Capone." Mariano retightens his tie. "A few weeks ago, your father was able to get a case dismissed, and that resulted in Colin Finnegan—the younger of the brothers—going to jail. Does that sound familiar at all?"

"Maybe." Anything that happened before Lydia went missing seems like a lifetime ago. How long has she been dead? How long has my search for her been pointless?

"All I'm trying to say is that your father riled the Finnegan brothers. And they're not known for mercy or turning the other cheek."

"What mobsters are?" I trace the hem of my uniform skirt, and my mind drifts to Lydia's uniforms hanging neat and useless in her armoire.

"Lydia was found still wearing your coat." Mariano crouches so we're at eye level with one another. He must sense I'm drifting. "Did you know she had it?"

"She had forgotten hers." A swell of emotion rises up in my throat and lodges there. I think of handing it to her that afternoon at my house. That afternoon when everything felt complicated and scary, and I had no idea the sky was about to fall. "She said she'd bring it back to me the next day."

"She also had a handkerchief with your initials in her pocket. It just makes me wonder if maybe . . ."

The breath whooshes from my lungs as I piece together his train of thought. "Lydia's hair is red and long, though."

"It could have been under the coat. Or under her hat."

"But surely as soon as they got close to her, they would see it wasn't me."

"One would think so." Mariano removes his hat, brushes off imaginary lint, and settles it back on his head. "I'm just wondering—combined with who your father is and the way the Finnegans keep coming up in this case—if this actually isn't about Lydia."

Mariano doesn't say the words, but they dangle out there anyway—*if it's actually about you.*

CHAPTER

TWELVE

CHICAGO, ILLINOIS

TWO WEEKS LATER—JUNE 5TH, 1924

At St. Chrysostom's Episcopal Church, on the same stage where Lydia once stood with the choir and sang hymns to her great God, the casket is closed. Mrs. LeVine had wanted it open, but the mortician had called this "inadvisable," considering the amount of time Lydia's body spent in the river. Instead, a framed photograph, the same one I showed Johnny Walker in my silly, girlish hope that Lydia was still alive, has been placed atop the casket lid.

I'm alone at church. Just me and the saints depicted in the stained glass.

As I make my way up the center aisle, the heels of my shoes silent on the thick red carpet, I see that the casket lid has been opened after all.

I quicken my steps, even as I ask myself if I really do want to see what's under that lid. But the temptation to see Lydia, to capture one last glimpse to carry with me through life, is too great to resist.

Only the corpse doesn't have Lydia's long red hair. Rather, it's a bobbed, honey color. And the cream linen dress . . . the same one I wore on the night she was taken.

When I peer at the face, I see why. It's not Lydia in the casket—it's me.

I scream and stumble down the carpeted steps. The church is full now. Father, my brothers, Walter, Emma Crane, Mariano, and even Alana Kirkwood of *The Kansas City Star*, all dressed in somber black. The look in their eyes is clear. *You. It was supposed to be you.*

I burst through the sanctuary doors, into the foyer, and find Lydia. She hovers in the air like an angel, radiant and beautiful in all white. Her red hair spills all around her, same as when we were girls, free to run and laugh.

"It was supposed to be me." The words feel like a long overdue confession.

Lydia nods and smiles, as if it's oh-so-good that I've come to this realization. "And you can't outrun death, my dear."

You can't outrun death, my dear. The words reverberate in my ears as I blink awake in my bedroom. The light streaming through my window is bright yellow, distinctly midmorning. My muscles ache, and I ease my knees away from my chest, my arms from my sides. It's as though my body tried to shrink, to disappear, as I slept.

When my feet bump Sidekick, he stands, stretches, and shakes, before leaping from the bed. Then he looks back to me, tail wagging and tongue hanging out.

"I won't begrudge you your happiness." I ease myself into a sitting position. "You're quite tolerant of my depression."

He paws at my bedroom door until it opens, and the

clicking of his nails against the floor fades as he makes his way downstairs.

I look at my pillow, still dented and inviting. *You need to get out of bed, Piper.*

I put my feet on the floor. *You have to do this day. Now, get up.*

The clock reads 10:02. So many hours between now and getting to close my curtains again. I can still smell breakfast. Sausage and biscuits. Father must be going into work late.

You need to eat breakfast, I coax myself, *and then you can come back to bed if you still want to.*

My mother was wrong. I can't trust myself—I have to lie just to get out of bed.

In the bathroom mirror, a thin, chalky oval stares back at me. Set against the paleness of my face, my dark brown eyes seem almost black. My hair has begun to grow out of the fashionable bob that once seemed so vital to my happiness, and it hangs at an awkward length. In the dream, Lydia had told me I couldn't outrun death, and the ghost of a girl I see in my bathroom mirror makes me think she's right. That I haven't.

I unhook my kimono from the back of my bathroom door and slip my arms into the silky sleeves. In the two weeks since Lydia's funeral, rare is the night that I don't dream of her. Sometimes I'm standing on the sidewalk of Astor Street, watching her get yanked violently into a car. I try to scream, but I can't. In other dreams, I'm there when the life-snatching seizure begins. There's a gag in her mouth, and I'm trying to pull it out, but it's never-ending. Like a circus trick.

The funeral dream, in comparison, isn't so bad. At least I get to see her alive and smiling.

The floorboards are warm beneath my bare feet as I make

my way downstairs. The conversation of Nick and my father—baseball, like it matters—reaches my ears before I see the two of them seated at the dining room table. Father is dressed for the day in shirt sleeves and trousers. Nick is still in his buffalo-check pajamas, picking at his breakfast. Even from the hall, I can see why he's eating so late. His face is pale and puffy, a sure sign that, yet again, he came home in the wee hours of the morning.

When they notice me, the conversation halts.

Father smiles. "Good morning, Piper."

"Good morning." I glance at Nick. His eyes are their new normal shade of red, from drink and lack of sleep. He doesn't speak to me.

Joyce comes through the door with a breakfast plate in one hand and a cup of coffee in the other. "Sidekick is so good to let me know when you're up and about." She smiles warmly and sets my plate on the table, across from Nick and Father.

"Thank you, Joyce."

With Walter returning to California the day of Lydia's funeral, and Father and Nick usually gone to the office, I'm accustomed to taking my breakfast alone or in the kitchen. It's strange to feel so awkward with one's own family.

Father sips at his coffee. "How did you sleep, dear?"

"The same."

They exchange a look that seems to be about me, and I pretend not to notice.

"Nick was just telling me about his plans to go to the lake with some friends. I think it'd be good for you to join him."

I involuntarily snort. Sure, relaxing on the shores of the lake. That will make everything better.

I reach for the jar of peach preserves. "I don't feel up to it today."

The silence is thick, like the weight of air just before it rains.

Nick leans back in his chair. "Do you have other plans?"

I shrug. "What's it to you?"

Sidekick pushes his way through the kitchen door and into the dining room. He stretches out on a plot of carpet beside me in a satisfied, full-belly way. He always eats his breakfast in about three bites, as if otherwise the food will vanish.

"I'd rather not watch you waste your life away." Nick's gaze holds a challenge. "Is that reason enough, sister? That I care about you?"

I could say the same thing to him, it seems. Perhaps he's wasting away his life in a more vibrant kind of way— speakeasies and race tracks and house parties—but it's wasteful all the same.

"I'm fine." I keep my voice level. "I'm grieving, but I'm fine."

"I don't believe you." Nick's tone is flat.

"Kids," Father says. "This time is difficult enough without bickering."

"We're letting her languish too much. She should be improving by now."

"Why, because you are?" I snap. "She was my best friend, Nick. And she was . . ."

The typewritten notes of the coroner's report swim before my eyes. *Fibers were found in the oral cavity of the victim, so it's likely the victim was gagged.*

I blink away the words, try to push out what I want to say. "And she was . . ."

The lungs were filled with not only water but emesis, leaving me to conclude that the victim aspirated before being bound and discarded in the river. Given the victim's history with seizures, it's my belief that—

"Taken." The word—so beautifully vague—finally comes out. "She was taken. Am I not supposed to grieve?"

"Grieve? Yes. Give up? No. You barely said good-bye to Walter when he left. You won't answer telephone calls. You won't come out with me and my friends."

Sidekick wedges himself between my legs. The tension in the air has set him trembling.

"I know losing Lydia hurts. It hurts me too, Piper." Nick's jaw quivers for a moment. "But there are still people who care about you. And I'm not just talking about that Cassano kid who keeps sniffing around."

There's a tinge of anger in that last sentence. Is this related to his hangover, or is he actually mad about the two visits Mariano has paid me since Lydia's funeral?

"*Detective Cassano* is the same age as you, Nicholas Sail."

"I think you know what I mean."

That I shouldn't be receiving attention from an Italian? Or a Catholic? Has studying the law turned my brother against immigrants?

"Nick." Father's tone holds a warning. "I think you're being unfair."

Nick turns to Father. "You can't possibly think it's a good idea for Piper to see him."

I slather preserves onto my biscuit with such force, it crumbles against my hand. "I'm sorry, but I thought this conversation began with you wanting me to live my life more."

"I do. I just don't think *he* should be a part of it."

"I'm sorry you feel that way, son." Father stands. "If Piper is interested in dating Mariano, she has my blessing. And I would encourage you to leave her alone about it. I'm afraid I have to leave now." He drops a kiss on my head. "Jane and I are meeting with the hotel manager to finalize arrangements, and I have a few things to take care of before I go."

Nick waits all of ten seconds after Father departs the dining room to press me further on Mariano. "Father doesn't want to be the bad guy, but this is a terrible idea, Piper. I don't trust him."

"If you would actually talk to Mariano, then maybe you would know he's not the bad fellow you make him out to be. This is all just stupid prejudice on your part."

"You don't know what you're getting into. Has he even told you about Zola?"

My heart thumps faster at the mention of another girl. Who is she? And how does Nick know about her when I don't? But I refuse to let on like I'm ignorant. "How do *you* know about her?"

"I make it my business to know such things."

I snatch my plate and coffee cup from the table. "Maybe you should pay less attention to *my* life and *my* friends and a little more to the choices *you're* making."

"Piper, come back." Nick's half-hearted plea reaches me at the door as I stalk away. Sidekick scurries alongside me. "Don't be so dramatic."

My coffee sloshes in the cup as I close the front door with my foot. Thank goodness the reporters have stopped loitering on our streets, or I might find photographs of me in my kimono and bare feet splashed across the society pages.

Sidekick barks as he romps after a squirrel. I'm grateful when the squirrel scampers to safety up the tree, because he's surprisingly good at nabbing them. Sidekick stands beneath the oak, staring up like the rodent could fall at any moment.

Behind me, the door opens.

"I'm sorry, but he's insufferable this morning." I set my coffee cup on the step. "I couldn't take it for one more second."

Father settles beside me, folding his long, thick body into the small space. "He's worried about you."

I lick a stray drop of jam from my thumb. "He should find better ways to show it."

"You really shouldn't be out here by yourself," Father says. "Especially dressed like this. That journalist has been hanging around here again."

"I haven't seen anyone for a week."

"This isn't a local one. Nick was talking to her yesterday because she was loitering around the house."

"Oh, her." I cram a large bite of biscuit into my mouth. "Hopefully, the people of Kansas City lose interest soon, and she'll leave us alone."

Sidekick abandons his pursuit of the squirrel and takes to rolling in a sunny patch of grass. Father and I watch him in silence for a few moments.

"I know you don't like Nick's lectures, and I didn't want to fan the flames and say so in front of him, but I do think you should exercise caution with Mariano."

I huff out an irritated breath. "What happened to your blessing?"

"You still have it. I'm just recommending you slow down a bit. I believe Mariano is a good sort of chap, but marrying two cultures is always tricky, especially with his type of fam—"

"Whoa." I put up a hand. "It's not like that. We've never even been on a date."

Father sucks in his lower lip, like he does when he's thinking something through. "In my day, if a fellow paid the kind of attention to a girl that Mariano has paid to you, it meant they were going somewhere serious."

"I'm not saying it isn't going somewhere serious."

"You're just saying I'm putting the cart before the horse."

"Yes. Miles away from the horse."

Father's mouth curls upward. "I won't pretend that's not a relief." He glances at his wristwatch. "Now I really will be late. I'm taking the Chrysler. I don't think Nick needs the Ford for his lake excursion, so if you want the car left here, you should feel free to ask him."

I wipe biscuit crumbs off my kimono. "Thank you, but where would I be going?"

"I would rather you not go anywhere. But Jane says I'm living too much in fear, that you're eighteen, and all that good stuff." Father clasps a hand to my knee. "Just be careful. Don't go anywhere alone. Okay?"

My own words from my dream—*it was supposed to be me*— shudder through my thoughts. "Okay."

S he's in heaven among the Lord's angels." Mrs. LeVine pauses stirring milk into her tea so she can dry her eyes with a handkerchief. "That's what I have to keep reminding myself. She's healthy again. She's with my mother and my sweet Rachel, God bless their souls."

Rachel. Born after Lydia, but who only lived to see a week.

"She'll like that." I stir my own tea because it's something to do. "Rachel's death was such a painful memory to her."

Mrs. LeVine gives me a watery smile. "And she's with *your* lovely mother, my dear. Just think. They might be standing together and looking down at us right now."

I try to smile back, but it feels brittle. I wish I could make myself believe what Mrs. LeVine does. That I could be satisfied with thoughts of Lydia floating on clouds and playing the lyre.

I settle my hand-painted cup onto the saucer. These are the dishes I've seen locked in Mrs. LeVine's china cabinet, which I've been shooed away from when being too rowdy. And now I've become the guest who deserves their use.

"How's Dr. LeVine doing?"

Mrs. LeVine's weak smile flickers and fades. Her fingers take to fussing with the outdated tulle jabot at her throat. "He's saddled himself with so much guilt, I'm afraid. As if he's some-how responsible for what happened to Lydia."

The back of my neck prickles as that old suspicion creeps into my thoughts—that perhaps Dr. LeVine actually *is* responsible.

Lydia's laugh fills my ears. *Oh, Piper, you can't think my own father would have done something like this.*

"He's the one who hired that wretched man, after all. But of course Matthew worked for us nearly eighteen months, and we never saw even a moment of suspicious behavior. Why, Lydia thought of him as an older brother. She probably"—Mrs. LeVine's chin trembles—"had no idea when he lured her . . . Excuse me."

She presses the handkerchief to each eye.

People can be so willfully blind. With hardly a glance, anyone could have seen that Lydia didn't feel *brotherly* affection for Matthew. While the LeVines have always been thought of as a good sort of family, truth telling has never been their strength. Not when the truth dares to color outside the lines of propriety.

I sip my tea and wait for her to lower the handkerchief. "I just wish they would catch him so he could be questioned and we could know the truth."

Because the truth coming out could only help Matthew. Couldn't it?

The aftermath has played out just as Mariano predicted that day he came to tell me the wretched news. Matthew had snuck out of town with such stealth, they couldn't even figure out how he left, much less track him to another location. And with the trail cold and Lydia just one of many dead bodies in the city, the department moved on.

"I said almost the exact same thing to Dr. LeVine just a few days ago. He tells me that even if they caught Matthew and sentenced him for it, it wouldn't change anything. That it's best for us to try to move past what happened." She mops her eyes once more. "He's right, of course. But what about the next family that man dupes? You know how it is with these sorts."

Or is there perhaps another reason Dr. LeVine doesn't want Matthew found and questioned? A motive for why he doesn't want Matthew's innocence to come to light? I can't imagine that these flimsy, patched-together stories about Matthew being a loose cannon could really satisfy a man like Dr. LeVine, who prides himself on scientific facts and details.

"I have a favor to ask, Mrs. LeVine." I settle my cup back into its saucer. Hopefully, Mrs. LeVine won't notice the way my hand trembles.

"Of course, my dear. What is it?"

The way Mrs. LeVine looks at me, with tenderness instead of reproach, still unsettles me. "I wonder if you'd please let me go up to Lydia's room."

Mrs. LeVine's eyes widen.

"Only for a minute or two. I just . . ." I fold my hands in my lap. "With the casket being closed, I don't feel like I ever really got to say good-bye. And I just wondered . . . I wouldn't touch anything, I promise."

Mrs. LeVine nods slowly. "If you promise to leave it all exactly where it is, then yes." She smooths imaginary wrinkles from the long, crisp skirt of her dress. "I understand why you're asking, Piper."

My heart hiccups in my chest. Does she?

"After the funeral, I spent more hours in that room than anywhere else. Even now, I often go up there for an hour or so. Sometimes, I even talk to her." Mrs. LeVine chuckles. "That's rubbish, isn't it? I've never been the sort to believe in spirits. Still, I can't deny that I feel better after I've been up there. So, of course, Piper. Take your time."

Take your time. Such beautiful words, ones I hadn't been sure I could count on. "Thank you, Mrs. LeVine."

I stand outside Lydia's closed door for a while. I don't know how long, really. I wish I remembered the last time I was in here, that I had some great memory to carry with me. Though it may be good that I don't. One less thing to become tainted.

I place my hand on the gold doorknob and turn. The door opens noiselessly.

"Hello."

I gasp and take a step backward.

Hannah, stretched out on Lydia's frilly white bed, props herself up on her elbows. "What are you doing in here?"

"Your mother said it would be okay. I didn't realize you'd be here, sorry." I reach for the doorknob to shut the door as I exit.

"You can stay. I don't mind." Hannah lays back down. "Sarah doesn't like to come up here. She thinks it's creepy. But I like it. I feel as if she's here. That if I listen hard, she'll talk to me."

The room is too warm and airless. Contrary to Hannah's impression, it seems as though the life has been suctioned out. And yet the Lydia-ness of the space nearly undoes me. Like my room, Lydia's is mostly pink. Unlike my room, it actually suits her. The frothy white curtains, the rosebud wallpaper, the pink gingham pillows.

"Will you please tell me what she was sick with?" Hannah's voice seems to glisten with tears. "Mother and Father still won't talk about it. They say it doesn't matter now."

I think of the china tea service downstairs, of the way Mrs. LeVine has been so kind to me. But Hannah's swimming eyes win. "She had seizures. Lots of them."

I pace the length of the room, taking it in. Lydia's knitting basket sits by a rocking chair, all the supplies tucked neatly inside. The armoire drawers are shut tight, as are the dresser drawers. The books are orderly on her bookshelves, alphabetized, spines aligned.

"Did you ever see one? Mother and Tabitha always shooed us out. Said she needed space to recover."

"I saw two." I turn from the window to Hannah's watchful blue eyes. "They were terrifying. You should feel thankful."

Hannah's jawline hardens, and she looks back at the ceiling. "I only feel angry. She shouldn't have been alone. If I had known, I would have walked with her."

"I wish all the time that I would have."

"Father's the one to blame."

Hannah's dark words make ice crawl up my back. I look at her. At thirteen, her body is still a girl's, and there's a hint of childlike roundness to her face. But her words are sharp like an adult's. "Why do you say that, Hannah?"

"He cared more about his stupid medical practice than he did Lydia's health."

I clamp my teeth over my lower lip, holding in the questions that want to spill out. I need to let Hannah talk.

"I even heard him say that to Mother one night." Hannah

shifts her gaze from the ceiling to me. "That he should've sent her to the Mayo Clinic earlier. That he felt guilty and responsible."

"And what did your mother say?"

"That he wasn't. But I can't get over thinking that he was."

Where was he the night she went missing? I knew what he had told Mariano, of course, but I wanted to hear it verified by his angry daughter. A daughter who had no problems accusing him of caring more about his reputation than his family.

"He called me that night, when she hadn't come home yet." I try to make my voice sound casual, conversational. "He was upset."

"He was." Hannah wipes at her eyes with the back of her hands. "I was actually there when he called you. He and Mother had been talking in private, and then they called Sarah and me in. They told us what we already knew—that Lydia was sick—and she would be going to Minnesota for a while to try and get healthy. We talked for some time, and then he realized she should have been home by then."

My focus blurs as I take in Lydia's view of the back alley. So Dr. LeVine couldn't have done it. He was with his wife and daughters, one of whom is so angry, she wouldn't hesitate to point a finger. Relief soaks through me.

I sweep my gaze across Lydia's desk. Her mementos are all in their normal places—the photograph of her grandmother, a vase full of seashells she collected when her family traveled to Florida, a stuffed bear I gave her back when we were children and she had the flu.

I know I told Mrs. LeVine I wouldn't touch anything, but I can't resist picking up the bear and letting the memories sweep over me. My mother had taken me to the toy store to purchase it for Lydia.

"Poor child," Mother had said on our way. "Father off at war all year long, and now this wretched flu."

I had been so disappointed that Mrs. LeVine wouldn't let me give the bear to Lydia myself that I had cried. "It's because she hates me."

"No, Pippy." Mother had cupped my face in her hands. "She doesn't want you getting sick too. That's all."

I put the bear back on Lydia's desk, eyes pooling from the memory of Mother's touch.

"Matthew wouldn't have done it." Hannah's words startle me—I had forgotten she was in the room. "He was in love with her."

She looks at me then, as if waiting. I nod. "He was."

Despite how her tone had invited no argument, her sigh seems relieved.

I slide open the drawer of Lydia's desk. Everything seems to be in its place.

"What are you looking for?"

I think about all the ways I could answer Hannah. I decide to go with the truth. "Clues."

"Clues of what? Who killed her?"

I wince at the word choice. "Yes."

Or, if I'm being honest, I'm looking to find no clues. Because if her kidnappers were really after me, there should be no evidence that points to Lydia.

"Do you want to know who I think it might be?" Hannah's voice is timid.

I turn to her, take in her porcelain doll face and round, blue eyes.

"If you don't, it's okay." Hannah toys with the end of her

braid. "Nobody else seems to care who I think it might be. Except for that detective. The cute one."

I perch on the edge of the bed. "I would like to know, Hannah."

"I don't have any real evidence." She sucks in a breath and draws her knees up to her chest. "It's just a feeling."

"That's okay. Who?"

She swallows. "David Barrow," she says to her knees. "Lydia didn't like him. And Lydia liked everybody. I think that means something."

"It definitely means he's a real creep." But why would he have killed her? What could he have gained from it?

"And she was supposed to be at his house," Hannah continues in a volume barely above a whisper. "Couldn't that be considered evidence?"

"I don't know." I think of Cole's sullen behavior several weeks ago. I haven't been to visit since the baby was born. Perhaps it's time I do my neighborly duty and bring them a casserole.

My gaze drifts to Lydia's nightstand, where a copy of *Persuasion* sits, forever unfinished.

"I hope, in heaven, she gets to find out how it ends," Hannah says.

"I hope it's too wonderful there for her to even care." But there's something unnerving about the thought—that everything that once mattered to Lydia may no longer—and I rush away from it. "You come get me if you ever need me, Hannah. Okay?"

She scrutinizes me, and for a moment I expect her to ask why I think she would need me. Or maybe to accuse me of not keeping Lydia safe when I knew she was sick. Instead she says. "Are you going after David?"

"I'm going to look into him, yes."

Her expression relaxes. "Thank you."

I close the door behind me as I retreat, leaving Hannah in the airless, suffocating room of her dead sister.

Downstairs, Mrs. LeVine's smile is polite and pasted. "How was it, dear? Do you feel better?"

After weeks of sitting in my room, grieving and stewing and jumping at every creak in the house, Hannah has given me a direction to go.

"Yes," I say. "I really do."

When I get home from walking Sidekick, Joyce springs on me that my brother won't be home for dinner tonight, because he's out on a date. A strange sense of betrayal billows up inside me. "What do you mean, he's on a date?"

She blinks at me over the steaming pot of potatoes she's mashing. "A date, Piper. Dinner, dancing."

"But . . ." But what about the way Nick used to look at Lydia? What about the way his face would fall if she didn't come home from school with me? "With whom?"

"He didn't share many details." Her forearm flexes as she resumes mashing. "She's a journalist. I guess they met because she's doing a story on Lydia and Matthew."

My teeth grind together. How long is this stupid reporter staying in town? And how can Nick go out with that pestering woman? Yes, she's beautiful, but is he really so shallow? Tears well in my eyes as I sink to a seat at the counter.

Joyce rests the potato masher against the edge of the pot. "I know." Her words are steady, comforting. "The two of you have always handled your grief in very different ways. This doesn't mean that Nick is over what happened. But, Piper, life has to be gotten on with."

Sidekick strains at the end of his leash, and I untie him.

Joyce picks up the potato masher. "Jane is coming for dinner—"

I groan.

"—so maybe it would be a good idea for you to call a friend and go out yourself. Or call Tim and see if you can spend some time with Gretchen and Howie."

I'd rather eat my own toenails than listen to my sister-in-law ramble about floral arrangements and how to knit the perfect booties. If I can't be with Lydia, then the only person I really care to see is—

I brush away the idea, but embarrassment still heats my cheeks. I'm not going to call Mariano, on a Friday no less, and ask about his evening plans.

Piper Caroline Sail, I can hear Lydia scolding. *Good heavens, who are you? Zelda Fitzgerald? Only a woman of loose morals would even think of something so brash as outright asking a man for a date.*

I mutter excuses to Joyce and leave the kitchen.

It's been several days since Mariano and I last talked. The department is a flurry of activity due to yet another missing adolescent. This one also ended in tragedy, and has caught the eye of the nation now that it's come out the boy was murdered for sport.

I shudder.

After the grueling days Mariano has had, the idea of going out probably doesn't even appeal to him. It doesn't interest me, certainly. I'm happy to stay home and listen to the radio at a volume high enough that I can't hear Jane and Father discuss a never-ending parade of meaningless wedding details.

And how would I even go about asking Mariano? I don't know how to do that sort of thing. If Mariano wanted to have dinner with me, I'm sure he would ask. He doesn't need me calling him up and pestering him about what he's doing tonight, or how work is going, or if he ever plans to give back my notebook . . .

My notebook. Mariano still has my notebook.

I don't particularly *need* my notebook. But it's mine, and I'd like to have it.

I close myself into Father's office, draw the telephone close, and dial from memory.

"It's me, Piper," I say when he answers. "Do you still have my notebook? The one I gave you when Lydia first went missing?"

"Hello, Piper." There's a smile in his voice. "I do."

"Will you still be there fifteen minutes from now? I'd like to pick it up, if it's no trouble."

"It's no trouble at all."

I catch sight of the lackluster dress I'm wearing, feel my uncurled hair. "What about forty-five minutes? Will you be there in forty-five?"

"I'll tell you what, Piper. I'm just about to wrap up for the day. How about I swing by your place on my way home?" His words are warm in my ear, and for the first time in a while, something besides anger, sadness, and fear quivers to life within me.

I'm just putting the finishing touches on my hair when Joyce calls up the stairs to me. "Piper? Detective Cassano is here to see you!"

He's here already? I stare at myself in the mirror for a moment, cataloging my paste-colored face, the circles under my eyes. My efforts to make myself look fresh and attractive have been wasted. And now I've manipulated him into traveling all this way just to return a notebook I don't even need.

Piper, this isn't like you at all, Lydia admonishes. *Put down the kohl pencil and go say hello to that nice young man.*

I take a deep breath. It's just Mariano. He's seen me at my worst—he can certainly endure this.

But I don't want him to *endure* me. I want him to like me.

I peek down the staircase. He stands in the entryway, one hand in his pocket, jingling loose change, and the other gripping my notebook, which I had once given him with such naïve hope.

"Hello," I say when I'm halfway down the stairs.

His head snaps up. "Wow. You're very quiet."

"It's a gift."

Mariano grins at me as I reach the last step. "Here." He stretches out my notebook. "Sorry I hung on to it so long."

"It's okay." I hug it to my chest. It smells like disappointment and the cigarette smoke that clouds Mariano's office. "Thanks for trying."

Mariano's eyes shine with regret. "I wanted to bring her home, Piper. I wanted to so badly."

"I know you did."

His dark gaze hangs on me. Can he see the fatigue? That simply existing is tiring for me right now?

If he can, he's too much of a gentleman to speak it. "You look nice. Are you heading someplace special tonight?"

My heart pounds, and I try to make my voice casual. "No. I'm completely free tonight."

Mariano's gaze sweeps over the length of me, and I know he's cataloging the evidence—my scarlet drop-waist dress that frees my legs for an evening of the Charleston, red lipstick and kohled eyes, my carefully marcelled hair. "You might be a little overdressed for an evening around the house."

My teeth press into my lower lip before I remember my lipstick. "Well, maybe I'll go out for a bit."

Mariano's smile hangs crooked as he leans against the banister. "You know, on the way over here, I got to thinking about this place that sells pizza in Little Italy, near where I grew up. I thought I might grab a slice and take a walk through the park there. There's usually music on Friday nights in the summer. What do you think of joining me? Seems like a terrible waste to leave you at home in that dress."

My yes catches in my throat, catches on a lump of guilt. How can I feel happy—excited even—with Lydia dead? How can I enjoy a night out with Mariano knowing that I never would have met him had I not lost Lydia?

Piper, I won't be any less dead if you go out and enjoy yourself.

Mariano's hand settles on the banister, beside mine so that our pinkie fingers brush together. "Or maybe it's too soon." The words are like a caress, and I want to lean in. Want to let myself be swept away by this man who knows that I'm trying, but struggling, and it's not about him.

The notebook is between us, still hugged to my chest. I lower it. "Let me fetch my hat."

The evening air is damp from the afternoon rain, and it smells of summer flowers and savory breads. Jazz music pulses from Vernon Park, as does loud laughter.

The world has continued to turn, hasn't it? Just like when Mother died, it will indifferently carry on without Lydia.

"*Buena sera*, Mariano!" calls the man behind the counter of Pompei's.

"*Buena sera,* Mr. Davino." The Italian rolls out of Mariano like a ribbon. "How are you? How's the family?"

But the man's eyes are fixed on me. "You've brought a lovely girl with you, I see."

"This is Piper." Mariano's hand grazes my back.

I offer an awkward wave. "Hello."

"Hello, Piper. My daughter will be very sad to hear that you're quite beautiful."

I blush. What does one say to that?

But Mr. Davino doesn't need me to answer. "What can I get for the two of you on this summer evening?"

Mariano buys us slices of bread and cheese pizza, which Mr. Davino wraps in butcher paper for us to eat in the park. "Have a good time. And, Mariano." He seems to hesitate a moment. "I believe I saw Alessandro heading over to the park earlier."

Am I imagining that this is a warning of some kind? The way Mariano says, "Ah, thank you," with a stiff smile makes me think I'm not.

Outside, we cross the street to the park, which is full of families and couples enjoying the mild evening. We settle on a bench near the fountain, where the music is loud enough to fill up the gaps in conversation without us having to yell over it.

"You grew up close to here?" I ask as I unwrap my gooey slice. I've never eaten this before, but if it tastes half as good as it smells, I think I have a new favorite food.

Mariano nods. "Just a few blocks over. We played soccer here as kids." He gestures to somewhere in the distance. "I still remember a magnificent goal I scored between those two trees. One of my first memories."

The park swims with young Italian boys, and it's not hard

to picture a pint-size Mariano rolling in the grass and playing soccer with his friends.

"Alessandro is one of my brothers." Mariano's words slice into my imaginings. "I'm sure you were curious."

"You don't have to explain to me."

His smile is strained. "Thank you, but I should before we run into him. I'm sure Mr. Davino only mentioned my brother because he's here with his girl." Mariano reworks the butcher paper around his pizza. "His girlfriend, Zola, she . . ."

Zola. I hear the name in my head, only spoken in my brother's razor-edged voice. *Has he even told you about Zola?*

"She and I used to be together. But . . ."

"You don't have to explain," I say again. But I'm not trying to comfort Mariano, am I? I'm trying to protect *me*. Because I haven't built a wall around my heart with Mariano like I have everyone else. And the vulnerability unnerves me.

"No, you should know." Mariano takes a deep breath. "We knew each other as kids, me and Zola, and we were engaged. Should've been getting married a couple weeks ago, actually."

"And why"—I try to swallow away the wobble that's in my voice—"didn't you?"

"She wasn't interested in being a detective's wife."

"Oh."

He slides his gaze to me. "Oh?"

But how do you say that you had hoped it would be more about a change of *his* heart rather than hers? On a first date, no less. My *first* first date.

It seems safest to not even try to explain. "That must have been very difficult for you."

Mariano hesitates. "It's gotten much easier recently. Though now that she's with Alessandro, it's hard again."

My heart twists in a way that makes me long for stone walls. How fast could I build one? Or once you've let someone in, is it impossible to wall them back out? "I'm sure it's difficult to see her moving on."

"No, I didn't mean it like that." Mariano's hand clasps mine. "I didn't mean that at all. It's only difficult because Alessandro chooses for it to be. He seems to think he bested me somehow, and it's hard for us to talk without it turning into an argument. I hate feeling pitted against my own family. More than I already am."

Mariano's grasp loosens, and he weaves his fingers between mine. "But—and I want to make sure this is completely clear to you, Piper—I have no lingering interest in her. And no regrets that I'm sitting here with you." He squeezes my hand. "Is this bothering you?"

When I look up from the captivating sight of his olive fingers entwined with my fair, I find Mariano's face is close to mine. "No." I squeeze back. "Not at all."

He grins and leans against the bench. "How's Sidekick doing? He's put on a good amount of weight the last few weeks. He actually *looks* like a decent sidekick now."

"I think he's doing well. Though if I leave the house for too long, he expresses his anger by dragging my shoes from the closet. I finally put them on higher shelves."

"Good plan." He licks olive oil from his thumb. "How are the LeVines? Have you seen them recently?"

I nod. "Yesterday, actually. Mrs LeVine and Hannah, anyway. They're . . . I don't know. They're very sad."

"I wish I could fix it all for you, Piper." His shoulders droop forward. "More than anything. And since I can't bring her back for you, I wish I could at least give you the answers you want."

"No one with the police is still looking, are they?"

Mariano shakes his head. "Even before everything with this new case, Matthew's trail was cold."

"Did you follow up with the Finnegans?" Just saying their name sends a tremor through me. "What were they doing at the time Lydia went missing?"

"Colin was already in jail. Patrick's alibi is solid—movie theater. Plenty of witnesses. But of course they have a lot of men under their influence . . ." Mariano crumples his empty butcher paper. "I haven't counted them out. I *did* keep an eye on Dr. LeVine in the week after. I think you're safe with him. I haven't found anything I normally would—no paper trail. No suspicious phone calls. No unexplained absences from work. The shady business of him not being forthright about Lydia's condition was really just a matter of his ego, I think."

"Did you look into David Barrow any further?"

"Ah, yes, David Barrow. I did a little digging and learned he's quite the fan of gambling. Spends a lot of time at the tracks and gin joints. Has a lady friend who keeps him company when he's there, actually."

I shudder as I think of pretty Mrs. Barrow with her newborn son. The way she always waves and says a bright, "Hello!" when I pass by.

Mariano sighs. "So while he's guilty of deplorable behavior, that's not exactly evidence or a motive."

"Lydia didn't like being around him. She found him to be creepy."

Mariano's mouth curls into a slight smile. "Creepiness isn't a motive."

A seed of an idea niggles at me. "What about the nanny who used to work for the Barrow family?"

"What about her?"

"Has anyone talked to her about Mr. Barrow? Lydia once told me she works at John Barleycorn."

He only blinks at me.

"It's a speakeasy, Mariano."

He rolls his eyes. "Yes, I know. I was waiting to see where you were taking this."

"Lydia was always suspicious about why she quit so suddenly. I just wondered if maybe this girl knew something." My knowledge of speakeasies is limited, all secondhand from Presley's girls who fancy it fun to sneak into what used to be male-only saloons, drink illegal booze, and dance the night away. "How does one get into a speakeasy? Do I still need a password? How does one learn the password?"

Mariano sighs. "I think you're going to give me an ulcer, Piper." He glances behind us, where the jazz trio plays "It Had to Be You." Mariano drapes his arm over the back of the bench, where it whispers against the fabric of my dress. "I've gotta confess something. I brought you here because I was hoping to dance with you. But if you don't feel like that tonight, that's okay. We could do it another time."

Another time. Like another date.

I glance at the couples who are already out there. The girls in their bright dresses, with skirts that twirl out like upside-down flowers, make my feet itch. "I'm a terrible dancer."

"I don't believe that."

"I am. I always try to lead."

Mariano huffs a laugh. "Now *that*, I believe."

I try to glare, but it's impossible with his fingertip tracing the slope of my shoulder.

"So we're doing this, then?" Mariano's face is solemn. "You and me?"

I nod. "We're doing this."

Mariano seems to hesitate only a moment before leaning close and brushing his lips against mine. And when the kiss is over, I can't help thinking how much I would have enjoyed telling Lydia.

CHAPTER
~ FIFTEEN ~

When I awake, the guilt is swift and sharp.

How could I?

My eyes press tight against the pale morning light. There had been no angel Lydia advising me that I couldn't outrun death. No sinister, faceless men snatching her from the streets before I could stop them. No gag that I attempted to pull from her mouth only to never reach the end.

There had been no dreams at all.

Sidekick nudges my cheek with his wet nose, urging me out of bed before he leaps to the floor.

But I make myself lie there and think about her. Make myself draw the coroner's report from my nightstand drawer, from its place beside Matthew's letter, tucked in Mother's Bible.

When I select my dress for the day, I choose one with pockets and tuck Lydia's photograph inside. I may have no choice about Lydia's life stopping while mine goes on, but I refuse to let her drift too far from my thoughts.

I tromp downstairs for breakfast and find Joyce scribbling out a grocery list as she finishes her coffee and toast. "Good morning."

"Good morning, Joyce." I reach up into the cabinet and pull down a mug.

"Your father is in his office. Said he wanted to see you. What can I fix you for breakfast?"

"I'll just have coffee for now, thank you."

Joyce moves her attention from her list to me. "You're not dieting, are you? You're a rail already."

"No. Just not hungry yet."

Because my stomach is too twisted in knots over last night—Mariano's smile, his lips, his hands—to consider anything more substantial than coffee. I fill Sidekick's food bowl and then carry my coffee to Father's office.

"Oh, good," Father greets me. "I have to leave to meet Jane soon, and I hoped you'd be up before I left. Have a seat."

I grab the chair that Nick often uses when they're reviewing a case together and drag it over to the desk.

Father scribbles his signature on some official-looking document as he asks, "What do you have planned for the day?"

"I thought I would pay a visit to Mrs. Barrow. I haven't seen their baby yet."

Father's pen stops moving. He looks up at me, eyebrows arched in amusement. "I'm sorry. I asked Joyce to send in my daughter, Piper Sail. You must be an imposter."

"Very funny." I sip at my coffee and curse my big mouth. Did I really have to be so vocal all these years about my distaste for children? "I'm just being neighborly."

"I think you'll have a chance to be neighborly very soon. Joyce was just telling me that Mrs. Barrow has an appointment of some kind and is bringing Cole here this morning. I'm sure she'll welcome your help with him."

I never thought the opportunity to look after a child would delight me, but this is perfect. Now I can observe Cole for extended time without the threat of David Barrow. "Oh, good. Do you know when?"

Father blinks at me. "You're scaring me. The daughter I know would have fled the house the moment she heard a person under the age of ten intended to enter it."

I grasp for a plausible lie. "Lydia used to look after Cole. I suppose I feel connected to her when I'm around him."

"That reminds me. I have something for you." He pats at his pockets. "I've had Joyce helping rearrange the bedroom to prepare for Jane, and we found something of your mother's that had fallen behind a dresser."

I sit up straight.

"Ah, here it is." From an inside pocket, Father pulls out a long silver chain with a pendant of some kind. "Actually, it wasn't exactly your mother's. It's yours. Mother bought it several weeks before she passed, intending it to be a present for your thirteenth birthday. She was so frustrated with herself for misplacing it. Joyce found it still in the velvet bag it came in. We're guessing it slipped back behind the dresser."

The oval pendant is actually a locket, silver and simple. My thirteen-year-old self would have been delighted to receive such a grown-up present.

One last gift from my mother. I must be the most fortunate girl in the world. "I don't know what to say."

"Open her up."

I slide my thumbnail along the seam and pop the tiny clasp. Lydia's beautiful face looks back at me. "Lydia." The word is a whisper.

"I planned to put your mother's portrait in there, but Jane suggested Lydia's. This way, you have a piece of both of them with you all the time."

I rub the pad of my thumb over my friend's face. "It's perfect, thank you."

Sidekick erupts with a string of barks, and his nails scrape against the wood floor as he scrambles out of Father's office.

"Cole must be here." Father smooths his vest as he stands. "Last chance to escape."

I tuck the locket into the pocket of my dress and stand as well. "Don't tempt me. I'm trying to grow, Father."

Cole's cries for his mother pierce the air.

Father grins at me when I flinch. "Have fun." He latches his briefcase and reaches for his fedora. "I'll see you at supper."

I grab my coffee and slip away to the kitchen. If I'm to endure a morning with a child, I cannot do it on an empty stomach.

"She'll only be gone for a bit." Joyce's tone is soothing as the kitchen door swings open. She has Cole by the hand.

Cole rubs a tear-filled eye. His cheeks are red, and his lower lip is pooched out. "But I want my mama."

"We're going to have so much fun that the time will fly by. Would you like a glass of milk?"

I take a deep breath. "Hi, Cole." My voice is high with fake cheer. Cole turns to look, one eye still covered by his fist. "Remember me? I'm Piper. Lydia's friend."

And that's when Cole does the last thing I would have expected.

He runs for me.

I stare slack-jawed as he comes nearer. There's no way he's actually coming for *me*, right? How could he consider me a better alternative than Joyce, who oozes maternal safety?

His skinny arms wrap around my waist. And while I would've sworn to China and back that I had no instincts at all with kids, I find myself lifting Cole up into my arms. Like I'd seen Lydia do a couple times when he'd scraped a knee or banged his elbow.

With his head on my shoulder, Cole takes a shuddering inhale and exhale, and the kitchen falls silent.

Cole studies the checkerboard before jumping over my red game piece.

"You're good at this game, Cole."

He shrugs his narrow shoulders. "Dottie and me play lots. But today she has a fever."

"I'm sorry to hear that."

"I had a fever on my birthday. Hey, your dress is blue and my shorts are blue. We match."

"We do." I don't recognize this high, cheerful voice of mine. I make a careless move on the board. "So how old are you now, Cole? Eleven? Twelve?"

His smile is faint. "Five."

He used to laugh so easily, Lydia whispers to me. *He used to bring frogs inside the house and break windows with stray baseballs. He's like a different child.*

Is having a new baby brother enough to turn a formerly rambunctious child meek and teary? Or could this be a byproduct of Lydia vanishing from his life? Have his parents talked to him about what happened? That would be enough to frighten any child.

Joyce bustles into the room with a tray. "Thought the two of you might enjoy some lemonade and cookies."

"Lemonade, yum." My words are sticky with forced cheer. "Thank you, Joyce."

"Are you winning, Cole?" Joyce asks.

He shrugs.

"He's a good checkers player. Aren't you, Cole?"

Again, he shrugs.

Joyce watches him for a moment, and lines form on her forehead. She glances at me, mouths *thank you*, and leaves.

"Maybe after our cookies, we could take Sidekick for a walk." Perhaps Cole will feel more talkative if we're outside and active. "How does that sound?"

"Okay."

I move my game piece and stand to put cookies onto individual plates for us.

A scream—Cole's—tears through the living room. I yelp, and the plate that had been in my hands shatters on the oak floor.

Cole has scrambled backward to the wall. The screaming has stopped, but now he cries with his knees tucked to his chest and his arms wrapped around his legs.

Joyce bursts into the room.

"Just me being clumsy," I assure her.

She heaves a sigh at the sight of the shattered plate. "Goodness. With all the fuss you two were making, I thought someone had broken in."

"I'll get the broom and dustpan and clean it up."

"You'll cut your feet if you move." Joyce is already bustling down the hallway. "Stay there, and I'll bring it to you."

I look to Cole, to his shaking shoulders. Then to the locket Father gave me an hour ago. It lies open in the middle of the

THE LOST GIRL OF ASTOR STREET

game board, revealing Lydia's smiling face. It must have fallen from my pocket when I stood.

"It's going to be okay, Cole."

But he doesn't seem to believe me. Or at least, he doesn't unroll himself. Instead, he keeps his arms wrapped around his knees, his head tucked as he rocks himself back and forth.

Cole knows something. And I need to know it too.

I attach the leash to Sidekick's collar. "Look at his tail, Cole."

A smile flickers on Cole's mouth as he watches Sidekick's furry tail brush back and forth on the wood floor. "He's a nice dog." He holds out a hand to Sidekick and then giggles when Sidekick bathes it with his long, pink tongue.

That sounds better. I find my hand settles on the back of Cole's neck as we head outside. When he leans into me, the feeling in my chest is akin to coming home to a warm house on a winter day.

We step outside to find Nick heading up the front walk. With that journalist.

The warmth of Cole settling his head against me is sucked away. Her red dress seems a bit much for before noon, and she's smiling at Nick, her teeth white and gleaming in the rays of sunshine slanting through the trees.

Her smile sharpens when she sees me. "Hello, Piper. I hoped I'd see you today."

I wait for Lydia's voice to tell me to be polite, to tell me that she's dead and she didn't love my brother anyway. But she's strangely silent.

205

Nick sweeps off his fedora. "You remember Alana Kirkwood, right, Piper?"

"Not really."

Nick's gaze commands me to be friendly, but I can't seem to make myself care. Stupid as it may be, having Alana around feels like a betrayal to Lydia.

Sidekick strains against the end of the leash. "I can't talk now. We're taking Sidekick for a walk."

"What a lovely dog," Alana coos. She rubs her fingertips together to attract him, but he winces away.

Nick glances at Cole, who has tucked himself between me and the handrail. "And who is this young man?" His tone is strange, high and too bright. He sounds as ridiculous as I do when I'm trying to talk to Cole.

Cole only slips his hand into mine and retreats farther behind me.

"This is Cole Barrow. You probably just don't recognize him because he's a big five-year-old now."

My brother looks at me as though I'm a foreign species, but Alana crouches low. "Hi, Cole. It's nice to meet you."

"Hi." Cole's word is no louder than a breath.

"Do you help Piper walk her dog very often?"

Cole doesn't respond.

"He lives one street over," Nick says to her. "In the house with the white fence that you asked about."

Of course she's asking all kinds of nosy questions about our neighbors. Surely her newspaper will bring her back home soon, right?

Alana stands to her full height, nearly a head taller than me. "I was admiring your home, Cole. You have a lovely yard."

Again, he doesn't answer her, and Sidekick strains at the lead. "We had better go. We'll see you in a bit."

"Piper, when you get back"—Alana touches my arm, and I use Sidekick as an excuse to step away—"I would still love to talk to you about Jacob and Lydia."

"I don't know anything that would be of interest to you."

"I don't think that's true at all. Nick was telling me that Jacob wrote you a letter."

I shift a glare to Nick. "Oh, he did?"

"Don't be angry with him. He wants the same thing I want— the same thing *you* want. Justice for Lydia."

I glance meaningfully at Cole. "*Now* isn't the time to discuss it."

"Of course. Later, then. Maybe after you get home? Do you have the letter here, or is it with the police? I would love to see it."

If Cole wasn't here, I would give this overbearing reporter a piece of my mind. What is wrong with my brother, that he can't see she's just using him to advance her career?

I turn on my heel without responding and race down the steps before the vicious words on my tongue spill out. Cole collected a stick while I wasn't paying attention, and he runs it along the wrought iron fence. A metallic *thunk, thunk, thunk* strides along with us.

I allow myself a few moments to silently seethe over crafty Alana Kirkwood, but I can't let her rob me of the opportunity I have to talk to Cole privately.

"Do you like having a little brother, Cole?"

He shrugs.

"Does he cry a lot?"

"Yes."

"Are you a good helper?"

Another shrug. Another fence. *Thunk, thunk, thunk* . . .

My chest aches with impatience. How does one go about making a five-year-old talk? How would my mother have tricked *me* into talking?

The answer is simple—she wouldn't have tricked me. She would have just asked what she wanted to know.

I glance at the child beside me, at his blond curls and his hand pocketed in mine. Maybe he just needs to be asked.

"Cole." He turns his big brown eyes to me. "Have your parents talked to you about Lydia?"

His hand goes stiff inside mine, and his eyes widen. Oh, great. I've scared him.

"You don't need to be scared." I squeeze his rigid hand. "I'm with you, okay? Nothing is going to happen."

"I can't talk about her." Cole's voice is so quiet, I have to lean closer to hear. "It's a rule."

I crouch beside him. "It's okay when you're with me."

He shakes his head. One hand covers his bottom, and he does a squirmy sort of dance.

Perfect. This is why I avoid being alone with kids. "Do you need a restroom?"

Again, he shakes his head, but his hand stays planted atop his bottom.

We walk on. Questions build in my head, and with the stick limp at Cole's side, I actually have silence to accommodate my thinking. Was he asking his parents too many complicated questions and they told him to stop? It would be hard—impossible, even—to explain what happened to Lydia without terrifying a small child. Especially one who knew and loved her, and walks the same streets she did.

Cole crouches next to the fence. "Look. A spider." He pokes it with his stick, causing the spider to scurry. "They eat other bugs. They catch 'em in their web and eat 'em."

"That's right."

"I'm very smart," he informs me.

I can't resist a smile. "Yes, you are."

When he turns back to the spider, he leans closer. And the hem of his shirt slides up high enough that I catch a glimpse of a dark blue line.

He's so focused on the spider, he doesn't notice me lightly adjusting the fabric of his trousers, where the bruise seems to come from. Doesn't notice the *whoosh* as my breath exhales from my chest at the sight of it—lines in all shades of purple, blue, and gray crisscrossing on his fair skin.

Lines from a father's belt make sense for a boy who tried to hide a frog under his bed to keep as a pet and who threw his dinner against the wall when he didn't want to eat it. But for this complacent and meek child? What could be the cause?

The answer comes swiftly, as if being presented on a platter. *I can't talk about it. It's a rule.* His hand protective over his rump.

And it's a rule I need him to break.

"I used to get whippings too, when I was your age."

Cole turns and looks at me with interest. "But you're a girl."

"Girls can get whippings. Actually, do you want to know a secret?"

Cole nods, and I make a production of crouching on the ground, of lowering my voice. "Sometimes, I still get whipped.

Not by my father, but at school. I have a teacher who likes to whack me with her ruler."

His eyes are bright. "Where?"

"On my knuckles, here." I shift Sidekick's leash to my left hand so I can show Cole my normally bruised right. "It's faded now that I've graduated."

"Was it because you tried to talk about Lydia?" Cole's voice has a solemn empathy to it.

My heart squeezes so tight, it feels as though it might burst. "Is that how you got yours?"

When Cole nods, it's all I can do to not weep. "I don't mean to, but it's awfully hard." His sigh makes him seem much older than five.

"Maybe you and I could make a deal, Cole."

"What's a deal?"

"A deal is when two people agree on something. So if you want, we could agree that when it's just the two of us, we can talk about Lydia." Cole's hand is already inching to protect his behind. "And no one will hurt us because of it, okay? You can ask questions or tell me stories about Lydia, and it'll be our secret."

There's a crease on the bridge of his nose as he studies me.

"I could go first, if you want."

Cole nods.

I settle against the fence. "Lydia and I used to walk this way all the time when we were kids." I point to the stone house on the corner. "There used to be an elderly woman who lived there. When it was nice out, she sat on her porch to knit, and she would give us peppermint drops if we passed by."

Cole frowns at the house. "What does elderly mean?"

"That she was old."

"Like you?"

"No. Like a grandparent. Do you have any grandparents?"

Cole nods. "And my grandfather always has peppermint drops."

I glance at the house. "Lydia was her favorite. I don't think she would have given them to just me. I was too loud."

Cole nods sagely. "I get too loud sometimes. And babies like quiet voices."

I smile, and try to seem serene despite the way my heart thumps wildly in my chest. "Okay, Cole, now it's your turn. To share something about Lydia."

He blinks at me. Then shakes his head.

"It's a secret, remember?" I use a whispering voice. "Just for you and me, because we loved Lydia so much."

Sidekick has given up on getting his walk. He lays his big head on my lap.

Cole pats him. "He's a nice dog."

"He is. And he won't tell anyone that we like to talk about Lydia when it's just the two of us."

Cole seems to think about this for a minute. His voice is small when he asks, "Do you know what this means?" Cole holds up his pointer finger.

I resist the urge to scream with frustration, to yell *Tell me what you know about Lydia!* "It's a one, right?" My cheerful voice is lined with impatience.

"Okay." Cole turns his pointer finger to himself and stares at it. "Mommy and Papa didn't know."

The skin on the back of my neck prickles. "Where did you see this, Cole?" I hold up my own pointer finger.

"It's what Lydia did to me." His eyes are round and woeful. "Before she got in the car."

CHAPTER
~ SIXTEEN ~

After Cole goes home, I sit on the porch with my notebook and write it all out. Digging the information from Cole had felt like looking for the proverbial needle in the haystack. I had to shovel past the "That stick looks like a seven," and, "Your eyes are brown and white," to get to what I hope is the real story.

The evening Lydia was taken, Cole was playing in his bedroom and saw her coming up the sidewalk. A car pulled up alongside her, and she started talking to the driver.

"Where did the car come from?"

Cole shrugged. "Maybe the store? That's where our car goes a lot."

"Did you recognize the car?"

"What does recognize mean?"

"Is it a car you'd seen before?"

Cole nodded. "Yep. Lots of times."

My heart had pounded, sure that I was a breath away from knowing who had taken and killed my best friend.

"I have one just like it at home. Santa Claus brought it to me. Do you know when Santa Claus will come back? Just Christmas. That's the only time he delivers."

"What did the car look like?"

"Black. Just like the one Santa brought me. Papa says they only make them in black. If I could pick any color for a car, I would pick orange. That's my favorite."

Not helpful. "Do you know what kind of car Santa brought you?"

"What kind?"

"No, I'm *asking* you. What kind of car is it?"

"Oh. Ford. Model P, Papa says."

I couldn't resist groaning. "Model T?" Only the most common car in the country. We'd seen seven just since we left the house, not counting the one that belonged to my family.

Cole had giggled. "Model T and Model P *rhyme!*"

So Lydia had been talking to someone—who could have been anyone—in a Model T. I asked if he saw what the driver looked like. Which had begun a long line of fruitless questions.

"Could you tell what color of hair the man had?"

"I don't know."

"Was there one person in the car, or more?"

"I don't know. Hey, look, an ant."

"Did you see what he was wearing?"

Cole shrugged. Poked at the ant.

But, finally, I landed on the right question. "When did Lydia do this, Cole?" I held up my finger like a one.

"I knocked on the window and waved to her. She did that and got in the car."

No struggle? "Did she do anything else with her hands? Or say anything?"

"No," Cole said. But then he pointed down the road. "Just this."

"Just what?"

"This." He kept pointing.

"She pointed at something?"

Cole nodded.

"At what?"

He shrugged.

"When did she do that?"

"When she was talking to the car."

"So she pointed down the street before she showed you the one? Did she do anything else?"

"Just some talking." Cole shrugged. "Butterfly!" And he was off to follow it.

My stomach clenched like a fist as I followed him on numb legs. She had gotten in the car. Willingly. The implications made my stomach feel sloshy. Had she known the driver? Could it be—I loathed to even think it—Matthew?

But it wouldn't take much to talk Lydia into a car. She was easy to convince, after all. Despite the questions pulsing in my head, I let Cole prattle on about other matters—rocks and colors and bugs—for another ten minutes. He seemed lighter than he had been before telling me about Lydia, and I wanted him good and relaxed before I dug for the answer to the big question.

A passing police car provided the perfect opportunity. I lifted him off the ground so he could see the car far down the road. "Have you ever gotten to talk to a policeman before, Cole?"

He frowned as he thought. "No."

"Even after Lydia made the one and got in the car? You didn't talk to any policemen about it?"

"No." He craned his neck, trying to watch the car at an impossible distance.

"Did you tell your mother about it?"

"She was sleeping. That was when she still had her big belly. Down, please."

I returned him to the ground. "What about your father?"

Instead of skipping ahead, he took my hand again. "I'm not allowed to talk about Lydia to Papa. But sometimes, I forget."

I thought of the stripes on his backside, and my stomach tightened. "Did you try to tell him about Lydia? I mean, a long time ago when you saw her get in the car?"

"I don't know."

I closed my eyes. *Yes, you do, Cole. It's in there, I know it is.* "Did your papa talk to the police about Lydia?"

"They came to the house when I was in my room with Dottie. I wasn't supposed to go down there, though."

"Did your papa tell them about what you saw?"

Cole's face scrunched. "I don't know. I don't think so, cuz he doesn't like to talk about her. When I do, he just says, 'You stop talking about that.'" Cole deepened his voice and made a lecturing motion with his pointer finger. "'You know not to do that.'" Cole sighed. "Sometimes, I forget."

I squeezed his hand. "It's okay to forget with me, remember? We can talk about Lydia together, and it'll be our secret."

Cole beamed up at me. "I like you."

"I like you too, Cole." And, oddly, I wasn't lying.

Cole squeezed my hand back. "Maybe when Lydia comes home, you can both come play with me."

I hadn't known what to say. Even now, sitting on my porch with hours of hindsight, the right answer eludes me. How do you explain to a five-year-old that a sweet girl who did nothing wrong was taken from this very street? That she was bound and gagged and killed for no clear reason. That she won't be coming home.

I flip through my notebook, to where I had described Mr. Barrow for Mariano's benefit. I don't like the man, but I find myself asking the same question Mariano posed last night. Even aside from the fact that Mariano has verified his alibi, what did he have to gain by kidnapping and killing Lydia?

But really, who had anything to gain from it?

"Hello, Piper."

I look up from my notes and find Emma Crane at the fence, smiling in that soft way of hers. Sidekick romps for the front gate and puts his paws up on the bars.

"Sidekick—down."

"What a sweet dog." Emma reaches to pat his head with a gloved hand, and he scurries out of reach. Some guard dog. "Could I join you for a bit?"

I put on a smile and set aside my notebook. "Of course."

Emma undoes the hinge and squeezes through so as not to let Sidekick out of the yard. Emma's face has more of a glow than normal. Perhaps it's the feminine pale pink of her drop-waist dress, or the effect of summer days spent on the lake.

"Would you care to go inside?"

"No, this is fine." Emma settles beside me on the step. "How are you doing, Piper? And please don't feel the need to be overly polite with me."

"I'm . . . okay, I suppose. It's a day-to-day thing."

"You've been on my mind a lot these last weeks. I won't pretend to understand what it feels like to lose your best friend in such a way, but I imagine it's too terrible for words."

My throat is tight as I hold back tears, and I have to wait a moment before I can squeeze out a watery, "Thank you, Emma."

"I know we've never been close, but I've always admired you and Lydia from a distance." Emma's smile is shy. "Especially you."

Her words remind me that she's a full year behind me in school. "I don't deserve admiration, Emma, but thank you."

"I disagree." Emma's eyes spark. "And my brother would too. He's quite taken with you, as I'm sure you realize. Since Jeremiah is about as subtle as a freight train."

A nervous laugh sticks in my chest. How would Lydia respond to something like this? A demure laugh, perhaps. Then she would redirect the conversation to Emma somehow.

But Emma doesn't seem to require my response. "You know, it was all over school that you've been investigating what happened to Lydia. That you even ditched school one day to help that detective."

I feel my jaw fall open. "How would anybody know that?"

"Just rumors. You know how it is. People have to talk about something." Emma shrugs her narrow shoulders. "So I came by today because I wondered how much you would charge somebody if they wanted you to look into something for them."

Emma's eyes, lake blue like Jeremiah's, have an unfamiliar gleam in them.

"How do you mean, 'look into something'?"

"I mean, if they had something they wanted you to investigate."

This is quiet Emma Crane, right? Emma, who's so reserved, I sometimes don't notice when she's joined a conversation? How can she be asking what I think she is? "Emma . . . ?"

She holds her gaze to mine, seeming to have no interest in answering my unasked question.

"What are you asking me to investigate for you?"

"I've been dating this guy, Robbie, since the spring. I was at the *Daily Chicagoan* offices, waiting for Jeremiah. Robbie was waiting for someone too, and we started talking, and . . . well, we really hit it off. We've had quite a few dates, and he's even come to family dinners a few times."

"But?"

Emma's wistful smile slips. "There's something he's keeping from me. He says he can't talk about his work, that it's a violation of his oath or something. Robbie tells me that 'in time,' it'll all come out. But meanwhile . . . I think I might love him. And I don't want to let myself get in any deeper if . . . Well, you know."

"It might not be something bad." But even I hear the doubt in my voice. "He might just work for the government or something."

"Maybe."

"What do your parents think?"

"Oh, they adore Robbie. But they think he works with the railroad. He told me ahead of time that he would have to tell them a fake story, but that he cares enough about me and will eventually tell me the truth. Or a part of it, anyway." Emma clutches her cloche to her head as a gust of wind sweeps down the street.

My hair breaks free of some of its pins, but I don't bother to capture it until the gust has passed. "So, eventually, you'll find out what he actually does."

"That's what he says."

"So you could just wait. Could just trust him to tell you when the timing is right." But I couldn't do that. If I thought Mariano were lying about who he was, there's no way I would just sit back and wait for him to tell me in his own time.

"I thought about that." Emma's voice is quiet, but strong too. "And I asked myself what you would do."

"What I would do? Emma, I'm no example to follow."

She cocks her head at me. "Says who?"

Anyone and everyone.

I take a deep breath. "You're so sweet and kind. You don't want to be like me."

Emma evaluates me for a moment. "How much would you charge?"

"I'm not a professional. I have no idea."

"What would make it worth your time?"

I sigh. "Seriously, Emma, I wouldn't know what I was doing. Yes, I did some poking around after Lydia went missing, but it's not like I figured anything out."

"How much would you charge to help me, Piper?" Her jaw has a determined set to it, like Jeremiah's gets sometimes. "Truly, who else could I ask? No one."

That's valid.

"If you'd like," I say in a measured voice, "I'll see what I can dig up on Robbie. But I'm not going to charge you for it when I have no idea what I'm doing."

She's already opening her small, beaded handbag. "Is five enough to get you started? Or should it be ten? Ten, right?"

"Emma, I said—"

She shoves the bill into my hand. "If you need more, let me know." Her bag snaps shut. "Robbie and I are seeing a movie this evening. You should join us so you can meet him."

"Okay." I slip the money into my pocket. Maybe the night out will provide the mental break I need to figure out how to proceed with David Barrow. "What time?"

"The movie is at seven." Emma rests her hand on her cloche as another blast of wind whips down the street. "It'll be so nice having someone to distract my big brother."

I blink at her several times.

"You don't mind, do you? If Jeremiah is with us?" She winks, clearly expecting that this is a welcome surprise.

And is it?

Emma's bright expression fades. "Oh, I'm sorry. I thought you liked my brother."

Get it together, Piper. "I do. I mean, he's very nice." I take a deep breath. "It's a little complicated, because I went out with someone last night. Someone who"—I can feel the color in my cheeks rising—"I like a lot."

Emma's eyes flicker with interest. "And would this someone happen to be an extremely handsome detective?"

My flush deepens. "Yes."

Emma's sigh is regretful. "Poor big brother."

"Do I need to tell Mariano about tonight, do you think?" I gnaw at my thumbnail. "We've only had one date. I don't want him to think that I think we're more serious than we are . . ."

"This is 1924, Piper." Emma shrugs, and somehow it seems saucy. "A girl has a right to explore options. And it's not like Jeremiah asked you out, right?"

Before this conversation, I would have described Emma as meek and a bit mousy. But when I wasn't paying attention, she grew up.

What else has changed while I wasn't looking?

"Cassano speaking."

I smile at the crisp sound of his detective voice. "Hi. It's Piper."

"Hi." His voice warms. "I didn't think I would hear from you today."

"Why not?"

"Aren't I supposed to call you?"

"Are you?"

Mariano's chuckle holds amusement. "Never mind. I was going to call after work, though. In case you wondered."

My stomach gives a surprised flutter. *You wouldn't have been able to reach me. Because I'll be on an investigation that turned into a double date.*

I'm not ready to talk about that yet. "I had an opportunity to talk with Cole Barrow this morning. I thought you'd be interested in what he had to say."

Glancing at my notes a time or two, I recount Cole's story for Mariano.

When I'm done, he mutters an expletive. Then, "Sorry."

"I live in a house full of lawyers. I'm fine."

Mariano is silent.

I stare at the stripes of yellow sunlight on Father's office floor, and my mind fixes on the purple and blue stripes on Cole's skin. "He beats Cole to keep him quiet. I hate him."

Mariano's exhale is shaky. "Please don't let yourself be alone with him, okay?"

"Cole?"

"No. David Barrow."

My heart hitches. "I thought you said you verified his alibi."

"I don't think he killed Lydia, but he's certainly a weasel."

"Definitely."

"Sometimes, I hate this job." Mariano's voice has a darkness to it, and I want to be able to hold him. Want to wrap my arms around his waist, squeeze, and say that it's all going to be okay.

Even if we both know it isn't. "I've got a front row seat to all the hurt, all the evil. And I can do nothing."

I pull the telephone closer to me. "Not nothing, Mariano. You help people all the time."

"We try. But it seems we're always too late. We're always working from behind."

"You can't right every wrong."

"I really wanted to right the wrong done to you, though." His voice is quiet, husky.

My eyes pool. "You did your best." Several tears roll down my cheeks and plop onto my gray skirt. "I wish we were having this talk face to face."

Mariano drags in a breath. "Do I sound too desperate if I ask what your plans are tonight?"

Oh. There's my open door. "I would love to see you, but I already agreed to see a movie with Emma Crane and her boy-friend tonight."

"Her name is familiar. Is she a neighbor?"

"Yes. And a Presley's girl."

"Her family owns the *Daily Chicagoan*, right? Her brother is . . . Jeremy?"

"Jeremiah." I wrap the phone cord around my finger. "I would ask you along, but . . . Well, this sounds silly, but Emma asked me to help her out with something. An investigation of sorts." My swallow is loud in Father's office. "And after I said I would, Emma told me that Jeremiah would be there too."

"Of course he will." Mariano's words are dry, but I don't think he's angry. Or maybe that's how he sounds when he's angry. There hasn't been time yet to find out. "What kind of investigation is this, Detective Sail?"

I smirk, but Sidekick is the only one who sees. "You're not asking me to share classified details, are you?"

"Of course I am. And now imagine me batting my eyelashes at you."

"It's something about her boyfriend. Emma just wants my opinion, I guess."

"And a date to distract her brother?"

"It's not like that. I told Emma about you. She knows we're . . ."

"We're what?" Now Mariano sounds amused.

"That we had a date last night." I release the cord that I'd wrapped around my finger, watch it unravel just like my control of this conversation seems to be. "That we're seeing each other."

"Well, I hope it goes well tonight. When you get in, will you call me?"

"Of course."

Mariano gives me the number to his apartment, and then we hang up.

The scent of Joyce's pot roast sneaks into Father's office, drawing out a memory of Lydia staying for dinner. "I think this is what pot roast must taste like in heaven, Joyce," she had said.

Part of me tries to push away the memory of my friend—her sincere smile, her face lit with the soft glow of the chandelier—and the lonely ache that comes with it. Another part of me wants to lean into the memory, play it again and again, wallow around in the words.

I unclasp my locket and look at Lydia's face. "I'm going to figure out what happened to you." My words are an unintentional whisper, as if Father's ordinary office has turned into a holy place. A place where Lydia might be able to hear me. "I will figure out what happened, and I will make them pay."

A toast." Father raises his glass of red wine high and beams at us all. "To my wonderful children, and to the beautiful woman who in one week will be Mrs. Sail. I'm a lucky man."

I turn to half-heartedly clink my glass against Tim's, and then turn to my right to clink with Alana, who somehow snuck her way into our family dinner. She smiles at me, all teeth.

I try to smile back.

"It's starting to feel so real with most of my belongings moved in." Jane beams at me from the head of the table. "Piper, you're such a sweetheart to let me store some of my boxes in your bedroom."

I don't recall being given a choice.

That's no way to talk to your almost stepmother, Lydia admonishes.

I smile and spoon myself a helping of mashed potatoes. "It's no problem."

The invasion began this afternoon while I was on the phone with Mariano. I had come out of Father's office to find thick-armed, sweating men unloading boxes. Of course I knew Jane must have items of her own that she would want at her new residence, and yet it had undone something inside me to find Joyce packing away all of Mother's china and replacing it with the new pattern Jane had picked out.

"I'll be sure to wrap this up nicely so it's ready for you, my dear," Joyce had said to me in that soft voice of hers.

They're only dishes, I had told myself. *Just plates, cups, and bowls. Nothing more.*

Still, I hid myself on the back porch and cried.

"I'm delighted that everyone was able to be here tonight for a family dinner." Jane slices her green bean into three equal parts. "This next week will be so busy that I imagine this is our last chance to be together before the big day."

I can only hope.

"It will be so wonderful to have another female in the family," Gretchen pipes up in her perky voice. I don't have to look to know she's wearing her practiced debutante smile. "Piper and I have been rather outnumbered all these years. Haven't we, Piper?"

"Piper must have been so glad when you joined the family, Gretchen." Jane smiles and shifts her gaze between the two of us.

It's clear we're all waiting for me to agree.

"Extremely." I put on my sweetest smile. I've no intentions of ruffling feathers this evening. Not when I still need to tell my father that I'm going out with Emma this evening.

My thoughts flit to Jeremiah. What, exactly, does he expect tonight? Does he also think we're two chums seeing a movie with his sister and her boyfriend? Does he believe this is a date? Did Emma tell him I'm seeing Mariano, or will I need to?

"Mother thought it was a terrible idea, but Father understands that this is part of the job." Alana's voice awakens me to a new conversation that's happening. "When your father owns the paper, you have to learn it all, whether you're a female or not."

Jane is nodding along with Alana as she continues to meticulously slice her green beans into thirds. "And do you have any siblings?"

Something inside me gives a twist at the sight of Jane playing the matriarch role. Of knowing that I had better get used to it.

"No, just me. Which is why I'll someday take over *The Star*."

"Quite a job for a young woman."

Alana's laugh is a throaty chuckle. "I've always been good with a challenge."

The last of her words are covered by Gretchen, who exclaims when Howie knocks over his glass of milk onto his food.

As the spill is being cleaned and Howie is being calmed, Alana's fingers feather against my arm. "Piper." Her voice is low in my ear. "I know we got off to a rough start, but now that I'm seeing your brother, I hope we can get along."

She's trying to be kind. I have to remind myself of that so I don't snatch my arm away from her touch. "Thank you," I murmur. Without Lydia's voice whispering to me, I have to tell myself to be politely appreciative. "I would like that too."

"I was wondering if you might be willing to talk about—"

But from my other side, Tim nudges me. He holds out the fresh plate that Joyce brought for Howie. "Could you spoon some mashed potatoes on here for me?"

"Sure."

Tim's eyes hold their characteristic tenderness. "How are you doing tonight, little sister?"

I angle toward him, thankful for the rescue from Alana's pestering. "I don't know."

He flicks his gaze toward Jane. "Same here."

I glance around the table. Father and Nick are discussing something baseball related, while Alana listens with either interest or a good imitation of it. Jane and Gretchen are commiserating about the stress of being a bride. Jane watches Howie with a look of obvious longing, and I'm struck with a new fear—will she and Father have children? I can't imagine Father wanting that, not now that he's already a grandfather, but Jane is so young . . .

"You know"—Tim's voice reaches out for me—"you're always welcome at our place. Gretchen would love it."

"Thank you, Tim. That's very kind of you."

Tim's smile says *I know you, sister.* "Howie no longer cries like he used to. Most of his teeth are in now. And"—he drops his volume even lower—"Gretchen has really relaxed. We had tried so long to have a baby, that . . . Well, I know her enthusiasm for motherhood grated on you."

As did her excessive enthusiasm for being a wife. And before that, for being a bride. And before that . . .

I glance at Jane and Gretchen, bonding over ballroom sizes and flowers. Things I can't imagine caring about. Despite Gretchen's obnoxious enthusiasm for all things feminine, she *is* kind. And thoughtful. I can't imagine *her* marrying a man solely for money.

Or is Jane? I touch my locket and think of Father crediting her with the idea to put Lydia's photograph in Mother's present. I push the thought away.

"Once they're back from their honeymoon, I imagine I'll be ready to get away for a few days." I wink at him. "Or years."

"Oh, Pippy. You'll be married and establishing your own house before too long, I imagine."

I snort and take a large bite of buttery mashed potatoes.

"You can't fool me. Do you think I'm unaware that you've been receiving attention from a certain detective?"

I'm glad I took such a large bite and can't be expected to immediately respond.

"You realize, don't you, that if Father wasn't otherwise occupied"—Tim nods to Jane—"you probably wouldn't be getting away with staying out until midnight with a man."

I roll my eyes even as my heart pounds in my chest. "What, are you spying on the place?"

Tim grins. "I have my sources."

"Nick should really keep his mouth shut."

Tim laughs as he forks a bite of pot roast. "So, has Father talked to you at all about Mariano, or is he counting on Joyce to rein you in?"

"Rein me in? Like I'm some wayward adolescent."

"Not wayward." Tim's smile is kind. "Just an adolescent. With her first boyfriend."

My stomach knots at the word. "If Father and I aren't arguing from time to time, then clearly I'm doing this whole thing incorrectly. Our generation is so vastly different than our parents', more so than any generation before, that some clash is inevitable."

Tim's eyebrows arch.

"I read that in a column," I admit with a laugh. "It was advice on wild young people, or something."

"On one hand, it sounded far too adult for my kid sister. On the other . . ." Tim takes me in with a serious gaze. "You've grown up a lot this last month, Pippy. You've been forced to."

A lump rises in my throat as Lydia's ghost settles between us.

Joyce bustles into the room and whispers something in my father's ear. His gaze travels across the table to me. "Piper, it seems there's a young man at the door for you."

I glance at the grandfather clock. But they weren't supposed to be here for another . . . Oh, wait. If the movie starts at seven, then of course they would need to pick me up now.

I lay my napkin beside my plate. "Jeremiah and Emma Crane have invited me to see a movie tonight. I didn't mean to surprise you with it, but I didn't think you would be upset."

Jane's lips pout, like Howie's when he's on the verge of tears. "Oh, I had so looked forward to enjoying a family dinner."

"And so we have, Jane, dear. We just won't have a family dessert." Father waves me away with a smile. "Run along, Piper. Have a wonderful evening."

Jeremiah stands in the entryway looking like his normal, well-groomed self. He sweeps his trilby from his head and nods to me. "Sorry to interrupt your dinner."

"Not your fault. Where are Emma and Robbie?"

"In the car." He grins down at me as he settles his hat back on his head. His blue eyes have a unique sparkle to them, one that I can't quite read. "You look beautiful, Piper." While he doesn't make my stomach swirl like Mariano, there's something undeniably fetching about him.

"Thank you. You . . . look very nice too." What an awkward thing to say. I reach for my handbag on the coatrack only to find it isn't there. "I must have left my bag in my room. This will only take a second."

"Take your time," Jeremiah says as I clatter up the stairs.

Yep, there it is, on my bed. I had loaded it earlier in preparation for my night out, including my notebook, Nick's pocket knife, and several other unorthodox items to take on a double date.

On a *fake* double date.

I snatch the bag, pivot toward the door, and pause.

My nightstand drawer is open.

Just an inch or so, but my most important belongings are in there. I never leave it open.

I slide the drawer open all the way and survey the contents. Everything seems to be here—several photographs of and cards from Lydia and Mother, Mother's Bible, and Matthew's letter are still in their places. Yet I can't shake away the unease.

I close the drawer and look around. There were movers in my room this afternoon, stacking Jane's boxes in the corner. Perhaps they bumped my nightstand? Or it could have been Joyce when she changed sheets. Maybe her skirt or the sheet snagged on the knob and pulled the drawer out?

Regardless of how it happened, nothing's missing. No harm done.

Right?

Downstairs, Jeremiah offers me his arm with a confident smile, and we leave the house.

When I've pulled the door shut behind us, Jeremiah bends his head close to mine. "I was relieved to hear you'd be joining us tonight. Robbie is a nice enough guy, but that's my sister he's getting cozy with, you know?"

I scrunch my nose, thinking of times that I've heard Jane gush about romantic gestures from my father. "I do."

Parked outside my house is Robbie's automobile, an older model with no top. My hair will be a wreck by the time we reach the theater. The driver—Robbie, I presume—has his hat pulled low, and Emma waves and smiles from the passenger seat.

Oh. I'll be riding in the back with Jeremiah. For some reason, I had imagined the boys riding up front. But this is part of the work I'm doing for Emma. It's fine. Mariano knows what's going on.

And how should I bring up Mariano to Jeremiah? Should I just say it? *You should know that I'm seeing someone. And that he carries a gun. Or should I be more subtle? Have you ever tried Pompei's? I had it for the first time last night with Detective Cassano.*

"My sister informs me that I have some competition." Jeremiah's words are low and almost playful as he holds open the front gate for me.

I pause and look up at him.

He grins, clearly pleased to have caught me off guard. "Did you not intend for me to know?"

"It's not that. I wasn't sure about the proper way to bring it up."

"Well, Emma did your dirty work for you."

He seems unaffected. Have I been wrong about his interest in me? This will certainly be much easier if I was.

At the car, Jeremiah holds the handle of the backseat door, but doesn't open it right away. "In my line of work, where competition is inevitable, you learn quickly that you have a choice about how to deal with it. You can wilt, you can grow paranoid, or you can use it as motivation to work hard and let the best man win." His gaze skims my face, lingering on my mouth before meeting my eyes again. "I choose the third."

I don't know how to answer, but that doesn't seem to bother Jeremiah. He opens the door and gestures for me to climb inside.

"Why, hello girls."

I look up from washing my hands and find Mrs. Barrow smiling at me and Emma in the bathroom mirror. "Oh, hello."

"It makes me feel very young and hip to be at the same place you are on a Saturday night." Mrs. Barrow offers a showy sigh.

"Though, David and I caught the earlier movie and are on our way home. The boys just don't sleep well if I'm not there."

"How nice it must feel to get out, though." Emma offers her lipstick to me, and I shake my head no.

"I don't want to give your brother the wrong impression."

Mrs. Barrow grins. "I wondered what girl was lucky enough to be here with Jeremiah Crane. You put that lipstick on, honey. He's a catch."

Emma snaps the lid back on her makeup. "She's already caught him. But Piper has a cute boyfriend. Detective Cassano, who helped with Lydia LeVine's case. That young one?"

Mrs. Barrow pulls out her own compact, clearly intending to prolong the girl talk. "He's cute all right, but a detective? You won't have two nickels to rub together, doll."

Better to be poor and married to someone honorable than wed to a rich devil in disguise like David Barrow. I wonder . . .

"Mrs. Barrow, maybe you could help us out with something. We're hoping to go out after the show. Someplace where we could dance and get a gin fizz or two. Surely you know of a good place."

I ignore the confused look Emma gives me.

Mrs. Barrow laughs, and her delight at being perceived as a lady who would know such things is obvious. "You two girls are so fresh and young, I imagine any place I've heard of, you've heard of."

"I don't know anywhere outside of John Barleycorn—"

Mrs. Barrow's mouth presses into a line—excellent. "Anywhere but *there* is fine with me. David goes there because the men from work like it, but it's awfully awkward when he runs into the nanny who used to work for us. Have you heard about this? Here I was, eight months pregnant, and she quit with no warning. As if working in a speakeasy was some lifelong dream of hers."

"Terrible." I infuse my voice with sympathy.

"Just awful," Emma adds.

Mrs. Barrow snaps shut her compact and thrusts it into her handbag. "You think you know a person, and then they just walk right out on you. David knows I hate him going there, but being invited to Friday night pool is a coveted thing. Good for his career, you know. How can I refuse that?"

"You can't, of course. I'm sorry to have upset you. I just thought you'd be the one to ask advice."

Mrs. Barrow seems mollified by the compliment. "Green Door Tavern. If David and I meet up with friends, that's where we go. Your father will have my head if he learns I told you that."

But she can't hide how pleased she is by the conversation.

As we leave the restroom, Emma murmurs, "What, exactly, did I just witness?"

I grin. "Nothing at all. Certainly nothing that should be repeated to anybody else."

Friday night pool. I wonder what Mariano would think about hanging around John Barleycorn next Friday and seeing if David Barrow shows.

Jeremiah and Robbie are waiting in front of the theater with popcorn and Coca-Colas. Robbie is pleasant but ordinary looking—brown hair, brown eyes, and skin that's neither tan nor noticeably fair. If I were trying to describe him to Mariano—goose bumps raise on my arm—I could just as easily be describing thousands of other American men.

When we settle into our seats, Emma arranges it so that Robbie and I are next to each other. Jeremiah offers me popcorn, but I wave him away. I only have a few minutes before the movie starts to talk to Robbie.

"I hear you're new to Chicago, Mr. Thomas."

"Call me Robbie, please. And, yes. I am."

"Where are you from?"

"Here and there." He shrugs and flashes an easy smile. "I've lived all over."

"Is work the reason that you move so much?"

"Yes and no. But I hope to settle in Chicago." He takes Emma's hand in his and squeezes it. She beams up at him as if he's wearing a halo.

And with those vague answers? My guess is he does *not*.

Robbie turns to Emma, and speaks in a voice so quiet that he undoubtedly means for their conversation to be private.

Hmm. What now?

"Why, exactly"—Jeremiah's whispered words are warm in my ear—"are you casing Emma's boyfriend?"

I turn to him and put on a smile. "Who, me?"

He chuckles. "It's nice that you're looking out for her."

He again offers me the bag of popcorn, but I would have to lean quite close to him to reach. I shake my head. With a roll of his eyes, he extends his arm farther, and I take a handful.

"How are you doing, Piper? Really?" The thoughtfulness of his tone makes me squash the temptation to lie.

"I don't know." I take a deep breath and think of all the ways I could expound on that. How sometimes, as impossible as it seems, I forget what happened to Lydia, and I think about calling her. Only to be crushed when I realize I never will again. Or I could say that I still think about that day and the days following, hunting for clues that I might have missed. Or that most mornings I have to lie to myself just to be able to get out of bed.

But nothing seems quite right, so I just shrug at him and say again, "I don't know."

"When I heard the news about Matthew, I couldn't believe it. Thinking about all the times I saw you girls get in the car with him . . ."

"Well." I pluck at the hem of my navy skirt, re-draping it over my knees. "Innocent until proven guilty, and all that jazz."

Jeremiah's blue gaze holds unnervingly steady on me. "Piper Sail, do you have another suspect in mind?"

"Who's asking? Jeremiah, my friend and neighbor? Or Jeremiah, the newspaper man?"

"To whom will you tell the honest answer?"

I laugh and stretch my hand out for the popcorn. "Neither of you."

Jeremiah pulls the bag closer to his chest, and grasps my reaching hand. "We'd be good together, Piper. Just promise me you'll think about it."

The smile drains from my face as I look at him. Had things gone differently, Jeremiah could've been the highlight of my summer. Handsome, smart, and not afraid to meet me quip for quip, he would've been everything I could have hoped for in a boyfriend. We should've had many dates like this, only with my thoughts full of *him* rather than Mariano.

Could've. Would've. Should've.

Losing Lydia, it seems, has left nothing untouched.

CHAPTER
EIGHTEEN

iper, honey, you really need to get your dress on," Jane says from the doorway of Father's office. "The seamstress is going to be here in fifteen minutes."

I keep my gaze on the phone as she speaks. "My dress fits perfectly."

"That can change from week to week. Even for a girl of your age. Now be a good girl, and come up to get your dress on."

"I will when I'm finished here."

"How much longer will this . . . this thing you're doing take?" Jane's voice grows ever sweeter, a sure sign that her patience with me is waning.

"It depends." I lift my eyes and beam a bright smile Jane's way. "How much longer do you intend to delay me?"

Her shiny red mouth purses. "Fine. Come up as soon as you're done. And, Piper . . . I'm not your mother—"

Well, this oughta be good. I raise my eyebrows at her—a silent challenge.

Jane presses her mouth shut as her gaze skims the kimono I've wrapped over my nightgown. "Walter will be here soon, you know."

The implications are as loud and clear as if she spoke them—*You're dressed indecently. Go put clothes on.*

I keep my anger shoved down in my chest and make my

voice sunny. "Thank you. Now, may I finish making my phone call, or would you like to belabor this conversation?"

I don't wait for a response, just start dialing Mariano's number once more.

"I'll see you upstairs, Piper." Jane's words are stiff, and her footsteps loud in the hallway.

I've nearly finished dialing when Joyce pads into the room, coffeepot in hand. "You'll have to learn to get along with her, you know."

I hang up the phone. Yet again. "I'm hoping to prove you wrong on this one."

She fills my cup with steaming black coffee. "She's doing a hard thing, marrying into a family with three grown children—"

"Well, nobody asked her to do that."

"Actually, Piper, your father did." Joyce lets this sit a beat. "You don't really want him rattling around this big house all alone, do you?"

I look away from her accusing eyes and draw Father's telephone close to me. "I'm trying to make a phone call."

Joyce's disapproval stings, like it always does. It's not that I want Father to be alone forever. Not if he's unhappy about it. What I want is for him to *want* to be alone. I want to know that he misses Mother more than he loves Jane.

What an unfair thing to ask of someone.

I shake the thoughts away as the operator transfers me to Mariano. "Hi, it's me."

"Let me guess. You want something."

His words cause hesitation. Denying the truth would be pointless, wouldn't it? "How do you know?"

"Your words are always a bit clipped when you call wanting something. What is it?"

"Well . . ." I feel inexplicably cross over him calling me out. "We don't have to talk about it immediately. You can tell me how your day is going or something."

Mariano chuckles. "My day is fine. What are you wanting?"

I sip at my coffee, wincing when it burns my tongue. "What are your plans tonight? What do you think of going to John Barleycorn?"

Mariano snorts a laugh. "You're aware I'm an officer of the law, right? That being seen in a gin joint might not be great for my career."

"If you're working, it would be fine, right?"

Now he sighs. "I know David Barrow is at the top of your list, but his alibi—"

"How'd you know?"

"Know what? That you're going after your favorite neighbor?"

"Yeah."

"Because Friday nights are his pool nights, and why else would you be going there?"

"Friday night pool is a real thing? I figured it was just a story he told his wife."

"I'm guessing he doesn't tell her that he meets his girlfriend there."

Yuck. "That's disgusting."

"But it's not evidence of homicide. No matter how much we wish it were."

I blow a limp strand of hair from my face. "Are you free tonight? I don't want to wait until next week."

Mariano sighs. "I'm not, actually. I have a report due, and

the office has been so crazy that I can't seem to get it done. But I could probably help you chase David Barrow next week, if you want."

I tap my fingers on Father's desk. Next week is awfully far away. "How does a person get in? Do you need a password still, or is that not a thing anymore?"

"Piper." He says my name as a warning.

Mother's words float back to me. *Trust yourself.* I can't wait a whole week. I just can't. "I won't even talk to him, I promise. I just want to . . . observe, I guess. It's a hunch."

"And your hunch can't sit safely at home for a few days?"

"I'll take Emma with me—"

Mariano snorts. "Pick a different person. Someone male and scary. Is Walter in town yet?"

"Yes, actually. Or he will be within the hour."

"If you can talk him into going with you, fine. So long as you're not planning to approach David Barrow. You're not, right?"

"I told you, I just want to watch him."

Mariano sighs. "You won't be the easiest girl to care about, will you?"

"I'm afraid you're in no position to complain, detective. Now tell me how to get in."

There's silence, and for a moment I think Mariano won't help.

"You won't need a password." His tone is resigned. "You're a pretty girl, so all you'll need to say is 'Joe sent me.' There's a Chinese laundry on the east side of the old saloon. Go through there. And call me at the office when you get home. And don't stay out late."

"Okay, thank you." Feminine chatter floats down the hall to me. The other bridesmaids must be here. "I have to go."

"So do I. Be careful."

"It's more likely that I'll die from boredom during my last dress fitting than I will from being out tonight."

Peels of girlish laughter reach me in Father's office. This afternoon may be destined to be a complete waste of my time, but I don't intend for my evening to be.

"This is ridiculous," Walter mutters as we navigate crowded Lincoln Avenue. "Hey, don't walk ahead of me."

"Then pick up the pace. Your legs are twice as long as mine. Surely you can walk faster than that."

"Forgive me for not rushing on this insane errand of yours." But Walter catches up and takes a protective hold of my arm. "You've never been in a place like this, Pippy. It'll be dirty. It'll be loud. There will be lots of drunks."

"Which is why I'm not going alone." My voice sounds brave, but Walter's words have me shaking in my core. In my beaded sleeveless dress, my diadem, and made-up face, I'm miserably far out of my comfort zone. Snitching a pastry from the teacher's room within the ivy-covered walls of Presley's is vastly different than sneaking into a speakeasy.

The boarded-up windows of the old saloon come into view. And there, just as Mariano said, is the Chinese laundry next door.

Walter stops walking and holds me in place there at the corner of Lincoln and Belden. Pedestrians—mostly other couples in their Friday night finest—stream around us. "Just let it go." His eyes plead. "What can David Barrow tell us that's so urgent, really? Lydia's already—" Walter swallows the word. "Sorry."

"You don't have to come in if you don't want." My words are ice. Here I'm already plenty nervous, and now I have to drag Walter in there with me. I pull my arm out of his grasp and don't allow myself to look over my shoulder to see if he's following.

To my relief, he is.

He holds open the door to the Chinese laundry and practically steps on my heels following me in. Inside, the air hums with the hiss and clank of washers and the chatter of foreign working women. The pungent scent of lye makes my head throb.

The man at the counter—olive skinned, with broad shoulders and beefy arms—stares at us.

"Um, hi." My thumb runs down the chain of my locket and back up. "Joe sent us?" The words curl into an unintentional question, and I wish I could snatch them back and try again.

But the bouncer jerks a thumb over his shoulder, toward a hall. "That way, doll face. Follow the others."

When I force myself to smile and say, "Thank you," I receive a wink.

Walter presses a hand into my lower back as I follow the echo of footsteps down the hall, and down the staircase. In the basement of the laundry, we find groups of giggling college girls, men talking loud and boisterously, and couples decked out to dance, all waiting to cram into a small elevator that will carry us back up to the old saloon. Most of the girls are dressed similar to me—sparkling, sleeveless dresses and painted mouths. At least I look okay.

"Let's make this as fast as we can." Walter's mouth is close to my ear. "This is no place for you to linger, Pippy."

"I'm doing what I have to in order to get the information I need." Words I never had to say to Mariano when we were on Clark Street.

His expressive eyes hold sadness. "She's not coming back. And you need to figure out how far is too far before you accidentally cross a line you never intended to."

I turn away, eyes blurred and heart hardened.

Inside John Barleycorn, the smoky air is rich with jazz music. On the dance floor, the sequins and beads of the girls' dresses sparkle when they catch on the stage lights. Despite several fans, the air has a stuffy quality to it, though perhaps it's only the boarded-up windows that leave me feeling slightly claustrophobic. Waitresses, showing a shocking amount of leg in their black dresses, saunter around the room with mugs of beer, shimmering cocktails, and plates of fried food.

I skim the crowd in hopes of spotting David Barrow quickly. "Let's pick a table," Walter says as he practically pushes me toward an empty high top. "I don't want to just stand here."

"Wait." I squint through the smoke. Near the stage is a girl that looks like the Barrows' ex-nanny. It's a little hard to tell, because the waitresses have an intentionally monotonous look to them—bobbed hair and mile-long legs—but she seems familiar. "Isn't that their old nanny?"

Walter follows my gaze. "Maybe."

"I think it is." I grab Walter's hand and pull him through the crowd.

"Pippy, there are no open tables up there!" He has to yell to be heard over the heart-piercing wail of the saxophone.

"I don't need a table. I need to talk to their nanny!" If only I could think of her name . . .

I press against the wall, and keep my gaze trained on her as best I can through the crush of people on the dance floor. Annie? That doesn't sound quite right. Anita?

Same as the night I danced with Mariano at Vernon Park, some couples are far more demonstrative than seems appropriate for public viewing. I glance at Walter, and find him watching the dancers with a wistful expression. He is far, far away from here.

"What are you thinking about?" I yell over the music.

He startles and offers a sheepish smile. "Audrey."

A feeling of betrayal jabs at my heart. Our thoughts used to be so aligned. "Thick as thieves," Joyce would describe us. "Attached at the hip." Now he has his world—Audrey and baseball and the lemony sunshine of California—and I have mine. Which is mourning Lydia, missing Lydia, and figuring out who killed Lydia.

In my peripheral, I catch the nanny breezing by us, and her name pops out of my mouth. "Annette!"

She whirls at the sound. Annette is older than me by a good five years, but she has the face of a girl—rosebud lips and wide eyes set in a heart-shaped face.

"I don't know if you remember me, but my name is Piper Sail, and I was friends with Lydia LeVine, who—"

"I know who Lydia is."

"I thought maybe you could help me. I'm trying to figure out what happened to her, and I think maybe David Barrow might know something, and that with you having recently been employed with the Barrows—"

Her face turns from blank to stony. "My boss doesn't care for me jabbering during work hours."

"It'll only take a minute." Behind her, a young, wiry boy wipes a table clean, loading the empty plates and glasses into a tub. "We'll sit right there. And we'll order drinks. And we'll tip well, I promise. Bring us . . ." I grapple for the name of the only cocktail I know. "Two gin fizzes, please."

She gives me a lingering look. "I can't help you. I don't know anything."

"I just want you to answer a few questions. Please." I play the only other card I can think to use. "You should see how devastated Cole is by the whole ordeal."

Annette's face flickers before going hard again. "I don't know anything." She turns her back to me and walks in a practiced way—all hips and clicking heels.

Walter holds out a chair at the empty table for me. "Is she coming back?"

"Yes." Even though I don't know that she is. "I ordered you a gin fizz. I hope that's okay."

"Nothing about this night has been okay with me, so why should it matter?"

It isn't until I sit that I feel an unwelcome ache in my bladder. "I wonder where they keep the powder room in this place." I crane my neck toward the entrance. "Think it's on the other side of the bar?"

Walter shakes his head. "You're not going to the restroom alone. Not here."

I put on a sweet smile. "Walter, dear, I can't take you with me. It's frowned upon."

But his scowl doesn't loosen.

"I can't help that I have to go, and I need you to save our table." I peek at Annette. She's chatting with the barkeep as she loads several drinks onto her tray. "If she comes back while I'm gone, try to keep her talking. Flirt with her. Whatever you have to do. I'll be back as fast as I can."

Walter opens his mouth, but I flee the table before he can argue. I squeeze my way through the crowd to the restrooms. The bathroom is full of girls checking themselves in their compacts and gushing about which men are the best dancers and who is going with who. I take care of my business as fast as possible, lather up my hands, and race out of there.

Straight into the thick chest of Mr. David Barrow. "Well, there you are, doll. I was looking for you." His mouth smiles, but not his eyes. He leans close to my ear. "We're going to walk over to that corner. You make a scene, and you'll wish you hadn't, do you understand? Now, smile and look like you're happy to see me."

Fear leaps to life in my heart as I paint on a smile. Does he know I came here looking for him? "Why, David. What a pleasant surprise."

"That's the ticket." His hand is low on my back as he presses me through the crowd, toward a corner of the room that's invisible to Walter. He edges me in, leans to the point his nose is just inches from mine. To the casual passerby, we are nothing more than a couple trying to steal a moment of privacy. "Rosie put you up to this, didn't she? However much she's paying you, I'll double it."

Rosie? I raise my eyebrows. "I have no idea what you're talking about."

"Don't be cute with me." The words are a growl. "I'm not a man you want to mess with."

"I wasn't trying to be cute. I actually *don't* know what you're talking about."

Doubt flickers in his eyes, and he draws back a bit. "Yes or no—Rosie sent you here to keep an eye on me."

"I don't even know who Rosie is."

"My wife."

Ah, of course. "And why would your wife ask me to keep an eye on you?"

"Annette said you were here to ask her questions."

It's all coming together now. Why Annette might have quit her nanny job so suddenly. Why Mr. Barrow would just happen to be a regular patron of the place where she works. He's here for her. The thoughts make my stomach pitch, but I pair an indifferent shrug with a roll of my eyes. "You think I care at all that you're having an affair? I'm here to talk about Lydia."

"Lydia?" The pressure of his fingers on my wrists eases. "Why would you want to talk to me about her?"

There's a part inside me that trembles with fear. That wants to run from this man, who might be capable of snapping me in half. But the other part of me—the part that insisted Mariano listen to me when Lydia first disappeared, that flirted with Johnny Walker, that would do whatever it takes to get answers about Lydia—won't shut up.

"I wondered if you might tell me why you're beating your son to keep him quiet."

A range of emotions—fury, sadness, bewilderment—fly

over Mr. Barrow's face before he wipes his expression blank. "What would make you say that, Miss Sail?"

"I've seen his bruises."

"As a father, I've got a right to discipline my son." The words come through clenched teeth. His hands are once again tight around my wrists.

"You're not disciplining. You're silencing. You don't want him to say what he knows. And why is that, Mr. Barrow?"

Mr. Barrow leans close, his beer-laced breath hot on my ear. "What good could come from Cole talking? I'm doing him a favor. No five-year-old needs to know just how nasty those Finnegan brothers are."

The words send a shiver through me. "What do you mean?"

"It's none of your business, girl. You keep sniffing around like you are, and you're going to wind up just like your friend."

"Well, if you don't tell me what you know, I might just have to pay a visit to Rosie tomorrow and—" My whimper of pain is drowned out by the brassy notes of "Tin Roof Blues."

His fingers press painfully into the delicate flesh on the underside of my wrists. "I told you I'd make your life miserable if you breathed a word of this to my wife."

"I could do the same for you too, you know." The words bleed with discomfort. "Let's make a deal. You tell me what you know, and I keep quiet about you and Annette."

"I don't want to see any cops knocking on my door, you hear? You've got a real nice dog, I've noticed. Be a shame if something happened to him."

My hands fist at my sides. It's imagining Mr. Barrow with a black eye that enables me to paint on a smile. "I won't send the cops your way. I just want to know what you know."

He stares at me. In the shadows, his narrowed eyes seem black. "I'll tell you what I know, but I don't ever want to find you around here again. You got it?"

I nod.

"I was walking back from the train station, and I saw the car take off. An armored Model T, custom job. I might've known just from that, but the Finnegans . . . they're as dumb as they are ugly. On the bottom corner of the door, they've got the two lions with the sword. And that red sticks out like a sore thumb. You can't help but notice it."

"I don't understand. What does that mean?"

"It's the Finnegan family crest. Look it up. They think they can be flashy gangsters like others have been and get away with it. They seem to forget—or maybe they just don't care—that the flashy ones get gunned down. They're idiots."

I shudder. "Dangerous idiots."

"But you're a smart girl, right, doll?" His fingers seem to press even deeper into my flesh. I hold in a cry of pain. "You know that it's in your best interest to keep this between us."

A threat—that I better not see him within ten feet of Sidekick—sits on my tongue.

"Piper." My name is sharp, like the rap on a snare drum, and Walter glowers at the two of us. "I think it's time that we leave."

David Barrow releases me and glares at Walter. "You'd be smart to keep a leash on her."

"Let's get out of here." Walter's fingers grasp my arm and pull me toward the exit like a disobedient child. "I think you've stirred up enough trouble."

"If you want me to stop treating you like a child, then maybe you should stop acting like one," Walter snarls as he pulls shut the car door. "Do you have any idea how scared I was at the table? Here I'm trying to help you out, and I find you cornered by that awful man."

"I was getting information—"

"Somebody needs to tell you that you're out of line, Piper." Walter's words roar out of him. "Your father is too ignorant, your brothers too distracted, and Mariano too smitten. You're acting like what you're doing won't have real consequences, but it will, and I'm trying desperately to keep you safe."

"I don't need you to keep me safe!" It's good that we're alone in the car, because I can't control my volume anymore.

"Yes, you do. Because you're so far in this, you don't even realize how dangerous it could be."

The adrenaline from being cornered by David Barrow, from fleeing the speakeasy, has worn off, and my limbs set to trembling. Even when I curl my legs up under me and cross my arms over my chest, I can't seem to stop the rattling.

"I know how you loved Lydia." Walter's voice has softened. "I understand it makes you crazy to not know what happened to her. But can't you see how crazy it makes *me* to think the same thing might happen to you? I don't know what I'd do if I lost you."

I stare out the front of the car, at the people on the sidewalk busy laughing and talking. Out for a fun night in a city that teems with danger. "Do you remember a few years ago, when you ran into the fence chasing down a fly ball? And I was so mad at you for injuring yourself to make a play?"

"I do."

"Do you remember what you told me?"

Walter shakes his head.

"You said that you didn't know any other way to play the game except to give it all. To leave it all on the field." I turn to him. "That's how I feel about Lydia. I don't know how to do anything else but leave it all on the field."

He only looks at me.

Other words sit on my tongue. I want to tell Walter about the Finnegans. About how Mr. Barrow—the lowlife—threatened my dog. But Walter doesn't want to hear that, does he? He wants me to go back to who I was before Lydia was killed. When Ms. Underhill and her ruler were my greatest fears.

I love Walter, so I pick a shade of the truth. "I'm starving."

He turns the key, and the Ford rumbles to life. "Then let's eat."

And he seems content to pretend the whole thing never happened.

CHAPTER
~ NINETEEN ~

t's undeniable that Jane makes a beautiful bride. Her raven hair gleams under the white veil as she turns toward us. Her mother and sisters gasp, and even my mouth falls open.

"Oh, Janie." Her mother adjusts how the veil drapes over her daughter's shoulders. "You're radiant."

Resentment falls like a hammer, having nothing to do with Jane being almost my stepmother, but rather with the way her mother looks at her on her wedding day. With Mother and Lydia gone, who will care enough to fawn over me when my turn comes?

A knock sounds on the bedroom door. "Piper?"

Never has Walter's voice been so welcome.

"I'll be right back," I say to Jane's family as I rush away.

"Careful in your dress," Jane calls after me.

I open the bedroom door just wide enough to slip through, and I grin up at Walter as I close it behind me. "Thank you," I whisper. "It was ridiculous in there."

Walter's gaze travels my peach dress, made of silk and heavy with beads, and down to my strappy, toe-pinching shoes. "I'm not sure I would've even recognized you like this. You look so . . ." He waves his hand, as if that's sufficient for completing his thought.

"It's not like I had any say in the matter." I can't keep my words from sounding cross. I actually thought I looked pretty nice. "This is just what she put me in."

"I didn't mean it in a bad way, Pippy. Just that you look different than normal."

"Did you need something?"

"Mariano is on the phone for you."

I clatter down the stairs to Father's office as fast as my pained toes will allow. When I reach the telephone, I say a breathless, "Hi."

"I'm trying to wrap up a report before I come to the wedding, so I don't have long, but I saw the message you left for me. Is it urgent?"

"Very." In a string of words, I detail what I learned from David Barrow the night before, ignoring as best I can the looks Walter gives me as he stands beside the desk. "So, obviously," I conclude, "we need to put together a plan to go after the Finnegans."

"Piper," Mariano and Walter simultaneously say. Mariano's tone is a warning, Walter's a chastisement.

"I said *a plan*. Which means I clearly don't intend to just rush into their headquarters."

"We can't go after them without convincing evidence," Mariano says. "We just can't. And it's not like I haven't already looked for it."

Walter has taken to pacing the room.

I angle away from him. "But why not? They're not so untouchable, are they? It's not like they're Al Capone."

"It should scare you that Al Capone is our measuring stick, Piper."

"We have an eyewitness who saw their car. That's evidence."

"He's also a witness who doesn't want to talk. That's a problem. We can discuss this more at the wedding, okay? As it is, I'm already going to miss the ceremony."

"It doesn't matter."

"Of course it does. This is a hard day for you. I want to be there."

"Oh." Seems a silly thing to say, but I'm too shocked by his thoughtfulness to think up anything clever. "Well . . . good-bye."

I place the ear piece back on the hook. Even without me saying so, Mariano knew today would be hard for me. He cared about that.

"Why didn't you tell me?" Walter's expression—jaw clenched, eyes narrowed—matches his rock-hard tone.

"About the Finnegans?"

"I was with you all night. How could you not tell me?"

I straighten my shoulders so we're not quite so unevenly matched. "Maybe I didn't want to get yelled at any more than I already was."

I walk past him.

He stays right on my heels. "I only yelled at you last night because it seems like you don't care at all about your personal safety. I know you want to find Lydia at all costs, but your life is too high a price to pay."

"You're being dramatic. It won't come to that."

Listen to him, Piper. Lydia's voice, soft and urgent.

My mind flits to finding Father with his gun, his chair facing the front door as if expectant. To the look in Mariano's eyes as he detailed that Lydia had been wearing my coat, carrying a handkerchief with my initials.

To my nightstand drawer, inexplicably open when it should have been closed.

I stop at the foot of the stairs and face Walter. "I'm not stupid. I won't go after them on my own."

Walter holds my gaze a moment. Opens his mouth. Closes it.

"Piper?" Jane's voice from above is like a blast of winter Chicago wind. "I need you up here."

I breathe out a private, frustrated sigh. "For what?"

Even from the first floor, I see the pinch of her expression. "It's almost time to go. We need to finish getting ready."

"I'm done."

"Piper, come upstairs now."

She's less than a decade older than me, but she thinks she can use the same commands my mother did when I was five?

"Piper." My name is a whispered admonishment on Walter's lips, and it's like a smack of betrayal. He turns to Jane in her snow-white glory up on the staircase. "You look lovely, Miss Miller. I'll bring the car around."

Just like at the speakeasy, I suddenly feel as though he's abandoned me.

"Thank you, Walter." Her dismissal is cool as she glides down the stairs toward me.

He slips away.

"Piper." Jane's voice is crisp, like a bite of sour apple. "I'm sure today isn't the happiest day of your life. And I know you're used to running this place—"

A snort escapes me.

"But today is my day." Her eyes are sharp. "I've watched both my little sisters get married, many of my younger cousins, and all my college girlfriends. Today is finally my turn, and you're not going to ruin this by making time with the hired help. Do you understand me?"

She doesn't wait for my answer—which would have been an

incredulous, "*Making time?*"—just holds her white lace skirts and marches upstairs.

I grip the banister as my head spins with anger.

"That lady is a real piece of work."

I startle at the sound of Alana's voice. She's tucked away in the living room, looking like the embodiment of the modern woman in her fringed lavender dress and crystal diadem. She is graceful and feminine, and beside her I'm a child playing dress up.

"When did you get here?"

"Joyce let me in a few minutes before you and Walter came down. I didn't know Nick was already at the church." Alana draws a silver cigarette case from her beaded purse. "Fancy a smoke?"

Bad idea, Piper, chides Lydia's disapproving voice.

"No, but air would be nice."

Outside, the early afternoon is glorious. A lake-blue sky full of fluffy clouds, the golden orb of the sun, and a warm, summery breeze.

"Don't take what Jane said too personally." Alana pops open her cigarette case once more, and holds it out like a tray of appetizers. "That was about her, not you."

"Thanks, but I don't care what she thinks." I wave away the offered cigarette, but note the engraved initials that wink in the sunlight. "M.B.?"

Alana blinks slowly. "Pardon?"

"The initials on your case. M.B."

"Oh." She smiles and snaps the case shut. "My mother's. From before she was married."

My mind drifts to Elsie Ann Sail, who was everything a

woman of her day was supposed to be. And who should have turned forty-six today, if the world was a place that operated as it should.

Happy birthday to you, happy birthday to you—the song flows from my heart, floods my eyes—*happy birthday, dear mother, happy birthday to you.*

"Nice that you have something to remember her by while you're away," I say. Alana turns to me, noting, I'm sure, the watery quality of my voice. "Today is my mother's birthday. Or would've been, of course."

Alana looks to the street, where Walter pulls the Chrysler alongside the curb. "I like you, Piper." She sighs, as if this is somehow a sad thing. "I wish all of this were better for you."

Jane barges out the front door and saunters past me without a glance. Her mother and sisters trail behind her, their shoes click-clacking down the front steps to the idling car.

"But girls like us keep moving forward." Alana stomps out her cigarette, and when she looks at me I notice she's not as beautiful as I initially thought. Rather, the way she appears and carries herself gives the illusion of beauty. Her voice is quiet, thoughtful, when she adds, "I hope you make it out of this okay."

"Piper, let's go!" Mrs. Miller—who already informed me I'm *not* to call her Grandma—calls from within the car. "We'll be late!"

I take a deep breath. *I love you, Mother.* And I force my feet to move down the steps and through the gate.

"Is there anything in this world more boring than a wedding?" I mutter under my breath to Tim.

"No. Especially when you're hungry," he says through his smile.

The flashbulb pops—finally!—and I let the smile fall off my face.

Gretchen turns to my brother, her eyes wide and the corners of her mouth downturned.

"Not *our* wedding, of course, dear." Tim squeezes her shoulder. "You had ours planned perfectly."

Gretchen seems mollified. She adjusts Howie on her hip. "Except for the carrot cake."

Her sigh is heavy, and she gives me a despairing head shake, as if we're commiserating together. As if I have the foggiest idea of what went wrong with the carrot cake at their wedding three years ago.

"Okay, all the family is dismissed," the photographer says in his pinched voice. "Only the happy couple needs to stay."

Thank goodness.

My shoes wobble beneath me as I attempt to speed walk up the front steps of the Congress Hotel. There are chairs in the ballroom, and I need a chair even more than I need something to eat. Would anyone notice if I went barefoot the rest of the night? Somehow, I think *yes*.

The golden ballroom is warm with chatter and laughter. The honey-colored tablecloths are still fresh, the fussy white flowers perky in the clear vases, and the food—slabs of beef, salads in lettuce cups, and an abundance of other colorful dishes—are still mounded on the buffet line.

And there's the head table, full of glorious empty chairs. I sink into one with a sigh and give thanks for whoever dreamed up tablecloths long enough to conceal that I'm removing my shoes.

More family—family that did not race as I did—filters into the room, causing a stir of excitement in the crowd, most likely because it indicates dinner will soon be served.

Gretchen takes the seat beside me, then giggles. "Oh, that's so cute! You want your auntie Piper, don't you?"

Howie's arms are extended, his hands trying to grasp me. Or, more likely, the sparkling beads on my dress.

"I'm sure it's just a fluke."

"No, he definitely wants you." With that, Gretchen plunks Howie onto my lap.

He looks up at me with large, dark eyes and an unsmiling mouth. It's like he knows I have no clue what I'm doing.

"You just love your auntie, don't you?" Gretchen coos.

He turns to his mother, and then back to me for more staring.

I give his curly head a pat, only to find my fingers mesmerized by his cloud-soft hair.

See? Babies aren't so bad, Lydia says to me as Howie grabs fistfuls of skirt in his chubby hands.

My stomach growls four times before Father and Jane are announced and enter the ballroom. (Heaven forbid Jane simply enter a room on her special day.) But at least they're here, and we can eat.

"How many people are you feeding off that plate, sis?" Tim asks as we settle into our seats after our turn through the buffet line.

I stick my tongue out at him, and beneath the shelter of the tablecloth, I again slip off my pinchy shoes. I shovel food into my mouth between chats with those who stop by to say a "brief hello" and fawn over Howie.

I've just swallowed a large bite of dinner roll when I sense someone standing beside me, and a rumbly male voice says, "You must be the famous Piper Sail."

I look up and blink into the dark eyes of a tall, imposing Italian man. He's not overweight, just solid. Broad shoulders, a thick chest, and powerful legs. With a scowl, he'd be intimidating, but his smile is full and his eyes indicate a man of good humor.

I dab my mouth with a cream-colored napkin. "I don't know that I'm exactly famous, but I haven't yet met another Piper Sail."

"You're famous at *my* house, anyway." The man sticks out his hand, which is massive, like a baseball mitt. "Giovanni Cassano. Mariano's father. Pleasure to meet you, Miss Sail."

Oh. *Oh.* "I . . . Yes, you too, sir."

His grip on my hand is surprisingly gentle. "My son speaks very highly of you."

And I have no idea how to respond to that. "Thank you. He does of you too." I think he does, anyway. Mariano doesn't seem to like talking about his family. "Is he here yet?"

"I expect him at any minute. He wasn't supposed to be long at the office today, but . . ." Giovanni shrugs his shoulders.

"Mr. Cassano." I startle at the sound of Tim's voice. He rises from the table, his hand outstretched. "Great to see you, sir. So glad you could make it."

"Glad to have been invited. I finally get the chance to meet your lovely wife."

How does my brother know Giovanni Cassano? A memory tickles at me, like a song you know, yet can't quite recall the exact tune. Is it Tim whom I've heard talk about the Cassano family? Or Nick? I think, maybe, I've heard Nick saying—

"Piper." Giovanni nods toward the entrance. "Someone finally broke free from his desk."

In the doorway, Mariano cuts a dashing figure in his silk top hat and cutaway coat. His gaze scans the crowd, and his mouth spreads into a smile when he spots me walking toward him.

In my stocking feet—whoops.

"Hey, beautiful."

"It's funny, but you look just like this guy I used to know."

"Way back last week, you mean?"

"Mm-hmm."

His fingers clasp mine, but with a ballroom full of people—including both our fathers—neither of us move closer. Gray smudges beneath his eyes give away how taxing his week has been.

"You need a good meal, detective."

He squeezes my hand. "I need time with my girl, Miss Sail."

My stomach seems to fold in on itself. "Maybe we could make both happen at once."

The band leader announces that Mr. and Mrs. Sail are going to enjoy their first dance—Jane's new name grates on my ears—and the band strikes up, "You Made Me Love You."

All eyes in the room lock on Jane and my father, who dances like you might guess a lawyer in his late forties would. Mariano's arm curls around my waist, and his mouth whispers against my ear. "Think they'd play 'It Had to Be You' if I ask 'em real nice?"

I grin with the memory of the Parmesan-scented evening at Vernon Park, the winking stars in the sky, and the warmth of Mariano's mouth on mine. "If not, I'll sic Jane on them."

His chuckle is a warm rumble against me.

I happen to catch Alana's eye—not everyone is tuned in to

Father and Jane, apparently—and I return her smile, hoping she sees that, like she had hoped on the front porch hours ago, I'm getting through the day just fine.

"Lydia getting into the car certainly implies that she knew the driver." Mariano twirls me out and then back against him. "That's the most disturbing thing to me. I can't get over it. You're sure David Barrow was telling the truth about the car?"

"Pretty sure. But you've spoken to the Finnegans?"

Mariano nods. "Jail and the cinema, remember? Rock solid."

My peach skirts swish against my legs as we waltz. "But what about beyond the brothers. Did you check out men who work for them? Because I could do some dig—"

"No." Mariano's hand presses into my back, and my heart hiccups in my chest at our closeness. "Please, no. After the week I've had and everything I've seen with this current case, I just really want to know that you're safe."

We've stopped dancing.

"Okay," I whisper.

He exhales, clutches me tight for a moment, and then spins me out. When he pulls me back close, his gaze has that faraway look. The one he gets when he's thinking. "But you still don't suspect Matthew at all?"

There's a tightness in my chest. "Should I?"

"I don't know. Sometimes, he seems to make the most sense."

"He has an alibi too, though."

"Not as firm as some others." We take several spins across the floor in silence. Mariano looks down at me, sadness in his eyes. "I'm sorry, Piper. I know you want to believe he's been falsely accused. It's just not in my nature to trust. Not anymore."

A sentiment I well understand. "The thought has crossed my mind, for sure."

"But . . . ?"

"But Lydia was as naïve as she was sweet. If someone wanted her to get into the car voluntarily, I don't think it would have been so hard, really. You could simply say you were hurt or lost or a friend of a friend or whatever, and she would've done it."

The song comes to a close, and Mariano rests his forehead against mine. "I sure know how to woo a girl, don't I?"

Around us, people applaud the quartet, and I mindlessly join them. "You're the only one who'll still talk to me about this instead of just telling me I need to move on. The only one who seems to care about the issue that matters more to me than anything else. That's . . ."

Love, Lydia whispers into my ear. *That's love.*

I swallow. "I'll take that over wooing any day."

Mariano grasps my hand in his. Smiles.

"Pippy." Nick's voice blasts into the moment. Alana trails behind him. "They're about to cut the cake. They want to photograph the wedding party in front of it first."

Of course they do. We wouldn't want a moment to go by that we don't photograph.

"Fine, I'm coming." I squeeze Mariano's hand before releasing it. "I'll be right back."

As I walk away with Nick and Alana, Nick emits a blustery sigh. "So you're really going to do this, huh? You're really going to date a Cassano."

My fingers curl into a fist, and if we weren't dressed in formal wear inside a ballroom, he would feel the full force of my right hook. "Why do you hate him so much? Is it just him, or are you prejudiced against all Italians?"

Nick shoots me a scathing look, but falls quiet as the photographer arranges us.

But the anger is too consuming for me to keep my mouth shut. "I like him, okay? And I don't see why that's such a big problem."

"Now isn't the time, you two," Tim says as the photographer steps back to survey his work.

"Smile, everyone!" he chirps.

"What did you expect, Piper?" Nick asks through his smile. "That we would all be okay with you dating someone from a mafia family?"

What? My head snaps toward my brother. "What?"

The pop of the flashbulb sounds.

Nick looks at me, his brow pinched. "What do you mean, 'What'? You know, right?"

"Brother, sister," calls the photographer. "Eyes up here, please! Let's try again!"

The memory that I couldn't quite grasp earlier rolls me flat. Dinner with Father and Nick the night Lydia went missing. Father had offered the wine to Nick, saying, "Nick, you help with the Cassanos' cases. You should enjoy some of the spoils."

Air rushes from my lungs as I breathe out the family name. "The Cassanos."

Clients of Father's. A name that I had probably caught snatches of when walking by his office, or if I came upon my brothers and him discussing a case. How could I not have put it together?

STEPHANIE MORRILL

"Sister?" calls the photographer. "Up here, please! Smile!"

Tim puts on his big brother voice. "Nick, Piper. Do this later."

I turn to the photographer. Beyond him, Mariano appears to be making polite conversation with Alana. Why didn't he tell me?

"They're our biggest client. We thought you knew," Nick mutters.

The flashbulb pops, and the metallic scent of magnesium fills my nostrils. "I didn't." I hate how stupid I sound. I had been so annoyed when Lydia fell in love with Matthew and became so illogical, and it turns out I'm no better. All the clues were there the whole time, and I just couldn't see.

"I'm sorry." Nick's countenance has softened. "I'm sorry to be the one to tell you Mariano isn't the white knight you thought he was."

I don't want to ask, don't want to hear the answer—but I can't bury my head any longer. "What is he, then?"

Nick's eyes hold sympathy as he deals a second blow. "Just another crooked cop."

TWENTY

P iper?" Mariano's voice rises above the cacophony of the busy city street.

I stiffen, but don't turn. I don't want to see him coming down the Congress Hotel steps with that confident gait I've admired. I don't want to see him, period.

"What are you doing out here?" He sits beside me on the cool concrete steps, close enough that his leg brushes against mine.

I yank away. "Don't touch me. Just leave me alone."

"Piper, what happened in there? What's wrong?"

A laugh bubbles out of me . . . or was that a dry sob? "Have you and your buddies been laughing about it behind my back? Or what's the official word for men like you? *Soldato*?"

Mariano goes rigid beside me.

I cut him a glare. "You and your fellow *soldatos* probably thought it was good and funny, didn't you?"

"Piper, what are you talking about?" His tone is one I've never heard from him—a low and dangerous sound that scrapes against me. "I'm a police detective, not some mob soldier."

I grind my teeth together to lock in the tears. The only thing that would make this worse is Mariano seeing me cry.

"Where did you even get that idea? Have you seen a single shred of evidence that I'm faking my way through this job?"

"No, but when would I? You'd be great at pretending. You'd have to be for the police force to actually buy it."

"Listen to me." Mariano's hand grips my bicep, tightens.

I look from his hand on my arm to his eyes. "Let me go, Mariano Cassano, or I'll be forced to throw a fit right here."

He lets go. "Yes, this kind of thing happens. Police officers get bought, Prohibition agents take bribes, but this is *me*, Piper. I thought . . ." Mariano's gaze soaks in my unflinching face. "I thought you knew me better than that."

"I thought I did too."

Mariano swallows hard and looks away.

"If you weren't hiding it, why weren't you honest with me, Mariano? Why didn't you tell me about your family?"

His words are frosty. "When, exactly, was I dishonest? I thought you *knew*. I thought, 'How could she not know her old man is an associate?'"

I cringe at his choice of words. My father, whose job should be upholding the law, protects criminals from suffering consequences for the laws they break. My house, my education, and my clothes—all paid for with money that costs too much.

I brush away the offense and take a deep breath. "You knew I didn't know."

"I didn't—"

"You did." I look him in the eyes. "Because I told you so when we were on Clark Street."

Mariano's larynx bobs, and I can see he remembers just as clearly as I do. *Your father doesn't talk to you about his clients, then?*

I let the memory settle between us. "You should've told me at that moment."

"Maybe I should have." Mariano pulls off his hat. Puts it back on. "But when I realized you hadn't figured out our family connection . . . I didn't know what to do. I didn't want you to think less of me."

"Is this why you won't go after the Finnegans? Bad blood between your families?"

His eyes snap. "I can't believe you'd even suggest that."

"Piper." Walter's voice booms from behind us, making me jump. "Your father's looking for you."

I turn and find Walter towering over us, a flat expression on his face. "Tell him I don't want to see him."

Walter doesn't budge.

"I said, I don't want to see him."

Walter looks to Mariano and then back at me. "Piper, he's about to leave for a month. You can stop whatever you're doing here for a minute and come say good-bye."

"No."

Walter's knees pop as he crouches behind me. "I'm not above begging, you know. Please don't make me tell your father bad news on his wedding day."

I lean back so my shoulders rest against Walter's knees. "My father is a lawyer for the mafia. Did you know this?"

Walter glances at Mariano, and then back at me. "Piper, *you* knew that."

"I knew some of his cases involved mobsters, but I didn't realize the extent of it."

"You said it yourself," Mariano says. "That they do horrific things, but they have a right to a fair trial too."

"Is that what my father provides?" I know I sound hysterical, but I can't seem to calm my voice down. "A fair trial?"

Walter's big hands clasp my shoulders. "Listen, Pippy. Just

put on a smile for another hour. Say good-bye, throw some rice, and then we can sort all this out."

"So Father gets to spend a month carelessly gallivanting around Europe while I stew over this? I don't think so."

"What's there to stew over? He's a defense attorney. This is part of his job."

"Fine." I stand abruptly. If I go inside, at least I can get away from Mariano. "I'll go talk to him."

"Cool off, or you'll wind up yelling," Walter cautions.

"Maybe that's not a bad thing. Maybe he deserves to be yelled at." I yank one shoe strap off my ankle. Then the other. "But not in these stupid shoes. I'm done with these."

"Piper—"

"Just let her be." Mariano's words are gruff. "She's smart enough to decide for herself."

"Don't flatter me." I brush imagined concrete dust from my dress, toss my wretched shoes into a wastebasket, and charge into the lobby in my stocking feet.

Father is engaged in conversation with the photographer when I tug at his sleeve. "I need a word with you."

"Ah, there you are!" He puts an arm around me and draws me to his side. "Smile pretty."

The flashbulb goes off.

I blink away the bright circle that clouds my vision.

"Perfect!" declares the photographer. "The wedding just wouldn't have been complete, Mr. Sail, without a photograph of you and your lovely daughter."

I demure in such a way that would win Emily Post's approval and then take my father's offered elbow. My head is so flooded with the words I want to lob at him, I can't seem to grab hold of a single one.

"I'm glad Walter found you. I wanted to have a moment with you before I left town," Father says as he leads me to the hall outside the ballroom. "Where have your shoes gone?"

I look down at my stockings. "They were hurting."

"You women and your impractical shoes." Father pauses along a row of windows and smiles indulgently at me. "How are you, my dear? I know it hasn't been the easiest day for you."

I look into Father's happy face. "Tired," is the answer that comes out. "I'm very tired."

Father nods with sympathy. "It's been an exhausting month, hasn't it?"

There's a war going on within me. I want to stomp my feet and yell and demand answers. Exactly how much of our life is bought by the mafia? How could he let me date Mariano?

And yet, I also find myself wanting to wrap my arms around him and sob against his chest while he reassures me. While he explains all the reasons why his professional choices have been about upholding the safety of our society rather than helping organized crime prosper.

"You'll be the lady of the house while I'm away, but I expect you to take some time off. Go to the beach. Go to the movies." Father winks. "Let Mariano spoil you a bit."

The suggestion stirs the anger brewing in my gut. Is my father in this so deep that he doesn't mind who Mariano is? "Do you really think he's the best guy for me to be seeing?"

Father blinks several times. "I thought you liked him."

"I do. I did. But . . . that was before I realized who his family is."

Father tucks his hands in his pockets and watches me without speaking. Lawyer trickery.

Lawyer trickery that I can't help succumbing to. "Why didn't you tell me?"

Father inhales slowly, and then exhales even slower. "Mariano is a good kid. He's not . . . in the family business."

I press my eyes closed as a strange mix of relief and confusion rumbles through me. "But don't you think that detail would've been pertinent?"

"These last few weeks have been the worst of your life, Piper. I guess I didn't want to do anything that might take away the one person who seemed to be making you happy." Father pitches his voice even lower. "I've known his father and uncle a long time. And Mariano is on the right side of the law. I knew you weren't in any danger."

"No danger." I huff a humorless laugh. "It's just the Sicilian mafia. That's all."

"Unless you have some bootleg operation I don't know about, you're perfectly safe." His smile is thin.

"Are you making a joke? Right now?"

Father sighs and looks out the window, at the snarl of shopping traffic on Michigan Avenue. "What should I have done? Banned you from seeing Mariano because of his father and uncle's business?"

"At the very least, how about some honesty? About Mariano, about you."

"About me? How have I been dishonest about me?"

"Your line of work."

THE LOST GIRL OF ASTOR STREET

Father seems exasperated. "Piper, you've known for a long time what kind of work I do. That was no secret."

"But I didn't know . . ." I didn't know what? "I didn't know you were defending . . . criminals."

Yep. That sounds exactly as stupid out of my mouth as it did in my head.

"That sounds dumb, I know. But I guess I always imagined that you spent your days defending people who were wrongly accused or didn't do anything *that* bad."

Father again averts his face to the traffic below, and pulls in his lower lip. I expect him to call me on this inconsistency—even to Mariano, I had said that I thought some of Father's clients were mobsters. The truth is that I had chosen to not think too deeply on it. I had chosen to stay ignorant.

"I'm sorry to be a disappointment. With the boys, their interest in law made it a natural subject to eventually talk about. With you, though . . ." Father turns his gaze to meet mine. "I suppose I wanted you to keep viewing me that way. I never lied, but I certainly omitted."

That's much more of an apology than I thought I would get. "Did Mother know?"

He hesitates for a beat. "My involvement wasn't as extensive when she was alive."

I blow a loose raspberry. "You're being evasive. Did she know, or didn't she?"

"She knew."

"And what did she think?"

Father holds my gaze. "She worried for the safety of our family."

I see him in my memory—his chair angled toward the front

door the night Lydia was taken. The gun within reach. "You do too."

"Of course I do. But I would no matter what my job was. It's part of being a parent."

"When Lydia went missing . . . what did you think had happened?"

Father blinks at me a few times. "I don't understand your line of thought."

"I told you that I came downstairs that night to get a drink. You were asleep in your chair. With your gun."

Father pulls his lip in again. I wonder if he knows he does that when he's crafting an answer.

"Did you think I was at risk?" I press him.

"Of course I did. Because I'm a father, though. Not because of my job."

I think back to what Mariano had told me about Father's case, and Colin Finnegan winding up in jail. "It had nothing to do with a big case you'd won?"

"I won't pretend that it never occurred to me that you or one of your brothers might be in danger because I had angered people—"

"The Finnegan brothers."

Father tries to shove away his surprise, but I see it before he can tuck it away. "Yes. They had certainly crossed my mind. But, obviously, I was being paranoid."

All roads in Lydia's disappearance seem to lead to the Finnegans. Is it merely proof of how far-reaching they've grown to be in this city? Or is it something more?

Father glances at his wristwatch. "I don't have long before our scheduled departure." He settles his hands on my shoulders, and waits to speak until I'm looking him in the eyes. "When I get home, I give you my word that we will sit and talk about this to your heart's content. I will be as open as I can without violating my clients' privileges. But for now, I just want you to know that I'm sorry you were caught off guard today, and I'm sorry for my part in that."

I want to keep my anger. Want to cuddle it close, where I can protect it and nurse its growth.

Yet I remember Lydia leaving my house on the day that turned out to be her last. How we almost parted in anger, and how I only escaped being saddled with that lifelong regret because she stayed long enough for us to work through our disagreement.

"I hope you have a good time on your honeymoon." The words are stiff, starched by my resentment.

"I love you." Father holds me in a long hug. When he lets me go, he adds, "And I hope you'll consider what I said about Mariano. I really do think he's good for you."

"No." He intentionally misled me about who his family was. How can I trust that he really is on the straight and narrow? "Being involved with him . . . It's just too risky."

Father takes hold of the locket around my neck, bought for me by my mother and bearing Lydia's image. "Piper, my girl. To love anyone is to risk."

❧ TWENTY-ONE ❧

t's after eight when Joyce, Walter, and I return to the house. The air inside feels strange, as if even the house can sense the change this afternoon brought. After making sure Joyce knows she's off duty this evening, I turn on the radio and perform an unladylike flop onto the couch. Nellie Melba's *Mattinata* pierces the haze that's surrounded me since my good-bye with my father. The higher her pitch-perfect soprano climbs, the harder I have to work to hold in the tears.

Walter returns from the kitchen with an odd assortment of appetizers left over from the wedding, along with two thick slices of wedding cake. Sidekick bounds along beside him, looking up at the tray with hope.

"So, earlier we ate a dinner that required about six different utensils. Now, we're doing this." Walter's smile seems wary as he settles onto the couch. "Is it just me, or do you feel like at any moment, Mother will come in here with a broom and chase us out?"

I hold out a cube of cheese to Sidekick and feel the comforting tickle of his muzzle. "There is something uncouth about eating in the living room, isn't there?" I pop a caviar canapé into my mouth. "But it isn't the worst thing we've done in this room."

Walter smirks. "It certainly wasn't my idea to play a game of baseball in here."

My mouth twitches with a smile. "I hated that vase anyway."

"Mother thought for sure she was going to get fired for her son being a bad influence."

"She had no idea that *I* was the bad influence." A memory comes—swift and painful—of Lydia being yelled at when I talked her into climbing the tree in her front yard. *That Sail girl is a bad influence on you*, Mrs. LeVine had snapped to Lydia.

"And then it turned out your father was so happy to see you acting like yourself again, he didn't mind at all."

I scratch under Sidekick's chin, and he groans his contentment. The aria fades to a close, and, for a moment, the room is silent. "I can't believe I didn't really understand about Father."

Walter stops chewing.

"I mean, I knew. But I didn't *know*. Not really." Frustration surges through me. "No wonder I can't figure out who killed Lydia. I'm too stupid to even notice what's happening under my own roof." I don't realize I've grown loud until Sidekick noses at my knee, trying to bury himself under my legs. "Sorry, boy. Didn't mean to scare you."

"Piper, you can't blame yourself for not being able to figure out what happened to Lydia. Even the police don't know, and they're professionals."

"But she was my best friend. And she was here right before it happened—I should be able to see the answer, and I just can't." The tears come with such a rush, it's as if a faucet has been cranked on. "Everything has been such a mess since I lost her. And it's like when she died, anything soft and kind in me died too."

Walter presses his clean handkerchief into my hands. "Pippy, that's not true at all. You're all heart. Just look at this dog who can't get enough of you."

"That's because I feed him."

"No, it's because you care for him. That's how you are. When you love someone, you're fiercely loyal. That's why you'll get through this thing with your father. You love him."

"But how do love and loyalty factor in when I think he's just plain wrong? I mean, he doesn't just work *with* them. He works *for* them. They were at his wedding, for heaven's sake!"

Sidekick whimpers as he trembles against me.

"I don't know," Walter says. "But I know you'll figure out a way. With your father *and* Mariano."

I scratch behind Sidekick's ear. I don't want to think about Mariano. "When does your train leave?"

"Tomorrow. Early."

"You'll be glad to go." The words make me feel achingly alone. Father off with his bride. Walter going back to California, to Audrey. And I'll stay here. Stuck.

"I won't be glad to leave you and Mother. I'm never happy about that." Walter regards me for a long moment. "What will you do about Mariano?"

I break a cracker in half. Then into quarters. "Nick said he's a crooked cop."

"What did Mariano say?"

"What else would he say? Of course he denied it." I shove away the memory of Mariano's hurt face.

"If he really were crooked, don't you think your father would have stopped you from seeing him?"

"Then why would Nick have said it?"

Walter snorts. "Because Nick is unhappy. And when Nick is unhappy, he tries to drag everyone else down in the muck. Especially you. He did the same thing when your mother died."

Sidekick licks the cracker from my hand. "Mariano had a chance to tell me about his family, and he didn't."

"Then I would ask him about it."

"I did."

"And?"

"He said he was embarrassed."

"And do you believe him?"

"I don't know." I think about saying more, releasing the jumble of words clogging up my brain. Instead, I just say again, "I don't know."

But I think I *do* believe Mariano. Does that make me stupid and naïve?

The thing is, if I'm being honest, I probably would have lied too in Mariano's situation. I think what really has me bothered is how this doesn't coincide with who I'd built Mariano up to be—a "what you see is what you get" kind of guy. I didn't want Mariano to come with baggage of his own, like an ex-fiancé or undesirable family.

An ex-fiancé, I can ignore.

This new facet of him, however, is too big to ignore. But is it too big for me to accept?

Nick stumbles through the front door, startling me awake. His laughter has a cruel edge to it. "Well, there she is. The star of the show."

I stretch my aching muscles. How long have I been sleeping in Father's chair? "And how was your evening, Nick?"

He responds with a glare.

"Did you and Alana have a nice time out?"

More glaring.

I fumble for my bookmark and close *This Side of Paradise*. "My evening wasn't great either, if it makes you feel any better."

Nick chucks his hat toward the coat rack and seems unaware that it falls to the floor. "It helps, yes."

I should've taken my book up to my room to read. When he's been drinking, Nick is downright intolerable. "I'm sensing you're mad at me."

He barks a laugh. "Because of your terrible behavior at the wedding, I had to hear about you all night." He pitches his voice high and mocking. "Do you think Piper's okay? Should we go home? Do you think she'd want to talk to me about it?"

I frown. "Who was saying this?"

"Alana." He fumbles in his coat pockets. "I swear, sometimes it's like she's two different people. Here I'm trying to get somewhere with her, and she wouldn't stop talking about *you*. She's obsessed."

"Well, maybe she didn't *want* you getting anywhere with her. You ever think of that?"

"Father lets you get away with too much, that's what I say." Nick pulls his package of cigarettes from his pocket. "All girls should be like Lydia LeVine. Sweet, timid little things."

"You won't hear any argument from me."

Nick's eyes slide closed. "Lydia." Hearing the way he speaks her name—wistful and heartbroken—melts away my anger. "It just still seems so unreal that she's gone."

"I know."

Nick holds up the package of cigarettes. "Want to keep me company?"

"Sure."

I nudge Sidekick off my lap, wrap the throw around my shoulders, and follow my brother onto the front porch. Astor Street is quiet at this hour, with just the occasional car rumbling by. Nick settles alongside me on the front porch step and takes a long drag of his cigarette.

I watch Sidekick sniff about the yard in a haphazard way. "If you still care so much about Lydia, why are you even bothering with Alana? She doesn't live here. Nothing's going to happen."

"Maybe it's just nice having someone who's interested in me." He flicks his cigarette, and ash dances away in the night. "Lydia sure wasn't."

"Are you so sure that Alana is interested in *you*? Seems to me, all she cares about is getting a good story."

Nick's shrug is sharp. Dismissive. "I can't believe you didn't know who Mariano was. Normally, you're the smart one in the family."

My teeth grind together, but I have nothing to say in my defense. The evidence was all there—who Mariano's family is, what my father's client list really looks like—and I just hadn't let myself think too deeply on it. Hadn't wanted to question for fear of what the answers might be.

Nick laughs—the loud and unaware laugh that comes from too much gin. "Didn't you ever wonder where all our booze came from?"

"The wine cellar, of course."

"And who do you think supplies our wine cellar, sister?"

"I don't drink any of it, so I guess I hadn't thought that far." It seems just as stupid now as it did when I said it to Father, but I tell Nick anyway. "I thought the men Father defended were mostly innocent." Nick smirks, and I ignore him. "Or that if they *were* guilty, it was of breaking a law that didn't really matter. I never thought they might be *really* bad guys."

"That's part of being a defense attorney, Piper. 'In *all* criminal prosecutions, the accused shall enjoy the right to a speedy and public trial.' The sixth amendment isn't just for good guys." Nick pauses for another puff. "And if you have to provide a defense for a man who's guilty, as a way of upholding the founding principles of our country, what's the shame in making decent money at it?"

"There's a difference between decent money and, well, *this*." I gesture to our house.

"You're still thinking about it wrong. Don't think of it as 'my daddy defends the mafia.' Instead, think of how our father works to protect one of the greatest rights we have as American citizens."

Nick will be a very good lawyer.

"And he's being paid ridiculously well for the verdicts he gets."

"Stop being so hung up on the money."

"Would Father still defend them if they were poor?"

"Absolutely."

Nick doesn't even flinch when he says it. And it's unsettling to see how it takes him no effort, how it costs him nothing, to lie.

"What would Mother have said about all this?"

Nick takes a final inhale of his cigarette before putting it out on the stoop. "I don't know. But it's not fair of us to speculate. To put words in the mouth of someone who can't speak for herself." Nick clasps a hand on my shoulder as he stands. "'Night, sister. Sleep well."

"Good night, Nick."

But when I don't hear the door open, I turn and find him with his hand on the doorknob and his gaze on the quiet street. "You won't stay outside too long, will you?"

"No."

"It's just that what happened to Lydia could've easily happened to you."

Maybe it was even *supposed* to happen to me. I pull the blanket tighter around my shoulders, as if my shivering has anything to do with the nighttime chill. "Not if it was Matthew."

"We both know it wasn't." Nick's voice has turned dark. "He loved Lydia. Alana says the same thing, that Matthew loved Lydia. She's working hard to find him. She's even traveled to places she thinks he might've gone."

"Why does she want him found so badly, if she thinks he's not guilty?"

"How else will we find the man responsible? Really, you should listen to her and work with her. You have the same goal."

I think of the predatory way she looked at me when we met, that day when it came out that Matthew had left town. No, I think Alana is all about herself on the issue of Matthew—her fame, her big break.

"Good night, Nick," I say again.

"Promise me you're coming inside soon. It's really not safe out here. Not these days. Bosses aren't content with just taking out the guy they want. They mow down entire families—wives, children."

Again, I shudder. But I don't want to give Nick the satisfaction of seeing me afraid.

"I'm not going to cower inside our home because of who you

and Father choose to do business with." I sound much braver than I feel. "If you don't like it, that's not my problem."

Nick mutters a terse good night and shuts the door firmly behind him.

I gaze up into the sky. This deep in the city, the sky is more of an ashen gray, even after midnight, as it reflects the city lights. There are stars up there. I don't see them—I rarely do unless I'm at Tim's—but I know they're there. I sit for a while, trying to spot a single star, but I can't. If I chose to, it would be easy to deny their existence.

They're there, I tell myself. *Even if your eyes can't perceive them.*

CHAPTER
❧ TWENTY-TWO ❧

I stare into my leather shopping bag—containing my notebook, several pens, Nick's pocket knife, a length of rope, and my F. Scott Fitzgerald novel for while I wait. I've never staked out a man's apartment. I'm not sure what all I need.

With all leads in Lydia's case pointing to the Finnegans, I'm at a bit of a dead end. I can't exactly go after them on my own, and even though I've thought of little else but Mariano and how to reconcile that he lied to me with my Father's belief that Mariano isn't mixed up in the family business, I still don't really know how involved with him I want to be.

So if I can't go after the Finnegans, I can at least help Emma solve the mystery of the very nice, but very vague Robbie Thomas. A consolation prize of sorts while I figure out my next move with Lydia.

There's a knock at my door.

I fold over the top of my shopping bag. "Come in."

I hold in a groan when Alana pokes her head in the door. "Hi, Piper."

"Hi."

She steps into my room, all grown-up glamour in a geometric-print dress and heels that make her even taller. "Your room is lovely."

Under her scrutiny, I feel even more aware of how it looks like a little girl's bedroom. "Thank you."

Sidekick sniffs at Alana, and she moves to pet him. He jumps back.

"He's very skittish around new people."

She crouches lower and holds out her hand. "I'm hardly new, right, Sidekick? You know me."

Sidekick seems unsure. He sits and stares at her.

"Did you need something, Alana? I'm actually getting ready to leave."

She stands to her full height and aims a bright smile at me. "Are you doing anything fun?"

"Just running an errand with a friend."

"How long do you think you'll be gone?"

Why, exactly, does she care?

I don't voice the question, but it must be obvious all the same, because Alana rushes on. "I know you've been feeling rather blue since the wedding. Nick and I thought it would be swell for the three of us to go have dinner together." Her smile rises impossibly high. "Someplace nice. My treat."

"That's very kind of you." I sling my bag over my shoulder. "I'm not sure how long I'll be with Emma, though. I'm sorry, but I need to go or I'll be late."

"Then tomorrow?" Alana asks as she follows me out of my bedroom.

I'm not trying to be rude, but I just can't think about a dinner with her and Nick right now, when my nerves are so tightly wound about venturing north with Emma. "I don't know. I think I told Mrs. Barrow that I would watch her kids for her."

"So Thursday, then? You can't possibly be busy *every* night this week." Alana laughs loudly as she patters down the stairs behind me.

Nick stands in the entryway, flipping through the day's mail. "What's so funny?"

"Your sister has quite the social calendar. I told her about our idea of going out to dinner, but it seems like it'll be impossible with how busy Piper is."

Nick narrows his eyes at me. "Surely one day this week can work for you." He holds my gaze a moment before turning back to the letters in his hands.

I can't get out of this without being outright rude, can I? And perhaps what Nick said a couple nights ago is right, that Alana's search for Matthew could maybe even help me. And if it turns out to be mutually beneficial, and she does get a great story out of the deal, what is that to me?

I tell myself to smile. "Now that I've thought about it, I bet I can make tomorrow night work after all."

Alana beams. "Marvelous. We can discuss the place later."

"And . . ." I'm at a dead end with Lydia anyway. What's the harm in offering this? "Maybe you should bring your notebook, and we could talk about Matthew like you've been wanting to. I don't know how much help I could be, but—" I shrug. "Some help is better than no help, right?"

Alana seems shocked by my change of heart. "Yes, that would be swell. Has he telephoned you?"

"No, nothing like that. And you should know that I believe Matthew is innocent. I don't want to get mixed up in a story where you make it sound like I think he's guilty."

"Of course not. But if not Matthew, who do you think killed her?"

"I don't know." The Finnegan name echoes in my head, but I can't vocalize that, now can I? Especially not to someone who would actually print it. If I hadn't been the true target to begin with, certainly that would seal the deal. "I need to go, or I'll be late. I'll see you at dinner."

"Mariano rang for you, by the way," Nick calls after me. "I told him you were unavailable."

I pause at the door, but don't turn around. "Thank you. I'm taking the Ford."

My heart thunders in my chest as I close the door behind me and clatter down the steps to where the Ford is parked along the curb. I just won't think about him yet. I won't think about how he called Sunday, yesterday, and now today. Or how I think if I see him, I won't be able to hold so tightly to my doubts.

And I certainly won't think about how deeply it scares me that if he *is* lying, I might be too hung up on him to perceive it.

"This is so exciting." Emma is almost bouncing in the passenger seat. We've been parked here about ten minutes, and this is the fifth time she's expressed her enthusiasm. "I've never been in the car with a lady driver. My mother says it's uncivilized for women to drive. She seems to think it's a gateway to rebellion. I doubt I'll ever have my own car."

"Sure you will. Just not while you live at home."

"Jeremiah let me practice once on his coupe." Emma beams at the memory. "I was terrible."

"I was too. Walter taught me because my brothers were too busy." I shift my hips to find a position that's comfortable, which is tricky with Nick's pocket knife digging into my side.

"It is so nice of you to do this for me."

"Well, you *are* paying me. It's actually the first money I've ever—"

"There he is!" Emma flails as she spots Robbie emerging from his apartment building. "And he's alone. Thank you, God, he's not secretly married."

Emma's enthusiasm has Sidekick turning circles in the backseat. "You know, most men don't take their wives to work."

"Oh." Joy drains from Emma's face. "I guess you're right."

Robbie heads east, away from his automobile. "Looks like we're going on foot." I make quick work of looping the leash through Sidekick's collar. "Ready to do some walking? How are your shoes?"

"I'll make do." Emma glances out her window at the sidewalk. "Is it safe?"

Much like the evening I dragged Walter to John Barleycorn, the sidewalks are crowded with hand-holding couples and groups of men and women dressed to flirt.

"We're not on Astor Street, to be sure." I bite my lower lip. "But, really, where is it safe in Chicago anymore?"

Emma's face broadcasts her fear, but she climbs out of the Ford anyway. She cranes her neck for a glimpse of Robbie on the opposite sidewalk. "We're going to lose him."

"No, we're not. Just be patient." I wrap Sidekick's lead around my palm several times. When Robbie is far enough down the sidewalk that I don't think he'd recognize Emma at a glance, I say, "Okay, let's go."

As we walk, Emma's gaze is locked on Robbie. She's not even watching what's ahead of her. "Emma, try to look more casual. Don't look right at him."

"Oh. Okay." She directs her gaze ahead of us. "Like this?"

"Much better. Just glance at him through your peripherals."

"It's rather hard to spot him like this. He looks like all the other men."

So I've observed. It's unnerving when I dwell on the kinds of professions where that ability to blend in, to be impossible to describe to the police, would be an asset.

Robbie stops at an unmarked door between a dress shop and a church. He knocks.

"Oh, look at these flowers over here, Emma." I pull her toward a flower box by a store window.

"Very pretty." Emma's words are polite but laced with impatience. "What are you doing? We're going to lose him."

"He's stopped too. See?"

Emma turns in time to see Robbie step inside the door on which he'd knocked. "What's that place?"

"No sign. Gin joint, maybe? Maybe he works there? Maybe he didn't want to tell you because he thought you'd disapprove?"

Emma's frown deepens. "I don't *like* the idea, certainly. But why would it be better to tell me in a few months? Now's as bad a time as any to learn your boyfriend's profession is illegal."

"You ladies lost?"

A man who's likely a decade older than us stands there, a cigarette smoldering between his lips. The cut of his suit is fashionable enough, though the sleeves are too long for tailor-made.

"No, sir, but thank you." Emma's voice rings appreciative, like she truly thinks this stranger is being kind to have checked on us.

"Where you girls headed tonight?" He pulls the cigarette from his mouth and holds it between his fingers. "My buddies and me, we want to hit the joint with the prettiest ladies."

Emma flushes.

"We're just taking our dog for a walk." Sidekick stands between me and the man, and I pat his head. "If we don't walk him often enough, he's prone to biting. And it's been a couple days."

The man's eyebrows arch. "Doesn't look like you're doing too much walking."

"We had only stopped to admire the flowers, and now we'll be on our way, sir. Thank you." I loop my arm through Emma's and carry on. "Infuriating man. Let's walk up to the corner. Hopefully, Robbie will come out soon."

"Yes, I hope so." Emma's words are breathy. "I don't care for strange men talking to us on the sidewalk."

"We're fine. We have Sidekick. And I have a knife."

Emma's feet stop moving. She turns to me with wide eyes, a dropped jaw. "You have a *knife*?"

"Keep your voice down. And, yes, just in case."

"How do you know how to do this?" Emma's gaze is admiring, and it creates an itchy discomfort in my chest.

I urge her farther down the street, to the other side of a street lamp. "What do you mean?"

"How do you know to watch someone across the street from your peripherals? To bring a knife? You didn't learn this at Presley's."

"No, I didn't." I glance at the door—still no Robbie. "I don't know, really."

"Did Mariano teach you?"

Just the sound of his name makes me flinch. "No."

"That Mariano is one good-looking fellow." Emma makes a show of fanning herself. "I told Jeremiah that, and I thought he might pummel me. As much as I like the idea of you and my brother—"

"The door's opening." And not a second too soon.

Robbie emerges, briefcase still in hand. Hmm.

"What does it mean that he's leaving? Does it mean he doesn't work there?" Emma's voice lifts with hope.

"He's crossing this way." I tighten my hold on Sidekick's leash. "We gotta move."

We hustle down the sidewalk, and I resist the urge to check over my shoulder.

"Should we duck into a store?" Emma huffs between breaths.

"That's tough with Sidekick." An idea sparks in my mind. "But I've got an idea. You go in to this store, and I'll stay here."

"But, Piper, he'll see you!"

"We're running out of time, and I can't explain. Go into the drugstore, wait until we've gone, and then go back to the Ford. I'll meet you there as soon as I can."

"Until you've *gone*? But—"

"Just trust me."

Emma blinks at me several times, looks down the sidewalk where Robbie will soon come into view, and then dashes into the drugstore in her impractical shoes.

I suck in a breath, breathe a prayer, and limp my way back the direction I came. Do I have enough time to conjure real tears? I should practice fake crying. That would be a handy skill in a pinch.

"Miss Sail? Are you all right?"

I look around, as if I can't fathom who would be talking to me. "Oh, Mr. Thomas. Thank heavens." I fall heavily against him and feel him brace.

He wears a gun. Fear lights up every nerve in my body.

"What happened to you?" Robbie looks around. "Are you out here alone?"

The alarm on his face makes me question the wisdom of leaving Emma on this end of town on her own. With no dog or knife.

I can't think about it now. I have a cover story to concoct. "I was with a couple of girlfriends, but they met these guys and . . . Oh, I just didn't like the look of them at all, but my friends wouldn't listen to me." I sniffle and choke out a sob. "I've been trying to find the closest L station, but then I twisted my ankle, and I don't know my way around here at all." I put on the face I would use to ask Father or Tim a favor. "Can you please help me, Mr. Thomas?"

"Of course." Robbie tucks his arm around my waist to support my weight. "Emma wasn't with you, was she?"

"Emma would never do anything like that. In fact, she told me I shouldn't go out with those girls. I should have listened to her."

"My apartment is just a block or so away. Can you walk that far?"

"Yes, I'll be fine, thank you."

"Instead of taking the train, someone should come pick you up. Who could you call?"

Time to get the attention off me. "Oh, you have your briefcase! I'm dreadfully sorry. I'm causing so much trouble for you."

His eyes are surprisingly kind. "It's no trouble at all, Miss Sail."

"But you were on your way to work, weren't you?"

After a pause, "Yes."

"Oh no." I stop walking. "You can't let me be the reason you're late to work. Please, Mr. Thomas, just point me in the direction of the nearest train station. I'll be fine."

"Emma would skin me alive if she heard I'd done that to her closest friend. Come on, now. No more arguing."

It takes a surprising amount of energy to pretend to limp, and by the time we arrive at Robbie's apartment building, my blue cotton dress sticks to me. I sneak a glance behind me as we go through the dingy double doors of the apartment building, but Emma is nowhere to be seen. She's going to be fine, right? It's a short walk back to the car, and I'll rejoin her in less than a half hour, I'm sure.

But I can't help seeing Lydia in my mind's eye, waving to me from her gate for the last time.

"I think I have a bandage from when I sprained my wrist." Robbie slides back the grate on the elevator door and helps me in. "We could wrap that around your ankle, and you could call for someone to come pick you up."

Sidekick nuzzles close to my leg and whimpers as the elevator gets going. I rub his ears. "It's okay, boy."

Robbie grins down at him. "How old is he?"

"I don't know, actually. I've just had him a month or so."

Robbie holds out his hand, but Sidekick only cowers. "He has a sweet temperament."

"He does. But I think he would turn on a man if I gave the word."

"That's a good trait in a dog, I say." Robbie releases the operating button as the elevator lines up with the third floor. He pulls aside the grate, then pushes up the sliding door and helps me off.

As soon as Robbie opens his apartment door, I see that Emma can put to rest her fears of him being married. It's a studio apartment with dull white walls, a single bed, and not a feminine touch in sight. I exhale a breath of relief.

"Here, Miss Sail." Robbie pulls out a beat-up kitchen chair. "Have a seat."

"Thank you. And you can call me Piper."

"I'll get that bandage for you."

As Robbie rummages around the bathroom, I soak in as many details of the room as I can. If only it were possible to take photographs with your mind. Of course, what would I photograph? There are no papers lying about—not even a pile of mail—no family pictures, and no mementos to suggest past vacations or even a favorite sports team. The place doesn't even have a scent to it. It's all very . . . stark. Maybe most bachelors have sparse apartments? I've never been in one before.

Or perhaps it's in Robbie's best interest to keep his apartment void of personality. Easy to pack up and make a clean getaway.

"Who can I telephone for you, Miss Sail?" Robbie asks as he reenters the room with a bandage in hand.

"I think I can make it to the station okay once we get my ankle wrapped."

Robbie gives me a skeptical look. "Miss Sail—"

"Piper."

"Piper, I can't in good conscience load you on a train by yourself in this condition. Not in this neighborhood. And as much as I would enjoy taking you back downtown, I can't afford the time."

"No, I wouldn't even ask it of you."

I wrap the bandage over my stocking. Who am I going to call? Tim would ask too many questions. Walter left for California on Sunday. Not only that, but I have the Ford, and Nick and Alana likely left the house with the Chrysler. Jeremiah? That could get Emma in hot water at home . . .

I wince. Mariano is the only person who won't be irate with me when he learns the truth. Who might even *help* me figure out what Robbie Thomas is up to.

"Can I dial a number for you?" Robbie asks.

Robbie's telephone hangs on the kitchen wall, a strange fixture in this apartment of no frills.

"No, I can manage, thank you."

Robbie moves to the kitchen, tidying a space that looks perfectly fine in an effort to provide me privacy as I spin the dial.

"Hello?" The male voice that answers at Mariano's apartment is unfamiliar.

"I'm calling for Mariano."

"He's at some dame's house."

"Oh." My gut clenches—Zola's? "What time do you expect him home?"

"I dunno. Late? Who is this?"

I hang up, my face hot and my heart hammering a painful beat. So Mariano's at a girl's house. That's fine. I've been ignoring him, after all. I take a deep breath as I lift the receiver to my ear once more. Maybe Nick and Alana are still at home. It's better, really, to call them. I certainly don't need to give Mariano the impression that I need him.

"Sail residence." Joyce's voice is crisp over the phone.

"Hi, it's Piper."

"Where are you calling from? Is everything all right?"

"Is Nick around?"

"No, dear. He and Miss Kirkwood left about ten minutes ago."

Blast. It'll have to be Jeremiah. I really hope this doesn't make life difficult for Emma.

"But Detective Cassano is here, if you'd like to speak with him."

My eyes fly open and my heart soars. "Mariano is there?"

"He's been sitting on the front porch the better part of an hour. Would you like to speak with him?"

Me. He's there for *me.* "Please."

I catch myself standing with weight on my supposedly hurt leg. Fortunately, Robbie is still in the kitchen, his back to me.

"Hi." Mariano's voice has a tenderness to it.

"I tried your apartment first, but you weren't there."

"No, I came here after work. Joyce said you were out with Emma, but would be back before too long."

"Yes, that was the plan." I swallow and try to infuse hysteria into my voice. "But then Mae and her sister went off with these terrible johnnies, and I refused to go with them."

"Piper . . . what's going on? Who are you with? You're not in the North again, are you?"

I swallow. Um . . . "But fortunately I bumped into someone. You know my good friend Miss Crane?"

"The longer you talk, the more nervous I get."

"Well, her boyfriend happened to be on his way to work—"

"I bet."

"—and when he found me limping, he was good enough to bring me up to his apartment so I could ring for someone to come pick me up."

"I thought you had a car with you. That's what Joyce said."

"I know, wasn't it fortunate? Downright providential, I say."

"Good grief, Piper. So you need me to come get you?"

"Quickly please. He needs to get to work, but he's being a gentleman and insisting he wait with me until someone comes."

"You still have the car though, correct?"

"Yes, I do." I pull the mouth piece away from my mouth. "Robbie, what's your street address please? My friend is on his way to come get me."

"703 W. Schubert. Right on the corner of Orchard. We can wait downstairs, if he likes."

"Mariano, the address is 703 W. Schubert, and we'll be waiting in the lobby." There's silence on the other end. "Mariano?"

"What are you thinking, Piper Sail?" Mariano's voice is coarse. "Do you realize where you are?"

My laugh rings hollow. "It's not like I planned this, Mariano."

"That's the same block Patrick Finnegan lives on. If they were to realize who you are . . . I'm coming. I'm coming now. Just stay there."

The line goes silent. I swallow hard. "I know it's an inconvenience, but I do so appreciate it. Thank you. Good-bye."

The Finnegans. Yet again.

"So your friend is on his way?"

"Yes." I make myself smile at Robbie. Is he associated with them? "Thank you so much for your hospitality, Robbie."

Together, we walk and fake-hobble down to the front door to wait for Mariano. I'm dying to check the Ford for Emma, but it's parked just out of view.

My gaze drifts to where I know Robbie's gun is holstered. All of this cannot possibly be a coincidence, can it? His secrecy about his job, the unmarked door from earlier, where he lives, and that he carries a gun?

I have to stop dwelling on it, or I'll be too nervous for the rest of our time together. That certainly won't help Emma and me get answers. "If you need to go to work, I'm sure my friend will be here soon."

"It's no trouble." But he's jingling the change in his pocket.

"I'm so thankful to know my friend is seeing someone kind-hearted like you."

Robbie's smile goes soft, and it stirs something in my heart. I want him to be a good guy. I'm not exactly sure when I decided I like Emma Crane, but I do.

"When you've moved around as much as I have, there's always a question of how long it'll take for the new place to feel like home. When I met Emma, Chicago finally felt like home."

"She's the best sort of girl."

Robbie ducks his head and smiles at his shoes. "I still can't believe she'd be interested in someone old like me."

Why thank you, Mr. Thomas, for opening up that window of opportunity. "You're hardly old, Robbie. Surely no more than twenty-five."

"Somewhere in there, yes."

"And lots of girls like the idea of finding a man who's already settled in a profession. What is it you do again?"

"I work for the railroad."

"How long have you done that?"

"A few years."

I gesture to the briefcase resting by the front door. "Do you always work in the evening?"

His smile is no longer the bashful variety, but rather the

kind a person wears when making polite conversation. "Trains run at all hours of the day, unfortunately."

"What exactly do you do for them?"

"Oh, I've done all kinds of things. I'm sure you're not interested in the details of my work."

"You might be surprised. Trains have always interested me."

"Me too. Their power is incredible, the way the ground trembles when they pass. It's fascinated me from the time I was a child."

He goes on to talk about how his father was a railroad man, spinning a story both interesting and vague. The man certainly knows what he's doing, knows how to cover up that he's revealing nothing.

When Mariano strides through the door, relief sweeps through me. Sidekick's tail thumps wildly, and I'm grateful God didn't see fit for humans to have tails.

"Oh, Piper. It's always something with you, isn't it?" Mariano sticks out his hand to Robbie. "Thanks for taking care of her."

No name, I notice.

"Just glad I was there to help."

Hmm. None from him either.

Mariano's gaze shifts back to me. He offers me a hand, his eyes sparking with amusement. "You really need to stop hanging out with those girls. They're more trouble than you are."

Robbie holds open the door, and Mariano hooks his arm around my waist to help me exit. On the sidewalk, I turn to Robbie. "Thank you for your help, Robbie. Again, I'm sorry for making you late."

"No trouble at all. I'll see you again soon, I'm sure." Robbie tips his hat and strides away.

"Where am I parked?" Mariano murmurs in my ear.

"You're the Ford by the street lamp. Emma should be waiting for us."

"You've dragged that sweet girl into this?"

"Actually, that sweet girl dragged *me* into this, thank you very much. Can you see her in the car? She was supposed to return when the coast was clear."

"See, this is just reckless enough to have your name written all over it." In a fluid motion, Mariano sweeps me up into his arms. "The car is too far for you to walk. With your bad ankle and all."

"You're a real cad, Mariano Cassano. Do you know that?"

He grins. "I know I've missed you."

When we get to the car and Emma's head pops up from the backseat, I release the breath I'd been holding. Her mouth falls open at the sight of me and Mariano.

"Hello, Miss Crane," Mariano says. "Fancy seeing you here."

She blinks from Mariano, to me, to my wrapped ankle. "Well. Clearly, I need to be caught up."

"Your friend here might be the death of me, Miss Crane." Mariano plops me into the passenger's seat and grins. "And I mean that in the nicest way possible."

Sidekick hops in, and Mariano shuts the door.

"I'll tell him it's my fault," Emma assures me from the backseat. "Did you really hurt your ankle?"

"No, I'm fine."

"It wasn't her fault, detective," Emma says as Mariano opens the door and slides in. "I hired her to tail him. This whole thing was my idea."

"Even without your aid, I suspect Piper would have

eventually found some way to stumble upon a lair of men who would take great pleasure in shooting her."

Emma's mouth forms an O. "Not Robbie. He wouldn't. I can't imagine . . ."

"I didn't mean Robbie. He took very good care of Piper."

"Wasn't she just brilliant?" Emma's eyes sparkle. "She comes up with the most creative things."

"Piper's creativity blossoms when it comes to finding new ways to get herself into trouble."

I smile sweetly. "That's because I have such a handsome detective to come to my rescue. A handsome detective who I'm sure knows just the right people to figure out what Robbie is—"

Mariano slants a glare my way as he pulls out into traffic. "I know what you're after, and it's not going to work. For one thing, word is the Prohibition bureau is building a case against the Finnegans, and I don't want to find you two in the wrong place at the wrong time and wind up in the crossfire."

Emma's hand grasps the Peter Pan collar of her dress. "Do you think Robbie is involved?"

"What I know is that this is a dangerous neighborhood to be in right now. When you go after these kinds of people, you better have a plan in place, or you'll wind up six feet under."

"You certainly paint a very vivid picture, detective," Emma says in a breathless voice. "It just seems like if they're breaking the law, and if you can prove it, that would be that."

Oh, sweet Emma.

"In a perfect world, that's how things would work. But this isn't a perfect world. This is Chicago."

His words seem to reverberate in the car.

"Robbie just seemed so nice . . ." Emma's voice is watery.

I turn in my seat. "Robbie *is* nice. It's possible he's mixed up in something bad, but I still believe he's a nice guy. Maybe he's trying to get out? Maybe that's the news he doesn't want to share with you yet?"

"Maybe." But Emma's face retains the kicked-puppy look. "Though that seems awfully optimistic."

"That's the funny thing about Piper. She seems tough. But really"—Mariano winks at me—"on the inside, she's as soft as they come."

"You may think it's crazy that she would want your help with something like that, but I don't." Mariano twists his fork to gather spaghetti. "Who else is she going to ask?"

"I've at least learned he's not married. So it hasn't been totally fruitless." I frown. Unless his wife and kids live in a different town . . .

"You found a smart way to get up to his apartment. That can be tough."

"But I couldn't figure out how to get back out without blowing my cover."

Mariano tilts his head. "Sure you did."

After a beat, I catch his meaning. "Well, yeah, technically. But I had to get outside help."

Mariano shrugs. "There's a reason policemen work in pairs."

I peek out the window to be sure Sidekick is still tied to the street lamp outside—he is—and then glance about Madame Galli's Italian restaurant. Tonight, the tables are bursting with young couples and groups of friends, mostly young professional types. I recognize a few judges, whom I met at Father's wedding. I guess it's no surprise considering our proximity to the courthouse.

"Can I talk to you about what happened at the wedding?" Mariano's question pulls me back to the table.

"Of course." I put another bite in my mouth despite my sudden lack of hunger.

He looks at me with those rich brown eyes of his. "First of all, I want to apologize for lying to you. I told myself I wasn't lying, but I was.

"Up until that moment on Clark Street, I honestly thought you knew. I wasn't thinking about you being a girl, and that maybe your father would try to protect you in some way from the kind of work he does. Because that's not the kind of house I grew up in."

Mariano takes a long drink of his Coke. "My father has always been very open about what he does. There was no reason not to be. While it may seem strange to you, being a *mafiasi* family is a proud thing in my culture. My father is the third generation of Cassanos to serve, and I would have been the fourth."

My heart leaps with that beautiful phrase—*would have been.*

Mariano takes several deep breaths, and his face seems to darken with each one. Then, quietly, "For as long as I can remember, my father has chided me for being too soft." When he looks at me, his face is boyish and vulnerable. "I'm built lean, like the men on my mother's side. Not like Father and Uncle Lucas, or my brothers. And I always enjoyed reading, which my father considered a hobby better suited for a girl. Because there was an expectation that I too would cut my own path in the mafia, Father would find ways—activities—to help toughen me." Shadows seem to cross Mariano's face. "Things I won't tell you about."

My hands reach across the table, grasp for his.

He smiles at the sight and raises his gaze to me. "Maybe, had I been of Father's generation, I would have stayed in the family business. But with Prohibition and bootlegging, the stakes have only gotten higher. Things like *omertá* don't hold the weight they once did."

"*Omertá?*"

"It's a value we hold as Sicilians. We protect our own. But with all these new players in the mix, like the Finnegans and Capone, and the obsession with territory, *omertá* is a dying ethic."

Mariano is silent for a bit, his mind clearly elsewhere.

"So you are—and I mean this in the best way possible—*just* a detective?"

Mariano grins. "Yes, Piper. Just a detective. Though it doesn't make my family as happy as it does you. Becoming a civil servant is equivalent to betraying the family name. I'm not a real man. I don't have what it takes. Etcetera." He shrugs, but I can read the hurt on his face as clearly as a bruise. "It's only gotten worse this year. They thought . . . Well, they thought my job could work to their advantage." The sentence tumbles out of him in a rush. "Don't judge them for that, please."

I squeeze his hands.

"They didn't ask for anything at first." His voice has dipped quiet and thoughtful again. "And then one of Doherty's men got gunned down. It wasn't us—not that time—but Uncle Lucas thought it could be a chance to expand our territory, to run the Finnegan brothers out. They wanted me to 'help' with the investigation, and . . ." Mariano shook his head. "When I wouldn't, there were a lot of words about family loyalty, my priorities. I thought Zola would understand, would be on my side, but when she gave me back the ring, she said she couldn't marry a traitor to the family. That was last fall. And I haven't been invited to a family event since."

"Oh, Mariano." The pain on his face has me itching to do something, to fix this for him. But there's nothing that can be done. "I'm so sorry."

He drains the last of his Coke. "It was hard at the time, especially when Zola walked away, but I see now that it was good. How much worse it would've been to marry someone who disapproves of me." For a moment, he stares into his spaghetti. "I suppose that's why I got so angry at the wedding. To Zola, I wasn't *mafiasi* enough. To you, I was too *mafiasi*."

"I shouldn't have assumed the worst. I've just never . . ." The options sit on my tongue.

I've just never cared about someone like this before.

I've just never been so vulnerable. So aware of how easily you could hurt me.

"This is all very scary to me," I hear myself say instead. "I don't want to be wrong about you."

"I don't want that either, Piper." His thumb rubs over the back of my knuckles. "And so long as you believe that I'm a detective who's too straight and narrow to make much money, who will never satisfy his family's expectations, and who values your safety above all else, then I can promise you won't be."

"I like that answer. Mostly. I think that safety thing might interfere with my hopes of going after the Finn—"

Mariano puts his hand up to halt me. "Could we fight about

that tomorrow? Tonight, I would really like to just enjoy being together and pretend that I'm not going to have to stop you from putting yourself in harm's way."

"Okay. Tomorrow. But that's it."

Mariano holds up his glass to cheers. "To tomorrow."

"To tomorrow," I echo.

CHAPTER
TWENTY-THREE

Would you like milk or a Coca-Cola?" Emma calls from the kitchen.

"Coca-Cola, please."

I clasp my hands on my lap so they'll stop trembling. What a silly thing to be nervous about, dropping in on a friend for a social call. I had claimed my visit was about discussing Robbie and our next move, but really, I hoped to talk to her about Mariano and just . . . be together. Have fun. Connect. Like I would have with Lydia if she were still alive.

I like Emma, and I can't keep holding it against her that she isn't Lydia.

When Emma returns to the living room, she balances a tray with two bottles of Coca-Cola and a plate of lemon bars that match the pale yellow of her dress.

"Maybe he doesn't have much money, so he never decorated." She settles the tray onto the coffee table, her skirts swishing around her calves. "Robbie is a very simple man. Which I mean in a good way."

"Maybe." I run my locket up its chain and back down again as I visit Robbie's place once more in my mind. "But no piles of mail? No old newspapers?"

"Perhaps he'd just cleaned them away. Robbie is very neat." Emma perches on the edge of the mahogany armchair, her back straight, her ankles crossed.

I take a bottle of cola and a lemon bar, and I sit up in a way that would please Joyce. "No photographs?"

"Do bachelors keep photographs?"

"I don't know. Robbie's is the only single man's apartment I've ever been in." The lemon bar is creamy and buttery. Crumbs scatter across my white linen dress, and I do my best to discreetly brush them into my napkin.

Emma nibbles at her lemon bar, somehow not creating a single crumb. "Does Mariano have his own place?"

"He has a roommate, but I've never met him. I think his name is Jack." I take a smaller bite of lemon bar this time. "When you meet under the circumstances that Mariano and I did, it's strange how you skip over ordinary details like roommates."

"It was dreamy, seeing him carry you out of Robbie's place. Like some great knight. And the way he looks at you." Emma grins. "He clearly thinks you're the bee's knees, Piper."

Coca-Cola fizzes down my throat. "Robbie too. He looked as though he might float away as he talked to me about you."

Emma's cheeks pinken, brightening her entire face. Seeing her like this makes it seem impossible that I ever thought her plain. "I suppose I'll just have to be patient now, won't I? With Mariano warning us away from the neighborhood, it hardly seems prudent to return." A frown flickers on her face. "I wonder if Robbie is safe there."

"I could ask Mariano, if you'd like. But I agree that we should do as he says. He's not the overprotective type."

"Well, I never thought I'd see *this* day." Jeremiah's words draw a gasp from both me and Emma, and he smirks in the doorway. "Sorry to startle you."

"What day is that, Jeremiah?" Emma's voice is edged with impatience.

Jeremiah removes his trilby from his head as he strides into the room. He swipes a lemon bar from the tray and selects the rocking chair across from me. "The day Piper Sail allowed herself to be stifled by a man." He shakes his head, making a *tsk, tsk* sound. "What would Zelda Fitzgerald think?"

I lock my gaze on my bottle of Coca-Cola.

"Don't be a sore loser, Jeremiah," Emma says. "It's not an attractive feature in a man."

But Jeremiah seems intent on ignoring his sister. "Are you sure about this, Piper?" The rocking chair creaks as he leans forward, elbows on his knees, hands clasped, and with something undefinable in his gaze. "I'm working on a story about the Cassano family for the *Daily*, and I'm worried about what you might be getting yourself into."

I've done some reading myself on the Cassano family, consisting mostly of trumped-up stories in the archived newspapers at the library. The articles had been what I feared I might find— territory battles with other families, gin joints being raided and shut down. And the story that had my father's name peppered throughout, when Lucas Cassano was accused of gunning down his own moll outside of her swanky Michigan Avenue apartment.

"I appreciate your concern, Jeremiah. But Mariano is on a different path than his family."

"Is he?"

My mind goes to the restaurant last night, to Mariano's earnest eyes as he assured me that he was *just* a detective. "Yes."

"What kind of story?" Emma's voice is low and fearful, her eyes wide.

Jeremiah looks to her. Takes a breath. The silence stretches tight between them.

"You're not doing anything foolish, are you?" Emma sounds like a scolding mother rather than a little sister.

"I'm fine, Emma."

Emma doesn't seem convinced. Perhaps it's because Jeremiah keeps twisting his hat in his hands. Or the way his smile doesn't quite reach his eyes.

He looks back to me and changes the subject. "Where have your father and his wife gone for their honeymoon?"

"Paris. Jane had never been."

Emma's plate clatters onto the end table. "Jeremiah Crane, what is your story about?"

Irritation gleams in Jeremiah's eyes. "Don't trouble yourself over it. I know what I'm doing."

"Do you?"

"I should go." I stand, and hope neither notice when crumbs sprinkle to the ground.

Emma jumps to her feet. "Piper, please don't."

The rocking chair creaks as Jeremiah rises as well. "Yes, don't let my rudeness drive you away."

"It isn't that. I'm having dinner with Nick and his girlfriend tonight, and I had better get dressed." I set my plate and empty bottle on the tray and pivot toward the front door.

"I think we saw them together in the neighborhood," Emma says as she follows. "Tall girl? Auburn hair?"

"That's Alana."

I reach for my cloche hanging on the entry rack, but Jeremiah's hand intercepts me. He lifts it from the hook and offers it to me without a smile.

My cheeks heat under his somber scrutiny. "Thank you."

"Neither of us recognized her," Emma says. "How did they meet?"

The question makes my heart ache a bit, like pressing on a bruise before it's completely faded. "She was one of the reporters who covered Lydia's story."

Emma frowns. "A woman?" She looks to Jeremiah. "Who in town has women doing such macabre articles?"

"She's from Kansas City, actually." My cloche pushes out one of my hair pins, and I tuck it back into place. "Because of the connection between Matthew and the organized crime down there, *The Kansas City Star* apparently felt it would interest their readers enough to send a reporter of their own."

Jeremiah leans against the wall, tucks his hands in his trouser pockets. "But a woman?"

"Someday, the two of you may be colleagues, actually. Her father owns *The Kansas City Star*. I suppose *that* is why she has the freedom to take on a story like this."

Jeremiah blinks, slow and considering. "Are you saying her *father* is Irwin Kirkwood?"

"If he's the owner of *The Kansas City Star*, yes."

"He is. But are you sure she said she was his *daughter*?"

"Pretty sure."

"Not his niece or cousin or anything?"

Emma sighs. "Jeremiah, really. Must you always be tiresome?"

But Jeremiah doesn't look away from me, and there's something foreboding in his eyes that prevents me from turning away either. I think back to that family dinner, and play Alana's words through my mind. "She said daughter," I confirm. "Why?"

He takes in a breath, holds it a moment. "Because Irwin and Laura don't have any children."

I stare at him, thoughts whipping through my brain too fast to grab a firm hold of any.

He stares back.

Emma's laugh rings high. "You must be remembering wrong, Jeremiah."

"No, I'm quite certain."

"Maybe I misunderstood her." My fingers draw my locket up the length of its chain. I can hear her words from dinner that evening as clear as if she just spoke them. *When your father owns the paper, you have to learn it all, whether you're a female or not.*

Why did she lie? Some kind of trick to win Nick's affections? Did she think my brother would only notice her if she had a family of means and power?

"Why would she have lied about that?" Emma's question is breathy with disbelief, and it brings a smile to my face. Lydia would have reacted exactly the same.

"I don't know, but I can't wait to find out." I wink at Emma. "Perhaps dinner won't be as dull as I had feared."

At home, I find Joyce forgot to lock the back door—so unlike her—and that Sidekick isn't in his usual place on the towel we keep in the pantry.

I groan. If he's chewed up my shoes again . . . "Sidekick? Where are you, you troublemaker?"

After a moment, I hear the distinct sound of Sidekick's nails scraping along the hardwood as he races down the stairs, makes a sliding turn in the entry, and barrels into the kitchen.

His front paws land square on my chest, and he gives a delighted yip.

I scratch his ears before nudging his paws off me. "Easy, buddy. Madeleine Vionnet dresses don't grow on trees, you know."

He dances a circle on the floor, his tail whipping back and forth.

Accusing Alana of lying is too big an allegation to hang on Jeremiah being "quite sure" that Irwin Kirkwood has no daughter. I could call the newspaper and learn her real last name, and then, if there's time, go to the library and see if I can get my hands on some archived issues. Seems like I should know everything I possibly can for when she inevitably denies the truth.

I settle at Father's desk and pull the telephone close to me. Sidekick lays his head on my lap and whimpers. "What's going on with you?" I hook my finger in the dial and pull until my finger aligns with the appropriate number. "You're acting very peculiar."

I rub by his ears while I wait. A woman comes on the line. "Long distance."

"Hi. I'd like to make a person-to-business call to *The Kansas City Star* in Kansas City, Missouri."

"Your name and number, please?"

"Piper Sail. LIN-0421."

"Thank you. I'll ring you back soon with your connection."

"Thank you."

My heart pitter-patters in my chest as I hang the earpiece back on the hook. Hopefully, Father makes enough long-distance telephone calls that the exorbitant expense won't be shocking enough for him to investigate when the next bill comes.

Sidekick presses his head deeper into my lap while we wait. I eye the ticking grandfather clock by the door. Supposing the call is quick, I *might* be able to make it to—

The phone trills, ratcheting up my heart rate. I shake my head at myself—I'm such a ninny sometimes. "Hello?"

"Your connection has been made."

"Thank you."

"*Kansas City Star.* How may I direct your call?" There's a click as the long-distance operator leaves the line.

"I'm calling for Alana Kirkwood."

Pause. "Did you say Irwin Kirkwood, miss?"

"No, Alana Kirkwood. One of your reporters."

The second pause sends a satisfying thrill through me. "We don't have any reporters by that name, miss."

I throw my stocking feet up on Father's desk. *Gotcha.* "Oh, really? I was sure that was her name. What about one of your other female reporters? Are they available?"

"We don't employ any female reporters, miss."

I sit upright, and my feet fall to the floor with a *thunk* that makes Sidekick scurry away.

"Miss?"

"I'm here. I . . ." None? "You don't employ *any*?"

"No, miss. What is your call in regards to? I'll connect you to the best party poss—"

I let my finger fall heavy on the switch hook.

No female reporters? Absolutely none? Does that mean—

"So." Alana smirks at me from the doorway, and a yelp escapes me. "You learned my little secret."

My heart thunders. "I didn't know you were here."

"I know."

The simplicity of her words and the mystery of her smile makes my stomach fold in on itself. "Why'd you lie?"

Alana saunters toward Father's desk, the late-afternoon rays of sunlight shimmering in the beads of her fine dress. "Haven't you ever lied to get what you want, Piper?"

I fight away an eye roll. "Nick is no sap. Don't you think he would've figured out that you're a fake before you dragged him down the middle aisle?"

Alana stands tall on the other side of Father's desk, looking down at me with a patronizing smile. "You really think I'd go to all this trouble for *Nick*?"

How dare she insult my brother. "If not for Nick—who, by the way, would be a catch for a girl like you—then why?"

"I'm going to ask you a question, and if you're smart, you'll tell me the truth." She rests her palms on Father's desk and towers over me, the smile wiped from her face. "Where is your friend Matthew?"

"Matthew?" The word emerges on a gusty exhale. "I've no idea."

Alana considers me. "I think you're lying."

"Well, then, you're going to be disappointed, because I'm not."

She straightens. "My patience has run out, Piper. And this time when I ask you, you'd better shoot straight." She undoes the clasp of her clutch, and a small, silver pistol glints in the light as she levels it at me. "Or I'll make sure *I* do."

The gun, which resides so comfortably in Alana's grasp, sends my heart slamming against my rib cage. "I-I'm not lying."

The words flop out of my mouth and lie pointlessly between us. They're no shield for me.

"I saw the letter." Impatience hardens her words. "He said he'd call. Now, where is he?"

Sidekick wedges himself under my legs and trembles. Some sidekick. "He never called."

"Enough with the lies, Piper. Where is he?"

"If I knew, I would tell you, but I don—"

There's a knock at the front door, which makes a startled scream stick in my throat. Sidekick barks, and scrambles out from under the desk to greet the visitor.

Alana seems alarmed as well. She holds the gun at her side, and I steal the moment to look about Father's desk. His banker's lamp could be a decent weapon. Why can't he keep a letter opener in plain sight?

Alana aims the gun at me once more. "Who's at the door, Piper?"

"I don't know."

"We're going to ignore them. You so much as whimper the word *help*, and I will pull this trigger. That understood?"

The look in her eyes—fury with a twinge of madness—is what sets my knees trembling.

"Is that understood?"

I nod.

"Do you want to live, Piper?" Her voice is cold and quiet, yet it roars above Sidekick's barking and scratching at the front door.

"Yes, I do." *Please come in here. Whoever you are, please come in.*

"Then all you need to do is tell me where Matthew is. You tell me that, and this has a happy ending for all of us."

"What's Matthew to you?"

Alana opens her mouth, but instead, Emma Crane's sweet voice fills the air. "Piper?" She's in the entryway. "Hello?"

My eyes slide closed as dread pierces my heart. *Not Emma.*

"Anyone home?"

I look to Alana, who presses her finger to her lips, the universal sign for *shh*.

But Sidekick's nails slide across the floor as he romps down the short hallway, toward the office.

"Blasted dog," Alana mutters. She tucks the gun behind her back. "Don't get up. Don't move. And get rid of her quick." Her voice morphs to the airy, social one I'm accustomed to. "We're down the hall, hon. In Mr. Sail's office."

Nick's words float through my ears—*sometimes, it's like she's two different people*—and a shiver courses through me.

"Forgive me for barging in, but the door was unlocked." Emma appears in the doorway, her dress sunshine yellow and her cheeks pink. Her smile falls when she looks at me. "Piper, what's wrong?"

I swallow. I don't need to look at Alana to know she's watching me with a warning gaze. I have to be calm. I have to lie.

"Nothing." My laugh trembles out of me. "I'm perfectly fine."

"Oh, good. You looked as though you'd received some sort of dreadful news!" She holds up my beaded handbag. "This is why I so rudely let myself in. I figured you'd need it for dinner tonight."

"Thank you." My gaze wanders to the barrel of the gun behind Alana's back, still pointed at me. "Why don't you just put it right there? We need to be going soon."

"I've walked it this far. Surely I can walk it ten more feet to you."

As Emma draws closer to the desk, I bite my lower lip to keep from screaming, *Run! Get out of here!*

Especially when Emma smiles at Alana and says a polite, "Hello."

I have to introduce them. It'll seem odd if I don't. "This is Alana Kirkwood, Nick's girlfriend." The words have a wobble to them that I can't seem to erase from my voice. "And this is my good friend, Emma Crane."

Emma holds out her hand, every bit the well-bred society girl. "How do you do?"

My stomach lurches as Alana shifts the gun to her left hand in order to shake Emma's. "Very nice to meet you."

How good of a shot is she? It's a single-action pistol. Does she carry extra bullets in her clutch as well? If I could somehow get to the gun and fire off a shot, I could do away with her advantage . . .

But I can't put Emma at risk. "Thanks for bringing my handbag, Emma, but we really need to be leaving for dinner."

"Of course. I hope you enjoy yourselves." She smiles at Alana. "So nice to have met you."

Emma bends to scratch Sidekick's chin, and in my peripheral vision, I see Alana shifting the gun back to her other hand. Her fingers seem to be tangled in the shift, and my gaze cuts to Father's banker lamp. I could yank it from its cord and aim for her temple.

I glance at Alana and find her piercing gaze on me, as if she read my mind.

The breath whooshes from me as I see it happening—the gun slips from her hand.

I reach across the desk and grasp the lamp base with both hands as Emma yelps, "A gun!"

I stand and push Father's chair back with one foot as I jerk at the lamp. "Run, Emma!"

She screams and scrambles for the door.

The lamp breaks free, and I stagger backward, right into Sidekick. He yips as I stumble over him, landing hard on my right hip behind Father's desk.

The crack of gunfire fills the room, cutting off Emma's scream. Through Father's desk, I see her crumple to the ground, her arms still stretching for the door. Crimson blooms on the back of her shoulder.

"No." I whisper the word. Or maybe I yell it. My ears ring from the explosion of the gun.

Fingers grasp my arm and yank me along the carpet.

"Get off me!" I claw at her hand. She used up her bullet— and her advantage.

I try to stand, but pain screams in my right hip where it connected with the wood floor. I grab hold of Father's desk, try to anchor myself there, and Alana grimaces as she tugs at me. "I don't want to hurt you, Piper."

The gunshot still rings in my ear, and her words seem distant, as if my ears are filled with cotton. "You shot Emma!" The circle of red on her back grows ever bigger, and she's eerily still against the wall. Is she alive? *Please, God.* "Emma!"

A scream overcomes the room, only it isn't me or Emma. It's Alana. She releases me and swats at Sidekick, whose jaws are clamped around her ankle. She raises her pistol, and before I can stop it, she knocks the butt of the gun against his skull.

He releases her with a yap and staggers away, handing me a window of opportunity.

I throw my left leg across her and collapse all my weight

onto her stomach. She groans as the air rushes out of her body. "What is wrong with you?" The girl yelling doesn't sound like me. I hold down Alana's arms and push her flat against the floor. "How could you shoot her? I told you, I don't know anything!"

"Don't protect him, Piper," she gasps out. "He killed Lydia."

He *what*?! My hands fall from her wrists. "That's impossible. Matthew loved her."

Alana's left hand snatches my collar, yanks me close. "And that's what killed her."

In my peripheral, I catch the shadow of something in her right hand—the lamp? Then the nape of my neck erupts in pain, and the world is dark.

~ TWENTY-FOUR ~

The world around me is shadowed. But at least I'm aware it exists. And that there are voices in it.

"The answer is no, Maeve." It's a male voice, graveled with a hint of Irish burr. "We're trying to run a business here."

Who is that? Where am I? Gray light filters through my eyelashes as I try to open them, and a blade of pain slices through my skull. I'm lying in something sticky. I raise my head, gritting my teeth against the searing pain, and force open my eyes.

Blood. And from the burning of my cheek and forehead, I would guess it's my own.

My hands instinctively reach to grasp hold of my head, only they're stuck behind my back. I tug, but they're attached at the wrists. Rope? Did that blasted Alana tie me up?

"I wouldn't ask if it weren't an emergency." Alana.

"You seem to have a lot of emergencies. We helped you out last time because I owed my cousin a favor, even if he is an idiot. And I loved Alan. But we already have the cops breathing down our necks. Another dead society broad is the last thing we need."

Fear streaks up my spine. I blink as my vision starts to clear. A car. I'm in the back of a car. Grainy light filters through the window, but it's too blinding to see any landmarks.

Is Emma here too? Wherever "here" is?

"Emma?" I try to call. But the sound never makes it past the rag shoved in my mouth.

"She knows where Jacob is, I can feel it." Alana's voice is high and desperate. "We could finally get justice for what he did to Alan. To our family name."

"Maeve." The name—Alana's name?—is sharp on his tongue. "No."

"It's Timothy Sail's daughter. Her dad is the reason Colin rots in jail. I'm handing you your best chance for revenge, Uncle Pat."

Pat? As in Patrick Finnegan? Panic fills my veins, and I strain at the ropes binding my wrists and ankles. I have to get them loose. If I want to survive this, I have to break free. I have to be clearheaded and smart.

But it feels as if my brain is wrapped in gauze, like I have to cut through layers upon layers to form a thought. And I *need* coherent thoughts right now. I need them like never before.

"I'm not your uncle. And even if I ignored that, the Cassanos would gun me down faster than you can say 'Mariano's girl.'"

My vision starts to edge in black as fatigue saturates my body.

No, not yet. I have to fight. I have to find *some* way to leave behind a clue for those who are looking for me. I force my brain to catalog every article of clothing I put on this morning. My feet are bare. I could try to tear my dress whenever Alana gets me out of the car, but that's a gamble I don't want to wait for. My knife is in my handbag, back in Father's office.

"But if you would just—"

"Am I being unclear, Maeve?"

My locket—has it survived so far?

The silver oval winks in the waning sunlight, and the stab of pain that shoots through my head is worth it. If I can get it off, maybe I can drop it on the ground when the door is opened. I have to try and leave some kind of trail.

"I just thought you'd care about your nephew, is all." Alana's voice has a childish, sulking quality to it.

"You bring me the guy who killed Alan, I'll slit his throat. But you keep bringing me society dames. I can't work with that."

If I could just get my hands free, I could yank the necklace off. But wriggling my wrists only makes them burn. Is there anything that I could possibly hook the necklace around to pull it loose?

"This discussion is over, Maeve. Move your car. We've got a big delivery shipping out just after sunset."

I'll have to try and work the necklace off. I trap the locket beneath my collarbone and push against the far end of the car with my feet. A burning ache flames across my right cheek as the raw skin rubs against the sticky, bloody floor. I have to ignore it. The chain cuts into my neck but doesn't give. I push harder. My muscles and face scream in protest.

"When my father-in-law hears about how I've been treated—"

"You tell Jimmy whatever you like about me. I don't know how my cousin works things in Kansas City, but I'm guessing he doesn't let little girls tell him what to do. And I don't neither. Now clear out."

The smells of sweat and strain fill my nostrils. My eyes slide closed, desperate for sleep. I think of Mariano, Father, Emma, Walter, Joyce, Tim, and Nick. I parade their faces in my mind's eye. I have to get this necklace off. I have to give people a chance to find me.

"Pat!" A new voice, masculine and panicked, bursts into the conversation. Gravel crunches—footsteps. Approaching fast. "Feds are here!"

I don't recognize the word Patrick Finnegan growls, but his footsteps race away from the car.

Will Alana—Maeve?—take me out of the car now? Shoot me and dump my body wherever it is that we're parked?

I push again with my toes, straining upward, but still the chain holds strong.

A door yanks open and slams shut. That must be Alana, right? The engine roars to life, and with a loud pop, the tires chew up gravel as we speed away. Each bump makes my bones rattle. The rear of the car fishtails from the high speeds on a poorly finished road.

The car makes a sudden turn to the left, sending my body tumbling out of control.

The snap of my chain is like music. The sound comes just before my head connects with the wall of the car.

And then the world is gone again.

An icy spray of water blasts my face. I try to suck in a breath, but there's still a rag taped into my mouth, and all I manage to do is breathe water into my nose. My eyes snap open just in time to see someone grab hold of a corner of the tape and rip it off my mouth. My cheeks scream in protest, and the air feels so good in my lungs, they ache.

"Emma!" I rasp out the word as the remnants of my dream—her yellow, flowered dress, the blood spreading outward—fade away.

"Finally." Alana towers over me, holding an empty glass. "I was starting to think you wouldn't come around. You must've lost more blood than I thought."

I rest my thumping head against the tall side of a bathtub. I pull a delicious amount of air into my lungs and exhale again. The rush of oxygen is dizzying.

Alana drags a wooden kitchen chair alongside the tub, like Mother would when bathing me as a child. "I took out the gag because I need answers from you. But I won't hesitate to put it back in if you decide to yell."

The lukewarm water filling the bath soaks my dress and makes me shiver. "What happened"—my voice scratches against my throat—"to Lydia?"

Alana's smile is tinged with sadness. "I *am* sorry about her. It sounds like she was a swell girl. Your brother was clearly still hung up on her."

My heart bucks against Alana's condolences, but my body is too weak to react as I want.

"I observed her for a while, you know. I would've liked her, I'm sure."

I can hear Lydia's voice in my head, confiding in me about her medicine. *It makes me paranoid too. I kept thinking this black car was following me. Or like at the store yesterday. I was convinced that woman was listening to every word we said. Following me.*

The tall woman who had watched us buy Walter's shirt and hat. I look at Alana, and it's so clear. If only I had realized it sooner.

"And I like you too, Piper. You think you're smarter than everyone around you, but I wouldn't sentence you to death for it."

"How thoughtful."

I'm not sure she hears my sarcasm above the roar of the water, but her smile has a wryness to it. "Would you like a drink?

You're probably thirsty." She leans forward to dip the glass in the bathwater, which has been dyed pink from my blood.

Sitting on top of the toilet tank is her silver gun.

"I had to leave you in the car for longer than I wanted," Alana says as she holds the glass against my mouth. "I needed it to be good and dark before I could bring you in, obviously. If I felt like I could trust you, I'd remove your bindings. We'll see how forthcoming you are."

My need for water overrides my detestation of accepting something from her hand. The corners of my mouth ache from where the gag strained them, and the water feels like a balm for my dry tongue and aching throat.

Far too soon, Alana pulls the glass away. She turns the faucet off, and then crosses one slender leg over the other. If she imagines she looks calm and glamorous, she's mistaken. Her bob of hair is disheveled, her face white like paper, and her movements jerky, like a marionette in an unskilled hand.

"I'll make you a deal, Piper. You give me the answers I want, and you get to go home. Back to your dog, your petulant big brother, and your very cute cop boyfriend. He must be out of his mind with worry."

"I'm sure that's a real concern to you."

"I'm not as cold as you might think. I've been in love before, can you believe that?" Alana reaches for the gun, and every aching muscle in my body goes taut.

But she only tweaks it so the handle is angled toward her. "I would prefer to not use this, but if you decide to get loud, I won't hesitate. And I wouldn't aim to kill, not the first time, anyway. Just something to keep in mind."

I stare at it, seeing Emma's body splayed on the floor, the

blood soaking her dress. Has anyone found her yet? Is there any chance someone arrived in time to save her? Where is my locket? Still in the back of the car, or dare I hope that it fell out?

"So do we have a deal? You answer my questions, and I don't kill you. We all get what we want."

"How stupid do you think I am? You'll never let me go. I know way too much."

"I don't want to kill you, Piper—"

A watery laugh wheezes out of me. "That's not the song you were singing to Patrick Finnegan."

Alana's eyes spark, and her lips purse. "I said what I had to so I could get the help I wanted. I think you're familiar with that concept, Piper."

"You think I don't realize you're doing the same thing to me? Dangling my life like a carrot so that I'll tell you what I know."

The smile on her face is broad and terrifying. "I *knew* you knew where Jacob went."

The victory in her words sends a shiver through my body. "I didn't mean it like *that*. I meant that you're trying to get me to share something that you *think* I know. Matthew, or Jacob—whoever he is—and I were never close. I have no reason to protect him."

"He said in his letter he would call."

"How many times do I have to say it?" My answer comes through chattering teeth. "He never called."

"I think you still have in your head that Jacob is the good guy, and I'm the bad. But I'm not. Not at all."

"You killed my best friend!" I try to scream it, but the words are a meager squawk. They don't even echo off the yellowed bathroom tiles.

"No, Jacob did."

"I don't recall him kidnapping her. Do you?"

Her mouth quirks. "Even now, you can't resist being snotty, can you? Jacob's letter to you was full of lies. Do you actually believe the man who lived next door to him just *happened* to be an undercover Prohibition agent? That the agent just *happened* to be ready and waiting for a pickup that Jacob was in charge of? That Jacob just *happened* to be one of the only people who didn't get killed? Sounds like a lot of coincidences, don't you think?"

She leans above me, her face hard and her eyes full of such a dark intensity, I look away. "Well, his coincidences stole my life. Everything I'd worked for and loved—my husband, my baby. And so long as there's breath in my body—and breath in *his*—I will make him pay."

Matthew had mentioned Alan's widow in his letter, hadn't he? By name, even. He had seen her in town after Lydia went missing, talking to Patrick Finnegan. Somehow, that detail had seemed inconsequential. The word *widow* had conjured up a mental picture of an older woman. Certainly not someone only a few years older than myself. Not someone who would have any motive to hurt Lydia.

"And it doesn't matter what collateral damage there is along the way, huh? The life of an innocent girl like Lydia is meaningless to you."

"Not at all. I'll regret her death every day of my life. I promise you that."

"Then why did you take her?" My voice sounds like it once did as a child, when I asked God the same thing about my mother. *I needed her. Why did you take her?* "Why did you kill her?"

"Jacob was always cunning." She sits upright in the chair,

her eyes glassy. "Or so I was told by my father-in-law. That's why the Burks hired him, of course. Never dreamed he'd double-cross them. The private investigators the family sent just couldn't seem to track him down, but I knew I could. I cared more, for one thing. And also as a woman, there was information I could get that no man could."

Her smile has a camaraderie that sours my stomach. "I know you understand that, Piper. They underestimate us. And the smart girl uses it to her advantage."

"So you found him."

"After a long year of searching, yes, I did." Pride shines in her eyes. "With all the women he burned through in Kansas City—they were quite helpful in locating him—I wasn't at all surprised to find he was carrying on with his employer's adolescent daughter. But to find he actually *cared* about the poor chit, and to see that she actually cared about him . . ." Her eyes glint, and her sorrow for what happened to Lydia seems to have evaporated. "I couldn't pass up the chance to make him feel even a fraction of what I felt when he took Alan from me."

Alana's sigh is heavy. "I regret it now, of course. By dallying with him, I missed my chance. I planned to return Lydia to her family the next day, only . . ." Again, she sighs. "She was dead that night when I came in to get her. After Lydia died, it was impossible to get close to him. There were reporters everywhere. I tried poisoning—figured better to get him from afar than not at all—but apparently, all I got was his cat. If only Lydia hadn't died, everything would've gone to plan."

"She had seizures." The words are watery, and I cough and shudder all at once. "She choked on her own vomit, thanks to you."

Alana regards me with a steady gaze. "I wish it hadn't happened." Her words are quiet, and yet somehow they seem to bounce all around the room. "Maybe my regret means nothing to you, but I hope you're at least smart enough to see that Jacob is at the root of all this. That telling me where he went is the best thing you can do."

"But I don't"—I cough and shiver—"know where he is."

Alana runs her fingers through her hair. Her hands tremble, or perhaps it only seems that way because my teeth chatter. "Come on, Piper, think. You rode in a car with the man for over a year. Where would he go?"

I would go to California or Arizona. Someplace warm. "Maybe he left the country."

"I don't need maybes." Her words are a dark snarl, and she grasps the sides of the tub, leans down over me. "I can come up with maybes on my own. I've searched all over for leads. I even went back to his mother's place in Arkansas. I need to know *real* places. I need to know where he called you from."

The words chatter out of me. "H-he didn't c-call me."

Her face morphs before my eyes, that inhuman look again. Her hands are around my throat as she presses me down into the water. The water which had once felt like a balm now burns. My arms and legs seem to forget they're bound; they press against the ropes, fighting for freedom. The world is splattered in black, and then I'm yanked back up. Air screams down my throat as water hacks its way out in an ugly cough.

"I am not going back without him." Alana's words come through gritted teeth, and yet somehow are being screamed in my ears. "I'm not going back to having nothing. Not when I had everything—*everything*—and that man ripped it away."

Breathe in, breathe out. That's all my body can manage to do right now. Breathe in, breathe out. There's a pounding in my head, an ache over my whole body. *I could be with Lydia and Mother. I could just let myself slip away.*

The pounding in my head is so loud, it seems audible. Like a knock on a door.

And maybe it is, because Alana suddenly straightens. She looks back to me, her expression calculated rather than demonic, and she shoves the gag back into my mouth.

"Our conversations seem to always get interrupted."

I sink against the edge of the tub and struggle to pull oxygen through my nose. *In and out, in and out.* Such an unconscious act until you find your airways blocked. *In and out.*

"Don't make a peep." Her face is so close to mine, it blurs. "Or I swear by my Alan that you'll regret it. We'll just let them go away."

In and out. In and out. The world around me is speckled with stars, but I have to keep breathing. *In and out.*

Another knock. "Police! Open up!"

Mariano. My heart seems to sing the name.

Alana's panicked face, her darting eyes, are framed in ever-growing black. She grabs her gun and slinks out the bathroom door, leaving me alone. I try to swing my legs over the edge of the tub. At least try to get out, to do *something* besides breathe. But breathing is just so darn hard. *In and out. In and . . . out. In . . . and . . .*

"Alana Kirkwood, we know you're in here!"

"Mariano!" I scream, but the word is tangled in the rag. I splash my feet, bang them against the edge of the tub. "Mariano!" I try again.

And then, as if by magic, he's there. Standing in the doorway with a gun leveled at me.

He lowers it immediately. "Piper! Thank God."

Tears heat my eyes as Mariano rushes to the edge of the tub.

He eases the rag from my mouth, and gives me a once-over. "What'd she do to you?" The horror on his face tells me that I look as terrible as I feel.

Detective O'Malley's broad frame fills the doorway.

"Alana." The words wheeze from my lungs. "She's here. She has a gun."

O'Malley turns down the hall, holds his weapon steady.

"You're burning up, Piper." Mariano's hand is like ice on my forehead. "We have to get you to the hospital."

"Get Alana." My mouth is so dry, it's like talking through a mouthful of cotton. "She's here. She . . ." The rush of oxygen has made me dizzy. There seem to be two of Mariano. "She has . . . She has a gun."

"We know. We're getting her, Piper. You're safe. Just relax. It's all going to be okay."

And I find that, miraculously, I believe him.

❧ TWENTY-FIVE ❧

The sunlight that filters through the stained glass windows of St. Chrysostom's Episcopal Church is soft and pink. The casket on stage is open, but I don't move from my spot on the front pew.

I already know who I'll find inside. Even from here, I can see the honey color of my hair. Can make out the profile I've seen countless times in my bathroom mirror.

Lydia reaches for my hand. She presses her palm against mine, wordlessly, just as she did all those years ago when we stood by my mother's grave.

"It doesn't feel so bad, does it?" I say.

She turns to me. It's clear that she's not a mere mortal—she's glorious, so bright that my eyes ache—yet somehow she still looks like herself. "You mean death?"

I nod. "I thought it might hurt, but . . ." I shrug. "I feel just fine."

Lydia's teeth gleam like pearls. "It's splendid, actually. Like you're finally whole. Finally perfect."

"I don't feel particularly *perfect*, but—"

Her laugh tinkles like a wind chime. "That's because you're not dead, dear Piper."

"Then what am I?"

"You're dreaming."

I stare at the casket. Empty. "How long do I get to stay here?"

"I'm not sure." Lydia shrugs. Her movements have a fluidity to them, rather than the labored grace she had on earth. "But you'll wake up eventually."

A sigh leaks out of me. "And then what?"

"How do you mean?"

"I mean, what am I supposed to do? All I've thought about since you went missing is figuring out what happened to you. Now what am I supposed to do with my life?"

"Whatever you like, of course." She smirks. "Though I wouldn't suggest anything that involves sewing."

I giggle. "Now there's a disappointment."

"What did you want to do?"

"You mean before you . . . you know."

Lydia laughs, the sound radiant and sweet. "You seriously think you're going to offend me? I know I'm dead, Piper. You can say it. Yes, what did you want to do before I was dead? Go to a university, right?"

"I don't know. It sounded bold and smart at the time, but I don't know."

"You wanted to find something that would help people. You didn't want to be just a wife."

The pew seems to feel harder as we talk. "It all seems so pointless now."

"No, it isn't. Giving away your life—helping people—is what will matter most in the end."

"I wanted to help *you*."

"I know you did, Piper." Her tone is one of amused appreciation. Like when an adult thanks a toddler for helping with a household chore—they didn't *really* help, but their effort was sweet. "However, only the living need help."

A headache creeps up the back of my neck. I move my arm to rub at it, and wince from the pain. "At the time, I thought you were the living. I hoped you were, anyway."

"I know." Lydia's voice has gone soft, and her image is nearly transparent. "But I'm okay. And you will be too."

A stab of pain hits my ribs. I'm waking up, I can feel it. "No! I'm not ready!"

"You are." Her voice is wispy, reassuring.

"I'm not ready!" But my words only echo off the high ceiling of the church.

She's gone.

Wherever I am, it's nighttime. Gray moonlight casts long dark shadows on the walls. My mouth feels as though it's filled with sand. The back of my head throbs, just like in my dream, and when I stir, pain blossoms all over my body.

I wince as I turn my head to the right. There are several empty cots—hospital beds?—and a window that reveals the city is asleep.

"Piper." My name is a breath of excitement from my left. Mariano jumps to his feet with enviable ease, a smile lighting his face. "You're awake."

The words scratch their way out of my throat. "Is there water?"

"I'll get you some. Be right back."

When Mariano seems to return half a second later, I realize I had dozed off.

He fumbles for the crank on the bed. "Let me help you sit up."

My body groans in protest, but it's worth it when the water washes over my tongue and down my throat.

"Not too much, now," Mariano cautions. "The nurse is calling your house, and then she'll bring in some broth. Joyce and your brothers were here all day, but I convinced them to let me take the night shift."

All day? "How long have I been asleep?"

"Over twenty-four hours. The doctor gave you some pretty strong stuff." Mariano's fingertips brush back my hair. "You were so brave, Piper. I'm so sorry for how long it took me to get to you."

"How did you find me in the first place? You seemed to magically appear. I thought I might be dreaming you."

"I was at your house when your friend Johnny Walker called. He found your locket, recognized the picture of Lydia, and called." Mariano's smile is wry. "He'd kept your number all these weeks. You make an impression."

"But how did *he* find it?"

"Alana—or Maeve, actually—lives above his lunchroom." Mariano's voice softens. "She was there that day. Do you remember? The waitress who dropped the mugs."

Yes. I see the moment clearly for the first time. Alana in her Johnny's Lunchroom outfit. Her long frame crouched over the ceramics she shattered when Johnny said Lydia's name. The sorrow in her eyes when she said she was sorry about my friend.

"You wouldn't expect it of him, but Johnny was near tears tonight after we found you. He said he thinks he even *saw* Alana take Lydia up to her apartment. Said she was carrying her up, unconscious. Alana claimed she was her niece from Kansas, who didn't know how to handle Chicago booze. I guess he was pretty ossified himself that night. Didn't put it all together until he found your locket in the stairwell, called your house, and learned Alana had taken you."

"But why were you at my house? How did you even know?"

"I hear our sleeping beauty is awake," sings a nurse as she bustles into the room. She carries a tray to the bedside, and smiles down at me. "You've given us all quite a scare. Your friend has been asking if you're awake every time I go in there."

"My friend?"

"Emma Crane," Mariano says. "She woke up from surgery this afternoon."

I didn't know I had the energy for it, but for the first time in my life, I burst into tears of joy.

"It was the most surreal experience I've ever had." Emma's cheeks are flushed as she recounts the details of that afternoon. "I must have been out cold for a bit, because when I woke up, you were gone."

I shudder involuntarily, and my body rewards me with a spike of pain in my two cracked ribs. Mariano frowns at me in the overly concerned way I've become accustomed to these last few days in the hospital, and I do my best to put on a smile.

It must be convincing enough, because Mariano turns back to Emma. "Fainting probably saved your life."

"Probably. Alana was clearly not in her right mind."

Leave it to Emma Crane to describe a woman wielding a gun in such delicate terms.

"From our understanding, Maeve hasn't been in her right mind for some time." Mariano pulls his notebook from his breast pocket and flips it open. "She's one of thirteen children born to a farmer out in Liberal, Kansas. Her father was a drinker, and her mother had a reputation around town. Maeve and her older sister escaped to Kansas City in their late teens to teach. Maeve met Alan Burk, the oldest son of small-time mobster Jim Burk, and they married pretty quickly.

"They had only been married a few months when Alan died during a delivery. The family blamed their employee, Jacob Dunn, who we knew as Matthew, for his death. Jacob knew enough to get out of town and to keep a low profile. From what we've been able to piece together so far—Maeve's older sister has been very helpful—Maeve went a little crazy after losing Alan. She lost the baby she was carrying, and fixated on revenge. She's spent this last year trying to find Matthew and make him pay."

A silence falls over the room, and Mariano tucks his notebook back into his pocket.

Pain pokes at my side, and I shift my weight. "And Lydia and Emma just got caught in the crossfire."

"You too, Piper," Emma says. "She did quite a bit of damage to you too."

"She didn't *shoot* me."

"Well, she didn't drag my face along the gravel and haul me off in her car."

My fingers brush the thick bandage covering most of my right cheek. "Anyway. You were telling a story. You had just woken up from being shot."

"Oh, right. In retrospect, it seems like I should have been thinking about the pain, but I really wasn't. It was like I hadn't discovered it yet, or something." Emma chuckles, and then flinches and repositions herself in her wheelchair. "I figured it

out when I tried to get up and go to the telephone, though. I'm
just glad she decided to shoot me in your father's office, where
the telephone was ten feet away, because even that took forever."

"Very considerate of her," Mariano says drily.

"I called Jeremiah, who thought you and I were playing
a prank on him. I swear, I thought I'd never convince him to
come over."

"You went to return her handbag," Jeremiah's voice breaks
in from the doorway. "What was I supposed to think?"

In many ways, he looks like his normal self. Fine-tailored
suit, hat slightly askew, a smile on his lips. But there are shadows
under his eyes, and in general he seems rather . . . wilted.

He strolls into the room, hands in his pockets. "I hope you
don't mind the intrusion. Your nurse told me you were off visiting. She asked me to bring you back upstairs, actually." He
nods at me. "Nice to see you awake, Miss Sail." His gaze flits to
Mariano. "Detective."

"Mr. Crane."

Jeremiah's gaze settles on me again. "How are you feeling?"

"Like one big bandage."

"You're interrupting me, Jeremiah." Emma's tone is teasing.
"And I can't go back upstairs until I've told Piper the whole
story."

Jeremiah makes a sweeping motion with his hand, indica-
tive of "go on," and perches on the empty cot beside mine.

"So I told Jeremiah as much of what happened as I could,
and then I must have blacked out or something. Because when I
woke up, Jeremiah was in the house, calling for me."

"Your dog is worthless, by the way," Jeremiah says to me.
"He just cowered behind a chair until Mariano showed up."

I think of the surprise and pain on Alana's face when Sidekick took hold of her ankle. "He's not worthless."

"We found Mariano's card in your handbag and called him." Emma leans her head against the edge of her wheelchair, her eyes noticeably heavier than they were twenty minutes ago, when the nurse brought her down. "And then we called Dr. LeVine over, since I was bleeding quite a bit. I feel terrible about your father's rug."

"Emma, I promise we do not care at *all* about the rug."

"We'll replace it."

I roll my eyes. "My brother's crazy girlfriend shot you. There is no need to replace the rug that you bled on in the process."

She yawns. "I don't remember much after Dr. LeVine came over."

"He stopped the bleeding, and then we came into the hospital for surgery." Jeremiah has his hat in his hands, and he rotates it clockwise. Then counterclockwise. "Mariano and his partner were at the house before we left, trying to get a hold of your brother or your housekeeper."

"It was a very long hour before Nick finally came home." Mariano's eyes hold traces of remembered panic. "And an even longer few hours before Johnny called."

Nick had hardly left the hospital these last few days. Guilt over letting Alana into our lives seems to be eating him up, no matter how many times I've told him he isn't responsible for her actions.

"She deceived us all, Nick," I had told him. "I had my doubts about her, sure, but I never thought she was *this*."

"I'm your big brother." Tears filled his eyes—so blue, like Father's. "What more important job do I have than to protect you?"

No matter what I say, he seems unwilling to be comforted. Always so stubborn.

"So, she's locked up now? Alana?" Jeremiah's question draws me back to the conversation.

"She is." Mariano's voice is brusque—all business. "No bail."

"What do you think will happen to her?"

Mariano smiles, allowing a beat of silence. "No comment, Mr. Crane."

Jeremiah's returned smile lacks its usual luster. "You can't blame a newspaper man for trying." He glances at Emma, whose eyes are closed. "I had better get her back upstairs in bed."

"I'm only resting my eyes," Emma says. "I don't sleep well at night."

I shudder. Do I ever understand that. "Neither do I."

Mariano's hand is warm on mine. "You're safe, Piper. I promise."

But it seems impossible that I'll ever feel that way again.

"We'll see you later." Jeremiah grips the back of Emma's wheelchair. "Any idea when you'll be released?"

"Hopefully tomorrow. But even then, it sounds like I won't be able to move from the couch."

Mariano huffs. "Do you want your broken ribs to heal properly, or no?"

"Oh, did you see the article in the paper on Robbie?" Emma smiles drowsily. "Didn't he look handsome?"

"I did. Very well written." I look to Jeremiah. "It's as if somebody had an in with Mr. Thomas."

Jeremiah barely even smiles at the compliment.

"One of the largest raids ever." Even in her sleepy state, Emma beams with pride. "I thought I would fall over from shock when I learned he had known Matthew in Kansas City. Or Jacob, I guess. What are we supposed to call him?"

My head had been spinning over that knowledge too. That Robbie had been the agent who infiltrated the Burk family. That his raid in Kansas City had set all this in motion. It's dangerous for me to think on it too long. I like Robbie. I don't want to feel resentful toward him.

Emma yawns behind her hand. "His picture's been splashed everywhere. I imagine his days of being undercover with the bureau are over. Not that I mind."

"He should be very proud." I haven't told Emma yet that I had a front-row seat when the raid at the Finnegans' began. That I received a good conk on the head as Alana squealed out of there. "Did you tell him about our stakeout?"

She giggles, and then winces and rubs where she was shot. "I did. He said he'll have to be more careful around you in the future."

"Well, fortunately for Robbie, my investigating days are over."

Emma's eyes widen as if I've said something truly shocking. "Oh, Piper! Don't say that."

"Why ever not? I've had enough excitement to last me a lifetime."

"You haven't either. You can hardly sit still in that hospital bed of yours."

"That's because they barely allow me to feed myself."

Emma gives me a look that intimates she knows me better than that. "I don't care what you say. I'll go on record as stating that I don't think Chicago's underbelly has seen the last of Piper Sail."

"Say good-bye, Emma." Jeremiah inches her chair forward.

"That cute nurse will have my head if I don't get you back upstairs."

Emma shakes her head—*can you believe this guy?*—but waves as Jeremiah rolls her out of the room.

"What will happen now with the Finnegans?" I ask when they're out of eyesight.

"What always happens. Patrick paid the fine for first-time Volstead Act violation and is already out."

Of course he is. I fumble with my tangled blankets. "This blasted city."

"I know."

"At the end of the day, how much can one person really do?"

Mariano watches me a moment before taking my hand between his. "Two people, right? You and me."

My heart foxtrots inside my chest under his gaze. "Right. You and me."

Mariano stands and fits his homburg onto his head. "I gotta get back to the office. Joyce will be here soon, though."

I force myself to say a calm, "Okay," as if the idea of being left alone and so defenseless in my hospital bed doesn't terrify me.

But Mariano hears it anyway. He squeezes my hand. "You're safe."

"I don't feel safe."

"But you are. Maeve is behind bars. You can rest, Piper."

"What about Patrick Finnegan?" I shiver at the memory of his voice. "You said yourself, he just paid his fine and walked."

Mariano shakes his head. "Are you kidding me? Did you read Jeremiah's article? Patrick Finnegan is probably balled up in a corner terrified that *you're* coming after *him* with how fierce you sounded."

I feel a smile inching out, and bite it back before it can stretch the bandage on my cheek. "Do you think we *could* go after him? I heard him say plain and clear that they helped Maeve. I suppose it's my word against his, but it seems like there must be evidence lying around somewhere."

"Let's table that conversation until you're out of the hospital, shall we?" Mariano brushes his lips over my forehead. "Nice to have you back, Detective Sail."

When he kisses me again, for a lovely bubble of time all the fear and pain is eclipsed by the one thing that is strong enough to conquer all.

"I really am fine, Nick. Truly." I lean forward so he can position the second pillow he insisted on behind my back. I'm happy to finally be home, but if Nick doesn't stop hovering . . .

"Another pillow isn't going to hurt." Nick takes a step back and frowns. "Are you sure you don't want a heavier blanket?"

"I really am fine." I tuck the blanket around me. "If I get cold, Joyce will be here to help."

"I'll grab one, just in case. Then if you *do* get cold . . ." Nick's voice trails off along with him down the hall.

"He's insufferable," I say to Joyce as she bustles into the room with a lunch tray, Sidekick at her heels.

"Oh, let him make a fuss over you. He's been so antsy for you to get home."

"He's going to be late picking up Walter if he keeps fetching me things."

"I'm as anxious as you, but Walter's train still doesn't come in for another half hour. Nick has plenty of time."

"Walter today. Father and Jane next week." No matter how much I had insisted they finish out their honeymoon, Father and Jane had started for home as soon as word had reached them. "This house is going to be crowded again very soon."

"I can't wait." Joyce settles the tray on my lap. "It's much calmer around here when you have plenty of people to keep eyes on you."

Nick rushes in with the other blanket. "Now, I'll put this right here on the back of the couch, Pippy. Can you think of anything else you need?"

"A face that doesn't have five pounds of bandages on it? Ribs that aren't broken?"

Instead of huffing about my lack of appreciation, Nick smiles affectionately. "Love you, little sister. I'll be back with Walter as soon as I can."

Joyce watches him go with a fond expression. "He cares about you so much."

"Right now, he does, anyway. And I'll take it." I lift my spoon. "Chicken and noodles. I'm spoiled."

"I thought you could use some of your mother's cooking." Joyce pulls over a footstool and draws the box of clean bandages onto her lap.

"Oh, Joyce, not now. You just gave me food, for heaven's sake."

"It's either now or right after Walter gets home, my dear."

I lay back with a gusty sigh.

My face and shoulders are battered from some quality time with the asphalt in our back alley, which must have happened when Alana dragged me to her car. Apparently, the doctor spent a decent amount of time digging grit and pebbles out of my cheek. Praise God that I was unconscious for that. The first time Joyce changed my bandages, she cried.

But today, her eyes are dry, happy even, as she peels off the tape and gauze. "And your father has done everything short of crawling out of his own skin to get back here. He couldn't be more proud of how you handled yourself, I'm sure. Your mama would be proud too."

I can't help snorting, which is quickly followed by a wince at the spark of pain in my ribs. "Oh, sure. I'm what every mother would want for a daughter. I can't sew, I'm not dainty, I'm loud, I—"

"You"—Joyce clasps my chin in her doughy hand—"are exactly who you're supposed to be, and that's why we love you. Your mama wouldn't have wanted you to be one of those prissy ladies, anyway. She wasn't one herself."

"She wasn't? She spent so much energy trying to get me to sit up straight and not run everywhere."

"She was a lady, mind you." Joyce smooths the edges of the bandage. "But your father speaks of a woman who laughed loud and lived life. Just like you, Piper." She snaps shut the bandage box and returns it under the end table. "I'll let you enjoy your lunch now."

I'm halfway done with my lunch, my mind floating listlessly from topic to topic, when the shrill ring of the telephone breaks into my thoughts. I reach behind me for the candlestick phone and pull it onto my lap. "Sail residence."

"Is Miss Sail available?"

The male voice makes my heart stammer. Matthew. "This is Piper."

"Do you recognize the voice of an old friend?"

"I do."

"I hoped so. I'm at a phone booth and don't have much money, but I had to call. I just saw an old issue of the *Daily Chicagoan*. It was like a nightmare come to life, seeing Maeve's picture with yours."

I run my thumb up the length of my repaired necklace. "It was a nightmare *living* it."

"If I'd seen Maeve any earlier, I would've left town." Matthew's words are laced with despair. "You have to believe me."

"You would have given your life for Lydia," I say in a quiet voice. "At least you've been cleared of murdering her. Did you see that in the paper too?"

"Only in a few of them," he says darkly.

All the papers had gone crazy over the detail that Robbie Thomas, of the famed Finnegan raid, had previously been involved in a raid in Kansas City, the one that had left Maeve Burk's husband dead and sent her packing for Chicago with her false name and thirst for revenge. A few of the papers were still calling for Matthew to be found, saying he and Maeve must have been in on it together.

"The reputable papers said you were innocent, anyway."

"I guess that's the best a guy like me can hope for. Thank you, Miss Sail"—his voice wavers—"for fighting for Lydia when I couldn't."

Emotion clogs my throat, keeping me from responding. But it doesn't matter. Matthew has already hung up.

I hang the earpiece back on its hook and hold the phone on my lap for a minute.

What now?

It's the question that won't seem to go away. The one that gnaws at me even in my sleep. What do I do now that Lydia's case has been solved? Now that I'm supposed to move on with my life?

I set the telephone beside me, on top of the morning newspaper, covering the picture of a suburban Chicago girl gone missing. I've already spent half my morning thinking about her, about her parents and siblings. The friends from school who aren't mentioned in the article, but who are no doubt terrified. I hate that there are more. That just as the mystery of what happened to Lydia comes to a close for us, the nightmare is only beginning for others.

Perhaps I could help out somehow.

I exhale a laugh. I'm laid up on the couch, face and chest bandaged. And I don't even know this girl. What on earth could I possibly do to help find her?

Yet the thought won't go away, silly as it is, and Emma's words from the hospital drown out my doubts: "I don't think Chicago's underbelly has seen the last of Piper Sail."

DISCUSSION QUESTIONS

1. If you had been alive in the 1920s, what do you think would have been the most exciting part?

2. Joyce suggests to Piper that her stepmother will never become a blessing to her if she doesn't open her mind to the idea. Have you ever had a time where you resisted change?

3. Piper's mother's last words were to tell Piper to trust in herself. How does this reminder help push Piper forward?

4. Piper struggles against the expectations society had for women of the day. When is a time that society's expectations influenced you or made you feel "less-than"?

5. Piper will go to the ends of the earth to solve Lydia's disappearance. What was a time you went above and beyond for a friend?

6. When Lydia disappears, Piper isn't interested in new friends, but Emma Crane becomes an unlikely ally. Have you ever met someone you didn't expect to connect with?

7. Piper is so not a dog person … until she meets Sidekick. How does Sidekick help Piper to start new after tragedy?

8. When Walter is angry with Piper for pursuing Lydia with such fervor, Piper likens it to a time when he played baseball

with such intensity that he hurt himself. She says, "That's how I feel about Lydia. I don't know how to do anything else but leave it all on the field." What is a time that you've left it all on the field and it's paid off? What about a time when you didn't try your hardest, and you regretted it?

9. Piper feels deeply discouraged by the corruption surrounding her. To Mariano, she voices, "At the end of the day, how much can one person really do?" Have you ever felt this way? How would you answer her?

10. Piper's father tells her, "Piper, my girl, to love anyone is to risk." Do you think this is true?

Check out these additional fun freebies for *The Lost Girl of Astor Street!*

The ultimate *The Lost Girl of Astor Street* music playlist: Cozy up with some of the best tunes from the Roaring Twenties!

http://bit.ly/LOSTGIRLMUSICPLAYLIST

The Lost Girl of Astor Street 1920s fashion guide: A guide for all the 1920s clothes, shoes, accessories, and hats you can handle. There are even some fashion tips for those dapper dudes in your life.

http://bit.ly/LOSTGIRLFASHION

Did you know? In the 1920s, women received the right to vote, Prohibition went into effect, and King Tut's burial chamber was opened. Find out more with these 1920s time period fun facts.

http://bit.ly/LOSTGIRLFUNFACTS

Toward A Secret Sky

by Heather Maclean

Toward a Secret Sky by *New York Times* bestselling author Heather Maclean is a fast-paced thriller that mixes reality with possibility, blending an epic romance with a breathless flight through the highlands of Scotland, the secret city under London, and history itself.

Available wherever books are sold!

BLINK

It Started With Goodbye

by *Christina June*

Not all stories begin with once upon a time ...

Tatum Elsea is facing the worst summer ever: she's stuck under stepmother-imposed house arrest and her BFF's gone ghost. Tatum fills her time with community service by day and her covert graphic design business at night (which includes trading emails with a cute cello-playing client). But when Tatum discovers she's not the only one in the family with secrets, she decides to start fresh and chase her happy ending along the way. A modern Cinderella story, *It Started with Goodbye* shows us that sometimes going after what you want means breaking all the rules.